CUNARD YANKS

Liverpool
New York City
Hamburg
The Beatles

CUNARD YANKS

LIVERPOOL
NEW YORK CITY
HAMBURG
THE BEATLES

John Winter

Troubador Publishing Ltd
Unit E2 Airfield Business Park
Harrison Road, Market Harborough
Leicestershire LE16 7UL
Tel: 0116 279 2299
Email: books@troubador.co.uk
Web: www.troubador.co.uk

ISBN 978-1-80514-491-5

British Library Cataloguing in Publication Data.
A catalogue record for this book is available from the British Library.

Printed and bound by CPI Group (UK) Ltd, Croydon, CR0 4YY
Typeset in 11pt Minion Pro by Troubador Publishing Ltd, Leicester, UK

This book is dedicated to my wife, Susan.

Without her invaluable support, and her always helpful advice and comments as it slowly took shape, this book would never have reached completion.

Grateful thanks are also due to my sister-in-law Rhona Winter, my sister Lin Stone, my son Robert Winter, and my very good friends Jim and Karen Kendig, all of whom very kindly read and commented upon the finished manuscript.

DISCLAIMER

This book is a work of fiction. There are however well-documented historical facts interwoven with the otherwise fictional story.

Real persons, both living and dead, who are named in this story including, but not limited to, The Beatles and their families, the Cunard Yanks, Ivan (Hayward), Ivan (Vaughan), Stuart Sutcliffe, Astrid Kirchherr, Tony Sheridan, Katharine Hepburn, Greta Garbo, George Schlee, Mrs G. Schlee, Tommy Steele, Fred Astaire, Bob Hope, Bing Crosby, Ronnie Scott, Pee Wee Marquette, Charlie Parker, Dizzy Gillespie, Dinah Washington, Jack Dempsey, The Quarrymen, Jim Gretty, Rory Storm (Alan Caldwell) and family, Johnny Byrne, The Hurricanes, Iris Caldwell, 'Kingsize' Taylor and the Dominoes, Buddy Holly and The Crickets, Pete Best, Mona Best, Allan Williams, Bruno Koschmider, Alan Sytner, Keith Hemmings, Manny Goldrich, Owen Bradley, Paul Cohen, Joe Zellin and Frank Hessy did not interact with any of the fictitious characters, or participate in any of the fictitious events, described in this book. The inclusion of their names within this story does not imply that they have approved, or that they endorse, any of the contents of this book.

All names, characters, places and incidents in this story are either a product of the author's imagination or are used fictitiously.

Any resemblance to the actual statements, opinions or actions of real people, living or dead, at past or existing locations is entirely coincidental.

CUNARD YANKS

Cunard Yanks were British men, mostly young, who worked on Cunard ships from the late 1940s to the 1960s on the transatlantic routes, mainly between Liverpool and New York.

The American consumer goods, fashions and music which they brought home to Liverpool at a time when rationing and import restrictions made them difficult to obtain in England gave the city a special awareness of popular American culture and played a part in the development of Merseybeat and The Beatles.

It is possible to debate just how influential the Cunard Yanks were. But in a world which was very much more compartmentalised than it is now, and America was a distant place which relatively few ordinary British people had visited, the links which thousands of men helped to establish with the United States must have had some effect.

John Winter
Liverpool

CONTENTS

LIVERPOOL – 1961

A Gretsch Duo Jet

The young lad who stood outside the front door couldn't have been any more than seventeen or eighteen. He was slim with a slightly pale face. The leather jacket which he was wearing over a black T-shirt had seen plenty of use. His pale-blue jeans were faded and well-worn, like his black boots.

The man who'd just answered the door bell was a little older. But no more than twenty-four or twenty-five. As he looked his visitor up and down he couldn't help noticing his eyes. They were a strikingly deep brown. Almost hypnotic. They suggested an underlying seriousness which didn't quite fit in with his otherwise youthful appearance.

The visitor spoke. And his voice was unusual too. His accent could only be Liverpool. And yet at the same time it wasn't. It was slower. More reserved. Peaceable. Confident. It was the voice of a thinker. Someone who was a little different. Special even.

But he possibly didn't quite know it yet.

"Sorry for disturbin' you," he said. "I've been told there's a taxi-driver called Ivan lives here. And a lad I know who plays with a group called the Delcardoes says this Ivan's got an electric guitar from America."

Ivan nodded his head. "That's me."

The young man held out a hand in greeting. "I'm George. George Harrison. From Speke. Upton Green." He hesitated for a moment. "The lad I spoke to from the Delcardoes said you might be thinking of sellin' it."

"I might," said Ivan. "But only at the right price." He gave George a smile as he shook his outstretched hand. "I'm in need of a bit of cash. So if you're interested you'd best come in and take a look at it."

George followed Ivan into the front living room. It was sparsely furnished with a couple of prints of the Liverpool waterfront hanging on the walls. But George didn't notice them. All he saw was the guitar. Propped up against the back of a small settee, it was beautiful. Beyond his wildest dreams. Unlike the settee it looked almost brand new. Brightly-polished and deep-black, with a pair of silver pick-ups and a solid-looking, Bigsby tremolo unit, the body was neatly edged in white. Etched on the small, white scratch-guard he could see the magical name 'GRETSCH'.

Thanks to post-war import restrictions American guitars were almost impossible to find in Britain, especially outside London. It was exactly what he'd been looking for. George knew at once. He had to have it.

Before leaving home he had stuffed seventy grubby and well-used pound notes into the inside pocket of his jacket. He'd been saving them up for this moment from the increasing amount of cash which he and his group had been making in Liverpool. Until they went over to Hamburg they'd been struggling to get bookings but countless hours of performing for noisy and demanding audiences of sailors and students, hookers and drug-dealers at seedy clubs in the red-light district of the German port city had transformed them. It had changed them from relatively immature and inexperienced teenagers, whose musical skills were little better than average, into the tightest rock 'n' roll outfit on Merseyside. Since their return from Germany the gigs at various clubs and dance-halls around the city had been coming in much more regularly.

But would seventy pounds be enough? It was a Gretsch Duo Jet. There certainly wouldn't be another in Liverpool. Maybe not even in the whole of England.

Ivan picked the guitar up from the settee.

"You can give it a try if you like. But you might want to give your hands a quick wash first."

George looked down. His palms and fingernails were indeed somewhat grimy.

"Sorry. I've been sortin' out a few plants. In our front garden. It's one of the things I enjoy. Being outside on my own. It helps me relax. Gives me time to think."

"The kitchen's next door," said Ivan. "There should be a bar of Lifebuoy in the saucer by the window. And a little scrubbing brush. Make yourself at home."

George returned a few moments later. His hands and nails were clean and dry.

Ivan handed him the Gretsch. "You play the guitar, then, do you?"

George nodded. "Yeah. A bit."

Slipping the strap over his head he let his shoulder take the weight of the instrument while he ran his left hand up and down the neck, pressing the individual strings with his fingers to see how easy it would be to play. The electric guitar he'd taken with him to Hamburg, and which he was still using, was similar to a U.S. Fender Stratocaster. Made by a British company based in Kent it wasn't bad. But George knew straightaway that if he could get hold of the Gretsch it would transform his playing. The action, the ease with which the strings could be pressed down against the metal frets on the neck, was in a different league.

Ivan watched him.

"What have you got at the moment?"

"A Futurama," replied George without much enthusiasm. "It's okay. But it's time I got myself something better."

"Well," said Ivan, "I've really enjoyed playing this Gretsch. It's a bit special. I'll be sad to see it go."

George took his hands off the strings for a moment and looked at Ivan.

"How long have you had it? You don't see many American guitars here in England."

"I used to know Tommy Steele," said Ivan, matter-of-factly. "Before he started making records and hit the big time. Tommy Hicks he was back then. We were shipmates on the Mauretania and it was him that gave me the idea of buying it. He'd got himself a guitar from Manny's Music Store on 48th Street when we were ashore in New York. Can't remember what sort it was but it wasn't that expensive."

Ivan stopped for a moment to think. Then he shook his head.

"No. It's gone. Tommy told me he'd have quite liked a Gretsch. But he didn't have much in the way of spare cash back then. It's a Hofner President he plays now. Very smart. Good mates we were but I've lost touch with him since he hit the big time. It was Tommy getting his guitar that got me thinking about buying one for myself. Back in the fifties you couldn't get hold of top-quality American guitars like this one in England. You still can't really."

As Ivan was speaking George had started once again to run his fingers up and down the strings and gaze at the highly-polished, dark-black body of the guitar. It looked and felt so good.

"If you've got a plec with you," said Ivan, "I'll go get my amp and we can plug it in. If you're going to buy it you'll want to know how it sounds."

George slowly nodded his head a few times and pulled a mottled-brown plectrum from the side pocket of his jeans.

"That'd be good," he said quietly.

His mind was elsewhere. He could already see himself on stage with the Gretsch. It would be another small step on the road to success. The long nights in Hamburg, high on Prellies and alcohol, had been wild. But it was exactly what they had needed. The perfect apprenticeship. And the reaction they'd been getting since they got home, particularly from the girls, told them they were now good.

But being the best on Merseyside wasn't enough. They wanted more. They needed better gear. And someone with contacts. Someone who could take them to the next level.

George was still lost in his thoughts when Ivan returned with the amplifier and took the guitar from him.

"I'll play you a quick tune to warm it up," he said. "Then you can have a go."

George watched as Ivan plugged the Gretsch into the amplifier. Then, after adjusting the volume and tone controls on the guitar, he ran through a slightly-shortened version of Duane Eddy's recent hit 'Because They're Young'.

George smiled to himself as the familiar, twanging melody filled the small room. Ivan was good. His fingers moved easily and quickly over the strings.

The Gretsch looked amazing. And the way it sounded was brilliant.

When it came to George's turn he sat on the arm of the settee and began to play an instrumental number he'd written a few months earlier.

"Nice," said Ivan as the tune came to an end. "I don't know that one."

"It's one of ours," said George. "'Cry For A Shadow'. I wrote it with one of the other lads in the group. John Lennon. He's on rhythm guitar mostly. We did a demo of it in a small studio run by a chap called Percy Phillips on Kensington a little while back."

"And this group of yours. What do you call yourselves?"

"We've had a few names since we started. When John first got together with a some of his pals from school they called themselves the Quarrymen. After the name of their school. Quarry Bank over in Woolton. The lads who went there were called Quarrymen in the school song. Then John asked a lad I already knew called Paul to join them. It was Paul who told John I was quite good on the guitar and got me into the group. Up 'til then I'd been playing on and off with various different people. After that, when a couple of John's schoolmates got fed up and said they were leaving, we changed our name to 'The Silver Beetles.'"

George smiled to himself.

"John says he got the name from a man who came up to him with a flaming pie. But that's just him. Playin' around with words and being daft. I reckon he got it from Buddy Holly's group, 'The Crickets'. But I don't think he'd ever admit it. Then after a while it got changed to 'Beatles'. Spelt with an 'A'. Like in 'beat music'. I can't remember exactly who came up with that idea. It might've been one of the beatniks from the Art College John was livin' with at the time. In Gambier Terrace."

Ivan nodded his head.

"The Beatles. That's neat. Easy to remember. The kids won't forget it. And how long've you been writing music?"

"A year or two, I suppose. But John does most of the song-writing. Along with Paul. They're both older than me so they reckon they're better at it."

George shrugged his shoulders and gave Ivan a slightly lop-sided grin.

"When we first got together they were both bigger than me too. They still think they are. So I don't get much of a look-in."

Ivan laughed.

"The Gretsch might impress them."

George smiled and held the guitar up by the neck, turning it round a couple of times and taking a good look at it as he did so. He nodded his head in approval.

"It probably would," he said. "I really like it. It's dead easy to play. And it sounds great. But I'm not sure I can afford it." He paused for a moment. "What did you mean when you said the right price?"

Ivan stopped to think.

"Well. As I say, I got it in New York. A couple of years after Tommy bought his. So that'd be about five or six years ago. We'd both left the Mauretania by then. Tommy to make his fortune as a pop singer and me back onto the regular sailings out of Liverpool. I was a Bar Steward on a Cunard ship called the Media and the tips were good. Especially from the Americans. Some of the Brits were a bit tight but the Yanks always tipped big. So I blew the lot on a guitar. That was before all the big jets came in and started killing the Cunard ships off. People wanted to get to New York quicker."

Ivan shook his head as if he couldn't believe it. Almost as soon as he started talking he was back on board one of the iconic, transatlantic liners.

"It's sad. I really miss that life. Over to New York and back every couple of weeks. It was brilliant. We were living the dream. We'd sail off down the Mersey leaving Liverpool behind us, all grey and grimy with its bomb sites and broken buildings. Then, just a week or so later, we'd be sailing into New York harbour and up the Hudson River to the Cunard Piers. The bright lights and the skyscrapers were right next to us. Sparkling clean and brand new. You could almost reach out and touch them. It was like 'The Wizard of Oz'. You know. At the start of the film. When Dorothy's black and white world suddenly goes all technicolour."

George laid the Gretsch back down on the settee. He was listening, but also wondering if his seventy pounds would be enough. Ivan was lost in his memories. He still hadn't mentioned money.

"Cunard Yanks people used to call us. Everything was still rationed back here in England and we'd be swanning round Liverpool in our smart, New York suits. Turning up at places like The Grafton and The Locarno with pockets full of cash. The girls used to love us. And our families did too. We'd bring back all sorts of stuff. Things people back here had only seen in the movies. Hoovers, fridges, washing machines, spin-dryers, record players. There was plenty of room in the cargo hold, especially on the trip back to England, so we brought home as much as we could afford. And American records from jukeboxes. They got sold off cheap as soon as they dropped out of the charts over there. A lot of them never made it into the hit parade in England so everyone wanted to hear them. They were a bit special."

George nodded his head.

"A lad I know from Southport called Ted Taylor's got a group called the Dominoes," he said. "'Kingsize' Taylor people call him because he's such a big guy. He got hold of a few American records from a mate who was a chippie on one of the Cunard ships. Ted told me he and his group would be playing these American songs and John Lennon used to sneak in an' write the words down." George laughed. "Ted wasn't happy. Up 'til then the Dominoes were pretty much the only group in Liverpool who knew them."

"You'd be amazed at some of the stuff which found its way here on those ships," said Ivan. "But I was the only one who came home with a Gretsch. My mates all said I was daft spending crazy money on a guitar. But I didn't have a wife to worry about back then. And she's been worth every penny." He gave George a smile. "The Gretsch, I mean. Not the wife."

He leaned down to pick up the guitar and cradled it in his arms.

"Only joking," he said. "The wife's great. I'd keep both her and the guitar if I could. But, as I said, I need the cash. I left Cunard when we got married. And after all the tales I've told her about how much better life is over there she fancies the idea of the two of us giving it a go in America."

He paused for a moment to think.

"It was just under three hundred I paid for it. Dollars that is. With the Bigsby and a fitted carrying case. So I wouldn't want to let it go for less than two fifty. That's about ninety pounds."

George started to do some mental arithmetic. If ninety pounds was two hundred and fifty dollars, how many would his seventy pounds be? Then, after a few seconds, he realised he was wasting his time. He didn't need to know. He had seventy pounds and that was it. Seventy was all he could afford. It was as simple as that.

He decided to be cheeky.

"How about sixty?"

Ivan shook his head.

"Sorry." He stroked the guitar affectionately. "I've looked after her well. You'd be hard pressed to find another one. No. Even if I'd like to help you out I can't give her away for sixty."

He waited to see what George would say. He liked the lad. But sixty was out of the question. The two of them sat in silence for perhaps half a minute, both thinking.

Then, quite suddenly, George decided to come clean. He pulled a tight wad of crumpled notes out of his jacket pocket and placed them on the settee beside him.

"There's seventy quid there. It's all I've got. I'd really love to have your Gretsch. But that's it. I can't give you any more."

Ivan looked at him. Then he picked up the notes and began to straighten them out. A few were torn in places and had corners missing but he'd still be able to make use of them.

Once he'd assembled them into a reasonably tidy pile he

began to count. As he put the last note down he turned to George.

"Exactly as you said. Seventy pounds."

Ivan looked at the collection of notes. He'd already decided he liked the lad. There was something about him. He had a feeling that having a really good guitar might be the making of him. He wondered what the other Beatles were like. If they were anything like young George they could be a bit special.

He looked again at the notes. Then back at George.

"I'm afraid I'm sticking at ninety. I really can't go any lower."

George looked crestfallen. But Ivan had more to say.

"Having said that, though, I think you could be someone who'll make the best possible use of such a fine guitar. You know. Take care of her the way I have. So I'll tell you what I'll do. I'll take the seventy. And you can sign me an I.O.U. for the other twenty. Give it me when you can. How does that sound?"

George couldn't believe his luck.

"Are you sure?"

"No," said Ivan, laughing. "I'm definitely not sure. In fact I must be daft. I only met you ten minutes ago and now I'm trusting you to turn up one day with twenty quid. That's a week and a half's wages. But I've said it now. So let's get it sorted before I change my mind."

On a blank scrap of paper Ivan scribbled out a receipt for seventy pounds. Then he added an I.O.U. for the balance of twenty at the bottom.

After they'd both signed it Ivan folded the paper up and put it in his pocket. As he was doing so George placed the Gretsch carefully in its custom-built, carrying case. Then, clutching his precious cargo, he headed off down the road.

They say it took a bit of time for the debt to be settled. But if Ivan still has that signed scrap of paper it must be worth many times its weight in gold.

And the Gretsch Duo Jet guitar?

George played it on many of the most iconic, early Beatles' recordings. Then he gave it away to a German friend from the early Hamburg days, Klaus Voormann, who created the cover of the group's 1966 album, 'Revolver'.

The guitar has now been returned to George's family.

And its value?

Priceless.

ONE

CABIN BOYS

August 1954

"Seasickness," said Dave sympathetically as he stood there and looked at me. "They say it's worst feelin' in the world."

It was day two of my maiden voyage to New York on the Cunard ship, RMS Media. The first time I'd ever been away from Liverpool. Unless you want to count a day trip with the school across the Mersey to New Brighton, that is.

According to Les, our Head Steward who'd been on the Atlantic run for over thirty years, the weather wasn't even that bad. A bit of a blow and a middling sort of choppy swell as the shallow Irish Sea gave way to the Atlantic Ocean.

Nothing to write home about.

But as I lay there on one of several bunks in a small stewards' cabin known as a 'glory hole', low down in the bowels of the ship, I just wanted to die.

Dave was my best mate. Like a brother almost. More than seventeen years we'd known each other. Since we were both nippers. He'd always lived a few doors away in St Bride Street, very close to the centre of Liverpool. One day the two of us had caught the bus down to the Pier Head and signed on together at the Cunard Building on Liverpool's historic waterfront.

So we were now shipmates.

Sir Samuel Cunard, originally from Halifax in Nova Scotia, had made his Cunard Line the very best in the transatlantic shipping business and the Cunard Building had been designed to impress his customers. Passengers who assembled in the grand lobby on the ground floor prior to embarkation found themselves surrounded by expensive Italian marble as they relaxed on the very finest leather seats and awaited the call to proceed to their ship. As they looked around at the magnificent interior décor, and observed the quiet efficiency with which the staff approached their various tasks, they knew that they were in good hands.

Dave and I, of course, hadn't seen any of this finery. We'd reported to the Cunard Building for duty the day before we'd sailed. And as crew members who'd just completed our basic training we were instructed to make our way down a set of stone steps from Water Street into the basement of the building where a grey-suited clerk sat at a functional, wooden desk. On his desk he had a ledger, and we joined the queue of men who were waiting to receive their orders.

He dealt with each of us very quickly.

"Name?"

"Stephen Crane, sir."

He ran his finger down a list of names in the ledger.

"Date of birth?"

"4th of August, 1936, sir."

"Cabin Boy. Report to RMS Media."

Dave followed me to the desk, and he too was told to report to the Media. We were very relieved. Until then we hadn't been sure that we'd end up on the same ship. And our plan was to see the world. Together.

That was three days ago. It was the beginning of what we hoped would be a great adventure.

As I did my best to forget about the constant motion of the ship Dave gave me a grin. Happy as Larry he was. I moaned at him while trying to stop myself from retching yet again.

Going to sea with Cunard had been my dream. And now it was turning into a nightmare.

"It's not bloody fair," I said. You're as right as rain and I'm feelin' like death."

Dave shrugged his shoulders.

"Luck of the draw I guess, Steve. Les says it's pretty normal for first-timers to suffer for a few days. Until they get their sea legs. After that they're usually fine. Though he did say that Nelson, you know, the admiral who won the Battle of Trafalgar then got himself shot and insisted on one last kiss from his mate, Hardy. Apparently he never got used to it. Sick as a dog he was for the first couple of days. Every time he put to sea. Every single time. Probably made him a right bastard to fight against."

Dave's relentless good humour was making me worse. But I felt too ill to say anything as he continued to witter away.

"It does make you wonder why he carried on, though, doesn't it." Dave shook his head in bewilderment. "I think I'd have jacked it in and found somethin' else to do with my life. Takes all sorts, I suppose."

He made as if to stop. But then he didn't.

"Les says we're lucky really. This ship used to be all over the place before someone came up with the idea of stabilisers. Cunard had them fitted a couple of years ago. Denny Browns they're called. The Media was the first of the transatlantic ships to have 'em. Before that a lot of the passengers weren't able to show their faces in the restaurant for the first couple of days. Which is a shame 'cos they'd be missin' out on all the delicious food."

He paused for a moment and started to rummage around inside his white jacket.

"Talkin' of which . . . "

With a flourish he produced a slightly battered, cheese and tomato sandwich from one of the pockets.

"They say you feel worse on an empty stomach, Steve. I swiped a couple of these sarnies off the buffet when no-one was looking. I've eaten one already. But we can split this if you like. It's a bit squashed but it tastes great."

I caught a whiff of the slightly warm cheese and an overwhelming wave of nausea hit me.

"For God's sake, Dave. Put it away and sod off. Please. You're just making me feel worse."

He turned away and opened the cabin door.

"Suit yourself, you miserable bugger. I get it that you're not feeling all that great, so I came down to try and cheer you up. Seein' as I'm obviously not helping I'll find out if the Doc can give you a jab or something. And if you don't make it we'll give you a decent burial. At sea I suppose it'll have to be."

As he stepped over the raised threshold into the corridor he quickly turned his head. He'd already taken a large bite out of the warm sandwich.

"Any last requests?" he said, taking another bite.

The sight of the half-eaten sandwich was the last straw. Another wave of nausea hit me and I began to throw up. Then Dave was gone.

About an hour later a doctor turned up with his medical case. It was the ship's surgeon, from Germany, Dr Hans Richter. His face looked kind and I guessed he was probably in his fifties. He sat down on my bunk.

"Your friend Robertson, he tells me you're suffering from the sea sickness," he said, taking hold of my wrist. I thought he was about to count my pulse but instead he began to stroke the back of my hand. "Judging by your look I think he is right. You have been sailing before?"

I shook my head and immediately retched.

"No, no no," said Dr Richter, still stroking my hand. "Keep the head still. It is moving about enough already with the ship. Shaking will not help. And you should not stay here. The best cure for sea sickness is out on the deck. In the fresh air. Staying indoors when you are feeling sick is no good. The balance organ in your ears is saying to your brain that the ship is moving around. But inside a cabin your eyes give a different message. So your brain it gets confused and you feel sick. Outside on the deck your eyes look at the horizon and see that your ears are right. The ship is moving. That makes sense to your brain. Yes?"

His theory might well have been spot on. But my brain was too scrambled up even to begin to understand it. And I was pretty sure that if I opened my mouth I'd throw up again. So I just nodded my head, moving it as little as possible.

"You can go outside on the deck now?" asked the doctor.

"No. I'm sorry," I said. "Not the way I'm feeling at the moment."

As soon as I spoke the nausea was almost overwhelming. But I managed to control it.

Dr Richter looked at me.

"Then I must give you an injection."

He opened up his medical case and took out what seemed to be an unnecessarily large syringe. Then he filled it with some fluid from a vial.

"Your trousers please. Down."

It was an order. Which I obeyed. Then, without any warning, the needle was stuck into my backside.

A Krakatoa Cocktail he told me it was. And it hurt.

After completing the injection the doctor started to rub my

naked buttocks with his hands. It will help with the pain was what he said.

Now, as you'll have realised by now, I was still young. And quite naïve. But I wasn't daft. What with the hand-stroking, and now the move to my buttocks as well, I pretty quickly worked out that the good doctor's activities probably didn't have an awful lot to do with pain relief. But I didn't care. All I wanted was something – anything – to get rid of the dreadful sickness.

And if that meant letting him play around with my bottom? Well, I could live with that.

Happily my generosity and understanding were amply rewarded. The treatment worked and the nightmare was over. By next morning I was up and about, scurrying around the ship with errands and messages for my first class passengers.

If anything the waves got bigger as we headed out into the Atlantic, but Dr Richter's treatment had done the trick. The crew called him 'Wandering Hans'. I understood why. But it was a price I was more than happy to pay.

From then on, whenever the sea got really rough, I took the his advice and got myself out on deck as quickly as possible. And unlike poor Horatio, 1st Viscount Nelson, I never felt seasick again.

●·+————●·+·●·+·●————·+·●

The RMS Media had set sail from Huskisson Dock, not far from Liverpool's Pier Head, on 7th August 1954. She was one of two smaller-sized ships which Cunard had commissioned to be built immediately after the war. Like their great ocean liners Queen Mary and Queen Elizabeth she was a product of the distinguished shipbuilders, John Brown, on Clydebank near Glasgow. So she boasted an illustrious heritage.

Our ship had made her inaugural voyage in the summer of

1947. She was what Cunard termed a combination passenger-cargo liner. And the prefix 'RMS' told the world that we were an official 'Royal Mail Ship', carrying letters and parcels as well as passengers and cargo. Across the Atlantic. To America.

On board we had a total of two hundred and thirty-one passengers. All 'First Class'.

Making the ship 'First Class Only', while also carrying cargo, was part of Cunard's strategy to remain competitive in the battle with jet aircraft. The company could see that passenger jets were beginning to take over from ships as the preferred method of transatlantic travel. And as the speed and range of the aeroplanes increased the competition would only get stronger.

Crossing the ocean at a leisurely pace on a relatively small, and exclusive, Cunard liner was being promoted as the most relaxed way to travel between Europe and America. It was the way the rich and wealthy made the crossing. The aim was to attract a clientele who had plenty of money. And plenty of time to spend it.

The new jets offered speed. Cunard's offering was the opportunity to spend eight or nine days at sea in pampered luxury with like-minded people. Unlike the airlines there was no limit to the amount of baggage which could be carried. Five, or even ten, large, and very expensive, Louis Vuitton trunks was by no means unusual.

The job of every one of the ship's crew was to keep our guests happy. To make sure they received the highest possible level of service. The sort of service they were used to at home. And which they expected.

The pay wasn't that great so we treated them like royalty. Our earnest hope was for very generous tips which would allow us to splash out when we reached our destination.

Dave and I were now Cunard Yanks.

Fellow Scousers who'd been serving on RMS Media for

a while assured us that if we worked hard and kept our noses clean we'd be well looked after by our wealthy passengers. Then, with a bit of luck, we'd have money to burn. In New York.

Who could argue with that?

In the early hours of the morning, nine days after leaving Liverpool, I stood alongside Dave on the top deck of the ship. None of our passengers were yet awake, and it would be an hour or two before we had to report for duty.

A few, scattered clouds in the eastern sky behind our vessel slowly and almost imperceptibly began to take on a reddish-orange hue. The sun was not yet visible but before long it would appear as a bright yellow dot on the distant horizon. Our eager eyes scanned the dark-blue, almost black, water of the ocean around us as the bow of our ship carved out a white-crested wave which appeared luminescent as it spread out to each side, gradually getting wider until it merged once again with the gentle swell. And to our stern the violent turmoil created by the thrust of powerful twin propellors left a wide, straight line which marked our passage.

Dave and I were watching for a light. A flashing light that would tell us we were approaching America.

The Ambrose Lightship marked the deeply-dredged channel which led from the Atlantic Ocean into the broad mouth of Lower New York Bay where our ship would pass between Coney Island and Sandy Hook, New Jersey. Numerous sand bars and shoals made the bay treacherous for vessels. But since 1908 the floating lighthouse known as Ambrose, along with a later radio beacon, had guided ships safely into New York Harbour.

More than five million immigrants seeking a better life in the New World had already been welcomed by her light.

"There it is, Steve!"

Dave called out excitedly, pointing about thirty five degrees to starboard to where something pale and white seemed to be flickering.

At first I wasn't sure. But as I continued to stare out across the ocean the flickering gradually became brighter and more obvious.

"I think I can just make out what looks like a ship," said Dave, continuing to point with his right arm and leaning out over the white-painted rail on the edge of the deck.

He was making me nervous. I grabbed the sleeve of his jacket.

"For God's sake be careful, Dave. It's a long way down if you lose your footing."

"Leave me, I'm fine. Just look. Out there. Below the white light."

I screwed up my eyes. Then I saw it too. The shape of a hull. Dave was right. It had to be the Ambrose.

My heart was beating fast. We were close to New York. The skyscrapers and the bright lights of the city that never sleeps would soon come into view over the horizon and we would make our way slowly up the Hudson River to our berth on Manhattan Island.

Cunard Pier 92, on the north side of which we would be docking, jutted out into the river alongside 12th Avenue. It was a few yards from the western ends of 51st and 52nd Streets, and a leisurely fifteen or twenty minute walk from Broadway and Times Square.

For six days, until it was time to set sail once again and return to Liverpool, our ship would be tied up close to the centre of the most exciting city in the world.

We were going to make the most of it.

TWO

NEW YORK CITY

The line for U.S. Immigration was long. It wound backwards and forwards, guided by a series of ropes, inside a large, metal-roofed shed which stood on the Pier, right alongside the ship. As we shuffled slowly forwards we could see we were being shepherded towards a row of glass booths occupied by serious-looking, uniformed men. All was quiet. The eerie silence was broken only by the sound, every few minutes, of an inked stamp being brought down upon a passport or other official document.

I looked at Dave. He didn't give me even a hint of a smile. I knew exactly how he was feeling.

"Watch yourselves, lads," Les had said to us as we were leaving the ship. He had many years of experience of entering the United States. "U.S. Immigration Officers won't put up with any nonsense. Just behave yourselves and answer their questions and you'll be fine. No jokes. Understood?"

Les was right. This was serious. We didn't have any nonsense planned. But being Scousers neither of us could be entirely sure what might suddenly pop into our heads. Or out of our mouths.

Dave went up to the booth first.

I watched as his documents were carefully studied. Then came a series of questions which I couldn't hear but which seemed to go on for ever. He stood there, looking anxious. After giving him one final look the officer picked up his passport and stamped it. Dave was through.

It was my turn.

As I approached the booth I could see that the uniformed officer, whose blond hair was cut very short, military style, was chewing lazily on a piece of gum. With his clean-shaven, good looks and smartly-pressed uniform he could not be anything other than an American.

He looked me up and down while flicking through the stiff pages of my very recently acquired passport.

"Good morning, sir. Brand new passport. Your first visit to the United States?"

I nodded my head.

The officer said nothing. He looked at me and continued to chew his gum. Then he pushed it into his left cheek with his tongue.

"You need to answer my question, sir. Your first visit to the United States? Yes or no?"

"Sorry. Yes."

"Just ashore for the day, sir?"

I nodded.

The officer's eyes narrowed and he gave me a frown.

"Bit of a slow learner, aren't you, sir. Nodding your head doesn't count. I said just ashore for the day?"

"Sorry. Just for the day? Yes. My friend and I. We've got to be back on board by five. We're on duty tonight."

He picked up the immigration questionnaire which I'd filled out on the ship before proceeding ashore.

"You've answered all these questions truthfully and accurately, sir?"

"Yes"

He scanned the form with his eyes.

"You've never been convicted of a crime?"

"A crime? No, never."

"And you've never used illegal drugs?"

"Yes."

He frowned again.

"To be clear, sir. You've never used illegal drugs?"

"Yes. That's right. I've never used illegal drugs."

The officer sighed.

"You're not making it easy for me, sir. But since it's your first time here I'll take it that you might just be a little nervous."

He picked up one of his stamps and planted it, very firmly, upon the blank page opposite the imposing red and blue, U.S. Visa in my brand-new passport.

"Welcome to the United States of America, sir. I suggest you act smart while you're ashore." He paused for a moment and looked at me a little pityingly. "Well, as smart as you're capable of, anyway, sir. Just keep your wits about you."

He paused again and leaned forwards, closer to me, speaking in a confidential half-whisper.

"You see, sir, not all of the folks here in New York City are as easy-going as my good self. Some of them, if they think you might not be quite as sharp as they are and not very familiar with things. Well, they might just try to take advantage of you. You remember that."

"Thank you, officer. I will. Is that it?"

"Yes, sir. That's it. Remember. Act sharp. And have yourself a good day."

I picked up my passport and slipped it quickly into my back trouser pocket. Dave was waiting by the entrance to Customs.

"What was all that about? You were with him for ages."

"It was okay. But I kept nodding my head instead of answering his questions. Which seemed to irritate him a bit. Then I might've said yes when I meant no about using drugs. In the end I think he just decided I was a bit dim."

Dave grinned at me. "Not a bad judge, then."

I made a face at him.

"Anyway," I said. "We're in. That's the important thing."

As we walked through the Customs Shed, following a series of arrows painted on the floor, there were no staff to be seen but the route took us past a series of long tables, a couple of which had empty suitcases lying open upon them. There were some darkened windows behind the tables and I found myself thinking someone must be watching. It made me feel uncomfortable. So I kept my eyes fixed firmly on a doorway marked '*EXIT*', doing my best to look relaxed. Which wasn't easy. Even though I knew I had nothing to hide.

Suddenly there was an urgent shout from behind us.

"You two. Stop. Both of you."

We turned round to see a uniformed officer hurrying our way.

"Does this belong to one of you?" he said as he approached us. In his hand he was holding what looked like a British passport. "Your full names, please."

It was Dave who spoke first.

"David Cuthbert Robertson."

The officer looked at the name on the passport. Then at me. "And you?"

"Er, Crane. Stephen Crane. Stephen with a 'ph' not a 'v'"

The officer gave a sigh and handed the document to me.

"You dropped your passport, sir. It was on the floor by my colleague's desk. If it'd been in the street outside I don't think you'd have seen it again. Not here in New York City."

"I'm sure I put it in my back pocket."

The officer shrugged his shoulders.

"Then I suggest your back pocket may not be the best place. You need a jacket with an inside pocket, sir. Ideally with a zip on it. Have a nice day."

"Idiot," said Dave as the officer was walking away. He stopped and turned back towards us.

Dave pointed at me. "Him," he said. "He's the idiot."

The officer nodded his head. I think in agreement. Then carried on walking.

"You can't get back on the ship without a passport," said Dave, turning back to me. "You'd have been stuck ashore."

"Fair enough. But I've got it back. So it's fine."

"Yeah. But what if you hadn't?"

"What if? What if? There's loads of what ifs in life. I've got it back. So it's not a problem."

Dave shook his head. "You were lucky."

"Okay. I was lucky. It could just as easily have been you, David Cuthbert."

I started laughing almost before I'd finished saying his second name. I couldn't help it.

"David Cuthbert Robertson," I said, still laughing. "What's that all about? You always told me your second name was Colin."

"It is. Cuthbert just happens to be what's on my birth certificate. So they said that's what had to go on my passport. But I've changed it. Okay? As far as you're concerned my second name's Colin. And if you ever call me anything else I'll batter you."

I grinned at him.

"I mean it, Steve."

I could see by Dave's eyes that he did.

"It was my grand-dad's name. Which was fine fifty years ago. But not now. So I really will batter you if you so much as mention it to anyone."

"Okay," I said. "I've forgotten already. We're in New York. Let's hit the sights!"

"My God, I feel weird," said Dave. "I keep wanting to jump."

"Well don't." I said. "We're a thousand feet above Fifth Avenue. You'd have an awful long time to regret it on the way down."

We were standing on the open-air observation deck of the iconic Empire State Building, the tallest building in the world. The elevator had whisked us up eighty-six floors in not much more than a minute and the view was unbelievable. There was another public area on the 102nd floor but it was completely enclosed behind plate-glass windows. Les, who'd been to both viewing points, had said the open-air one was better.

"You get a better feel for how high up you are, being outside," he'd said. And he was right.

The tickets weren't cheap. But we'd probably never do it again. And the tips had been good.

The deck wrapped itself all the way round the building offering a 360 degree panorama of the city. A set of tall, metal railings, with inward-curving spikes, had been very securely embedded into the stone parapet.

I guessed it was to stop people like Dave discovering too late that flying was for the birds.

A few coin-operated telescopes on little steel platforms with steps leading up to them were available for anyone who fancied a close-up view of the city which lay below us.

"Did you see the picture of Edmund Hillary on the corridor leading to the elevators?" I said to Dave. "Down on the ground floor. You know. The bee-keeper chap from New Zealand who got to the top of Everest last year. Him and a Sherpa called Tenzing. Just before the Queen's coronation."

Dave shrugged his shoulders. "What about it?"

"The label on the picture said he was up here with his wife. Earlier this year. He was leaning against one of the telescopes and pointing out the Chrysler Building in the background. He told a reporter it was like being on top of a man-made Everest. A good quote for the papers even if he didn't really mean it."

"I can't understand why anyone'd want to climb a mountain," said Dave. "Even Everest. It's great seeing New York spread out below us. But I definitely wouldn't have bothered if we'd had to use the stairs. Come on. Let's see the rest of it."

We made our way slowly around the deck, taking in the spectacular views of the city. To the west was the Hudson River. Our ship, easy to spot thanks to the red and black Cunard livery on its single funnel, looked so small. It could have been a child's toy. It was difficult to believe it had carried us safely all the way across the Atlantic.

Five miles away to the south, beyond where the Hudson joined the Inner New York Bay, we were able to make out the Statue of Liberty. It had looked so impressive when we had sailed past it just a few hours earlier. Now, from our high and distant viewpoint, it was tiny.

Moving round to the other side of the deck we could see the East River, spanned by the Brooklyn Bridge which carried thousands of commuters to and from the skyscrapers of Lower Manhattan at the beginning and end of each working day.

To the north was Central Park, a large, oblong expanse of green. It gave the residents of the densely-populated city some very welcome and precious space for relaxation and recreation.

"See Central Park," said Dave, pointing towards the distant, straight-edged shape with a lake at its centre. "They say the guy who designed it got the idea from Birkenhead Park. Across the Mersey from Liverpool. He visited it and decided New York needed something similar. Of course, because it's America, they made it a lot bigger."

"I've never been there," I said.

"Where?"

"Birkenhead Park."

"Me neither."

"We should jump on a ferry across the Mersey and take a look at it sometime."

"You're on," said Dave. "If this is just a copy we should definitely see the original."

He looked at his watch.

"It's nearly two o'clock. Let's give it ten more minutes. Then we need to head off if we want to grab ourselves a drink before going back to the ship."

The Market Diner, close to the Cunard Piers, was packed. The low building, with a line of windows looking out onto the street and its name in neon lights up on the roof, couldn't be missed. Half of the interior was laid out as a diner while the other half, the main attraction for thirsty seafarers, was kept for drinking. A long, curved bar ran down the centre of the room and many of our shipmates had made a beeline for it as soon as they were allowed ashore. As far as they were concerned they'd seen all there was to see in New York. They'd be spending their time ashore eating and drinking until it was time to set sail again for Liverpool.

Sitting on a stool alongside the bar, talking to a smartly dressed, Italian-looking man with neatly-styled, dark hair, we could see our Head Steward, Les. The man with him was wearing a navy-blue jacket over a light-blue shirt with a soft, button-down collar. A white pocket handkerchief was tucked neatly into his breast pocket.

Les gave us a wave and shouted above the noise.

"Hey, boys. Come over and meet my friend, Joe."

Dave and I made our way towards Les, squeezing past groups of rowdy drinkers in the crowded bar. His companion stood up as we reached them and held out a hand in greeting.

"Joe Zellin," he said as we shook hands. "Les and I go back a long way."

Les put an arm round my shoulder and turned towards Joe. "The name of this fine young man is Steve. Stephen Crane. And his companion, who is an equally fine young man, is Dave. David Robertson."

'David Cuthbert' I thought to myself. But I didn't say anything.

Les surveyed the crowd.

"Joe owns this place, boys. The finest, and busiest, diner and bar in the whole of New York City."

"We do our best," said Joe, laughing. "And if Les approves, I'm happy. What would you like? On the house as it's your first visit."

Dave and I looked at each other.

"Coca Cola?" said Dave.

"Okay," I said. "That's fine with me."

Joe turned and lifted his hand. One of the bartenders reacted immediately and hurried towards him.

"Yes, boss?"

"Two Cokes and a couple of Hamm's, Danny."

The man scurried away and quickly returned with our drinks. The Coca Colas, along with the blue, gold and white cans of beer, were ice-cold and straight from the refrigerator. The word, Hamm's, was written on the side of each beer in a swirling, red typeface.

Joe passed our Cokes to us and gave one of the beers to Les.

"The Theodore Hamm Brewing Company," he said as he opened his drink with a can-piercer. "Based in St Paul, Minnesota. They were one of the first breweries to get themselves organised and start up again after prohibition."

He lifted the can to his mouth and took a generous swig, nodding approvingly.

"They like their beer, those folks up there in Minnesota. And they sure know how to make it. It's a shame for you two boys that here in New York City you can't legally enjoy it until you reach the grand old age of twenty-one."

No problem, Joe," I said. "We can wait. Coke's good."

"And what about your day, lads?" asked Les. "Did you get to the Empire State Building?"

"We certainly did," I said. "A bit expensive. But well worth it. And thanks for the tip about the view from the outside deck. It was great. Dave was telling me it's something his grand-dad always wanted to do. What did you say his name was, Dave?"

I knew I was skating on very thin ice but I couldn't help myself. Fortunately, as Dave gave me a look which I took to be a very final warning, Joe put his drink down on the bar.

He had a question for us.

"Were the pictures of the airplane which flew into the Empire State Building still on display?"

"A plane flew into the Empire State Building?" said Dave. "I never knew anything about that" Joe's question had distracted him. "There weren't any pictures there today were there, Steve?"

I shook my head. "No," I said. "Definitely not."

"It was just over nine years ago," said Joe. "July 28th, 1945. Just before ten in the morning. On a Saturday. It was my daughter's birthday which is why I remember the date. Usually on a Saturday I'd have been down here getting things ready for the lunchtime crowd. But we were all at my mother's apartment. On East 49th and Third. The whole family. Having a birthday breakfast. We had some music playing on the radio. And then over it we could hear the sound of an airplane engine. Very loud. There was a lot of mist around but we looked out and there was a plane, flying real low."

He paused for a moment, as if he was suddenly seeing it all over again.

"We couldn't believe our eyes. It just missed the Chrysler Building three blocks south. And it looked like it was going to hit the offices by Grand Central but it swerved away at the last minute and we lost sight of it. Then there was this huge explosion. Everywhere was shaking. Like the city was being bombed. I thought we were being attacked because we were still at war with Japan. What we didn't know back then, of course, was that we'd just built an atomic bomb and successfully tested it in New Mexico. And the war would soon be over."

He paused for a swig of Hamm's.

"Anyway, thinking we might be in danger, we hung around in the apartment for maybe ten or fifteen minutes. Then I rang one of my managers down at the diner here to see what was happening. It was him who told me the plane we saw had hit the Empire State Building. High up, just below the observation deck. I told him I was on my way over. And as I was crossing Fifth I could see the smoke. There was what looked like the tail of an airplane sticking out of the Empire State Building on the north side. The streets were all crowded with people trying to see what had happened. It turned out it was one of our military planes. A B25 Mitchell bomber. It had flown into the building at 79th floor level. Just below where you guys were standing. And the fuel tanks had exploded. So it had set off a big fire."

Joe scratched his head. There were tears in his eyes.

"I don't talk about it much," he said. "If I close my eyes I can still see that plane. As I said, there were some pictures on display last month. For the ninth anniversary I guess. But maybe they didn't want to leave them up too long. Just like me, people still get upset. One of the plane's engines shot right through the building and landed on the roof of a nearby penthouse studio, starting another fire which completely destroyed it. The other engine and part of the landing gear ended up by one of the elevators. The elevator operator, a lady called Betty Lou Oliver, was badly burnt. After the first aid team had stabilised her they put her in one of the other elevators to take her to hospital. What they didn't know was that the supporting cables had been damaged when the plane hit. And when the elevator car started to move it plunged all the way down to the basement."

"My God," said Dave. "What a way to go. And after surviving the initial crash too."

Joe looked at us and shook his head.

"You two are probably going to think I'm making this up. But she survived the fall in the elevator. Seventy-five floors she went down. They say it was the cables bunching up under the elevator car which acted like a sort of spring. And maybe a cushion of pressurised air built up as it fell. I don't think anybody knows for sure. But whatever the reason nobody has ever fallen further than Betty Lou Oliver in an elevator car and survived. She was pulled out with just a broken pelvis, a broken back, and a broken neck."

"Poor thing", I said. "But at least she was alive."

"Fourteen people died that morning," said Joe. "Three in the airplane and eleven in the building. It's a miracle it wasn't many more. But this is New York. The city that never sleeps. And never stops. Remember I said it happened on a Saturday morning?"

Dave and I nodded our heads.

"Now I'm not necessarily saying I think it was right," said Joe. "Maybe they should've been a bit more respectful of the dead. But first thing on the Monday. Less than forty-eight hours after the accident. The Empire State Building was open again for business."

THREE

ROCK AROUND
THE CLOCK

It was soon after sunrise.

I watched the flagship of the Cunard fleet, RMS Queen Mary, as she passed the Statue of Liberty and headed towards us, up the Hudson River. An early morning arrival at the Port of New York has for many years been one of the most iconic and spectacular of maritime experiences. I could see hundreds of passengers lining the rails of the upper decks, eager not to miss a single moment as their ship neared port.

The mighty ocean liner, which had been designed and constructed for that very passage, had carried them safely across the North Atlantic, one of the wildest and most challenging oceans on our planet. Now, having navigated her way through the Narrows and crossed the sheltered waters of New York Bay, she gradually reduced her speed and, shepherded by three tugs, edged her way carefully towards the Pier.

Cunard Pier 90 had been built to accommodate the Queen Mary which, until the very slightly larger Queen Elizabeth came into service, was the biggest ocean liner in the world. Passengers taking their daily exercise on the Promenade Deck were advised that three circuits was equal to one mile. The Media's Pier 92 was far too small for such a vessel. When she was finally tied up alongside, after making a very slow and deliberate turn through ninety degrees to line up with the dock, the Queen Mary's twelve decks towered over us.

I gazed up at her as the two thousand passengers on board began to disembark. One day, I thought to myself, I shall try and get myself a job on that ship. Being a member of her crew would be hard work. Les had worked on her for a couple of years before moving to the Media and he was full of stories about life on board. About the Hollywood stars and the famous sportsmen and women he had looked after. And about the jazz greats like Count Basie, Ella Fitzgerald and Oscar Peterson who would sometimes give impromptu concerts to entertain the passengers as they travelled to or from New York. There would be many tales to pass on to my grandchildren.

For the eleven hundred crew members the day in port would be hectic, unloading and loading supplies and baggage, refuelling, sorting out myriad engineering and general maintenance tasks, changing the sheets on the beds, and cleaning all the cabins and suites. Everything had to be checked and rechecked to ensure that the ship was fully ready for her return voyage to Southampton.

New passengers would be boarding within hours, and the Queen Mary would be leaving that same evening. Passengers expected to reach their destination on time. The return passage across the Atlantic had to go to plan. A rapid and efficient turnaround was essential. Time in port was unavoidable, but for such a large ship the fees were expensive and they had to be kept to a minimum.

Until 1952 the Queen Mary, as Cunard's flagship, had been the holder of the coveted 'Blue Riband' for the fastest Atlantic crossing. After carrying a group of war brides to Halifax, Nova

Scotia, she had completed the return journey to Southampton in just three days, 22 hours and 42 minutes, achieving an average speed of almost 32 knots (59 kms per hour). For almost fifteen years, until the launch of SS United States, she had remained the swiftest ocean liner of them all.

Life on our smaller ship, just half the size of the Queen Mary, was much more relaxed. Our first class passengers expected the best but they understood that RMS Media's cruising speed was slower. Our transatlantic voyage took three or four days longer, a pace which suited our passengers. And a very generous six days were allowed for the turnaround. Unlike the crew of the Queen Mary we had time to take full advantage of the many delights of New York City as well as keeping Joe Zellin and his staff at the Market Diner fully occupied.

Day two of our stay in New York was taken up by work. We had a job to do, caring for the needs of the mostly older passengers who had decided to remain on board and make full use of the ship's many comforts as well as the fine dining. But on day three we were free. We had money to spend. It was time to hit the shops.

"Head for the Thrift Stores," Les had said.

Back in post-war Liverpool, as in most of England, life was still 'make do and mend.' Little or nothing was thrown away. The rationing of bacon, sugar, cheese, margarine, cooking fats and eggs had come to an end only twelve months earlier, in 1953. And just one month before our ship had set sail for New York the UK Government had announced that from the morning of 4th July 1954 the very last thing which had still been restricted, fresh meat, would at last be freely available from butchers' shops across the nation.

It had been fourteen long and difficult years. Ration books were no more. They had been consigned to history. But the rebuilding of the country's bombed cities would take years. Life in England was still a very long way from returning to normal.

In the United States things were different.

War-time food rationing had been abandoned very soon after hostilities had come to an end. By the 1950s America was a full-blown, consumer society. The Thrift Stores in New York City, which were the U.S. equivalent of British charity shops, were packed with many perfectly serviceable goods which could not be found in Britain. American housewives with plenty of money to spend had donated them to charity after upgrading to newer models.

"Try the Salvation Army Thrift Store on West 46th," had been the suggestion from Les. "Half-way between 10th and 11th Avenues on the south side. It's less than ten minutes from the Pier. And they've got everything."

It was very good advice. The store was an Aladdin's Cave. As well as the usual clothes and small household items the three-storey building was packed with refrigerators, washing machines, dishwashers, Hoovers, radios and televisions.

And records.

"Take a look at this little lot, Steve."

Dave had found something interesting. It was a pile of seven-inch, 45 rpm singles, all with large holes in the centre. It seemed that they had just been thrown casually onto a table.

I picked up a couple at random and looked at the labels. One was a Decca recording.

"The song on this one's called *'Thirteen Women'*," I said, showing it to Dave. "By Bill Haley and His Comets whoever they are."

I turned the record over.

"The other side's called *'(We're Gonna) Rock Around The Clock'*," I said. "That sounds like it might be a bit more interesting."

"I dunno," said Dave. "Thirteen women could be pretty interesting. At least if they're the right kind of women."

"Thirteen'd be unlucky," I said.

"And knackering," said Dave with a grin. "But it could still be a lot of fun."

We were both still laughing as we shuffled through a few more of the records.

"I reckon this lot must have come from a jukebox," I said. "There's one in the Kardomah on Stanley Street in Liverpool. And the records on it have got these big holes in the middle."

"I suppose they've got to get rid of records which aren't getting played any more," said Dave. "So they end up in places like this."

He took the Bill Haley record from me and studied it carefully, moving it around from side to side so the light hit it from varying angles.

"This one's not in bad nick," he said. "If it's from a jukebox it must have been played quite a few times but I can't see that many scratches. D'you fancy seeing how much they want for the lot? None of our mates in Liverpool have got records from America. They'd be dead jealous."

We were up on the third floor. The cash desk was on the ground floor, by the door.

"I'll nip down," I said. "You wait here and keep an eye on the records."

The girl sitting by the cash-till looked surprised when I asked her how much it'd be for the whole pile of records.

"People usually just pick a record they like for ten cents. They cost sixty from a record store. So it's not a bad deal."

"Okay," I said. "But if I did want to buy them all would it work out cheaper?"

"I'm not sure," she said. "Nobody's ever asked. Give me a minute. I'll check with the store manager."

She pressed a button on her desk.

"He won't be long. How many records are there?"

"I don't know. We didn't count them. My friend's still up there so I could run up and check if you like."

"No. Don't worry. We can wait for the manager and see what he says."

The girl gave me a smile.

"I'm Julie, by the way. I like your accent. Where are you from?"

"England. Well, Liverpool to be exact. I'm Steve. And my friend upstairs is Dave."

"The two of you must be off one of the ships then. We get a quite a few guys in here from Liverpool. You know. Buying stuff to take home. Some even take away big stuff like fridge-freezers and washing machines. They say there's always plenty of room in the cargo hold on the return voyage to Liverpool." She paused for a minute. "I couldn't understand it at first. But they told me you can't get things like that over in England."

"That's right. You can't."

Julie shook her head, as if to say that she still couldn't understand it.

"That's crazy. I can't imagine always having to wash your clothes by hand. Or not being able to keep your food cold."

I thought of telling her about the many washboards, dolly-pegs and mangles that were still in daily use in some parts of Liverpool. Then I decided she probably wouldn't believe me. So I kept it simple.

"Some people back home have places they call larders," I said. "Like sort of cool rooms where they can store food." I shrugged my shoulders. "But keeping your food cold's not usually a problem in England. The weather's miserable. So the stuff we eat is mostly cold and wet anyway."

Julie laughed, and as she did so a slightly older man appeared. He was wearing the sort of light-brown work-coat that I associated with foremen in factories. He looked at me before moving protectively alongside the girl. I guessed he must be her manager.

"What's the problem, Julie?"

"It's okay. No problem, Mr Thompson. This chap, Steve, is from England. And he wants to know about the pile of records up on the third floor. The ones from the jukebox. I told him they're ten cents each. But he and his friend might want to buy all of them and he was wondering if that'd make them cheaper. His friend's still up there."

Mr Thompson looked at me again.

"To take back home to England?"

"I suppose so." I shrugged my shoulders. "I don't know what else we'd do with them."

"How many are up there?"

"I'm not sure. Thirty maybe? We haven't counted them."

Mr Thompson thought for a moment.

"Let's go take a look. Then I'll see what I can do."

Up on the third floor Dave was still guarding the records.

"This is the store manager, Mr Thompson," I said. "He wants to know how many records there are so he can give us a price."

"Thirty three," said Dave. "I've just counted them. Some look quite interesting."

"Quite interesting?" said Mr Thompson, giving him a smile. "I'm not sure that's the smartest way to start off a negotiation, young man."

He glanced at the pile of records.

"Thirty three you say?" He looked again. "Seems about right. I'll take your word for it."

He paused to think. "At ten cents each that'd be three thirty. I'm feeling generous. How about we say two dollars for the lot?"

Dave, who was good with numbers, did a few calculations in his head.

"Two dollars," he said to himself. "That's a bit less than a pound in our money. Which makes it about sixpence for each record." He nodded his head approvingly. "Seems pretty fair to me."

He looked at me to see what I thought.

"That's fine," I said. "Let's take 'em."

The deal was struck. Without realising it we had just purchased, along with thirty-two other seven-inch singles, an American copy of what would turn out to be the world's very first, smash hit, rock 'n' roll record.

As we made our way out of the store carrying our precious acquisitions in a canvas holdall which Julie, who had continued to be very chatty and friendly, had said was going spare, we came across several of our shipmates. They were spending freely with the aim of filling up at least some of the empty cargo space aboard RMS Media on the return voyage to England.

Electrical goods would have to be converted from the U.S 110 volts to the British 240 volts standard. But that wasn't a difficult job. Most of their purchases would be snapped up eagerly by family and friends, as they would dutifully explain to UK Customs. Being second-hand there wasn't usually any significant duty to pay. And there was a ready market in Liverpool for any American items, big or small, which were surplus to their own requirements.

We were very pleased with our little collection of American records. We would definitely not be selling them.

But we weren't quite finished.

In New York the very latest fashions in men's suits, shirts, shoes, hats and ties were on display in department stores such as Macy's and Bloomingdale's which had both been in operation for almost one hundred years. Within those same stores could also be found nylon stockings, the latest perfumes, and the most up-to-date styles in jewellery.

"We'll be proper Cunard Yanks by the time we get home,"

said Dave. "Citizens of the world. We'll get ourselves a couple of smart outfits. And pick up a few bits and pieces that you can't get hold of in Liverpool. You know. Stuff like lipstick. And stockings. For the girls."

He looked at me with a big grin.

"We'll be able to take our pick."

⁙

"Don't waste your precious dollars in those expensive Fifth Avenue stores," said Les as we were getting ready to go ashore. "Get yourselves down to the market stalls on Orchard Street. Sid Ginsberg's or Harry Finkel's. Their suits are half the price. And just as classy."

It was Thursday. In just over twenty four hours the engineers aboard RMS Media would be firing up her engines and we'd be on our way back to Liverpool. If we were going to find ourselves some natty suits we'd need to be quick.

Orchard Street on Lower East Side was busy. Shoppers laden with bags, which were stuffed full of purchases, hurried past us as we slowed down to look more closely at the myriad items which were on display. Wire baskets on the stalls were piled high with shirts. Brightly-coloured ties were pinned to painted, plywood boards. Some were narrow. Others wide. Above our heads the very latest in fashionable mohair and gabardine suits and jackets, protected from the weather by see-through plastic covers, dangled from their hangers on metal poles which stuck out at right angles from the brownstone walls of the tenement buildings.

A middle-aged New Yorker who was standing next to me pointed up at one of the jackets.

"Let's take a look at the dark-blue jacket. That mohair one."

The stallholder reached up to fish it down using a large hook on the end of a long, wooden pole. Dave and I watched as the potential purchaser examined the material and checked the seams and lining before trying the jacket on. It was a good fit and a few dollars changed hands. The stallholder checked each individual note very carefully before gathering them together and securing them with a metal clip. The jacket was neatly folded into a brown paper bag and the sale was complete.

"Have you seen anything you might fancy?" said Dave. "I reckon one of those mohair suits might look good. What d'you reckon?"

"Yeah, maybe. I'm not sure yet. Let's keep going and see what turns up."

We moved on to the next stall.

"We need to get something, Steve. We can't go back to Liverpool wearin' the same gear we had on when we left. If we want to stand any chance with the girls we need to get hold of some stuff like stockings and perfume as well. I don't know about you, but as well as not having to do National Service one of the reasons I signed on was to improve my chances with the ladies."

"You're still a virgin, then?" I said with a grin.

"I might be."

"Come on, Dave. Either you are or you're not."

"What about you, then?"

I shrugged my shoulders. "It depends. I might've done a little bit of this an' that. You know."

We both started to laugh.

"Forget a little bit of this an' that," said Dave. "Let's find ourselves some nice American gear. And with a little bit of luck we'll get some proper action with the girls back home."

FOUR

BACK TO LIVERPOOL

It was Friday 20th August. RMS Media would very soon be leaving New York and embarking on her long, transatlantic passage back to Liverpool.

For several hours Pier 92 had been a hive of frantic activity. Refrigerated lorries appeared on the dockside carrying last-minute perishables which had to be moved as quickly as possible to the on-board cold-store, next to the kitchens. Rope cages containing steamer trunks and expensive suitcases hung from the jibs of cranes as they were swung aboard. As soon as they hit the deck the cages had to be emptied, ready for the next consignment.

Dave and I were given the job of identifying the owner of each piece of luggage and ensuring that it was delivered promptly to the correct cabin or suite. Embarking passengers were already making their way along the gangway from the Pier to the ship, and they liked to get their cases and unpack them as soon as possible. Then they could then start to relax.

Even though the day was warm all the crew on duty and dealing with passengers had to be kitted out in full uniform according to Cunard's standing orders. Newly-arrived passengers would be guided to their accommodation by their personal

Cabin Steward so smartness and efficiency were essential. First impressions counted. For many years the ships of the Cunard Line had been regarded as the only way to cross the Atlantic and passengers expected the very highest of standards.

One of the Senior Stewards, Vince, had the task of ensuring that a very expensive set of Louis Vuitton cases arrived safely in the ship's most luxurious and expensive suite. And Dave, who never missed much, had spotted the name tag.

"I had a quick decco at that smart luggage Vince was handling," he said to me. "I think Katharine Hepburn might be on board."

He whispered the news to me as we were manhandling a very heavy and awkward steamer trunk to one of the smart suites on the upper deck. There was a leather handle at each end, designed to make it as easy as possible to move, but even with two of us sharing the weight it was hard work in the heat.

"Well if Miss Hepburn is on board I hope she's been more considerate than whoever packed this one. God knows what's in it. Gold bullion I shouldn't wonder knowing how rich some of these people are. It weighs a bloody ton. There should be some sort of weight limit on these trunks. Or they should be fitted with a set of wheels. Why hasn't anybody thought of that?"

"You just have," said Dave. "Patent it and you'll make a fortune."

I stopped and lowered my end of the trunk to the floor. We were half-way along the top corridor. Dave seemed to be okay but I needed a breather. The sweat was pouring off me.

He gave me about thirty seconds.

"Come on, Steve. One last effort and we're there."

I looked at the label on the trunk.

"Mr and Mrs J. C. Forsyth. Suite 403. That's two along on the left."

"Okay then," he said. "Let's go for it."

As we reached the door to Suite 403 it opened and a head popped out. It belonged to an elegant-looking lady who gave us a cheery smile.

"Ah!" she exclaimed, sounding both surprised and relieved. "You've got it. We were getting a bit worried it might have gone astray."

Stepping back inside she called out, presumably to Mr Forsyth. "It's here, Jim. The big trunk. A couple of the young Stewards are just arriving with it. Shall I see if they can bring it in and put it by the wardrobe?"

Her head appeared again. She was still smiling.

"Do you think you'd be able to pop it next to the wardrobe? Then my husband and I can get it unpacked."

Dave and I manoeuvred the trunk into position as requested.

"Will there be anything else, madam?"

"No. I think that's it. The rest of our luggage is already here. And Peter, our steward, called in a few minutes ago to show us where all the light switches are and so on. So thank you, but I think we're fine."

She turned towards the dressing table and opened the top drawer. Pulling out two twenty dollar notes, she pressed them into our warm and slightly sweaty hands.

"You boys look as though you've been working very hard. We really do appreciate it."

Dave and I looked at each other. Twenty dollars each. It was by far the most generous tip we had received since leaving Liverpool.

"Thank you, madam," I said, bowing my head slightly to show my very genuine gratitude.

Dave did the same.

"Yes, madam. Much appreciated. Thank you very much."

The door closed behind us as we left.

"Wow!" said Dave as we went to pick up our next consignment

of luggage. "What a lovely lady. Twenty each. That's almost two weeks' wages."

I looked at him.

"We're rich, Dave. Maybe it really was gold bullion?"

That evening the open deck at the stern of the ship was crowded. The weather was perfect for a sail-away and many of the passengers had decided to make the most of it. I wasn't officially a drinks waiter but with it being so busy I'd been roped in to help with the pre-dinner cocktails. The job wasn't that difficult. The staff behind the bar did all the mixing. I just had to circulate with a silver tray of glasses, each one decorated with a slice of orange or lemon, or a cherry on a cocktail stick, and try not to knock anything over.

Dave was jealous. He'd been given a job down below so he'd miss all the fun.

As six o'clock approached everyone moved towards the railings on the starboard side, drinks in hand. Still holding my tray I watched the men on the quayside as they removed the last two mooring ropes from the great, steel bollards and RMS Media started to move away from the Pier. For the first minute or two the ship's motion was so gradual that I had to fix my eyes on the jib of one of the dockside cranes to be certain we were actually under way.

There was a palpable air of anticipation and excitement among the passengers on the deck as the stern of the ship, still moving very slowly, edged its way out into the Hudson River while a pair of tugs hovered alongside us, ready for any mishap. Then, as we cleared the Pier and the New York tugs took their leave, the Captain up on the bridge moved the brass lever on the Chadburn telegraph to full ahead.

The power to the engines increased and the Media picked up speed, heading down the river past Battery Park and the southern tip of Manhattan. Not many minutes later we were passing the Statue of Liberty, from where a gentle turn to port would take us through the Narrows between Brooklyn and Staten Island.

As we entered Lower New York Bay a slight swell rocked our ship. The Atlantic Ocean lay ahead but the forecast was fair. All the signs were that we would be enjoying a pleasantly smooth passage.

By nine Dave and I were off duty, enjoying a drink in The Pig. Les was there with Peter, the steward responsible for Mr and Mrs Forsyth's suite.

The crew bar and eating area on all Cunard ships, as well as on most other British Merchant Navy ships, has long been referred to as 'The Pig'.

"Why do you think we call it 'The Pig'?" said Les with a smile.

Dave and I looked at each other.

"Pig and Whistle," said Dave. "But I suppose that isn't the full story. Come on, Les. You know everything. And you're dying to tell us. Fire away."

Les took a deep breath. Then he began.

"The origin of The Pig? Well, like so many other things to do with the sea it goes back a long way. And it has a link with Liverpool."

Les was a good story-teller. By mentioning our home city he had immediately grabbed our attention.

"But for the very beginning of the story you need to go back a bit further. Back to the fifteenth or sixteenth century when the English language sounded very different. At that time a 'piggin', was a word for a drinking bowl. And 'wassail' was another old English word."

He looked at us to make sure we were listening.

"You must've heard of people going wassailing around Christmas time," he continued. "You know. Getting together and having a good time. Usually helped along by a few drinks. Well, 'wassail' was a type of spiced ale which people used to drink in England. Particularly around Yuletide. Although it originally came from Norway."

"'Wassail' as in Shakespeare," said Dave. "In Macbeth. And Hamlet."

I looked at him in amazement.

"I've no idea where that came from," he said, laughing. "Half-forgotten English lessons at school probably."

"Your English teacher was right," said Les. "Shakespeare did use the word. Even though it wasn't one of the many which he invented. And if you put 'wassail' together with 'piggin' you've got 'piggin wassail'. Which was spiced ale in a drinking bowl."

He paused for a moment.

"You're probably ahead of me now. Say it quickly. 'Piggin wassail'. 'Piggin wassail'. 'Pig and wassail'. 'Pig and Whistle'"

I nodded my head.

"Great story, Les. But I don't see how it links up with the bar on a ship. Or Liverpool."

"The Pig and Whistle in Liverpool," said Les. "Down by the Pier Head."

"Of course," I said. "My Dad was a regular down there when he worked on the docks before the war. He said it was always packed out with sailors. Off the ships."

"And it's been that way for a hundred years or more," said Les. "Going back to when Liverpool was one of the busiest ports in the world. The crew on pretty much all the ships used to end up there. So 'The Pig and Whistle', or just 'The Pig', started to mean anywhere they could get themselves a drink. Which included on board their ships."

Dave reached into a pocket and pulled out a twenty dollar bill.

"Talking of getting a drink, Les, you must be ready for another. There's a tip here from a very generous passenger which says it's beers all round."

"Mr and Mrs Forsyth in 403," I said, turning to Peter. "They're yours aren't they? Dave and I were delivering a steamer trunk to their suite earlier on. And she gave each of us one of those lovely twenties."

He gave me a knowing smile.

"She slipped me ten just for giving her a two minute rundown on how everything in their suite worked."

"They must have a bob or two then?"

Peter nodded his head.

"Someone said he's big in films. Not acting or directing. Something in the background. On the money side. So we wouldn't necessarily have heard of him. But it looks like they've got plenty."

"Draught beers," announced Dave when he returned a few minutes later. "It's been a long day. We've earned 'em."

He lifted his tankard.

"Cheers!"

"She's on her way to Venice," said Dave.

"Who?"

"Katharine Hepburn."

We were collecting together the wooden, steamer chairs on the Promenade Deck and roping them together before covering them with a smart, blue tarpaulin. This task had to be carried out as a precaution every evening in case a swell built up overnight. It was a two-man job. So it gave us a chance to gossip.

"Who told you that?"

"A couple of passengers were going on about her," said Dave. "They were out here taking a stroll before breakfast when I was gettin' these steamer chairs ready for the day. You know, making sure they were all lined up properly. I didn't catch everything they were saying but apparently she's in a film called '*Summertime*' which is being shot over in Italy. She's travelling with another lady and they keep themselves to themselves most of the time. They usually turn up in the swish restaurant at about half-seven for dinner. But otherwise they get meals sent to their suite. I don't blame 'em really. Those suites have got pretty much everything you could possibly want."

"I think I'd probably do the same if I was in their shoes. Being so well known you'd probably feel people were staring at you all the time. I wouldn't mind the money of course. But apart from that I don't think I'd really want to be famous."

Dave leant towards me.

"The other thing." His voice dropped to a conspiratorial whisper. "The other thing they were sayin' was that she wears tailored trousers in the evening. Katharine Hepburn that is. She's the only woman on the ship who does. And the lady who's with her always wears very feminine dresses."

"So what?"

"So nothing. I'm just tellin' you, that's all. What those passengers were saying. They seemed to think it was a bit strange. You know. With the two of them sharin' a suite as well I suppose."

To encourage him to carry on I gave him a wink. He took the bait.

"And there's only one bedroom in those suites. The passengers can ask Cunard for the beds to be set up either as two singles or a double. It'd be interesting if it turns out they've got them made up into a double. We could ask Peter I suppose. But then again maybe they're just good friends. Who knows?"

"And to be perfectly honest, Dave, who cares?"

"Lots of people. The Hollywood gossip magazines wouldn't exist if they didn't. I remember readin' somewhere she got married and divorced when she wasn't much more than a teenager. An' she was living with Howard Hughes at one time. You know. The American billionaire guy who owns TWA. They say she's also been havin' an affair with Spencer Tracey for years. Ever since they were in a film together."

"So she must be into men," I said.

Dave thought for a minute.

"Maybe she's into both? They say some people are. Peter said he saw her before lunch today. Katharine Hepburn that is. Mr and Mrs Forsyth asked him if he could get together a few cocktails and nibbles for some people they'd invited to their suite. And when he took them in she was there. Along with her friend. Chattin' away the four of 'em were. Ten to the dozen. Like they were bosom buddies."

"Maybe they are," I said. "Mr Forsyth might have something to do with the film she's in and they're all off to Venice together. They might be getting a private limo when we arrive in Liverpool and heading for London to catch the Orient Express. That's how I'd do it if I had their money."

"Me too," said Dave. "Just imagine it, Steve. Across the Atlantic in a couple of smart suites. Being looked after hand and foot all the way. Then London to Venice on a luxury train." He shook his head. "If that's what they've got planned I'm dead jealous. I've wanted to go on that train ever since I read '*Murder on the Orient Express*'."

"The Simplon Orient Express," I said. "The original Orient Express didn't go to Venice. It was in a quiz on the radio."

"What was?"

"The fact that the original Orient Express didn't go to Venice. Agatha Christie should really have called it Murder on the Simplon Orient Express. Not the Orient Express."

Dave frowned at me.

"Forget it," I said. "It's not important."

Dave grinned at me. "It is if you're hopin' to see Venice."

"Okay. Yeah. Very funny."

As I made a few adjustments to the blue tarpaulin and started to rope it down I was trying to remember something else from the same quiz. Then the name came to me.

"Hercule Poirot."

Dave looked at me. "Who?"

"Hercule Poirot. I couldn't remember his name. You know. The detective in her books. He's a real character. They were saying on the radio she might kill him off one day."

"Why would she want to do that?"

"She might decide she's getting fed up with him. Like if you were in a book I was writing I could decide to get rid of you."

"You can forget about that," said Dave, looking a little miffed. "I thought we were good mates."

"In theory, Dave. Just in theory. Mind you some people think the whole world could be that way. You know. That we don't really exist at all and the universe is something that's been dreamt up by some all-powerful person who's just playing games with us. Or a super-intelligent machine. Like the big computer someone said they've just got at the university in Manchester."

"You mean like God?"

"Yeah. I suppose so."

I pulled hard on the rope over the tarpaulin.

"Can you hang onto it for a second, Dave? Keep it taut while I get this last knot tightened up."

With the final knot securely tied, the job was finished.

"That's it. We're done."

The two of us made our way down the white-painted, metal stairs which took us to the crew area. We weren't allowed to use the elegant staircases in the passenger areas unless a job for a passenger required it.

"What're we going to do to celebrate when we get back home?" said Dave. "We're going to have pretty much a whole week to kill before we're due back on the ship."

"What d'you reckon?"

"Well, we definitely shouldn't waste any time. See family obviously. But once that's out of the way we've got the mohair suits. We've got New York shirts and ties. We've got New York shoes. And we've got those sexy New York stockings for some lucky ladies to put on. As well as the perfume."

"So we need to find ourselves a couple of nice girls who'll appreciate them."

"And us too."

"Oh yeah. And us too. Those stockings and the other stuff we got weren't cheap. We're not giving 'em away and getting nothing back."

"Nice girls. But a bit naughty as well then."

"Oh, I think so," I said. "Or even very naughty."

"An' don't forget we've got to work out what we're going to do with those records we bought."

"Listen to them, I suppose. Then it'll depend what they're like."

"We'll need a record player."

"Okay. So we find ourselves a couple of girls," I said. "As naughty as possible. But nice. Who've also got a Dansette record player. Sorted. But we've got an ocean to cross first."

For more than four days the sea remained calm. Any waves which did put in an appearance were little more than ripples. Our ship hardly noticed them as we sailed north-east from New

York, keeping roughly parallel to the coast of Nova Scotia. Then we turned east and followed a course to the south of Greenland.

An old hand chatted away to us as he sat in The Pig one evening.

"I remember it being like this for three weeks solid one time when we was down in the Doldrums," he told us as he nursed his pint tankard. "Out in the middle of nowhere, just south of the equator. Drifting around and not a breath of wind. The sea was like a mill-pond, and my God it was hot. I've never known anything like it."

The sea around us wasn't quite a mill-pond, but for the North Atlantic it was as close to it as many of the longer-served members of the crew could recall. But they were also saying the weather around Greenland had a well-deserved reputation for being unpredictable. Even in the summer. It was only a matter of time before it turned nasty.

Earlier in the year, in April, May and June, enormous icebergs tear themselves free from glaciers in the north and drift south on the Labrador Current. Very slowly they melt and get smaller as they encounter the slightly warmer air to the east of Canada and Nova Scotia. But, as Captain Edward Smith so unexpectedly and tragically discovered on the 'unsinkable' RMS Titanic, they still pose a very real danger to even the greatest of ocean liners.

Iceberg Alley has to be navigated with care.

Our North Circle route across the Atlantic would take us very close to the site of that terrible loss. It was a sobering thought that somewhere on the ocean floor, in the eternal darkness thousands of feet beneath our keel, that mighty vessel would still be resting.

The offices of the White Star Line, who'd commissioned the Titanic to be built at the Harland and Wolff Shipyard in Belfast, were in Liverpool on the Strand, very close to the waterfront and a short walk from the Pier Head. Quite soon after that tragic sinking White Star were obliged to merge with the Cunard Line. So, as we were travelling on board a Cunard ship, those momentous events of April 1912 felt very close to home. Many of our passengers gathered together on deck as we approached the site. Wreaths were cast onto the water and prayers were said for the many who lost their lives.

Back in 1912 the one hundred and twenty-one dead bodies which were recovered from the sea had been transported by ship to Halifax in Nova Scotia, the birthplace of Cunard. There they were laid to rest in The Fairview Lawn Cemetery on a gently sloping hillside. Four rows of simple, dark-grey granite markers, one at the head of each grave, still stand there in the cemetery. Poignant reminders of an event which shook the world.

After the prayers the Commander of RMS Media, Captain F.G. Watts, led the assembly in a heartfelt rendition of the hymn 'For Those In Peril On The Sea'.

Years ago, back in Liverpool, when I told him it was one of my favourites, the vicar at our local church, Reverend Bates, had said it was based on Psalm 107. I've no idea at all why I remember that. It's strange the way random facts which will probably never be of any practical use lodge themselves in your head.

Our more experienced shipmates told us that Iceberg Alley tends to be free of such hazards in late August and that we were unlikely to come across any life-threatening icebergs. But Captain Watts posted an extra watch, just in case, and the wisdom of his decision was confirmed soon after the Titanic commemoration when a large berg was spotted drifting towards us from the north.

There was never any danger of a collision. But at sea it is wise to be cautious and take nothing for granted.

As the old hands had predicted might happen the weather changed late in the afternoon on our fifth day out of New York. We ran into a moderate swell as we were passing over the Mid-

Atlantic Ridge, south of Iceland. This hidden mountain range which rises almost ten thousand feet from the deep ocean floor stretches from the Arctic almost as far as Antarctica. As the massive tectonic plate on which North and South America sit continues to move slowly westwards, and the Eurasian and African tectonic plates move eastwards, the ocean floor is opened up allowing hot, volcanic magma to rise from beneath the earth's crust and solidify as lava, forming yet more underwater peaks.

I remembered looking at a map of the world when I was younger and thinking how strange it was that if they could be pushed together the western edge of Europe and Africa would slot very snugly against the eastern edge of North and South America. Any suggestion back then that it was more than a coincidence, that the continents were actually on the move over the surface of the planet, would have been dismissed as the ravings of a lunatic.

This astonishing geological process, which has been termed continental drift, began one hundred and eighty million years ago at a time when the Americas were joined to Europe and Africa. They were all part of one gigantic supercontinent called Pangea.

And the continents are still drifting. Each year the distance across the ocean between New York and Liverpool increases by two to three inches.

As the winds grew stronger and the swell increased I spent as much time as I could out on deck, staring at the distant horizon as it rose up and then dropped down with the movements of the ship.

Happily it seemed that 'Wandering Hans' was right. Because

my brain was getting the same signals from both my eyes and my ears I felt fine.

No more Krakatoa Cocktails.

Despite the good doctor's strange penchant for buttock massage I was deeply grateful for his excellent advice. I would never again allow my brain to get confused and scrambled.

On Sunday 29th August in the early hours of the morning our ship entered the North Channel between Ireland and Scotland. It marked the point at which we were leaving the deep ocean. Ahead of us lay the Irish Sea. And on the far side of that sea, after passing to the west of the Isle of Man, we would reach the River Mersey and Liverpool.

Dave and I hadn't been able to sleep. We were both experiencing a strange combination of apprehension and excitement as we got closer to home.

We'd been away from Liverpool for just twenty-two days. But it felt like a lifetime.

How much can two young people change in such a relatively short space of time?

We both knew the answer.

There hadn't been much time for sleep anyway. Our passengers, who had spent nine relaxing days being very well looked after, had been instructed to leave their packed suitcases and bags in the corridor outside their cabins no later than midnight. Our task as cabin boys was to get the luggage down to the lower deck where it would all be gathered together ready for loading into the rope cages which would be swung ashore the following day.

Having delivered the last pieces of luggage to the lower deck at just before three o'clock in the morning we were up again at five.

"Reveille! Reveille! Come on you lazy lot. Rise and shine for the Cunard Line!"

It was Les, striding along the corridor and banging a copper saucepan with a metal spoon, shouting us awake. He was well aware that we had been very late to bed. But there was more work to be done.

Breakfasts had to be delivered on silver-plated trays to passengers who had decided not to eat in the restaurant. Final accounts had to be collected from the purser's office and placed in the clips outside each cabin or suite. Last minute messages had to be rushed here and there within the ship. Passengers who were wandering around looking confused and lost had to be guided to their destinations. And their anxious, last minute queries and problems had to be addressed and sorted out.

RMS Media and all her passengers had to be ship-shape and ready for disembarkation.

We would soon reach the Mersey Bar, an elevation of the sea bed created by the movement of sand and sediments where powerful Irish Sea tides fight against the constant outflow from the River Mersey. Dave and I were instructed to go out on deck and check that all loose items were safely stowed away. The Irish Sea can be deceptively treacherous and rough. Before our ship crossed the Bar a pilot from Liverpool would have to join the ship.

We pushed against the self-closing hinges on the outer door and emerged onto the deck. There was almost no wind but a thin, early morning mist made the air feel cool. Peering through the mist we could just make out the flat shoreline of Lancashire with its beaches and sand-dunes. And in the distance, pointing up at the sky through the mist like a skeletal finger, was the unmistakeable outline of Blackpool Tower.

We would soon be home.

As we busied ourselves with our tasks a motor launch

appeared, travelling fast from the direction of the Mersey. The launch was the Liverpool pilot-cutter. It made a wide turn through 180 degrees and approached us, exactly matching our speed. As the cutter continued to move forwards through the water in tandem with our ship, maintaining a position alongside an open hatchway in our hull, a man wearing a life-jacket and carrying what looked like a briefcase stepped out of the cabin.

For a couple of moments he stood precariously on a narrow walkway, steadying himself by gripping a wooden rail which ran along the roof of the cabin with his left hand. Then, as the two vessels moved closer together until they were almost touching, he stepped off the launch and onto our ship. His transport then increased the power to its engines and peeled away from our hull, heading back towards the Port of Liverpool.

Our pilot was on board. We could now make our crossing of the Mersey Bar.

His highly-skilled task, one that Les told us had been carried out by the Liverpool Pilot Service for almost two hundred years, would be to guide our ship safely through the constantly-shifting sandbanks and channels of the Mersey Estuary. The Atlantic tides cause huge volumes of sea-water to flow in and out of the relatively shallow Irish Sea every day. This daily movement of water gives the Mersey Estuary, and the lower reaches of the river itself, one of the biggest tidal ranges in the world although it can't quite match the Bristol Channel, or compete with the Bay of Fundy between Nova Scotia and New Brunswick in Canada.

Dave and I had been ordered to report back to Les for further instructions as soon as we had finished checking the open deck. So we were down below and didn't see the two Liver Birds, Bertie and Bella, emerge from the mist as the Media made her final approach to the dock. Perched high above the river on the Royal Liver Building, Bella, the female Liver Bird, faces the sea. She watches the ships as they make their way back to port, while Bertie, the male, looks inland across the city. His job is to make sure that the girls who are left behind in Liverpool when the ships set sail, often for many months, behave themselves while their menfolk are away.

⬥⬥⬥⬥⬥⬥⬥⬥⬥

"Come here you two."

Les had a job for us.

"I want you to take the luggage belonging to Miss Hepburn and her companion to the limousine on the other side of Customs. They're being driven down to Claridge's Hotel in London with Mr and Mrs Forsyth. The four of them are leaving for Venice on the Simplon Orient Express tomorrow morning."

Dave and I looked at each other and nodded. Our guess had been right. As had the quiz-master on the radio.

"We thought that might be what they were planning, Les."

But Les hadn't finished.

"Your job isn't to think. Or gossip. Your job is to keep yourselves busy. The Forsyth's cases should already be there. Alongside the car. Their chauffeur'll be keeping an eye on them. But you're to wait with the luggage until the Forsyths, along with Miss Hepburn and her companion, are all safely through Customs and Immigration. Then, when they arrive at the car, you will very politely ask them to check that all their bags are there. Understood?"

"Yes, Les. Understood."

"I'm making the two of you personally responsible for every single item of luggage until it's all been loaded into their limousine. And don't you dare leave until every last case has been checked and safely locked away in the boot."

Dave and I stood there, awaiting further instructions.

Les looked at the two of us as if we were simple.

"What are you hanging about for?" he shouted. "Haven't I made myself clear? Move yourselves. Now!"

FIVE

REST AND RECREATION

My mother, who was half-lying on the settee in the front living room with her feet up, put her knitting down and gave me a smile.

"Oh my Lord. Look at you! Three weeks away and you're not my little Stephen any more. You've turned into a man."

"What's up, Ma?"

"Nothing, love. Nothing at all. It's just that you've changed."

"It's only a suit, Ma."

"I know. But you don't see suits like that here in Liverpool. And what about that shirt. And your tie. You look. I don't know."

"American?"

She nodded her head.

"Yes. I suppose so. Like you see in the pictures."

"And you don't like it."

"Oh no! It's not that. Not at all. I love it. You look so smart and mature. It's wonderful. But all of a sudden you're growing up. So very fast. And if I'm honest I'm not altogether sure I like that."

She was still smiling but her eyes looked a little tearful.

"I suppose I'm worried I might lose you," she said. "And you're all I've got left now apart from your two uncles. You know. With your sister falling for that young American airman from Burtonwood and going off to the United States. And then your Dad disappearing."

"Don't be daft, Ma. I'm not going anywhere. Just into town with Dave."

I bent forwards and she moved her legs to one side so I could sit alongside her.

"Come here."

She gave me a kiss on the cheek. And a big hug.

"It's only a few days before we leave again for New York, Ma. So we've got to make the most of it."

"Don't worry. I understand, love. You've got your whole life ahead of you. And you only get one stab at it."

I put an arm round her shoulders.

"Thanks, Ma. And if me and Dave hadn't signed up with Cunard we'd have been called up for National Service. And probably sent off to fight the Mau Mau in Kenya or something. Then you might really have lost us. For good."

"I know, love. I know. You're right."

I gave her a hug and a kiss.

"And what about Dave?" she said briskly, picking up her knitting again and pushing the stitches along the pair of needles. It was a message that she was fine. "Will he be all dressed up in smart New York clothes too?"

"I guess so. I've not seen him since the cab dropped us off last night. But he got himself a suit and so on too. So I reckon he'll want to wear it. No sense in buying a nice suit and just hanging it in the wardrobe."

"Bring him in to say hello before you go. I'd like to see the pair of you together. Two young dandies. Out on the town." She smiled to herself. "I never thought I'd see the day."

I glanced at my watch.

"I'd better go. Dave's expecting me to give him a knock in

about five minutes. We'll see you before we go. But it'll have to be quick. Just a couple of minutes. We've got a cab booked and we're meeting a couple of girls outside The Grafton at eight-thirty. We can't be late."

I gave her another kiss.

"Back in two minutes."

As I stood up she squeezed my hand.

"That's fine, love. Just fine."

<hr />

"Your Mum's starting to look her age, Steve."

Dave was staring out of the cab at the Victorian terraces which we were passing on our way to The Grafton. It was getting late and most of the windows were already curtained against the coming darkness.

"You're right," I said. "She does look older. I feel a bit guilty about leaving her. I couldn't have done it if my two uncles hadn't been living there with her. As you know, Georgie's never left home. And Jimmy moved back in last year after he fell out with his wife. A right bitch she was according to Ma. She said it was a mistake him ever marrying her. I never met her, but Ma normally sees the best in everybody so she must be a really nasty piece of work. She says there's no chance of them ever getting back together. So it looks like Georgie and Jimmy will be living in St Bride Street permanently. Which is good. There's plenty of room. The two of them have got their own space upstairs so they're no bother. And it means they can keep an eye on her. You know. Be there to help if Ma gets herself into any sort of trouble. To be fair to her she's never tried to tell me what to do with my life. Never. But I could tell she was a bit upset at the idea of me going off to sea."

"National Service would be worse," said Dave.

"That's what I said to her. But we've got to do six years with Cunard or they can still call us up."

Now it was me staring out at the passing houses. And thinking.

"I wish she still had my Dad and Jean at home, though," I said. "As well as her two brothers. It'd make things a lot easier."

I started counting on my fingers, working my way back from December 1949.

"D'you know it'll be five years ago this Christmas that my Dad went missing," I said.

Dave turned away from the window and looked at me.

"And you still don't know what happened to him? It's weird him just disappearing like that. No note. No messages. Nothing. It doesn't make sense. A grown man can't just disappear." He shook his head as if he didn't understand it. "Are the police still looking for him?"

"I don't think so."

We sat in silence as the cab made its way towards The Grafton along the evening streets.

For nearly five years the whole family had buried my father's disappearance away. We'd always changed the subject if someone asked questions or tried to talk about it.

Was I going to change the subject yet again? Or was I going to tell Dave what I'd found? When he'd said 'no note' it had got me thinking. I was pretty sure he wouldn't mention it to anybody else. And it'd be good to talk it through with someone I knew I could trust.

"I've just found a letter," I said, breaking into the silence. "My Dad sent it to Ma after he disappeared. It was tucked away inside an old book in the parlour. Up on one of the shelves. I think Ma must've hidden it. It looked like it'd been there for a while. There was a date on it. 24th January, 1950."

Dave looked puzzled.

"That's over four years ago. Are you sure? I mean are you sure the letter was from your Dad?"

"Yeah. I probably shouldn't have read it. But I did. And it was definitely his writing."

"So he's alive?" said Dave.

"It looks like it," I said. "Or at least he was four years ago. I'll show it to you tomorrow. There's no time to talk now. We'll be there in five minutes. Forget about it and let's enjoy ourselves. Okay?"

We sat in silence again as The Grafton got closer.

"Peacocks," said Dave, relieving the slight tension and giving me a grin. "That's what your Ma said we were. A pair of peacocks in smart American outfits."

"I think she was quite proud of us though." I said, pleased that Dave had come up with something else to talk about. "You know. When she said peacocks. I reckon she meant like when they display their feathers. All bright and colourful. Trying hard to impress the ladies."

"That sounds like us," he said. "So let's hope we do."

Dave looked down at the sleeve of his mohair jacket and rubbed the material gently between his fingers.

"This American gear's good, isn't it. If we can't score lookin' like this we might as well give up. You know. Accept we're always going to be virgins and sign up as priests."

I laughed as he carried on.

"Do you think they're really celibate, Steve? You know. Priests and monks?"

"Don't even go there, Dave. There's enough problems in the world. Religion's complicated."

I looked at the gold-coloured watch on my left wrist with its light brown, leather strap.

"If this was a real Rolex it would've cost a small fortune," I said. "Let's see yours."

Dave tugged at the cuff of his shirt to expose his wrist.

His watch was less heavy than mine but it looked equally expensive. Finely inscribed on the face, below the thick bar which marked twelve o'clock, I could see the words 'GRUEN PRECISION'. Attached to the platinum-coloured case was a black strap, tooled to resemble crocodile skin.

Dave looked at his watch. I could tell he was thinking.

"People sometimes get their hands chopped off," he said. "So expensive watches like these can be stolen."

"Brilliant," I said. "But hopefully not at The Grafton."

Dave was still thinking.

"It'd be a real drag to lose one of your hands for a watch. And the thief'd be pretty gutted too. Goin' to all that trouble and then discovering he'd nicked a fake."

"Forget it, Dave. It's not going to happen. As long as the girls think they're the real McCoy and we're loaded. That's all that matters."

Our teenage dates for the evening would never know that in a few days we'd be making a visit to a pawnbroker friend up on Everton Brow to get a bit of cash for the two watches. The guy in the shop was a decent bloke. He wouldn't be fooled by them. If we got a tenner for the pair we'd be happy. It'd still be more than we'd shelled out in New York.

Hopefully, before then, the two girls would have been impressed enough to think we were decent prospects. And want to keep us happy.

The Grafton Rooms were at the city end of West Derby Road in the Kensington area of Liverpool. For more than thirty years the large dance hall, with its ornate marble staircase, scarlet and gold décor, and canopied bandstand, had been a place where locals could meet up and dance the night away.

And sometimes get to know each other a little better.

The cab dropped us at the main entrance, above which was a triangular canopy. A row of lights had been attached to it to brighten up the immediate surroundings. The evening was reasonably warm and dry, and dozens of young people were milling around on the pavement.

Dave was the one who'd set up the meeting. But he didn't seem to be entirely sure about the exact arrangements.

"What do the two girls look like?" I said.

He scratched his head.

"It's been quite a while since I saw Pamela." He stopped to think. "She's got dark hair and she looks a bit like her brother, Greg. I know what he looks like."

"So do I," I said. "And if Pamela looks anything like her brother I'll take a chance on her mate. What's her name?"

Dave furrowed his brow.

"Sylvie," he said.

"What?"

"Sylvie. I'm pretty sure that's what Pamela said her mate's called. Her mother was French."

"Nice," I said. "I like French."

"So you're happy?"

"Yeah. I'm fine. But we've still got to find them. You fixed it up. What exactly did you say?"

"That we'd meet them by the main doors at eight-thirty."

"Brilliant," I said. "There's at least fifty pairs of girls out here who could be them."

"It was Greg I spoke to. I told him we'd have smart American mohair suits on. Dead expensive. And Greg said he'd mention it to Pamela."

I looked at Dave's outfit. Then at the crowd.

"Stop me if I'm stating the bleeding obvious, Dave. I'll grant you our suits are smart. And they do look expensive. But it's getting a bit dark. And in the dark they don't look all that different from the bog-standard outfits most of the other lads are wearing."

"Trust me. It'll be fine."

"That's what you always say," I said. "Next time I'll do the organising."

But Dave wasn't listening. He was staring at an attractive girl who was walking towards us, looking slightly nervous. She was wearing a loose-fitting, sleeveless dress with a narrow, matching belt which drew the material in around her waist. It made the most of what was a very good figure. The material was pale cream, with a gold and yellow floral design. She had chosen well.

"You wouldn't be Dave, would you?" The girl had stopped next to him. "I was looking round and I thought maybe I recognised you."

"Yes," said Dave, sounding relieved. "That's me." He pointed in my direction. "And that's Steve. My mate."

"I'm Pamela," said the girl. "Greg's sister. Sylvie's in the lobby."

I looked closely at Pamela. She was very obviously Greg's sister. She had dark hair, as Dave had said. And there was a definite family likeness. But she had drawn the lucky straw when the genes were being handed out. She had all of Greg's best features. And few, if any, of his less attractive ones.

Dave had already told me in the cab that he fancied Pamela as his date for the evening. And as he'd fixed everything up I'd agreed. Having seen her I almost suggested a swap but I quite liked the idea of Sylvie. I was wondering if she'd have a French accent. It would be the icing on the cake. French accents were so sexy. Even the very slightest trace would be enough.

Pamela shook hands with each of us and we kissed, demurely, cheek to cheek.

"Let's go and meet Sylvie," said Dave, placing himself firmly between me and Pamela and holding out his hand to indicate that she should lead the way.

He'd staked his claim. Any idea of a swap was off the cards. But that was fine. As I say, I liked the idea of Sylvie.

The lobby was no more than about half-full and a girl approached us as we entered.

She gave Pamela a smile.

"So," she said. "You found them."

It was Sylvie. Her hair was shoulder length and fair. Her face was delicate with just a hint of make-up. And she had the most perfect, slightly tanned skin. She was wearing a metallic, brocade dress, dark gold in colour with a pale blue, butterfly motif.

And she spoke with the most gorgeous French accent.

Oh my God! I'd struck gold.

If we hadn't left the perfume and stockings at home the evening would have been a complete success.

I was totally smitten by Sylvie and her French accent. As well as by the way she kissed me as we got to know each other a little better. Dave, however, who had known Pamela since she was very young, seemed to be slightly less certain, overawed maybe by the way she had blossomed into an extremely attractive teenager.

Both the girls seemed to like us which was a plus. They were definitely impressed by our sophisticated American outfits. And by our expensive-looking watches.

I'm not sure what Pamela thought, but as far as Sylvie was concerned the fact that Dave and I would, in a just few days, be returning to New York City seemed to be an added bonus. It made us just that little bit exotic. And attractively dangerous to know. It was a shame. The perfume and the stockings would almost certainly have sealed the deal.

But not to worry. I'd whetted Sylvie's appetite by describing all the wonders of America and the multitude of beautiful things which could be found in the big stores like Bloomingdales and Macy's.

We'd definitely be seeing each other again. And maybe next time?

I met up with Dave outside his house the following morning. I'd already removed the letter from its hiding place in the parlour and we headed down to town for a coffee.

Once we were sitting at our table I gave the letter to Dave and watched his face as he read through it.

Amsterdam
January 24ᵗʰ 1950

My dearest Barbara,

It is now just over a month since I left England, and I thought very long and hard before writing this letter. As you can see, I am alive. And I wanted you to know that. Even though we shall almost certainly never see each other again.

As we discussed many, many times after my return home, the war changed me. You said I was a different person. And, as always, you were right.

I talked to you about a young French Resistance fighter. Her name was Anna. We were lovers, as I am sure you must have realised.

When the war finished I thought that would be the end of it. Then in July last year I received a letter.

It was from Anna. She told me that she had a four year old daughter.

My daughter. Her name is Karin.

When I said to you back in September that I was going to travel to France to meet up with some old wartime comrades it was the truth. But it was not the whole truth.

Anna was there, as I was sure she would be. And as soon as I saw her I knew that she was much more than just a comrade.

She lost all her family in that terrible war. She and Karin were alone in the world. You still have your family, and they needed me in a way that you did not.

I am now with them.

I hope, and believe, that you will understand.

The three of us will be leaving Amsterdam very shortly for another country. We are living and travelling under assumed names and we have constructed a foolproof, but completely false, past life.

I doubt that you will wish to try. But you will never track us down.

This is the only letter I shall write. If you want Jean and Stephen to know that I am alive, then you must tell them.

I am truly sorry, but I have done what I thought was best.

With my love, and my heartfelt thanks for the many good times we shared.

John

When he came to the end of the letter Dave just sat there for a few moments, looking stunned. Then he turned to me.

"Have you told your Ma you've found this?"

"No." I shook my head. "I wouldn't even begin to know what to say to her."

"So what are you going to do?"

"Put it back in the book and say nothing," I said. "Look at the date. January 1950. That's only a month or so after he disappeared. And he says he's leaving Amsterdam. He could be anywhere by now."

Dave didn't say anything. He just nodded his head.

"It looks to me like Ma decided there wasn't much she could do about it," I said. "And she might've been too ashamed to tell me that my Dad had gone off with another woman. You know. Like she'd failed in some way. So she just hid the letter away and forgot about it."

"You're right," said Dave. "Stick it back inside the book and say nothing. End of story."

"We need a spider," said Greg.

It was Thursday morning. In two days we were due to report back to the ship and we were sitting in the living room of Dave's house with Greg. On the floor around us were the vinyl records we'd brought home from New York. Greg's sister, Pamela, was the proud owner of an almost new Dansette record player and she'd agreed to let us have it for the day.

Greg had just turned up with it.

Apart from the three of us the house was empty. Dave's father was out at work and his mother had sadly been killed in an air raid during the May 1941 Blitz on Liverpool.

She'd been staying with her sister who lived in Bootle, close to the docks which were the target of much of the German bombing during that dreadful month. In the middle of the night, when the family were sheltering in the basement, the house had suffered a direct hit. Dave's five year old cousin had been pulled out alive but he'd died a few days later. All the others had been crushed beneath tons of falling masonry.

By the end of the Blitz only fifteen percent of the houses in Bootle were left standing. Over 4,000 civilians on Merseyside had lost their lives, and more than 70,000 were homeless. It was a tragedy which affected many, many families. Dave and his father were not the only ones to suffer.

It was all-out war. But life had to go on.

"We need a what?" I said.

"A spider," said Greg. "It's a little plastic thing you slot into the jukebox-sized hole in the middle of a record to make it smaller. Then it fits nicely over the small spindle on the turntable. Ideally you need one spider for each record. Otherwise you've got to keep switching it from record to record. Which is a bit of a faff. And they're not all that strong. They tend to break if they're being changed all the time."

"So it's thirty odd spiders we need or we can't listen to the records?" I said. "And we haven't even got one."

Greg looked thoughtful for a moment.

"We might have one," he said. "There was this white, plastic thing came with the Dansette. Pam said she thought it might be something to do with playing records off jukeboxes. But I wasn't really listening. Now I'm thinking she might've been right."

He picked up one of the records and studied it.

"Yeah. It was about the size of that big hole. And there was a small hole in the middle which fitted the spindle on the turntable. We were playing some of Pam's English records so we didn't need it."

"Where is it then?" I said. "You haven't chucked it out, have you?" I couldn't believe it. "You must've known it was there for a reason."

"No problem, Steve. Pam wouldn't let me do that. She's one of those people who never throws anything away."

"Okay. Let's go and get it. Where is she this morning?"

"At the Meccano toy factory in Old Swan. Binns Road. She's got a part-time job there. Packing Hornby Double-O trains into boxes. She clocks off at lunchtime."

I looked at Dave.

"How d'you fancy shooting over there and seeing if she's still got it?"

"Sod off, Steve. It's about four miles to Binns Road. Who d'you think I am, Roger Bannister? Even at his speed it'd take about twenty minutes. So for me it'd be an hour at least. Just to get there. And if there's loads of people clocking off I probably wouldn't be able to find her anyway."

"I'm sure we can sort something out," said Greg. "There's no point in poor Dave going all the way over to Old Swan on the off-chance."

He had a smile on his face. And while he was talking he'd reached out with his right hand and started to tickle my left ear.

"Bugger off, Greg. What the heck d'you think you're playing at?"

As I moved to grab hold of Greg's hand he pulled it away with a flourish.

"Magic!" he said triumphantly. "I've found it!"

Between his thumb and forefinger he was holding a white plastic spider.

Dave began to laugh. I wasn't amused.

"Bloody hell, Greg. When're you gonna grow up?"

"Never if I can help it," he said, picking up one of the records and joining Dave in his laughter. "Anyway, you should be impressed. Close-up stuff like that takes a lot of practice."

Very deftly he fitted the white spider into the hole.

"Okay then," he said. "Let's see what this American music of yours is like."

The Dansette sounded good. Better than we expected. But the verdict on the records was mixed.

Bill Haley's recording of 'Rock Around The Clock' was undoubtedly the pick of the bunch. We played it about ten times in succession. It wasn't like anything we'd ever heard before and it was very difficult to understand why it hadn't been a massive hit in America.

As we sat there, mesmerised by the totally new rhythm and

sound, we didn't know that we were probably among the very first teenagers in England to hear it. What we also didn't know was that it hadn't received any worthwhile publicity in America. It hadn't even been released as an 'A' side. For some strange reason 'Thirteen Women' had been selected, and promoted, as the 'A' side.

It wasn't until 'Rock Around The Clock' was chosen for the soundtrack of the hit film 'Blackboard Jungle' that it rocketed to the top of the charts.

Several of the other records were already familiar to us. 'Stranger In Paradise' by Tony Bennett, 'I believe' by Frankie Lane, and 'That's Amore' by Dean Martin had all been hits in England.

There was also a novelty record called '(How Much Is) That Doggie In The Window'. The version we had brought back on the ship, though, was by an American singer called Patti Page. The hit record in England had been by a Liverpool singer called Lita Roza. As often happened back then she had recorded a cover version specially for the UK market. And it had outsold Patti Page's recording several times over to become the very first UK Number One for the city of Liverpool.

After we'd got through all the records the three of us were in full agreement on one thing.

"That 'Rock Around The Clock' is just incredible," said Dave.

His judgement was spot on. Within twelve months millions of youngsters around the world would buy the record, while older people would be horrified by the disorder and fighting which Bill Haley and His Comets seemed to trigger everywhere they performed.

'TEDDY BOY RIOTS' screamed the newspaper headlines.

It was a new kind of music. And it was waking up a generation. The press were now calling them teenagers. And they were determined to make themselves heard.

It was Bill Haley who lit the touch paper. But he was nearly thirty years old. 'Rock Around The Clock' was tame and almost old-fashioned compared with what was to follow.

Hidden away among the next batch of Julie's jukebox cast-offs would be the record which really started to change things. The original, overtly sexual lyrics had been cleaned up so radio stations would play it. Without the changes the record would have been banned. It would never have been accepted by a mainstream audience.

'A-wop-bop-and-a-good Goddam!'

The song was 'Tutti Frutti'.

And the singer was Little Richard.

'A lot of people call me the architect of rock 'n' roll. I wouldn't say I started it all. But I don't remember anyone else before me playing that stuff.'

Richard Wayne Penniman ('Little Richard')

SIX

RETURN TO NEW YORK

The passenger lounge on RMS Media was very smart with décor and furnishings which gave it a pleasantly relaxed atmosphere. Four metal-framed windows were equipped with aluminium handles which allowed a narrow, upper section to be opened for ventilation. The windows looked out onto the Promenade Deck and a sheltered, sunbathing area.

Comfortable armchairs and settees, all upholstered with a patterned material depicting large tropical leaves, were dotted around the room. Low round tables, each with an ashtray, were placed in such a way that one of them would always be within easy reach of a passenger who needed to flick some ash from a cigarette or put down a cup of coffee. Nearer the middle of the room there were two small, square tables with four upright chairs, suitable for card games such as bridge, whist or canasta.

The largest item in the room was a baby grand piano. It stood to one side of a slightly elevated stage with a proscenium arch which was used for small-scale drama productions and evening recitals by the seven piece, on-board orchestra. The piano had been faced with Formica which had an elegant 1940s design. People would lean against it with drinks or coffees in their hands as the ship's pianist was playing in the evening. Thanks to the practical Formica the inevitable drips and spills were quickly wiped away leaving no trace.

On one side of the room, facing the windows, there was a small bar. Alongside it was a small galley where simple snacks along with tea and coffee could be prepared.

The style of the windows, and the absence of any direct view of the sea, made the room feel more like a luxury apartment on shore than a ship's lounge but it was still a popular meeting place, particularly after dinner. Our well-travelled guests would order cocktails, or one of the special Cunard blends of filter coffee, while exchanging gossip about their fellow passengers or competing with each other in the telling of extravagant tales about their journeys to various exotic parts of the world.

As lowly Cabin Boys, Dave and I had not been allowed to enter the lounge on our first transatlantic voyage. But when we'd reported for duty at the Cunard Building before the voyage I had unexpectedly been promoted to the role of Lounge Steward. So on this second voyage the elegant passenger lounge would be my place of work.

My unexpected elevation was not because of any special skill or merit that I might have demonstrated as a Cabin Boy. It was a stroke of luck. And I felt a bit guilty that Dave had not been similarly fortunate.

Paul Lewis, one of the regular Lounge Stewards, had been taken ill two days before we were due to sail. A routine x-ray had shown some shadowing on his lungs which was diagnosed as pulmonary tuberculosis. In the 1950s this debilitating illness was sadly still quite common and Liverpool had a large hospital in Fazakerley, north of the city centre, devoted solely to its treatment.

The role of Lounge Steward was much sought after. The passenger lounge was a pleasant working environment and, even better, there was the opportunity to get to know passengers and provide them with excellent service. Such service would hopefully be rewarded with equally excellent tips.

Lounge Stewards on Cunard ships usually received a period of training before taking on the role but the last minute nature of my appointment had left no time for such preparation. I would be jumping in at the deep end without knowing for sure if I could swim but hopefully there'd be no disasters. Graeme Moffatt, the Senior Lounge Steward, seemed to be friendly. So I was fairly confident he'd show me the ropes. And point me in the right direction if he saw me struggling.

An older lady with permed, blonde hair who was sitting on her own in the lounge lifted a hand and called me over. It was our first morning at sea and I was on duty in the lounge with Graeme.

"My husband has gone back to our suite for a moment," she said. "When he returns we'd like two filter coffees, please?"

"Certainly."

I bowed my head very slightly, just as Graeme had instructed me to do.

"Thank you." The lady looked at my name badge. "And where do you live when you're not working on this lovely ship, Stephen?"

She spoke with a delightfully soft American accent.

"Liverpool, madam."

The lady nodded her head thoughtfully.

"My husband and I enjoyed our visit to your home city very much. The buildings on the waterfront. The Pier Head I think you call it. They're very fine. But we were both shocked to see how much damage some other parts of the city had suffered during the war. We were fortunate in America. Apart from Pearl

Harbor in Hawaii our country was never bombed so we haven't had to face the enormous task of rebuilding."

"I suppose it'll take a bit of time," I said. "But to be honest when you're living with the damage all around you every day it sort of becomes normal. You don't really notice it. I was only about three when the war started so I don't remember the city being much different. My family have had a house in St Bride Street, very close to the city centre, for many years. Luckily we're a mile or two away from the docks which was where most of the damage occurred but there were still bomb sites everywhere. To be perfectly honest they were great playgrounds for us kids. We'd mess around in them for hours."

As I was speaking the lady's husband returned.

"Stephen here lives near the centre of Liverpool," she told him. "We were talking about the damage the city suffered in the war and he was saying how he and his friends used to play in the open spaces where buildings had been completely destroyed." She turned to me. "What did you call them?"

"Bomb sites," I said. "But for short we used to call them 'bombies.'"

Her husband raised his eyebrows.

"Very different from my childhood in Pennsylvania," he said. "Farming country was where we lived. Wide open spaces to run around in. A wonderful place to grow up. My father was a chicken farmer. So I was very lucky."

He smiled to himself at the memory.

My Dad used to keep chickens," I said. "After the war. So we could have fresh eggs. All you could get was powdered ones because of rationing. He built a wooden hen-house in the back yard."

"And how many chickens did your father have?"

"About fifteen," I said. Which I thought was rather a lot.

"We had about fifty thousand." The American gave me a friendly smile. "It was a big farm."

He wasn't bragging. Or putting me down. They just did things big in America. It was simply a fact.

Although I'd have been more than happy to carry on chatting it was time to go and make the couple their drinks. Scousers are born with the gift of the gab and I was no exception. Cunard liked us to be friendly and talk to our guests. But the rule was never to overstay your welcome.

"It's been a pleasure talking with you," I said as I turned to leave. "I'll be back with your coffees in a moment."

While I was at work in the galley Graeme told me that the couple were a Mr and Mrs Allenby. They had a large suite on one of the more exclusive decks.

"Be on your very best behaviour, Stephen. The Allenbys are regulars on this ship and they're the most generous tippers I've ever known. Look after them. Give them extra special service and you'll be very well rewarded. Trust me. They'll ask you for your name if they haven't already. And they'll remember it. They like to get to know the members of the crew who are looking after them. They'll want to hear about your family. What you're planning to do in the future. That sort of thing. They're a very nice couple and they're genuinely interested in hearing about other people's lives. So by all means chat with them. But don't overdo it. Keeping passengers like the Allenbys happy is the name of the game. If you can do that I won't complain. And nor will Cunard."

When I returned to our guests with their coffees, carefully laid out on a polished brass tray, Mr Allenby had more to say.

"My wife and I were over in your country for almost a month, Stephen. We both know London quite well so this time we decided to do something a little different. My family, the Allenbys, were originally from Lancashire. So we thought we'd arrange a little trip around the north-west of England to see if we could track down any of my ancestors."

"And did you have any success, sir?" I asked as I lifted the glass coffee jug, which I had been told by Graeme was called a French press, from the tray and placed it carefully on their table. The coffee was followed by two fine Art Deco, Grosvenor design, demi-tasse cups and saucers manufactured exclusively for Cunard by The Foley China Company and supplied to the ships by Stoniers who had retail shops in both Liverpool and Southampton.

The Liverpool branch of Stoniers was justifiably proud of its association with Cunard. I could remember, as a small child, seeing a full set of Foley China Company cups and saucers on display in the window of their elegant shop near The Playhouse Theatre in Williamson Square, each one decorated with the famous Cunard logo. Back then I could never have imagined that I would one day be using them to serve morning coffees to wealthy Americans on a ship in the middle of the Atlantic Ocean.

"Do either you or Mrs Allenby take sugar with your coffee?"

"No thank you, Stephen." The reply to my question came from Mrs Allenby. It was her role to supervise refreshments. "I'll be mother. If you could just leave us the milk please that'll be fine."

Mr Allenby continued to chat as his wife picked up the small jug and poured a little milk into each cup, leaving the coffee in the French press to brew a little longer.

"So, you were asking whether we'd had any success in our hunt for ancestors, Stephen. I think I'd have to say the answer is 'yes.'"

He looked at his wife who nodded her head in agreement.

"We live just outside the city of Lancaster in Pennsylvania," he said, "and we came across some very interesting information when we visited your fine English city of Lancaster just last week. We called in to take a look at the ancient priory, right by the castle, and got talking to one of the church wardens who just happened to be in there, preparing for a service. It turns out that a branch of my family lived in a house not very far from that same church. About a hundred and fifty years ago. Unfortunately the owners were away so we were unable to take a look inside."

Mr Allenby stopped for a moment and took a sip of his coffee before continuing with his story.

"One hundred and fifty years ago would have been around the time that Robert Allenby, my great, great, great grandfather, left England to begin a new life in America. The warden told us that the youngest son of those Lancaster Allenbys was called Robert. So maybe he was the same Robert? It's too early to be sure but it certainly seems to be a possibility. I plan to do a little more research when we get back home to Pennsylvania."

"I wish you luck, sir. It'd be wonderful if it turned out that you've tracked down one of your English ancestors. And in the place which gave your Lancaster its name, too. It would certainly mean your trip had been worthwhile."

"It would indeed," said Mr Allenby. "But our trip has been well worthwhile even without such a bonus. We had no idea at all how beautiful the north-west of England can be. We spent two nights in the Forest of Bowland, staying at a place called The Inn at Whitewell. We were told it dates back to the sixteenth century. It was where the horse-drawn mail coaches used to stop overnight on their way from the North of England to London. The inside of the building was just as we'd imagined such a place would be with its dark oak beams and inglenook fireplaces. And there was a lovely, sheltered terrace at the back of the inn, overlooking the River Hodder. Your English weather was kind to us so we were able to eat outside in the evening. It was quite magical."

"I can't say I've ever visited that part of Lancashire," I said. "Perhaps I'll get up there one day."

"The other place Mrs Allenby and I both loved was the Lake District. We stayed at a hotel called Sharrow Bay, overlooking Lake Ullswater. It had been recommended to us and it turned out to be the perfect choice. We were there for a week and we couldn't fault it in any way. Francis Coulson, the owner, told us that he purchased what used to be someone's lakeside, weekend home about six years ago and turned it into what he now calls a country house hotel. A friend of his by the name of Brian Sack teamed up with him about two years ago and they make an excellent pair. Francis is a truly inspired chef. All his meals were delicious. And Brian is a most thoughtful and kind front of house manager. I'm sure their little venture will be a great success. We enjoyed every minute of our stay with them. And we managed to see quite a lot of the Lake District as well."

"We're both book lovers," said Mrs Allenby. "So to be able to make a visit to a place like Dove Cottage in Grasmere and pay our respects at the great William Wordsworth's grave. And see John Ruskin's home overlooking Coniston Water. It all felt very special. It's just a shame it wasn't the right time of year for the Ullswater daffodils to be putting on a display."

"I went up there one spring," I said. "And saw the daffodils which they say inspired the famous poem. After William Wordsworth had been out walking with his sister, Dorothy."

Mrs Allenby smiled to herself. "Fluttering and dancing in the breeze," she said quietly with a faraway look in her eyes. "What a picture."

"Anyway. That's enough about our travels, Mary," said Mr Allenby. "What about you, Stephen? Have you seen anything of the United States apart from New York City?"

"Not yet, sir. This is only my second voyage with Cunard. I signed on with my best friend from home earlier this year. He's one of the Cabin Boys. When we were ashore in New York last month we mostly just walked around the area close to the ship.

But we did treat ourselves to a ride up the Empire State Building. The view from the top was amazing."

"Do you know," said Mr Allenby, looking at his wife, "that's something Mrs Allenby and I have never done. It's a strange thing, isn't it? You always make sure to tick off that sort of thing when you visit other countries. But when you're at home you never seem to get round to it. I suppose when it's close by you always think there'll be some time more convenient."

"There's lots of places in England I've never seen," I said. "But I'm definitely hoping to see more of your country. My sister, Jean, married an American airman who was stationed at the big U.S. Air Force Base at Burtonwood, not far from Liverpool, during the war. Jean's a few years older than me so I don't know all that much about how they met. Maybe her husband, Carl, used to go into Liverpool when he had some time off? I don't know. But anyway she's now happily settled in America with her husband and two young children."

"And where exactly does she live?"

"I'm a little ashamed to say I don't really know. But my mother did say Jean put something in one of her letters about some people living near them called the Amish. She said they're strict Christians and they prefer not to make use of modern conveniences like cars and televisions. I remember thinking it was a bit strange."

"Many of the Amish settled in Pennsylvania when they first arrived in America two or three hundred years ago," said Mrs Allenby. "A lot of them around Lancaster. Much of the land in the area is devoted to farming and you see the Amish driving along the country roads in their horse-drawn buggies. I don't think they have any particular religious objection to modern technology. It's just that it doesn't fit in too well with their traditional lifestyle. They believe that things like cars and televisions tempt people to focus their attention on the outside world rather than working to support their own community. And they might well be right. Their lifestyle is different but we're mostly God-fearing folk round our way. So we all get on fine."

Mrs Allenby smiled at her husband.

"Mr Allenby is always saying it's a small world, Stephen. If it were to turn out that your sister, Jean, is now living not very far from us that would be quite some coincidence."

"It would indeed, madam. And if you'll excuse me, I'll now leave you and Mr Allenby to enjoy your coffees."

"Thank you, Stephen. I'm sure they'll be excellent. My husband and I will be taking coffee here in the lounge every morning so hopefully we'll have a chance to talk some more before we reach New York."

I bowed my head as I turned to walk away.

"That would be a great pleasure."

Later that day Dave and I were off duty and grabbing a much needed bite to eat in The Pig. I'd been telling him about my chat with the Allenbys and his opinion was clear.

"It's a no brainer, Steve. When we get back to Liverpool you should find out from your Ma where your Jean's living. You never know, we might be able to meet up. It'd be nice to see her again."

"To be honest," I said, "it never occurred to me that gettin' together with Jean might even be a possibility. America's such a massive place. She could be living hundreds of miles from New York in which case I can forget all about it. But it won't do any harm to find out."

"I've probably asked you before," said Dave. "But how many kids has your Jean got?"

"She was already pregnant when she left and she had the

baby not long after she got to America. A boy it was. He'd be six or seven now. And then she had a little girl a year or two later."

"So you've got an American nephew and niece who are growing up fast and you've never met them. You never know. With all these Amish folk being in Pennsylvania your sister, Jean, might be living there too. And I'm pretty sure Pennsylvania's not all that far from New York. It's definitely not out California way or anything like that. What're the kids called?"

"The boy's Richard. It was my Dad's middle name and Jean always liked it. Although I think they call him Ricky." I stopped to think for a moment. "And the little girl's Susan. Yeah. That's definitely it. Susan."

"There you go then," said Dave. "Ricky and Susan. Nice sensible names. They go well together. It'd be great if you could see them. And maybe I'll tag along too."

• •‒‒‒ • • • • • ‒ • •

The very first time you do anything is almost always the most special. So the passage of RMS Media through the Narrows and into New York wasn't quite as exciting as it had been four weeks earlier. But Dave and I were still out on deck to enjoy it.

"You know, Dave," I said, turning towards him. "Arriving here by sea and getting this view of the Manhattan skyline is always going to be special. No matter how many times we experience it."

I looked around. The number of passengers who were out on the deck with us, despite the early morning, mid-September chill, showed that the feeling was widely shared.

I had said my goodbyes to Mr and Mrs Allenby when serving them their after-dinner coffees and cocktails in the lounge the previous evening. We had continued to have our daily chats during the long, Atlantic crossing and we had got to know each other quite well. Mr Allenby jokingly called me the man with fifteen chickens and told me that his family now owned none at all. Farming, he said, could be a precarious business and he had decided against following in his father's footsteps. He had, instead, qualified as a lawyer; a much more secure, and lucrative, way of earning a living. The farm had been sold. And prior to his retirement Mr Allenby had been the senior partner in a highly successful legal practice in Lancaster.

The gratuity which he pressed into my palm as we shook hands for the last time was extremely generous.

●·•————●·•·●·•·●————·•·●

During our time ashore in New York a small group of us whiled away a number of happy hours in Jack Dempsey's Broadway Bar. The great man himself came over from his regular chair in one of the corner booths to greet us in person, a routine which he liked to follow with all his customers, and we all very cautiously shook the still-powerful hand of the former heavyweight champion. It was the hand that had floored the French challenger, Georges Carpentier, back in 1921 at Boyle's Thirty Acres in Jersey City in the world's first 'million dollar fight'.

We called in at Birdland, 'the jazz corner of the world', at the junction of West 52nd and Broadway where the diminutive Master of Ceremonies, Pee Wee Marquette, took to the stage to introduce Charlie Parker, Dizzy Gillespie and Dinah Washington. They were just coming to the end of a three-week engagement.

We caught the A-train to Coney Island where we braved the wind and ate hamburgers on the boardwalk while gazing at the silver sand of Jones Beach and the big, Atlantic breakers.

We went to the movies and laughed at the antics of Phil Silvers in the film, 'Top Banana', which had been released earlier that year.

And we headed over to Ebbets Field where we saw the legendary Jackie Robinson hit a home run for the Brooklyn Dodgers.

Dave and I were starting to feel like proper Cunard Yanks.

And New York City was starting to feel like our second home.

SEVEN

A LETTER TO PENNSYLVANIA

When I got back to St Bride Street nine days later after an uneventful return crossing my mother was in her usual place on the settee, still knitting. I took a seat opposite her in one of the armchairs.

"I've been thinking, Ma. Maybe me and Dave could try and meet up with our Jean one time when we're over in America? If you give me her address I could write to her and see if we can fix something up. That's if she's living not too far from New York."

"Your sister lives in a place called Manheim, Stephen. Her husband, Carl, was brought up there and that's where they decided to settle down. Meyers is Carl's surname. So your sister is now Jean Meyers. Before they left for America Carl told me his family were originally from Germany. Which I thought was a bit odd. You know. Him coming over here to England to fight against his old country. But I suppose it must have been several generations ago that his family left Germany. So he wouldn't really see himself as being anything other than one hundred percent American."

"Manheim," I said. "That does sound a bit German. And did

you once tell me there's some religious people called the Amish near where Jean lives?"

My mother nodded her head. "Yes. I think that could be right."

"The thing is," I continued." I was talking to this American couple on the ship. They live in a place called Lancaster. In Pennsylvania. And they were saying there's quite a lot of Amish people round their way."

"Jean did mention something about them in one of her letters. She said she quite liked their simple lifestyle."

"So this Manheim?" I said. "Is it anywhere near Lancaster? Because the American couple said Lancaster's not that far from New York. Me and Dave might have enough time to get there by train or something and see Jean and her family if it is."

"I really don't know, Stephen. I've never had any reason to find out. I certainly can't see myself going all that way to visit them. I've always hoped that Jean might come over here with the children one day. Perhaps when they're a little bit older. It'd be nice to meet them. You never quite know how long you've got left."

There was an unmistakeable sadness in my mother's eyes. She never really complained about anything so I'd not given it much thought. But as I looked at her I suddenly realised how hard it must be. She was just like over sixty thousand other British mothers. Her daughter had married an American serviceman. And she had grandchildren who were growing up thousands of miles away. With no certainty that she would ever get to see them.

"Give over, Ma," I said. "You're not even fifty. You've got years ahead of you. Give me Jean's address and I'll write to her. It's not right you never seeing your own grandkids."

"Pass me that little black address book," said my mother, pointing to the dark, wooden sideboard on the far side of the room.

I went over to the sideboard and gave her the book. She quickly leafed through it.

"Here it is," she said. "Jean's address. Have you got a pencil?"

"No need, Ma. I'll remember it."

"You won't. There's some unfamiliar words in these American addresses. Come on. Write it down or you'll get it wrong."

My mother handed me a loose slip of paper which was in her address book along with the pencil which she kept slotted into the spine. As she read out my sister's address I jotted it down. Then I read it back to her to make sure I'd got it right.

"*Mrs Jean Meyers, 64, East Ferdinand Street, Manheim, Pennsylvania*"

"That's it," she said.

"So she does live in Pennsylvania," I said. "Maybe it's not all that far from New York?"

"Get a letter done then. And airmail it to Jean before you go back to the ship. With a bit of luck we might get a reply before you're next home."

She closed the address book and as she leant forwards to hand it to me she gave a little wince. She was holding on to her stomach.

"What's up, Ma. Are you alright?"

"It's nothing, Stephen. I'm fine."

"You're not fine if you're in some sort of pain."

"Leave me. It's just a bit of wind. I'll take an Alka-Seltzer or something."

"I don't want you ignoring things, Ma. If you've got some sort of problem you should see the doctor."

"Don't you be bothering yourself about me. I told you. I'm fine. Doctors are busy people. They've got more important things to be doing than treating me for wind."

"Okay, Ma. But I'll be upset if you're not telling me something."

"I'm okay. I don't want you worrying about it. If I've got any problems while you're away Georgie or Jimmy will sort it out. Please. Just forget it."

Something wasn't right. I could tell. But I knew my mother. She'd always been a very stubborn woman and she didn't like asking for help.

For now, at least, I'd have to let it go.

The comedy '*Doctor In The House*', based on the best-selling book of the same name, was the biggest movie of the year in England. It was still on at The Futurist Cinema in Lime Street even though it had been out for several months. Over fifteen million people, almost one third of the British population, had already seen it.

I didn't want to miss it. And when I asked her to join me, nor did Sylvie.

"The chap who wrote the book, Richard Gordon, was a junior doctor," I said to her as we stood in the queue waiting for the box office to open. "It's supposed to be based on his own experiences in hospital. And with it being such a huge success I don't suppose the NHS is going to be seeing all that much of the good Dr Gordon from now on."

Sylvie took hold of my hand and gave it a squeeze.

"Thanks for asking me along."

"I wasn't sure you'd be free. I didn't give you very much notice."

"I'd have found a way to be free," she said. "Even if I wasn't."

She squeezed my hand again as the queue began to move slowly forwards.

"D'you know," I said, "the last time I was in a queue for this cinema was just before Christmas last year. With a few lads I knew from school. We were all keen to see this documentary called '*The Conquest of Everest*'. About how Hilary and Tenzing made the first ascent. Just before the Coronation. Which reminds me. When Dave and I went up the Empire State Building in New York there was a picture of Edmund Hilary up there. Anyway, the film was really good. But what I remember most about the evening was standing in this queue and smoking a Sobranie. Have you ever tried one?"

Sylvie shook her head. "No."

"Then don't," I said. "They're black Russian cigarettes. Really strong. Smoking them is supposed to be dead cool which I suppose is why I wanted to give it a try. But they're absolutely disgusting. The good thing about it is I'll never touch a cigarette again."

"That's fine with me," said Sylvie. "My Mum was a very heavy smoker." She paused for a moment as if there was something she wasn't sure she should say. "She got lung cancer and died two years ago."

I immediately regretted mentioning the Sobranie and I wasn't sure how to react. Just to say I was sorry didn't seem to be adequate. But what else was there to say?

"I didn't realise," I said. "I'm sorry."

"Don't worry," said Sylvie, giving me a wry smile. "You weren't to know. It was awful at the time but I'm mostly fine about it now. Before she died my Mum said it was the cigarettes so it was her own fault, and she asked me to make two promises. First, not to be sad. And second, never to start smoking." She shrugged her shoulders and gave me another smile. "The second was easier than the first. But I've mostly managed to keep both of them."

"The cigarette companies all say smoking's perfectly safe."

Sylvie laughed. "They would, wouldn't they."

As we reached the box office she put her arm round my shoulders.

"Let's not talk about it," she said, "or we won't enjoy the film."

The cinema was no more than half-full, which was good. And there were very few smokers. Which was even better. Sylvie and I both enjoyed the film. Parts of it were very funny indeed and it was easy to see why it had been such a success.

At just after nine-thirty we walked through the foyer and emerged onto Lime Street.

"What now?" I said. "It's a bit early to call it a night. Do you fancy going somewhere for a coffee? The Kardomah on Whitechapel should still be open."

"Perfect," said Sylvie, smiling.

The Kardomah was quiet. In the 1950s there wasn't much in the way of night life in Liverpool. In provincial cities there were very few meeting places available in the evening other than the traditional public houses. And they were mostly the preserve of men.

Even in London things were only just starting to change. The Italian actress, Gina Lollobrigida, had just opened her Moka Espresso Bar in Soho, bringing the very first Gaggia coffee machine to London from her native country. Also in Soho there was another coffee bar, The Two I's. It was run by the two Irani brothers, and aspiring young pop singers like Tommy Steele, Adam Faith and Cliff Richard used to perform live on a small stage there. It quickly developed a reputation as the place to be seen if you were an ambitious youngster who wanted to be discovered. Impresarios such as John Kennedy, and record producers like George Martin from Parlophone, would call in regularly on the look-out for new talent.

As Sylvie and I sat down with our coffees in sleepy Liverpool I realised that I knew very little about her. At The Grafton we'd spent most of the evening dancing rather than talking. And this evening had so far been taken up with watching the film.

"We could talk about *'Doctor In The House'*," I said to her once I'd taken a sip of my coffee. "Or you could tell me a bit about yourself."

"I don't think I'm all that interesting," she said. "But I don't mind. You choose."

"We'll talk about you then," I said. "For a start I don't even know how old you are."

"Have a guess."

There was no doubt Sylvie was very attractive and amusing. And bright too, which only added to her attractiveness. But how old was she? Seventeen seemed the most likely. But could she be eighteen? Or even nineteen? I wasn't sure. So I went for what I thought was the safest number.

"Seventeen."

"Not bad," she said. "But before I tell you if you're right, what's my star sign."

"I know nothing about star signs," I said. "I don't think I could even name them all. Surely you don't believe in them?"

"Sometimes I do. If it suits me."

"Okay then. How about Gemini?"

Sylvie frowned at me. "How did you do that?"

"What?"

"Get my star sign right."

I shrugged my shoulders. "It's a one in twelve chance and if you are a Gemini, I just guessed right. As I said I can't even name all the star signs. I've got no idea at all what month Gemini is."

"And you got my age right too."

"So you're seventeen. The perfect age." I gave her a grin. "I promise you I'm not psychic. So when's your birthday?"

"The 3rd of June."

"Okay, give me a minute. Add three years to 1954 and take off twenty."

Sylvie said nothing but the look in her eyes suggested that

she could see the cogs in my brain rotating very slowly. After a polite interval she took pity on me.

"The 3rd of June, 1937," she said. "My full date of birth. I presume that's what you were trying to work out."

I laughed. "Sorry. Mental arithmetic was never my strong point. And that's Gemini is it?"

"Yes. Late May and early June. So when were you born?"

"The 4th of August, 1936.

Sylvie's response was almost immediate.

"Which makes you eighteen. And Leo the lion."

"That was quick," I said, genuinely impressed. "Gemini and Leo. Does that mean our relationship is doomed? Or is it a match made in heaven?"

"I could find out. The friend who'll be going to college with me won't do anything without checking her horoscope. But it's what we think that matters."

She leaned across the table and gave me a kiss.

"I think it's a match made in heaven. Whatever the stars might say."

"I'll second that," I said. "But forget star signs. What's heaven for me is that French accent of yours. Don't ever lose it. As soon as I heard it I was madly in love with you."

Sylvie looked at me.

"Only my accent? Is that all you like? Not my figure? Or my face?"

"It was definitely your accent that got me first," I said. "And then a fraction of a second later I fell for everything else. Including your personality and your brain. Which is very important."

She laughed. "That's okay, then."

"And talking of brains, you said college? What will you be doing at college?"

"Physical Education." She paused for a moment and caught

my eye. "I loved P.E. lessons at school and I enjoy watching most sports. So when I was trying to decide what to do I thought why not become a P.E. Teacher? And it'll be brilliant."

"I like sports too," I said. "Football and Liverpool Football Club in particular. But I don't think being a teacher would suit me. I haven't got the patience. I'd end up losing my rag with some poor kid for no reason."

"I'm doing it for my Mum a bit as well. She always wanted to be a teacher but never got the chance. Her parents weren't well off. So as soon as she was old enough to leave school she had to get a job. She was working in a bar in Paris when she met my Dad."

"I'll have to buck my ideas up if you're going to be a teacher," I said, laughing. "You make me feel as if I should be making more of an effort. All I've got is five O-levels. Otherwise I haven't got any qualifications at all."

"But you're a Cunard Yank," said Sylvie. "That's more than enough for me."

"In which case," I said, "I'd better give you these."

I reached into my jacket and took out a slim packet.

"Stockings," I said. "From New York. You were supposed to get them when the four of us went to The Grafton. But I left them at home."

Sylvie looked at the expensive New York packaging.

"I won't take them out now. But they look really nice. And I'm sure they'll feel really smooth and silky when I've got them on. You'd have to pay a fortune for them over here. If you could even find a pair that is. Thank you." Her eyes were twinkling as she smiled at me. "I love them. And hopefully you will too."

As she continued to smile I removed a small, almost square glass bottle, with classic bevelled edges, from the same pocket.

"They say you can't go wrong with stockings and Chanel Number Five."

Sylvie moved closer and gave me a kiss on the cheek.

"They're right," she whispered. "You can't."

"And such luxury items are currently available in this country only from a Cunard Yank. Never forget that."

"I won't," said Sylvie. "And if you've not found yourself some exciting American lady and lost interest in this rather ordinary Liverpool lass I'll be waiting on the dockside wearing the stockings and the perfume when you get back from New York."

"I couldn't possibly expect that," I said, laughing. "Not at the crack of dawn on Huskisson Dock. But you can definitely wear them the next time I take you out."

"It's a promise," she said. "I can't wait."

⋅⋅⋅⋅⋅⋅⋅⋅⋅⋅⋅⋅⋅⋅

Next morning, just before midday, I was standing in the hallway at the bottom of the stairs in St Bride Street, putting on my coat. Sylvie and I had chatted for hours, and it had been well after midnight when I'd finally got home.

A voice came from the living room.

"Is that you, Stephen? For a while I thought you were going to spend the whole day in bed."

"Yes, Ma. It's me."

"Have you sent that letter off to our Jean yet?"

"Not yet, Ma. I didn't get in 'til late."

"A typical sailor," said the voice. "A girl in every port. Just mind you don't catch anything."

"She's called Sylvie, Ma. She's half-French. And she's lovely."

"Half-French? That's all I need. Your sister's gone off to America. Your father's disappeared to goodness knows where. And I suppose it'll be you next. Telling me you're off to Paris or some other such place. Then it'll just be me rattling around in this house with your two uncles."

"Rattling around?" I said. "I think it's great you've got Georgie and Jimmy here to keep you company. I'd be much more worried about you when I was away if they weren't. Anyway, Sylvie may be half-French but she lives in West Derby. Just off Queens Drive. With her Dad."

"And what about her mother? Where's she?"

I decided not to mention that Sylvie's mother had died. It would only make my mother feel bad about what she'd just been saying. Details could wait.

"Her Mum was French. But she moved to England when she met Sylvie's Dad and got pregnant. Sylvie was born in the Maternity Hospital here in Liverpool. A couple of hundred yards from this house. So apart from her French accent, which I suppose she must've got from her mother and which I happen to think is very attractive, she's as Scouse as you or me."

There was no reply so I put my head round the door. My mother was sitting in her usual place on the settee and the knitting needles were working away furiously.

"I'm sorry I've not got round to doing the letter yet, Ma. I've been a bit busy."

"I've noticed. Spending every minute of your shore leave with your new French girlfriend."

I didn't take the bait. It wouldn't have been fair.

"I'll get it done today, Ma. And take it down to the Post Office in Hardman Street before the last collection."

The furious movement of the needles slowed down a little as she looked over at me.

"Just make sure you do. It'd be nice if you and Jean could get together."

1st October 1954   *19, St Bride Street*
Liverpool 8

Dear Jean,

I hope this letter won't come as too much of a surprise. I know it's a while since we were last in touch, but Ma gave me your address in America. I hope everything is going well over there for you.

To get straight to the point, I've signed up with Cunard along with Dave from down the street. I'm sure you must remember him. At the moment we're both on the transatlantic run between Liverpool and New York on one of Cunard's smaller ships called RMS Media. It's a 'first class only' vessel, so the passengers are mostly very well-heeled and the tips are good. Particularly from the Americans.

The Media is in New York every few weeks, berthed at one of the Cunard Piers on the Hudson River. We're there for several days between crossings and I was wondering if maybe I could catch a train or a bus to Manheim and see you and the two children. And of course Carl, your husband. Dave might join me if that's okay. We wouldn't stay long, probably just one night, because we'd need to get back to New York promptly to catch the ship.

It would be very good to see you again and catch up.

I hope to hear from you before too long.

Ma sends her love, and she says she can't wait to meet up with her two grandchildren one day.

Love from me too,

Stephen xxx

Next morning Dave and I were in the basement of the Cunard Building, waiting for confirmation that we would both be sailing for New York that evening as planned. We had both been told to report back for duty when we had left the Media six days earlier so it was unlikely that anything had changed. But until we'd actually been given the order to proceed aboard nothing was certain.

"Well," he said. "How did your evening with Sylvie go?"

I was about to answer Dave's question when our names were called.

"Crane and Robertson."

The two of us went over to the desk.

"Stephen Crane?"

"Yes, sir."

"Lounge Steward on the Media. Senior Lounge Steward Graeme Moffatt gave you a good report after the last voyage, Crane. He was very pleased with your performance and he received quite a few positive comments from our passengers. So well done. Report to him in two hours in the Passenger Lounge."

"Thank you, sir."

"And keep up the good work."

"Yes, sir".

I had managed to hold on to my job.

"David Robertson?"

I looked at Dave, who I knew was desperate for a promotion. The administrator behind the desk looked down at his list.

"Cabin Boy on the Media." Poor Dave looked crestfallen. "Report to Senior Cabin Steward Les Moore in two hours. Outside the Purser's Office."

I felt very sorry for him.

"Don't let it get you down," I said as we collected the crew passes which we would need to show to board the ship. "Something's bound to turn up soon. The important thing is you've still got a job. And we're both on the same ship."

"Whatever," said Dave morosely.

With our passes securely in our pockets we made our way round the back of the Cunard Building towards Pier Head Station on the Liverpool Overhead Railway. Four stops in the direction of Seaforth Sands would bring us to the Huskisson Dock where RMS Media was berthed.

My first attempt to cheer Dave up didn't seem to have worked. So I tried something else.

"Sylvie and I went to The Futurist to see '*Doctor In The House*' on Wednesday night. It was good."

"I've not seen it," said Dave without looking at me.

It was like getting blood out of a stone.

"For God's sake, Dave. What's the matter with you? I get it that you're a bit fed up that I'm up in the lounge and you're still working the cabins. But I can't do anything about it. I wish I could. But I can't."

"Sorry, pal," said Dave, shrugging his shoulders. "It's not you. It's just that I've got something on my mind."

Dave didn't immediately explain. He was thinking. Then he spoke.

"I saw Greg on Thursday night. I was asking him what Pamela was up to and he said she's been goin' out with this older chap called Eddie."

"And that's upset you."

"No. It's not that. I've known Pamela since she was a kid and she's always been Greg's little sister. I thought when we went to The Grafton that maybe I could fancy her. But I was kiddin' myself. She's great. But she's a good friend more than anything else. To fancy someone there's got to be a little bit of mystery about them. She looks amazing but I think I've known Pamela too long to properly fancy her. You know what I mean. And I reckon it's best kept that way. I haven't talked to Greg about it but I'm pretty sure he'd say the same."

"So what's the problem?"

"It's this Eddie guy. He deals in the stuff that comes in on the ships. You know. Things people can't get over here because of the stupid way everything's rationed and restricted. Greg says he's loaded and he's always lookin' out for people like us who go to New York and back. There's good money to be made if you're willing to take a bit of a chance with Customs."

Ahead of us we could see the stairs which would take us up to the platform. There was a cool breeze but the weather looked promising and a crowd of people, including a number of families with small children, were making their way up the steps ahead of us. The train was going to be busy.

Dave looked around.

"I'll tell you a bit more when we get off the train," he said. "There's too many day-trippers and kids who might be listening."

Ever since it first began operating in March 1893 a trip on the Liverpool Overhead Railway had been a popular weekend activity. It was one of the world's first overhead, electric railways, along with those in Chicago and New York.

As a child I'd travelled the whole six-mile length of the line, from the hidden-away Dingle Station in the south of the city to Seaforth Sands in the north, on numerous occasions. For a small boy it was a magical experience. Ocean liners and cargo ships from every corner of the globe could be seen from the train, berthed in Liverpool's extensive system of docks. And as the ships set sail for faraway places, to be replaced by new arrivals, the scene was constantly changing.

No two trips on the Overhead Railway were ever the same.

On a fine day the view over the network of docks, with the River Mersey providing a route to the Irish Sea and the Atlantic beyond, was breathtaking. It very clearly demonstrated the stature of Liverpool as one of the great seaports of the world.

For a small boy it was a tantalising glimpse of the

opportunities which life could offer to the adventurous. I was probably unaware of it at the time but it must have helped to create a longing within me to get out there and make the most of them.

The train which would take us to Huskisson Dock pulled into the station almost as soon as Dave and I reached the top of the stairs. Proudly displayed in cream and white lettering above the very generous windows were the words *'LIVERPOOL OVERHEAD RAILWAY'*, and the narrow, hinged doors to each of the carriages were marked either *First Class* or *Third Class*.

Third Class suited us fine so Dave and I found ourselves a seat on one of the slatted, wooden benches. From it we would have an uninterrupted view of all the docks and ships as our train made its short journey, stopping on the way at the stations for Princes Dock, Clarence Dock and Nelson Dock.

Princes Dock was where the steamers of Coast Lines were berthed. These ships offered a regular and much used service between Liverpool and the Irish ports of Belfast and Dublin.

Leaving Princes Dock Station we passed the Stanley Dock Tobacco Warehouse on the shore side of the railway, thirteen stories high and the largest, brick-built tobacco warehouse in the world. Sacks of tobacco were being loaded from the adjacent dockside onto cargo ships which would take them to ports big and small on the continent of Europe.

On the approach to Huskisson Dock Station we caught sight of the Media, berthed alongside vessels from the Leyland Steamship Line which shared the dock with Cunard. Their ships carried goods to and from Boston, Mexico, New Orleans and ports in the West Indies. The company's large storage sheds were packed with ham and timber from North Atlantic ports, along with cotton, sugar, grain and citrus fruits all the way from the ports further south.

Over the past couple of centuries a never-ending flow of

ships, people and cargo had made the merchant families of Liverpool very wealthy. And victory in the Second World War meant that their fortunes were secure.

For the time being at least, it was back to business as usual.

As we got off the train at Huskisson Dock a sudden squall of rain blew in on the brisk, north-westerly breeze. Looking up I could see a collection of dark clouds that were the source of the downpour but beyond them the sky was blue. They were moving quickly so the rain wouldn't last long.

We hurried down the stairs, away from the exposed platform, and took shelter beneath the broad, cast-iron girders and wooden planking which carried the railway. The massive structure acted as a very effective shield from the rain, and within weeks of its construction the ever-inventive Scousers were calling it 'The Dockers' Umbrella'.

The name was well-chosen. And it had stuck.

As we waited for the rain to ease off Dave started to tell me a bit more about Eddie and his little enterprise.

"Just out of curiosity more than anythin' else," he said, "I asked Greg if he could arrange for me to meet up with Eddie."

I looked at him and shook my head.

"Please tell me you've not agreed to do something daft, Dave."

He shrugged his shoulders.

"He seemed like a nice guy. And he asked me if I'd be interested in bringin' a few pairs of stockings in for him from New York."

"You're crazy. What if you get caught?"

"That's what's been worryin' me. But Eddie says it's money for old rope and he's never known anyone get stopped. The Customs in Liverpool are seriously short of staff so they haven't got time to be bothered about little bits and pieces the crew might be bringing in."

"So he says. But the Franconia got taken apart a couple of years ago. That's a Cunard ship. Les told me the Customs spent five days searching it after they got a tip-off. It was all over the Echo. They found forty thousand pairs of nylons stashed in the engine room. And then another ten thousand hidden behind the timber lining of the main cargo hold. Two quid a pair they sell for. So that's a hundred thousand pounds."

"Which is Eddie's point," said Dave. "The Customs just concentrate on the big boys. I won't be bringin' in thousands of pairs. Eddie said even a hundred would be good. And he's gonna give me a quid for each pair. That's a hundred quid."

"Fair enough. But it's not all profit."

"It is if you can get 'em cheap. Well, pretty much. Eddie's given me the name of a guy he knows in New York who'll sell 'em to me for twelve cents a pair if I'm buyin' a hundred pairs. That's twelve dollars for the lot. About a tenner. So I'll have ninety quid profit. Cash in my pocket. Basically for doin' nothing."

He turned and looked at me.

"And Eddie said if I know anyone else who might be interested they can do the same. Lay out ten quid and get a ninety quid profit. It's a no brainer, Steve."

The rain was easing off and so we headed towards the Huskisson Dock gates.

"Do whatever you like, Dave. It's your choice. But it's not for me. I don't mind bringin' in the odd pair of nylons and a bottle of nice perfume for Sylvie but you can count me out as far as Eddie's concerned. Buying a hundred pairs in New York to sell on at a profit is different. That's proper smuggling. Maybe you wouldn't get done for it but you'd definitely lose your job. It's not worth it."

"Speak for yourself. I haven't even got a decent job to lose at the moment."

"It won't be long before you get a promotion. Les is a decent bloke. He'll see to it that you're alright."

At the dock gates we showed our passes and made for the gangway. It was almost midday.

In just over an hour we were due to report for duty.

And at six o'clock, once all the compulsory safety drills had been completed, the Media would cast off her moorings and head west once more.

Towards the setting sun.

And New York City.

EIGHT

BROOKLYN

"I'm off to the Market Diner with Graeme and a couple of the lads from the main restaurant," I said to Dave. "Are you going to join us?"

He shook his head.

"I might see you there later. But I'm meetin' the guy Eddie told me about at four o'clock. In a place called Park Slope. Over in Brooklyn."

"Are you sure you don't want me to come with you?" I said. I couldn't help being a bit concerned about Dave's plan to get himself involved with New York's black marketeers. "I don't mind. You know. Just in case you run into problems."

"Thanks, Steve, but I'll be fine. Eddie said he's done a lot of deals with this guy over the past year or two and there's never been any trouble."

"Okay. But be careful. A group of lads I was chatting with in The Pig were saying there's over six thousand gangs in New York. They've each got their own patch an' they hate each other's guts. No one outside the gang is allowed on their territory and disputes are settled by organised fights. They call 'em 'Rumbles'. There's twenty or thirty on each side. Mostly in their late teens. And it's serious stuff. They don't use guns but they tool themselves up with baseball bats and knives. And they wear winklepickers with sharpened, steel toecaps. One poor kid got kicked to death not that long ago."

"Don't worry, Steve. I'm not gonna take any chances. I'll keep my wits about me. I'll only have the twelve dollars on me. So I'm not riskin' a huge amount of money."

"It may not be a fortune. But it's still a couple of weeks' wages."

"Look. If there's any trouble I won't be hanging about. I promise. I'll just scarper."

"Okay," I said. "Make sure you do. I'll see you when you get back."

When we arrived at the Market Diner that evening Joe Zellin asked me why Dave wasn't with us. And when I told him he was meeting someone over in Park Slope he looked worried.

"That's a rough area, Steve. Even for Brooklyn. Most of the houses are historic brownstones but they've been sub-divided into apartments for the Italian-Americans and Irish Catholics who now mostly live there. There's a gang of teenage kids over that way who call themselves The Jokers. And trust me, they ain't funny."

<hr />

It was almost eleven o'clock. The others had left the Diner and gone back to the ship two hours earlier. I was about to give up and do the same when Dave walked in. He was carrying an oblong, brown paper package, tied up with string.

"Sorry to take so long. I hope you weren't getting worried." He put the package down on the bar. "Mission accomplished. What I need now is a nice, refreshing drink."

I waved a hand towards Joe who was busy chatting to one of his regular customers at the far end of the bar and pointed a finger at Dave. He gave me a thumbs-up and indicated he'd be over in a minute.

"I wanted to let Joe know you were back," I said to Dave. "He was worried when I told him you were meeting someone over in Brooklyn. Particularly when I said it was Park Slope. Apparently it's not the nicest part of the city. There's a teenage gang over that way called The Jokers who've got a bit of a reputation."

Dave gave a wry laugh.

"I think I just met a few of 'em. They were with Eddie's friend, Spike. And they made it pretty clear they wouldn't stand for any messin'. One of 'em had a baseball bat and the way he was handling it sent out a definite message. And another had what looked like a gun in his coat pocket."

Joe came over.

"Good to see you back in one piece, Dave. What can I get you?"

"A couple of really cold Cokes please, Joe," he said. "And a Hamm's for yourself."

He took two dollars out of his pocket and placed them on the counter.

Joe picked the notes up. "Give me a minute and I'll be back."

When he returned with the drinks he turned to Dave.

"So, Dave. What crazy idea took you over to Park Slope?"

Dave pointed at the package. "It's to take back home."

Joe picked it up. "Not a lot of weight in there," he said, giving it a squeeze. "Soft too."

He replaced the package on the counter and laughed. "My guess would be you've got a fair number of best American stockings in there, Dave. You must have quite a few lady friends back home."

"Yeah, well, it's not that easy to get hold of nylons in Liverpool. So I'm taking a few pairs back as a bit of a favour. It keeps the girls happy."

"I'll bet it does," said Joe, giving him a wink. "Just be sure those lucky girls keep you happy too."

"They've already told me they will, Joe."

Dave picked up his Coke and took a drink before pushing the second can towards me.

"It must be twenty years since I was last over in Park Slope," said Joe. "It used to be a nice area. Lots of nice professional families. Decent people. But it's a bit scary now. There's too many gangs. They fight over territory. They fight over money. And they fight over girls. It's getting out of hand. They face up with each other in a park. Or in one of the playgrounds with the high, wire fencing. With baseball bats. Switchblades. Bike chains. Anything at all they can use to injure the other side. The fights are so violent they don't last long. Sometimes it's just a few minutes. When it's all over those who can still walk melt away into their apartments before the cops appear. And it's getting worse. If the city can't work out a way of controlling it a lot of youngsters are going to get seriously hurt. Some of them might even lose their lives."

Joe swigged down the last of his beer.

"Take my advice, Dave. Steer clear of that area. You're back in one piece this time but next time you might not be so lucky. The kids are bad enough but it's the slightly older guys you really need to avoid. Stockings are small time stuff but they might be testing you out. Next time it could be something serious. Like drugs. The problem is they suck you in and it's hard to get out. Once they've got you hooked they threaten to hand you over to the cops who are on their payroll if you don't play ball. And if they decide they really don't like you there's a very real possibility of ending up with a few bullets in your back. I know people who've seen it happen."

Looking at Dave I could see Joe's little lecture had hit home.

"Thanks, Joe," he said. "I'll be careful."

"Come on," I said, looking at my watch. "It's after half eleven. We need to get ourselves back to the ship."

⬦⬦⬦⬦⬦⬦⬦⬦

The evening before we were due to leave New York Dave and I were having a drink in The Pig when Les walked in. He got himself a tankard of beer and came over to the table where we were sitting.

"There's something we need to sort out, Dave," he said. "I was going to speak to you tomorrow before we sail. But as you're here we might as well get it over with now."

I immediately thought of the stockings. One hundred pairs of them. Sitting in a locker by our glory-hole. Dave had gone pale. He was obviously thinking the same thing. Les and Joe Zellin had known each other for years. They were as thick as thieves. Joe could easily have said something to Les about the package from Park Slope. Or maybe he'd just told Les he was worried Dave might be getting himself into something he didn't properly understand.

I looked up at Les.

"Do you want me to leave?" I said. "So you can talk to Dave in private."

If it was about the stockings I didn't want to get involved. It was Dave's problem and he was the one who'd have to sort it out. Buying a hundred pairs of stockings from a shady operator in Brooklyn might be unwise but it wasn't illegal. So if that was what Les wanted to talk about Dave could probably come up with a good story.

Les smiled at me and shook his head.

"Thanks, Steve, but it's fine. I've got a bit of good news for Dave and I'm sure he won't mind you hearing it."

He put his beer down on the table and took a chair next to Dave who suddenly looked more relaxed.

"Right, Dave," he said. "I'm sorry to butt in on your chat. But I've been wanting to offer you a step up. Like Steve. And I'm pleased to say something's turned up which I think might interest you. One of the waiters in the main restaurant, you may know him, Billy Atkins. Well, he's sent us a message to say he's just got himself married to a girl who lives in Harlem and he won't be coming back with us to Liverpool. Billy never mentioned anything about getting married before he went ashore so it all sounds slightly dodgy".

Dave looked understandably relieved and happy, but as Les continued to explain the situation I was thinking about poor Billy. He was a decent bloke and he seemed to have got himself into a bit of trouble.

"Whether he's got permission to stay here in America we don't know," said Les, "but we think probably not. So we've had a word with U.S. Immigration and they're looking for him at the moment. If they find him before we sail they might just tell us to take him back to Liverpool. But if it's after we've gone he'll be arrested and taken into custody while they look into what he's been up to."

He turned to Dave.

"It's a shame. But that's Billy's problem, Dave. Either way, I'm afraid he's lost his job. Which gives you an opportunity. That's if you want to take it of course."

Dave had a big grin on his face.

"Thanks, Les. Yes. Of course I'll take it."

Les gave him a smile.

"Poor old Billy has probably been taken in by this girl in Harlem. I just hope she's worth it. But the plus side is I'm able to give you a chance at last. You know Jack Dixon, the Head Waiter?"

Dave nodded his head.

"You'll need to report to him at eight o'clock tomorrow

morning," said Les. "So he can go through a few of the basics with you before the passengers start arriving on board."

He drained his tankard and stood up.

"Well, lads. That's me done. Enjoy the rest of your evening. I'm off to get some much needed shut eye."

Dave watched as Les made his way out of The Pig.

"Honest to God, Steve, I thought I'd been busted."

"Me too," I said. "But didn't I say Les was a good bloke and he'd see you okay? You've got yourself a decent job now. Are you sure you still want to take the risk of smuggling in those stockings? You've got something to lose now."

"I'll have to think about it, Steve. Some of the guys on the ship walk through every time with brand new suits and shirts mixed up with their dirty washing. And all sorts of other stuff like washing machines. One of the Bar Stewards, a chap called Ivan who lives in Speke, has just got himself a really smart electric guitar from a place on Music Row here in New York. He was playing it in here last night. Graeme, your boss in the lounge, said it looked and sounded amazing. A Duo Jet I think he said it was called. Nearly three hundred dollars he's supposed to have paid for it. His tips must be really good if he can run to that sort of money."

"But a guitar's different," I said. "If it's been played it's no longer new. The Customs Officer could be persuaded it's just for personal use and turn a blind eye to it. A hundred pairs of stockings is different. Nobody's going to believe they're for your personal use. You know. Like you'll be swanning around Liverpool wearin' 'em. Apart from anything else you're not pretty enough."

I dodged backwards as Dave took a big swing at me. And missed.

As we stood together in the Customs Shed at Huskisson Dock Dave had a large rucksack on his back and he was carrying a soft holdall. I just had a rather battered suitcase which had done service for various members of the family over the years. It was definitely showing its age. The two locks which kept it closed had a tendency to jump open at the slightest jolt so I'd knotted a length of rope around the outside as a precaution. Going through Customs was stressful enough without the added worry of all my belongings, and some stockings, suddenly being scattered all over the floor.

Ahead of us we could see four Customs Officers on duty. More than usual. And it looked like most of our shipmates were being stopped and questioned. Several of them had already been asked to lift their cases onto one of the desks and open them for inspection.

"Either they've had a tip off about something or we've picked the day they've got all their staff on duty," I whispered to Dave as we waited to be called forward.

Dave turned to look at me. "It looks like I'm stuffed, mate."

He'd decided that he didn't want to leave all the stockings on the ship. Apart from anything else he couldn't be absolutely certain he'd be sailing on the Media again. Cunard sometimes moved crew to a different ship at short notice to stop us drifting into lazy routines and becoming too comfortable.

He'd thought of throwing them over the side in mid-Atlantic. But that seemed like a bit of a waste.

So he'd decided to take the chance.

I wasn't carrying anything ashore apart from my own things so I'd agreed to put ten pairs in my suitcase, hoping it'd make it slightly easier for him to argue that his were all presents for family and friends if he got stopped.

We'd even thought about wearing a few pairs under our trousers. But that plan was abandoned when Dave pointed out that as well as making us sweat like pigs they'd be stretched and unsaleable. And we'd already decided to wear our American suits, shirts and shoes as we hoped that would technically make them second-hand. And thus not liable for duty.

"Next!"

One of the officers pointed at Dave and beckoned him over to the nearest desk. It was no more than ten feet away so I could hear every word.

"Passport, please."

Dave handed the document over. The officer opened it up and flicked through the pages. Then he held up the photograph page and looked at Dave.

"David Cuthbert Robertson?"

Dave nodded his head.

"Yes, sir."

"Looking at the U.S. Immigration Stamps you've been over to New York three times now."

"Yes, sir."

"And you had a good time over there?"

"Yes, sir."

"I'm told things are very different in New York. The shops are full of things you can't get hold of over here."

"Yes, sir. That's right."

"And what might you have brought back?"

"Just a few pairs of stockings. As presents."

The officer looked straight at Dave for what must have been almost half a minute without saying anything. I could see the side of Dave's face and he hardly reacted at all. He looked unbelievably calm.

"Presents," said the officer eventually, still staring at Dave.

"Yes, sir. Presents. I've got a lot of cousins and there's quite a few birthdays coming up in the family. And it's Christmas in a few weeks."

Without taking his eyes off Dave's face the officer slowly handed his passport back to him.

"Enjoy your shore leave, Mr Robertson. You can go."

It was my turn.

"Passport, please."

The initial routine was the same. My name and passport photograph were checked and I was asked a couple of questions about my time in New York.

"And have you got any items you'd like to declare, Mr Crane?"

"Stockings, sir. Presents."

Just as he had done with Dave the officer stared at me without saying anything. I felt like a criminal and one of the muscles in my left cheek started to twitch. It was noticed.

"Stockings seem to be very popular presents today. I think I'd like to take a look. Would you mind opening up your suitcase for me?"

As I lifted my suitcase up onto the desk one of the dodgy locks sprung open, just as I'd feared it might. Fortunately the rope kept the lid closed and I started to work on the knots. I'd tied them very securely and one of them proved to be a bit stubborn.

"Take your time," said the officer. "I've got all day."

He continued to watch me as I did my best to loosen the tightly-knotted rope.

"That suitcase has definitely seen better days. Perhaps you should consider investing in a new one next time you're over in New York? Rather than stockings."

As he was speaking the knot suddenly decided to come loose and I was able to open the case for inspection. Ten pairs of stockings, still in their smart packs, lay neatly on top of my own rather less than smart clothing. I'd decided when packing the case that there was no point in hiding them. If the suitcase was checked they'd certainly be found and I thought it'd look better if I hadn't tried to squirrel them away.

The officer picked one of the packs up and studied it.

"Gold Mark Seamless. Fifth Avenue, New York City. You've got expensive tastes."

"Not me. But the ladies seem to like the nice ones," I said.

"And who are the lucky ladies, might I ask?"

"There's a few pairs for my girlfriend. And a couple for my mother. My Dad walked out on her a few years back so I thought they'd cheer her up a bit. I'll probably keep the rest of them back for Christmas."

"And there's nothing else hidden away among all those clothes?"

I shook my head. "No, officer. All I've got is the stockings."

He thought for a moment. "I should probably charge you some duty on these stockings. But I'm in a good mood today. And it'd only be a few shillings. You've been honest and declared them so if you promise me you'll put the duty I'm not charging you towards a new suitcase I'll let it go on this occasion."

He placed the pack of stockings on top of the others.

"I appreciate that," I said. "Thank you."

"You can close your carrier up now, Mr Crane. Forgive me, but given the state of it I hesitate to continue calling it a suitcase. Enjoy your shore leave."

I got outside to find it was raining. I could see Dave waiting for me under The Dockers' Umbrella as I made my way out of the dock gates.

"I got searched," I said. "But I think the bloke felt sorry for me. He said he wouldn't charge me any duty on the stockings as long as I got myself a new suitcase."

Dave laughed.

"Thanks for doin' that for me, Steve. I'll buy you a drink as soon as I get the money from Eddie."

"Very generous. Thank you." I looked him in the eye. "I'm only going to say this once, Dave. If you want to do any more smuggling, you're on your own."

NINE

MOTHER

I arrived back at St Bride Street to find my mother sitting downstairs with both Georgie and Jimmy which was most unusual.

"It's good to see the three of you together having a natter," I said, giving them all a smile. "You should do it more often."

None of them smiled back. It was my Uncle Georgie who broke the silence.

"Your mother's been to see the doctor, Steve. It was a bit of a battle but we finally persuaded her to go yesterday. She's not been herself for a while as you know."

I looked at my mother.

"Oh dear, Ma. I knew something wasn't right. I was saying you should see the doctor before I left for New York, wasn't I? About that pain. What's the problem?"

My mother didn't say anything. She just sat there as Uncle Georgie went over to the settee and sat down alongside her, holding her hand.

"Your mother's frightened, Stephen. The doctor examined her and told her she needs to go for some tests. I was with her and he said he could feel a lump in her stomach where the pain is. He thinks it's something called an abdominal aortic aneurysm which is a weakness in the wall of the main artery. He wants her to see a specialist to see what can be done about it."

My mother shook her head.

"No. I don't want any treatment. I'll just wait and see what happens."

Uncle Georgie put his right arm around her shoulders and gave her a gentle hug.

"You know you can't do that, Barbara. I've got a friend who works in the x-ray department at the Royal Infirmary. She says if it is an aortic aneurysm and it gets bigger and starts leaking it's a serious matter."

"The doctor said that could take years."

Uncle Georgie shook his head.

"Yes. But I was there, Barbara. And he also said the bigger it gets the more risk there is."

"So what's the doctor going to do?" I said.

I knew my mother well, and how very reluctant she would be to agree to any sort of medical intervention or treatment. I wanted to be sure this didn't mean the problem would simply be ignored.

"As I said, he wants an expert opinion, Stephen. So he's referring Barbara to see a specialist. She'll be seen within the next couple of weeks."

I joined my mother and Georgie on the settee.

"You've got to go and see the specialist, Ma," I said, gently holding her right hand. "We all just want the best for you. There might be an operation or something which could put you right. You can't just sit here and do nothing."

"I've already said to Georgie I'll see the specialist, Stephen. But I'm not going to let him start messing around with me."

"That's fine, Ma." I gave her shoulders a reassuring squeeze. "One step at a time. We'll see what the specialist has to say and then take it from there. Okay?"

My mother nodded her head reluctantly.

There was nothing more to be said. It was time for a cup of tea.

Georgie and I made our way down to the kitchen which was hidden away in the basement of the terraced house. As I filled the kettle and placed it on the old-fashioned, cast-iron hob my Uncle Georgie told me a little more about his visit to the doctor with my mother.

"I didn't mention it upstairs, Stephen, because I didn't want to make your mother even more worried. But the doctor told me there's probably not very much that can be done. He said he was reading in the British Medical Journal that some specialists in America have been trying out various ways of strengthening the weak area in the last few years. But they've not had much success. And there's nothing like that happening here in England."

"So Ma might just have to wait?"

"It looks like it, I'm afraid. But I think she should still see the specialist. Just so we know. She wouldn't agree to any treatment anyway. So if there's nothing they can do it won't make much difference."

"Thanks, Uncle Georgie." I gave him a weak smile. "I understand."

Sylvie's Dad had gone fishing with a couple of friends so she'd invited me over to her place in West Derby. She was very sympathetic when I told her about my mother.

"We won't know for sure what's happening until she's seen the specialist," I said. "That's if she doesn't refuse to go at the last minute. Which could easily happen. But if my Uncle Georgie is right about what the doctor said, and he's usually pretty much on the ball when it comes to this sort of thing, the swelling in her stomach isn't going to get any better. It could stay the same. Or it could get worse. So every time I leave for New York I'll be wondering how she's going to be while I'm away. You know. Worrying about something happening without me being there to help."

"She's always got your two uncles, Steve. Your Ma won't be on her own. And according to your Uncle Georgie the doctor said she could be okay for years. It'll be fine."

We were sitting on a very comfortable couch with our arms round each other.

"Thank you," I said. "I needed someone to say something positive."

Sylvie rested her head on my chest as I pulled her closer and hugged her tight.

Is that better?" she said, giving me a smile and kissing my cheek.

"Much better."

"What do you want to do this evening? There's some food in the fridge if you'd like to eat."

"Maybe later," I said. "I'm not really hungry yet. We could wait for your Dad if you like. What time is he due back?"

"He isn't," said Sylvie. "He and his friends have gone up to Scotland for three days because the fishing's better up there. They only left yesterday."

"So we've got the place to ourselves for a couple of days?"

Sylvie gave me a slightly naughty look and then laughed.

"I suppose we have."

We were both thinking the same thing.

"You are unbelievably attractive," I said. "I don't quite know what you see in me but I'm very happy just being here with you."

"What I see is a very interesting Cunard Yank who is equally attractive," she said, putting both her hands around my head and gripping my hair. "Someone I want to kiss. Right now."

She pulled me towards her and I felt the softness of her lips against mine. It wasn't our first kiss but this time it was different. Our lips stayed together and I could taste her. Our hands began to explore each other's bodies, pushing clothes aside to reach bare skin.

I ran my hands up both her legs, beneath her flared dress, and found the top of her stockings.

"A gift from a Cunard Yank, I hope."

"Ah," she said softly. "Mais oui, monsieur."

I kissed her neck and caught the scent of her perfume.

"And that would possibly be Chanel Number 5?"

"Ah, monsieur. Tu est tellement intelligent. C'est vrai."

Sylvie hadn't spoken to me in her mother's native tongue before.

"Oh my God," I said, laughing. "Your French language is so sexy. I'm not sure exactly what you're saying but you'd better stop now or I might not be able to control myself."

"Quel domage," she said, putting on a serious face and pouting her lips.

Then she laughed again.

"Mais je suis tres heureux, monsieur. I am happy. Very, very happy."

Her eyes sparkled as she spoke which made her look even more desirable and beautiful. She put her lips close to my ear before very gently nipping the lobe with her teeth.

"I want you to undress me," she whispered. "Now."

I turned to look at her.

"Except the stockings," I said. "I'm going to leave the stockings on."

Sylvie lowered her eyes.

"If that is your wish, monsieur, it is my command."

Nothing more was said.

We understood each other.

I was still at Sylvie's three days later when her Dad arrived home from Scotland. We'd never met before, and for some reason he was taller than I'd imagined him to be. Almost six foot. He had a friendly, tanned face and he was still wearing what looked like his fishing clothes.

"You've got a visitor, I see," he said, looking at me before turning to Sylvie with a smile.

"This is Steve, Dad," said Sylvie, giving him a hug. "He's just popped over to say hello. He's a friend of Greg's. You know. Pamela's brother. That's how we first got to know each other."

Her Dad gave us both a knowing look.

"Pleased to meet you, Steve. I'm Frank." He held out a hand in greeting. "As Sylvie may have mentioned I've been doing a bit of fishing with a couple of friends in a small town called Crieff. Up in Scotland. Not far from where the Highlands proper start. Beautiful place. So clean and fresh. It's like a different world up there."

"I hope you all had a good time," I said, shaking his hand.

"We always do." Frank gave me a smile. "You can't beat the Scottish rivers for the fishing so we try to get up there as often as we can. There's a marvellous place in Crieff called The Hydro on the edge of the town. It's been there for nearly a hundred years so they've got access to Atlantic salmon fishing on the River Tay. And also fly-fishing for rainbow trout on a loch about twenty minutes away. It's the best place we've ever come across. By a country mile. Have you ever done any fishing?"

I shook my head.

"Not yet. But I've got a few friends who are keen. If they're anything to go by fishing seems to be something which is very difficult to give up once it gets into your blood."

"It is indeed. And if you and Sylvie stay together I'll take you both up to Scotland with me one day and treat you to a stay at The Hydro. We can go fishing to see if you like it. And if you don't, the two of you can do whatever you please and leave me in happy solitude on the river. How does that sound?"

Sylvie laughed.

"Early days, Dad. Steve's a Lounge Steward with Cunard on one of the New York ships. So he's away quite a lot of the time."

"A Cunard Yank, eh? I've got a mate who was an engineer on the Queen Mary for about ten years. He did war service on her. Said it was a bit hairy at times. Being hunted by Hitler's U-boats. Sinking a ship like that would have been a real feather in their caps. But it never happened, thank God."

"I'm a bit of a new boy," I said. "I've only been going to sea for a few months."

"But you're enjoying it I hope. Seeing the world and being paid for it. Can't be bad."

He gave Sylvie a fatherly kiss.

"Now, if you don't mind, I must get my things ready for work tomorrow. I'll see you again, Steve, I hope."

Two days before I was due to leave Liverpool on my next trip to New York my mother gave me a letter which had just arrived from Manheim in Pennsylvania. She knew who it was from, of course, but she had left it for me to open.

October 23rd 1954   *64, East Ferdinand Street*
Manheim

> *Dear Stephen,*
> *How lovely to get your letter. An unexpected surprise, but very welcome. Mum writes regularly as you know,*

but I was beginning to fear we'd permanently lost touch. Life here in America is good. I'm very happy, and lucky, to have met and married Carl. He's a wonderful husband and a great father to Ricky, who is now seven, and Susan, who will soon be five.

It'd be great to see you, and Dave too if he's able to join you. The journey from New York City to Lancaster by train takes about three hours and Carl says he could pick you up at the station. We're only about half an hour from Lancaster by car. So, as long as you've got at least two days free while your ship is in New York, I'm sure a trip out here to Manheim would be possible. If you could let us know when you think you might be able to come and visit us, maybe giving a couple of weeks' notice, we can have everything ready for you.

With love to you. And, of course, to Mum.

Your sister,

Jean xxx

My mother didn't take her eyes off me for even one second as I read the letter.

"What does she say, Stephen?" The question came the moment I'd finished reading. "Are the two of you going to be able to get together?"

"I think the easiest thing is if you take a look at it yourself, Ma."

I passed the letter to her. She donned her reading glasses and read it very slowly and carefully, absorbing every word. As she came to the end she lifted her head. There were tears in her eyes.

"That's wonderful, Stephen. It'd make me so happy if you could meet up with Jean. And the two children as well, of course. I doubt I'll ever see them now with this problem I've got, but at least I'll know you're in contact with each other. And hopefully you'll stay in touch. That'd be a huge comfort to me. And much better than nothing."

"Nonsense, Ma. Once I've been to see Jean and the kids, and made sure the journey is possible, there's no reason why you shouldn't do the same. As a member of the crew I'm sure I can get you a reasonably cheap fare across the Atlantic. We could travel together and then get to Jean's from New York by train. It'd be exciting. You'd be able to see a bit of the world."

"See a bit of the world, Stephen?" My mother shook her head and gave me a smile. "And how long does it take to get to New York by ship? A week? Ten days?"

Then, without any warning, she began to sing.

"*I sail the ocean, like Fred Astaire. And all that I see. Is lots of sea.*"

I laughed.

"Fair enough, Ma. There is quite a lot of sea between here and New York. But you'd see something of America. And spend a bit of time with Jean and the kids. I'm sure with you travelling all that way they'd be more than happy to put you up for as long as you wanted. There'd be no need for you to rush back home."

"Let's just take it slowly, Stephen. One step at a time as you said to me about the specialist. It was good advice. And I took note of it. You go and see Jean first. And then we can maybe think about me."

I smiled to myself. My mother was certainly stubborn. But she was also very wise. We should listen to her.

TEN

MANHEIM

It was half an hour on foot from the Cunard Pier to Pennsylvania Station. Up 50th Street from the Pier and then right along 7th Avenue. Dave had decided against joining me so I was on my own. Jean and I had agreed that the best thing would be for me to catch the first train out of New York City. Getting to Manheim as early as possible would maximise our time together. And leaving their place after lunch the next day would give me plenty of time to get back to the ship.

I couldn't risk missing it. It'd cost me my job if I wasn't on board for the return voyage to Liverpool.

Not long after reaching 7th Avenue I got my first glimpse of Penn Station. For forty-five years it had been New York City's main railway station. The largest transportation hub in the Western Hemisphere. Les had said it was amazing but his description hadn't remotely prepared me for what I could see ahead of me.

"There's nothing like it in England, Steve. It's massive. It looks more like a Greek temple than a railway station. We think some of our buildings back home are big and impressive, but Penn Station is in a completely different league. Half a million passengers pass through it every single weekday. Half a million. That's pretty much the population of Liverpool."

To say that the building I was now approaching was big and impressive didn't even begin to do it justice. At ground level its design had been inspired by the classical styles of St Peter's Square in Rome and the Bank of England in London. And beneath this astonishing building were hidden eleven platforms and twenty-one railway tracks. It was difficult to get my head round it.

I entered through the main entrance from 7th Avenue, passing between rows of Doric columns which, as Les had said, wouldn't have looked out of place around a temple on the Acropolis in Athens. Once inside I found myself standing in a vast shopping arcade. All around me were numerous expensive boutiques and shops. It was early in the day so most of them were closed but I didn't feel I was missing out. Just a quick glance at the window displays told me that most of the items were way above my price range.

The arcade led on to a main concourse which was dominated by a large clock supported by elegantly crafted, steel pillars. And the whole area was protected from the New York weather by a roof of glazed sheets contained within a plain, steel framework.

Several stairways led from the concourse down to the platforms below. The departures board confirmed that the first service to Lancaster would be leaving on time in just ten minutes so I hurried down. My train was already waiting and, like the station, the locomotive and the carriages seemed to be substantially bigger than the ones we had in England. Even the coach-class seats, upholstered in what felt like genuine, brown leather, were unexpectedly spacious and comfortable.

It was a pleasant and relaxing journey, and several hours later I arrived at my destination feeling fully refreshed. The extremely comfortable seats, and the gentle, rocking motion of the train, had caused me to drift off into a very welcome sleep for much of the way.

Leaving the platform I made my way through the high-ceilinged waiting room of the railway station which was located in downtown Lancaster, close to Franklin and Marshall College. Elegant Art Deco light fittings were suspended from the ceiling and a number of antique, wooden benches were lined up on the terrazzo floor. They provided practical, although possibly not all that comfortable, seating for passengers who were awaiting their trains.

I stepped outside the red brick, classical revival building and a man in his mid-thirties who looked vaguely familiar approached me. He was wearing a striped, red and white scarf which identified him as Jean's husband, Carl. The almost identical scarf which I had wrapped loosely around my neck before alighting from the train, as instructed by my sister Jean, told Carl that I was his brother-in-law, Steve.

Carl held out his hand.

"Steve. Welcome to Lancaster. And Pennsylvania Dutch Country. You've chosen a beautiful day for your visit. It can get a bit cold and wet here in the wintertime. But not today. I believe there's an old-English word for it. Apricity. The warmth of the sun in winter."

I looked up at the clear, blue sky. It was early December. But in the sun it didn't feel all that cold.

"That's a new one on me, Carl. But we don't make much use of old-English in Liverpool. As you may remember, our main language is Scouse."

He laughed as I took hold of his outstretched hand and shook it warmly.

"It's great to see you again," I said. "Although I'm not sure I'd have recognised you without the scarf."

"Your sister, Jean, is full of good ideas. The red and white scarf trick is one of her more useful ones."

"A little nod to her favourite football team," I said. "We're

'Reds' in our family. Liverpool supporters. And you never abandon your team. Even if you're thousands of miles away on the other side of an ocean. Our rivals in the city are Everton. They're the 'Blues.'"

"No need to explain, Steve," said Carl, laughing. "Your sister has given me a very thorough indoctrination. The kids too. And I know for sure she still keeps an eye on how Liverpool are doing."

"Not too well at the moment," I said ruefully. "As I'm sure Jean must know. We got relegated to the Second Division at the end of last season after fifty years in the top flight. Everton are the team who are riding high just now. As we went down they passed us going the other way. Which made it particularly hard to take. But we live in hope that things might change. We badly need a new manager. That's the real problem. Don Welsh, the manager who just got us relegated, is a bit of an eccentric. He was given the job a couple of years ago and it's been downhill ever since. It's a shame because the board also interviewed a chap from Scotland called Bill Shankly. It was between the two of them. And Bill Shankly's been doing very well since, managing a club called Grimsby Town over on the east coast. Everyone's been saying they chose the wrong man. But that's water under the bridge now. We've missed out on Shankly and that's it. And anyway, I'm probably boring you."

While we'd been talking Carl had guided me to the parking lot alongside the station where his maroon, Buick Roadmaster Estate Wagon was parked. With chrome mouldings on its sides and white-walled tyres it was exactly what I expected an American car to look like.

And, as I was beginning to learn was normal in the United States, it was big.

Carl opened the tailgate.

"Put your overnight bag in there and let's hit the road. It's not far to Manheim. Thirty minutes at most."

We took our places in the front seats. The soft leather upholstery, in a pleasing shade of light tan, made for another comfortable and relaxing ride as we left the parking lot and headed north-east.

"I'm taking Fruitville Pike," said Carl. "It's as good a route as any. And when we reach Manheim it's straight through onto South Main Street and along East Ferdinand Street to our home. Taking the Pike also means there's a good chance we'll come across one or two horse-drawn, Amish buggies on the way. Particularly on a fine day like this. Jean said you might find them interesting."

We were in luck. About two miles out of Lancaster, as we drove along a straight length of road between empty cornfields, Carl pointed out a dark shape heading towards us.

"A family of Amish," he said. "Off somewhere together. Maybe to pick up a few provisions."

The road wasn't wide so Carl slowed the Roadmaster down. As we got closer I could see that the dark shape was an open, four-wheeled wagon. It was being pulled along at a nice, steady pace by a beautiful, chestnut-brown horse which had a very striking white triangle between its eyes, extending down its nose. Sitting in the wagon, in two neat rows, were eight people. In the front seat was a man with a neatly-fashioned, dark beard beneath his chin. He was holding a pair of reins loosely in his hands and wearing a heavy black jacket and trousers. A dark-coloured hat with a wide brim shaded his eyes from the sun. Seated alongside him were three teenage boys, similarly dressed but with hats that had narrower brims. Behind the four men were two women and two young girls, all wearing white bonnets. Like the men the two women were dressed warmly in black, while both the girls were wearing dark-brown jackets. One of them had a light-blue dress on. The other girl's dress was plain white.

The driver of the wagon turned towards our car and

acknowledged us with a very slight nod of his head as we passed. The three boys also turned their heads towards us. But the ladies continued to stare straight ahead.

"There you go," said Carl. "You've now seen some of our local Amish. They're good, honest people who follow the teachings of Our Lord, working hard and looking after each other. Some of their customs might seem a little old-fashioned and strange in this modern world. But to my mind their hearts are in the right place."

Even as he spoke another Amish wagon approached us. Also with four wheels, its seating area was fully enclosed by a soft, grey canvas material supported by a square frame. The driver was peering ahead out of a rectangular gap in the canvas through which the reins to his single, black horse also ran. Even as the wagon passed by it wasn't possible to see whether he was carrying any passengers.

As we continued along the road the dark soil on either side was mostly broken up and bare. But one or two fields which had not yet been ploughed were still dotted with stubble from the autumn harvest.

"If you'd visited a few months ago we'd have been surrounded by fields of ripe corn," said Carl. "Right up to the edge of the road on both sides. And high as an elephant's eye as a pair of clever Broadway songsmiths said a few years ago. Their song was about Oklahoma. But the corn grows just as high round here."

The road to Manheim was quiet. Apart from the two Amish buggies only one other vehicle passed us, a small lorry, heavily loaded with timber, making its way towards Lancaster.

"Our little town gets its name from a village in Germany called Kerpen-Manheim," said Carl. "It was founded by a man called Henry Stiegel who arrived here from Germany in 1762 with a number of other Lutheran and Mennonite immigrants. Two years after arriving he started up a glassworks to provide employment for the local people and once the small settlement was established he gave a plot of land to the local congregation. This was twenty years before the dollar came into being and he charged them just five shillings for the land. Along with a yearly rent of One Red Rose. The Lutheran Church which was built on the land is still in regular use. Your sister Jean and I worship there every Sunday. Its proper name is the Zion Lutheran Church. But because a Festival of the Red Rose takes place there every year at which a red Lancastrian rose is presented to one of the heirs of Henry Stiegel everyone round here knows it as The Red Rose Church."

In less than twenty-five minutes we had left the open fields behind us and we were passing the first of Manheim's neatly-kept houses.

The small village in Germany after which the town was named would in future years become famous as the childhood home of Michael Schumaker, the Formula One Racing Driver. He was born in the village of Kerpen-Manheim and practiced his skills on the local Go-Kart Racing Circuit with his younger brother, Ralf, before leaving home to become World Champion and one of the best drivers his sport had ever seen.

"Nearly there," said Carl as we made our way along South Main Street and then turned into East Ferdinand Street.

He brought the estate wagon to a halt outside a cream-coloured, frame-built house with three large windows and a glazed front door. A tiled canopy above the front door and downstairs window, which matched the roof, gave the building a very pleasing, symmetrical appearance. A small front garden had been planted with evergreen bushes which softened its appearance. And, running between the bushes, a neat path led to the front door.

"Your big sister's American home," said Carl. "I hope you approve."

"It's really nice," I said, turning to him with a smile. "I definitely approve."

He gave a little laugh of pleasure and smiled back at me.

"Well, Jean and I certainly like it," he said. "And Ricky and Susan too, of course. We've been here about three years now. Before that we were in a smaller place a little bit out of town. We'd been thinking for a while about getting somewhere bigger but as usual we hadn't got round to doing anything about it. Then someone I know told me he'd had this house built. And just as he was about to move in with his family he got an offer of a job in New York City which was just too good to turn down. So he asked me if Jean and I might be interested. It was as if it was meant to be. The price was right. And when we took a look at the house it was almost exactly the sort of place we'd have designed for ourselves if we'd been starting from scratch. It was perfect. And everything was sorted out within a few weeks." Carl shrugged his shoulders. "I believe some things are meant to be. And we've been thanking the good Lord for looking after us ever since."

He opened the driver's door and swung his legs out of the car.

"If you're ready, Steve, we might as well go on in and say hello."

Jean had been nearly eleven years old when I was born in 1936, and by the time I was a teenager she'd already been living in Manheim for a couple of years. So, as often happens when there's a big age difference between siblings, we'd never really got to know one another. But it was lovely to see her again. And with us both being a few years older the age gap seemed smaller. It wasn't long before we were chatting away like long lost friends.

"So Dave decided against making the trip?" she said as we sat together in their comfortable lounge, enjoying a coffee and a few home-made cookies. We were on our own. Carl had taken the two children down to a local playground to get a bit of fresh air and run off some of their surplus energy.

"I think he'd have liked to come and see you," I said, "but he was a bit worried about travelling so far away from New York. He didn't want to risk missing the ship. And he said it'd probably be better if I was on my own anyway. So you and I could make the most of our time together. You know. Catching up and sorting out the problems of the world."

"That's why Carl's taken Ricky and Susan out," said Jean. "To give us a bit of peace and quiet."

She leant back in her chair.

"So," she said, "how's everything back home? I've got a good life here but I do miss the family. I often think about those gatherings we used to have in St Bride Steet at the weekend when grandad and grandma were still alive. Grandad sitting there in his chair by the range in the kitchen. All warm and cosy down in the basement."

"And grandma busying herself with Sunday lunch," I said, smiling at the memory. "We'd get together down there, round that big, square table. Always a roast it was. With all the trimmings. Roasties and carrots and peas. And stuffing as well if it was chicken. And really thick, rich gravy. I'll never forget that gravy. I don't know what her secret was but grandma made the best gravy in the world."

"And sometimes if there was more than about ten of us she'd do two sittings," said Jean. "With apple pie and custard to follow. Great times. There wasn't much money about but we were happy."

"We certainly weren't rich," I said. "But I don't think we were on the bread line. I'm pretty sure we were the first house in our street to have an inside toilet. Which I suppose Georgie and Jimmy must've paid for. Neither of them were married when we were kids. And they both had good jobs. So they probably had a bob or two between them."

"But I'm sure I remember an outside toilet," said Jean, turning to me with a questioning look.

"That's right," I said. "We kids all used it. The posh toilet was up on the third floor and we couldn't be bothered climbing all the way up those steep stairs. It was easier to nip out quickly to the one in the yard. Even if it was a bit basic. So that's what we did. And after lunch, once he'd had a smoke, grandad used to cover copper coins with the thin, silver paper from his tobacco. I can still see him sitting there, rubbing away at the coins until it looked like they were made out of real silver."

"And then he'd give you one and say it was half-a-crown," said Jean, laughing. "You were made up."

"And you were too," I said. "When you got yours."

"Ah," said Jean, laughing even more. "But mine was always the real McCoy. A genuine half-crown. I was his first granddaughter, you see. And a few years older than you. He used to tell me it was our little secret. And you never cottoned on."

"The sneaky old devil!" I said, as Jean continued to laugh. "Ah, well. God bless him. He was still lovely."

"And how are Mum and the two uncles?"

"Uncle Jimmy and Uncle Georgie are fine," I said. "Jimmy's separated from his wife so both the uncles are living in St Bride Street now. Which is good because I wouldn't have been happy going off to sea and leaving Ma on her own."

As Jean smiled and nodded her head I decided it was time to mention our mother's illness to her. I'd been waiting for the right moment.

"What's not so good, I'm afraid, is that Ma's had to go and see a specialist about a bit of a problem with her circulation."

Jean's smile changed to a look of concern. I think she could tell by the tone of my voice that it might be rather more than a bit of a problem.

"It was when I was on shore leave," I said, "I'd noticed Ma seemed to be getting some pains in her stomach. And as usual she was insisting it was nothing and wouldn't do anything about it. Then, when I was away at sea the time before last, the pains got worse and Uncle Georgie insisted on taking her to see Dr Roxburgh. He examined her and said he couldn't be a hundred percent sure but he thought it might be something called an abdominal aortic aneurysm."

"Which is what?" asked Jean.

"As I understand it, it's a sort of weakness in the wall of the main artery which causes it to swell up," I explained. "Like a balloon. And it can sometimes get painful. Ma saw the specialist a couple of weeks ago and he's confirmed that's what it is."

"So what are they going to do about it?"

"The specialist said her blood pressure was a little bit higher than he'd like it to be. So he's put her on some tablets to bring it down which might help by taking some of the pressure off the aneurysm. But apart from that there isn't really any treatment. He said some surgeons over here in America have been trying out one or two ways of strengthening the weakened artery. Like wrapping it in cellophane. But it's just experimental at the moment. They gave it a try with Albert Einstein but but it didn't save him, sadly. So it wouldn't be of any help to Ma right now."

"So there's nothing they can do?" said Jean.

"I think that's right," I said. "Apart from the blood pressure tablets that is. I was half-way across the Atlantic on the Media when Ma went for the appointment but Uncle Georgie was with her. According to Georgie the specialist said the aneurysm might get bigger and start leaking. And if she's very unlucky it could even burst. But I don't think Ma fully realises that. Or at least if she does she's in denial. Which I suppose might be for the best."

"And that'd be it?" Jean looked shocked. It was a lot for her to take in at such short notice.

"I suppose it would," I said. "Then again the specialist said she could be okay for years. He couldn't say for sure what's going to happen. He's going to see her again in six months to check if the aneurysm's getting any bigger and take it from there."

We sat in silence while Jean mulled over what I'd just told her.

"I'll have to speak to Carl and work out what we should do," she said. "He's very good. He'll go along with whatever I think is best."

"The only helpful thing I can say is that I know Ma would love to see you. And the kids too, of course. But she understands you can't just drop everything and zoom over to Liverpool at a moment's notice."

"No. It wouldn't be easy." Jean thought for a moment. "Do you think there's any chance she'd be well enough to come over here? You know. If Carl and I paid."

"I don't know. I did sort of suggest it to her a while back. But that was before we knew about the aneurysm thing. And even then she wasn't certain about making such a long journey. I think she'd be worried now that something might go seriously wrong while she's away. But I'm not sure."

As I was speaking Jean had started to cry.

"It's awful, Steve, being so far away. I knew when I came over here with Carl that this sort of thing might happen. That it was something I'd probably have to face one day as Mum got older. But I didn't think it'd be quite so soon. I mean it's hardly as if she's old."

"I know," I said. "But life isn't always predictable. Unexpected things happen. I suppose we all know that but mostly we avoid thinking about it. Otherwise we wouldn't be able to cope."

For a few minutes Jean was lost in thought. Then she turned to me.

"It'd be easier if Dad hadn't disappeared. Do you ever wonder if he might still be alive?"

I looked at her. "That's the other thing I need to talk to you about."

Before leaving for New York I'd taken the book down from the shelf in the parlour. The letter from my father had not been touched. It was still in exactly the same place. So I'd decided to bring it with me to Manheim and show it to Jean.

"Dad wrote a letter to Ma four and a half years ago." I said. "About a month after he disappeared. I came across it completely by accident. Tucked away inside a book. Ma must've hidden it away for safe keeping. I don't think it'd been touched for ages. I suppose she might even have forgotten all about it."

I took the letter out of my jacket pocket and gave it to Jean.

"The best thing is if you just read it," I said. "And then we can talk."

Jean removed the letter from its envelope and unfolded it. As she began to read her eyes moved up and down the page, revisiting a particular sentence or word before moving on. When she had finished she folded the piece of paper up.

"Well I never," she said as she looked down at the folded paper. "This must have come as a real shock for Ma. But I have to say it's not a complete surprise to me."

She paused. As if she was working out exactly what she should say. When the words eventually came they were a question.

"Did Dad ever talk to you about the war?"

"A little bit," I said. "But not much."

"He probably thought you were too young. I don't think he said very much to Mum either. But we were very close. At least I thought we were. So he did tell me one or two things.

After the war this was. Not while the fighting was still going on." She paused again. "Have you heard of the Special Operations Executive?"

I shook my head. "No."

"They were soldiers who were specially trained to work behind enemy lines," said Jean. "Dad told me he was one of them. And in the spring of 1944 he was parachuted into France to work with the French Resistance. They'd been ordered to sabotage the German defences and create as much chaos and confusion as possible in the run-up to D-Day."

"D'you mean like a spy?"

"Not exactly. He was a soldier. But not in uniform. So I'm pretty sure he'd have been shot if the Germans had captured him. He told me that Winston Churchill took a particularly keen interest in what the Special Operations Executive were doing. He wanted them to set Europe ablaze. According to Dad those were Churchill's exact words. 'Set Europe ablaze'. He seemed to be very proud of that."

I suppose I should have felt proud too. The idea that my father had been involved in such secret wartime events was completely unexpected. It explained some of the things in the letter. But it also told me that he wasn't the person I had once very confidently believed him to be.

"I knew he was in the army," I said. "And that he fought in France. But nothing more than that. Did he tell you a lot about what he was doing?"

"It was mostly unconnected stories. As if he needed to share them with someone and get them off his chest. You know. Relieve some of the burden. Maybe it helped, me listening to what he had to say? I don't know. But he always insisted I must never say anything to anyone else."

"And you haven't? Not even to Carl?"

"No. You're the first person I've mentioned it to."

She stopped and looked a little guilty.

"Look. I don't think Dad told me all that much to be honest. There must have been a lot of stuff he couldn't talk about. Which he had to keep secret. But I've found it quite hard, having to bottle it all up. Particularly with me moving over here to the States and then him disappearing. And because of what he'd told me I did wonder if his disappearance might have been related to something that happened during the war."

Jean stopped again, deep in thought.

"There was one thing he kept going back to. As if it was really important to him. And having read that letter I now understand why."

Jean took a deep breath.

"It's difficult to believe," she said. "He told me it was after D-Day. In the autumn of 1944 when the Allied armies were trying to fight their way into Germany itself. For some reason which he never explained he was with General Patten's American troops near a place called Metz. Very close to the border between Germany and France. And the Germans were fighting hard to defend it. He was with a group of French resistance fighters and one of them was a young girl. Which according to Dad wasn't that unusual. Quite a few of the French resistance fighters were young women. But he kept going on about this particular girl. Saying they got on really well and that I'd have really liked her. Which I thought was strange. Because how old was I at the time? Nineteen I suppose."

"And it was Anna?"

"Yes. He told me her name. And from the way he described her she can't have been much older than me. Dad would have been, I don't know, thirty-seven or thirty-eight. So almost twenty years older than her. I kept thinking is he trying to tell me they were more than friends? But he never actually made it clear. And I couldn't pluck up the courage to ask. Maybe he wanted me to? I don't know. But they were fighting a war together. And I suppose when you don't know if you're still going to be alive the next day you do things you wouldn't do if circumstances were different."

She looked at me. Her face was troubled.

"Is that it?" I said.

"No," she said, shaking her head. "Dad told me he was still with this resistance group when they got involved in a fight with some German soldiers. And he ended up killing this girl's twin brother."

"What?"

"According to him it was a mistake. It was dark and everything was confused. Dad heard a noise behind him and thought it was a German soldier. So he turned round, you know, almost without thinking And shot him in the head. But it wasn't a German. It was Anna's brother, Pierre."

I could hardly believe what my sister was telling me. Could this really be something that had happened to my own father in real life?

"Dad kept telling me how he begged Anna to believe it was an accident. But the problem was he'd had a big argument with Pierre just a few hours earlier. Something to do with how they should handle German prisoners. And Dad had accused him of wanting to go easy on them. Which wasn't true, but it was enough to make Anna and some of the French fighters think the shooting might not have been an accident. That Dad might have taken advantage of all the chaos to get rid of someone who he thought was sympathetic to the enemy. Anyway, to cut a long story short Dad said Anna did eventually believe him and they carried on fighting the Germans, moving around from place to place until the war ended. By that time they were in a village on the River Elbe, not all that far from Hamburg. But unless by some miracle Dad decides to reappear and tell us, I don't suppose we'll ever know the full story."

The two of us sat in silence again. I didn't know what Jean was thinking. But I was certainly starting to understand that I hadn't really known my father at all. And I probably now never would. It was a lot to take in.

"I don't believe in miracles," I said. "He's not going to reappear. At least not by choice."

"Do you think there's anything we should do?" asked Jean, handing me the letter which she had returned to its envelope while she'd been talking.

I shrugged my shoulders. "I just thought you should know about it, that's all."

"Thank you," said Jean. "Even though it's upsetting to read, I'm glad I've seen it." She shook her head. "Poor mother. What must she have made of it?"

"I've no idea," I said. "When I read it I couldn't believe it had been written by my own father. I just felt numb. And then angry. How could he do that to Ma? I'm sure she'd have been in a complete turmoil when she received it. I just wish she'd told us. It might have lessened some of the burden."

"I think I can understand why she didn't," said Jean.

"Can you? I'm not sure I can."

"I think maybe she felt it was her burden to bear. That it wouldn't be fair to unload it onto us. Maybe she hid the letter away thinking that one day she might tell us. Or even let us read it. And the time was never right so it just sat there in the book. As you say she might even have forgotten about it by now. They say people do if something's very traumatic. Even when it's important." She paused for a moment. "What are you going to do with it?"

"Put it back where I found it, I think."

"That's fine with me," said Jean.

Later that evening Jean told me that she'd had a quiet word with Carl about our mother's illness. In a couple of weeks it would be Christmas, after which Carl's business would be involved in a very big project for five or six months. So they had decided that the whole family would fly over and visit Liverpool later in the year, probably in early September. That would fit in best with Carl's work commitments. And she was sure they'd be able to clear it with the children's school.

"Thank you," I said, giving her a big hug. "Ma will be over the moon. She's never been one to complain but I'm sure she thought she'd never see her grandchildren. Wait 'til I get back home and tell her."

⸱━⸱━⸱●⸱━⸱●⸱━⸱●━━⸱●⸱━

My journey back to the Media next day was trouble-free. Dave needn't have worried about missing the ship. And when we got back to Liverpool it looked like I needn't have worried too much about my mother either. She was back to her normal self, insisting that her pains had completely disappeared. Uncle Georgie told me he had noticed she was no longer holding on to her stomach.

It was very strange. There didn't seem to be any reason to doubt the specialist's diagnosis. But he had said that bringing her blood pressure down could take some of the pressure off the aneurysm. So hopefully that was what was happening and it wasn't going to get any worse. Maybe she was going to be one of the lucky ones?

I really hoped so. She certainly deserved to be.

And when I told her that in just nine months she'd be meeting her two American grandchildren she burst into tears. They were tears of joy and happiness. At long last things seemed to be going well for her.

ELEVEN

WOMEN AND CHILDREN FIRST

Over the next few months life on board the Media dropped into a regular routine. Even the early morning arrivals at New York every few weeks became almost normal. Almost, but not quite. The appearance of that very special skyline after eight or nine days at sea would never completely lose its magic.

Our shore leave in New York City itself also became more routine. Dave and I found ourselves spending more time in the Market Diner and less time exploring. But we still managed to have plenty of fun.

Then, in the middle of the summer, news arrived from Manheim that the planned visit to Liverpool would have to be delayed. Carl's business venture had not gone well and the pressure of it all had made him ill. Jean explained that his doctors were still unsure whether his medical problems were primarily physical or psychological in origin, but the bottom line was that he was undergoing tests in hospital and he had been advised against travelling abroad for the time being. Jean, understandably, did not feel able to leave him.

The good news was that the specialist reports on mother had

been very positive. The size of her abdominal aortic aneurysm was unchanged and there was cautious optimism that as long as her blood pressure could be kept under control she would be fine. They could offer no long-term guarantees, but there was no immediate cause for concern. The future was looking good.

It was a shame, but the delay could not be helped. As long as all went well with Carl, the Meyers family would arrive in Liverpool the following September.

Twelve months later than originally planned.

⚫·⚫·————⚫·⚫·⚫·⚫·⚫—————·⚫·⚫

One of the very regular and most important routines on RMS Media was the compulsory safety drill which all passengers had to attend at the start of every voyage. It could not be avoided, no matter how many times they might have attended one before.

"This is the bridge. For exercise. For exercise. For exercise. The general emergency signal is about to be sounded for guest exercise purposes only."

Seven short, high-pitched signals were then sounded throughout the ship, followed by one long blast.

"The signal you have just heard was the general emergency signal. If you have not already done so you should go to your cabin and collect your life jacket, warm clothing, head covering and any medication which you regularly use. You should then proceed to the Assembly Station which is specified on the inside of your cabin door. Please note that in accordance with international law all passengers must attend this emergency drill even if they are regular travellers. Please ensure that your

name has been ticked off on the passenger list which a designated crew member will have available at your Assembly Station. Any passengers who are not marked as present at their designated Assembly Station will be required to attend an interview with one of the senior officers."

As members of the crew we all had specific tasks. Familiarity with the drill ran the risk of it feeling routine and unimportant. But people's lives were at stake so the whole operation was run very strictly and with military precision.

Wearing our life-jackets, and peaked caps which specified our role, some of us would stand at the top and bottom of all the stairways and direct passengers to their designated Assembly Stations where their attendance would be noted. Others would be out on deck by the lifeboats. Passengers would be assisted, if necessary, with the slightly awkward business of putting on their life-jackets. The various belts and buckles had to be fitted securely and correctly if the life-jacket was to do its job in a real emergency. There was no room for half-measures.

Once the names of all the passengers had been ticked off and they had successfully donned their life-jackets in the approved manner there was a further announcement over the Tannoy.

"This is your Captain speaking. On behalf of the entire ship's company and Cunard Line may I welcome you all aboard and I hope you have a most enjoyable voyage with us. As your safety and well-being is our highest priority I would now request your complete attention while I outline some important information.

The signal you heard a few moments ago was the general emergency signal. It is the only signal that requires you to take action in an emergency and it is used to call you to your Assembly Stations. Please note the general emergency signal is not the signal to abandon ship.

In the early stages of any emergency, you may be instructed to return to your cabin where you will be accounted for by your Cabin Steward. If for any reason you are unable to reach your cabin you should proceed immediately to your designated Assembly Station where a life-jacket will be given to you from the additional supply of life-jackets which is kept in the vicinity of the Assembly Station. You should then remain there, calmly and quietly, and await further instructions and information from the officer in charge. This officer may decide to take a roll-call.

In the event that it becomes necessary to abandon ship the order will be given from the bridge. Members of the crew will then divide you into groups and guide you to the ship's survival craft.

In the event of a fire on board the ship some routes may be closed off by fire-proof doors. Alternative routes are available from all cabins and you are advised to spend a little time familiarising yourself with the area around your own cabin. In the event of such an emergency alternative lighting may be switched on automatically throughout the ship.

Should you smell smoke, or discover a fire, press one of the fire alarms situated around the ship. Please note you will not immediately hear an alarm but pressing the fire alarm will notify the bridge and action will be taken. If visibility is reduced by smoke so that you cannot see the signs on exit doors you should keep close to the edge of any corridor and crawl if necessary.

If you should see anybody fall overboard throw a life belt or anything else that will float in order to assist the person in the water. Shout 'Man Overboard' and inform the nearest crew member.

The safety of our passengers and our crew is our utmost priority. To this end all Cunard Line vessels operate under the highest level of security awareness. When boarding and leaving the ship you will be identified and hand baggage may be searched. Please do not bring items on board at the request of any stranger.

Some areas of the ship are marked 'Crew Only'. You should not enter such areas, even if invited, and members of the crew are not permitted to visit passenger staterooms or cabins other than in the course of their normal duties.

Never sit on the ship's side rails and please do not throw any items over the side. Whenever you are smoking please use the ashtrays and other facilities provided and ensure that cigarettes and other smoking materials are fully extinguished after use to minimise the risk of fire.

I would like to thank you all for your cooperation with this important exercise. And if you have any questions, please contact the Purser's Office.

This announcement marks the end of the safety drill. Passengers should now return their life-jackets to their cabins. As soon as the Port Authorities here in New York have completed their usual checks and formalities we shall be leaving on our passage to Liverpool.

I will be making an announcement from the bridge at noon each day while we are at sea, and I would once again like to wish you all a very pleasant and enjoyable voyage."

As I was about to leave Assembly Station 'B', which had been my post for the emergency drill, an older couple who had needed a bit of assistance with buckling up their life-jackets came up to me. They were two really delightful people.

"Thank you so much for your help just now," said the gentleman. "You'd think with the number of times we've been across the Atlantic on this ship we'd have worked out by now how to put on a life-jacket and do up the various bits and pieces. But it always seems to be so complicated. With all the different straps and buckles having to be in exactly the right place."

"It's a pleasure to be of assistance," I said. "That's what we're here for."

"I'm Mr Tierney," he said. "Jack. Jack Tierney. And my wife here is Ena."

"I'm pleased to meet you both. As it says on the badge, my name is Stephen. I'm one of the Lounge Stewards. Perhaps I'll see you in there sometime during the voyage? I can highly recommend the coffee. It's Cunard's very best. And I'll make sure to look after you myself."

"We will definitely call in, Stephen," said Mrs Tierney. "My husband and I love Cunard. We try never to sail with anyone else."

"And on the one occasion we did use another shipping line," said her husband, "there was a real emergency. It's the only time we've ever had a problem on a ship."

"And you got cross with me," said his wife.

"Not really, dear. I wasn't cross. Just a little bit firm." Mr Tierney smiled at her. "It was only because you weren't following the Captain's orders."

He turned to me.

"I can't even remember which ship it was now. But it definitely wasn't one of Cunard's. Anyway, we were on our way from New York to the Caribbean. It was about three o'clock in the morning and we were out in the Atlantic somewhere, heading towards Puerto Rico. Mrs Tierney and I were both fast asleep when all of a sudden we were woken by the emergency signal. The same one we heard just now. Even before the Captain started speaking we were wide awake. And you could tell straightaway by the tone of his voice that he was worried. When it's a practice the Captain always sounds very assured and professional. Like he's totally in control. That night it was very different. The Captain's voice was shaking. He sounded really concerned. He said there was a fire in the engine room and that if they couldn't contain it we'd have to abandon ship. He told us to follow the instructions we'd received during the emergency drill a couple of days earlier in New York. Put on warm clothing and a head covering. And then your life-jacket. You know. All that palaver. So I said to Mrs Tierney get yourself moving, dear, it's a real emergency. I knew it was because I could smell the smoke in our cabin. I went into the bathroom to collect together our regular medication. Following orders, you see. When I came out, I expected to see Ena getting into her warm clothing as instructed. But no. There she was. Standing there in just her nightdress. She'd opened up the safe and she was putting on all her jewellery. I couldn't believe it."

I started to laugh and Mrs Tierney took me by the arm.

"The thing is, dear, I had this beautiful diamond necklace which Mr Tierney had bought for me in New York. It was an early anniversary present. And I'd never had the chance to wear it. Not once. Well, I certainly wasn't going to let it go to the bottom of the ocean without me ever putting it on. If we were abandoning ship it was coming with me."

"Women, children and diamonds first," I said.

It was Mr Tierney's turn to laugh.

"If you ever decide to write a book about your experiences at sea, Stephen, that's the perfect title."

"So, what happened?" I said, turning to Mrs Tierney. "Did you end up sitting in a lifeboat, dolled up in all your expensive jewellery, looking like Elizabeth Taylor?"

"Thankfully, no," she said. "We were very worried because the smell of smoke seemed to be getting worse. But after about half an hour there was an announcement that they'd managed to put the fire out. And we just carried on to San Juan which was our next port anyway."

"You know I always thought these compulsory drills were a waste of time," said Mr Tierney. "But that real emergency taught me a lesson. They aren't. As I said, you could tell by the Captain's voice that he was really worried. And it would have been a lot more frightening for us if we hadn't been familiar with what to do."

"I've got a friend on board," I said. "One of the Deck Stewards. And when he first went to sea as a young lad his Mum was very anxious about him. She told him he had to write home regularly. Every week without fail. He did his best to keep her happy but as you can imagine he was soon running out of things to say. There's only so many words you can use to describe the sea and the sky. And as both of you know there's not much else to write about a lot of the time. So to liven it up a bit he ended one of his letters by writing, '*Sorry Ma. Got to go now. The ship's on fire.*' Then he got his cigarette lighter out and held the letter above the flame until the bottom of the paper was all singed and burnt. And posted it home to his poor mother."

When we'd all stopped laughing Mr and Mrs Tierney turned to go.

"We'll see you in the lounge, Stephen."

"The coffee is exceptional," I said. "You won't regret it."

That evening, after dinner, I was on duty in the lounge. I'd noticed that on the first night of a voyage many passengers tended to drift off to their cabins quite early. Perhaps they were tired after a long journey to the ship? Or maybe they wanted to get things properly settled down and organised in their cabins or suites, ready for the transatlantic voyage?

By ten o'clock just one couple were still sitting there, drinking cocktails. Manhattans. They'd each had at least four. The gentleman, who I guessed was probably in his mid-sixties, had chosen to wear a smart tuxedo for dinner while his extremely attractive lady companion, who appeared to be at least thirty years younger, was dressed in a very low-cut, and obviously very expensive, little black dress. Her outfit was set off with some gold and diamond jewellery which even I could tell had to be from somewhere top-notch like Tiffany's in New York or Garrard & Co in London. They were sitting at one of the corner tables and he looked over to where I was standing, tray in hand, and raised his arm to call me over.

"Yes, sir?"

"Mrs Cox and I will have two more of those fine Manhattans, please."

He glanced at the lady who I now knew to be his wife and she almost imperceptibly nodded her head.

"It's very quiet in here tonight, Stephen," she said, looking up at my name badge and smiling at me, "so why don't you join us and have one yourself?"

"I'm afraid we're not allowed to drink alcohol when on duty, madam. But I'll have a coffee if that's alright."

"Slip a tot of whisky into it then," said Mr Cox. "On me. Nobody's going to know."

"Thank you, sir. I'll be back in a moment."

When I returned with the two Manhattans and my coffee, neatly arranged on a tray, Mr Cox stood up.

"Thank you, Stephen. I'm James. Here." He touched the edge of the table with his right hand. "Put the drinks down and I'll get a chair for you."

While I was transferring the three drinks from the tray onto the table, James moved a nearby chair over and placed it next to his wife's.

"That's it," he said. "We've got a long trip ahead of us so we might as well get to know each other. Sit down, Stephen."

As I took a seat he gestured towards his wife.

"My wife is Christine." He gave me a smile as he sat down. "Christine Cox."

I'd served the Manhattans in the traditional lowballs. James picked up his glass and took a very generous sip.

"Here's to a voyage the three of us will remember."

His wife, who had already taken several sips, clinked her glass against his and put it down.

"Mmmm," she said. "That's a wicked cocktail you've mixed, Stephen. I think you might be trying to make me tipsy."

She smiled at me. Then she put her hand on my leg. Just above my knee.

In an instant my mind was racing. What was happening? Was this very attractive lady making a pass at me? With her husband watching. Or was it just too much alcohol? I knew she was on her fifth Manhattan. Or was it her sixth? My mind had gone blank and I couldn't remember. And how many glasses of wine might she have had with her dinner?

Only one thing was certain. Graeme hadn't covered this sort of situation in my training. And I had no idea at all how to handle it.

"We are advised not to serve our passengers with excessive amounts of alcohol," I said to her, still trying to work out exactly what was happening and what I should do about it. "I mixed the Manhattans using the standard Cunard measures of bourbon, Italian vermouth and aromatic bitters, madam."

I didn't want to make a scene. So I tried to ignore the hand which was now working its way a little further up my leg.

"How boring," she said, giving my thigh a squeeze. "And I'm sure you're not boring, Stephen."

"I just follow the rules, madam."

"Always?"

"Well, almost always."

What was I saying? The last thing I wanted to do was encourage her. Mrs Cox looked at her husband.

"There you are, James. Didn't I tell you earlier that Stephen looked like a young man who'd be happy to bend the rules and have a bit of excitement?"

"You did, Christine," said her husband. "And I think you might be right."

"I'm just like you when it comes to excitement, Stephen," said Mrs Cox, giving my thigh another squeeze. "Mr Cox will be getting together with three of his friends to play some bridge very shortly. They stay up ridiculously late so I'll be retiring to our stateroom on my own. And I think another of your wicked little cocktails would make the perfect night cap. Perhaps you'd like to bring it to me?"

The chair that James had pulled over was facing away from the door. And just as Mrs Cox was asking me the question I heard someone enter the lounge. Turning my head I could see it was Graeme.

I stood up quickly.

"I'm very sorry," I said, "but I'm afraid you'll have to excuse me. It's Graeme, my Senior Lounge Steward."

James and Christine both smiled at me. It was Christine who spoke.

"Don't worry, Stephen. I'm sorry too. I wouldn't want to get you into trouble. But we've got eight sea days ahead of us. And nights. Or is it nine? Anyway. I'm sure we'll have plenty of opportunities to get to know each other a great deal better."

I bowed my head slightly.

"Thank you, madam."

"Jesus, Dave. I think I've just been chatted up by a nymphomaniac."

Dave had finished his shift in the restaurant and we'd arranged to meet up for a drink in The Pig as soon as I was free. He picked up his beer and gave me a funny look.

"I'm being serious," I said. "Her husband was saying we need to get to know each other. And my wife here is Christine. Then he tells me to sit down with them for a drink. He actually pulled a chair up for me and put it right next to his wife's. So the two chairs were touching."

"Bloody hell, Steve. You jammy bastard."

"No, look Dave. It was terrifying. I was on my own in the lounge with just the two of them. And they were drinking Manhattans like they were going out of fashion. They'd just ordered a couple more and before I know it I'm sitting there and she's got her hand on my thigh. Half-way up. Squeezing it and working her way upwards. I didn't know where she was going to put it next. And her husband – at least that's what he said he was but he must have been at least thirty years older than her – he didn't say anything. He just sat there smiling. Almost like he was egging her on. And she was dead attractive too. Wearing a low-cut dress and a whole load of really expensive jewellery."

"You get all the luck, Steve." Dave was shaking his head ruefully. "Why doesn't that sort of thing ever happen to me?"

"Come off it, Dave. This is serious. I was panicking. I didn't know what to do. She was saying she thought I probably liked a bit of excitement and maybe we should get to know each other better. Then she said her husband was going to be playing cards with some friends and she'd like me to bring her a Manhattan. To her stateroom. Where she'd be on her own."

Dave now had a broad grin on his face.

"So," he said. "What does the beautiful lady get from her very wealthy husband? Lots of money, obviously. But maybe not much else I guess. You're definitely on there, mate. She's lookin' for a young stud who's still got what it takes. You've hit the jackpot."

"Wonderful," I said. "And after collecting the jackpot I lose my job. You know the rules. No fraternising with passengers. And no going to their staterooms. Especially not on a small ship like this."

"Who's goin' to know?"

"On this ship, Dave? Pretty much everyone. Within five minutes. Some of them in the lounge go on about what other people are up to the whole time. It's all they seem to talk about. And they're dead loud when they've had a couple of drinks. If it's busy after dinner the whole place is nods and winks and jungle drums. I can tell you I was mighty relieved when Graeme walked in so I could get away from the two of them without it bein' rude. But they're going to be in the lounge every night until we get to Liverpool. I know they are. And I'll have to serve them. I don't know what to do."

"If you're not interested just mix a Manhattan and give me her stateroom number. I'll sort her out."

"We never got as far as her stateroom number, thankfully. All I got to know was her name. Christine. Mrs Christine Cox."

Dave looked at me, and I thought for a minute he was going to drop his tankard.

"You are having me on, aren't you?" he said and started to laugh.

I looked at him blankly.

He was still laughing as he took a deep draught of his beer.

"Are you soft or something, Steve? Mrs Cox. A nymphomaniac called Mrs Cox. Wait 'til I tell the lads!"

I had no idea at all what was amusing him so much. But

talking, drinking and laughing at the same time was more than Dave could cope with and I watched him as he choked and coughed and spluttered.

Then the penny dropped.

"Oh for God's sake, Dave, grow up. It's Mrs Cox. Spelt C-O-X. And unless you're a grubby-minded kid in short trousers it's not funny."

Dave was still coughing up his beer and laughing.

"Come off it, Steve. Not funny? It's brilliant. The lads'll be in stitches."

"You can laugh as much as you like," I said, "but I thought as a good friend you might at least be a little bit sympathetic. The lady's a nympho. And I don't want to lose my job."

Dave looked at me. He could see I was serious and he stopped laughing.

"Okay, Steve, I'm sorry. If you really are worried you should tell Graeme."

"I already did," I said. "Before we locked up the bar. He just said it happens. And if I don't fancy taking her up on the offer the best thing is to be very polite and ignore any suggestive comments. And never sit down with the two of them."

"There you are then. Sorted. If you want to give the lovely Mrs Cox the full benefit of your youthful vigour, you're on. And with Graeme's approval too. And if you don't fancy the idea he'll look after you."

"What would you do?"

Dave looked at me and started laughing again.

"Daft question, Steve. Get a couple more beers in and stop worrying. It'll be fine."

TWELVE

HEARTBREAK HOTEL

Thursday 2nd February 1956

January and February are always the coldest months in New York. After finishing my breakfast I peered out through one of the portholes in The Pig. A yellow haze hung over the Cunard Piers. It was a common sight during the winter months. A toxic mixture of icy fog and smoke from thousands of chimney stacks.

As in many British cities the citizens of New York covered their faces with scarves as they made their way about the streets doing their best to protect themselves from the deadly effects of the smog. On such days the city authorities advised people with heart and lung problems to keep their windows tightly closed and stay indoors.

I turned away from the porthole. Dave was just tucking into his third round of toast and I caught his eye.

"It looks pretty miserable out there," I said. "D'you want to give it a miss today?"

We were off duty, and free to go ashore, but a lazy day in the warm comfort of the ship suddenly looked like a very tempting alternative.

"I'm not sure," he said, adding extra marmalade to his half-finished toast. "Julie said they'd probably be gettin' a whole load of new records in and she was going to put 'em on one side for us. I'd feel a bit guilty if we didn't at least go and take a look. If you like we could walk straight there, pick up the records, and then head back. If it gets too cold we can always stop off at that coffee shop on the corner of West 45th and 11th to warm up."

"That sounds okay to me," I said. "I don't really want to let Julie down."

"Me neither." Dave grinned at me. "With a bit of luck I might get invited round to her place again."

I looked at him.

"Don't get me wrong, Dave. I'm only asking because of my natural concern about a very good friend's mental and physical health. But do you ever think about anything other than sex?"

"Not very often." He grinned at me. "Which I think means my mental health is fine. And nobody's put in any complaints about my physical performance either. So you've no need to lose any sleep over me. It's you I worry about. I still can't understand why you kicked that Mrs Cox into touch. She might've taught you a trick or two."

"And I might've have given her a couple of surprises as well, Dave. You never know. Anyway, it's too late now. Come on. Finish your toast and let's get going."

It was several degrees below freezing as we walked down the gangplank, faces covered and wearing several layers of thick clothing to combat the damp, bone-chilling weather. Underfoot it was icy and we took care not to slip as we hurried down 11th Avenue towards West 46th. By the time we got to the store my nose and ears were starting to feel painfully numb and the warm blast from the blower above the door as we entered was very welcome.

Julie was at the till and she gave us a wave. I stood in the comforting warmth just inside the doorway and watched as Dave walked over and gave her a big hug.

"Hiya, sweetheart. Great to see you again. 'Have you got anything interesting for me?"

She grinned at him.

"If you mean cast-offs from the jukeboxes, I've got plenty. But the way the temperature is today anything else'll have to wait. I'm well wrapped up, and that's how I'm staying. Hang on for a minute and I'll go get them."

Julie disappeared through a door marked 'STAFF ONLY' and returned with a sports bag. It was three-quarters full.

"There you go," she said, placing the bag alongside the till. "We've had three deliveries since you guys were last in so I put them all to one side. You don't need to take the lot. But since you seem to be so keen, I thought I'd let you have first refusal. If there's any you don't want, I'll just put them out for sale as usual."

She took hold of the two handles and slid the bag across the counter towards Dave.

"Take your time. There's no rush. You can make use of that big table over there." She pointed to a large, square table on one side of the floor. "We've had it in for at least six months so I don't think anyone's likely to turn up and want to buy it on a day like this. Go through them and let me know which ones you want to take. I'll be here."

Dave gave her an affectionate peck on the cheek.

"Thanks, gorgeous. I'll be back."

"What comes after sweetheart and gorgeous?" I asked as I followed him to the table, feeling a little less cold thanks to the blower.

"I'm not sure yet," said Dave with a smile. "It might depend how flexible the lovely Julie turns out to be with her pricing on the records. If she's generous then I'll be generous too."

He emptied the bag out onto the table and we started to go through the contents.

Many 'Billboard Top 100' records from the previous twelve months were there, some of which had also been hits in England.

'The Ballad of Davy Crockett' by Bill Hayes, 'Unchained Melody' by Roy Hamilton, 'Ain't That A Shame' by Fats Domino, 'Sixteen Tons' by Tennessee Ernie Ford, 'Maybelline' by Chuck Berry, 'It's A Sin To Tell A Lie' by Somethin' Smith And The Redheads, 'The Bible Tells Me So' by Don Cornell and 'Mr Sandman' by The Chordettes. The singers were sometimes different but the songs were all familiar.

We knew they weren't going to be expensive so they all went in the bag to take home to England, along with fifteen or twenty others that we hadn't heard of but which had been recorded by artists we knew were good or whose titles sounded interesting.

'I've Got A Woman' by Ray Charles, 'Only You' by The Platters, 'Hound Dog' by Big Mama Thornton, 'Bo Diddley' by Bo Diddley, 'Fool For You' by Ray Charles, 'All By Myself' by Fats Domino, 'Reconsider Baby' by Lowell Fulson, 'My Babe' by Little Walter, 'Shake, Rattle and Roll' by Big Joe Turner, 'Money, Honey' by The Drifters, 'You're So Fine' by Little Walter, 'I'm Ready' by Muddy Waters, 'I'll Be True' by Faye Adams and 'You'll Never Walk Alone' by Roy Hamilton.

We'd selected about half the records, twenty-five in all.

I looked at the ones which hadn't been put in the bag, still lying there on the table. On top of the random pile was a record with a very striking yellow and white label which said 'SPECIALITY RECORDS'. The title of the song was 'Tutti Frutti'.

It looked interesting so I picked it up.

"Look at this one," I said to Dave. "It's by some guy called Little Richard. Ever heard of him?"

Dave shook his head.

"Me neither," I said. "But if we leave records like this behind we might be missing out on some gems. Why don't we see how much Julie wants for the lot? It's not likely to break the bank."

Dave picked up the bag and we went back to speak to Julie.

"Right, beautiful," he said with a big smile, putting the bag down in front of her on the counter. "Tell me all about '*Tutti Frutti*'."

Julie laughed and grinned back at him.

"You're too young to understand. Come back when you're twenty-one. And what's with all the 'beautiful' stuff anyway? I suppose you think a bit of flattery might bring the price down."

"Not at all," said Dave, putting the bag on her desk, "You need to make a profit so just give it to me straight. There's twenty-five records in that bag. And another twenty-five or so over on the table which we're not yet sure about. If the price for all fifty is right we're prepared to save you a whole lot of hassle and take 'em all off your hands."

He looked at Julie and gave her a smile.

"And as a bonus," he said, "you and I could meet up for a meal tonight. On me. That's my last and best offer."

Much as it bugged me to do so I had to admire his style. And Julie didn't have to think for very long.

"Mr Thompson says two fifty for the lot," she said with a grin. And we'll throw in the bag. Where d'you want to meet?"

"I'll go get the other records," I said, grabbing the bag and leaving Dave to pay up and sort out his love life.

After stopping for a moment under the blower by the door to enjoy one final blast of warm air we stepped out onto the pavement. The temperature outside seemed to have dropped even further and as we headed back towards the Pier our breath formed white clouds in front of us. I could feel the tip of my nose getting colder as the scarf across my face started to ice up.

"I think my nose is getting frost-bite," I said. "I'd rather not lose it so let's stop off for that coffee and warm up."

There were just two other people in the coffee shop, sharing a table in the corner and deep in conversation. One of them looked as though he might be in his mid-twenties, with a rather unkempt appearance and dark, tousled hair. He was dressed for the weather in a buttoned-up jacket and thick, woollen trousers. His companion was older with wide-rimmed glasses which gave him a more intellectual appearance. He was also dressed for warmth in a brown and red check jacket, and a similar pair of heavyweight trousers. The two of them kept glancing over at the door as if they were expecting someone.

Dave and I ordered large American coffees and chose a table as far as possible from the cold air which hung around the window and the door. We sat down, hunched up, warming our hands on our mugs.

"So," I said to Dave, "are you all fixed up with Julie?"

"I am indeed," he said, nodding his head. "She still seems to be keen."

"What's the plan?"

"It's a bit chilly to be eating out. So we're meetin' up at her place on Cornelia Street in Greenwich Village. She's gonna get the place really warm so we can get comfortable. And then maybe rustle up something to eat."

"You'll freeze walking all the way down to Greenwich Village."

"Don't worry. There's no way I'm walkin' in this weather. Julie said to jump on the subway. If I catch a train at 50th and get off at West 4th by Washington Square I'm only a couple of minutes from her place. And if get cold on the way she knows how to warm me up."

He gave me a wink.

"Oh, and by the way. She said to tell you she's got a new flatmate called Carol who's just arrived in New York from Florida. She's lookin' for a boyfriend if you'd be interested."

"So you don't have to cope with both of 'em, I suppose."

Dave laughed.

"Trust me, Steve. I could if I had to. But I think it's a genuine offer if you fancy the idea."

"What's she like, this flatmate?"

"I've no idea. She wasn't livin' there when I was at Julie's before Christmas. She could be stunning. Or she could look like the back end of a bus." He shrugged his shoulders. "It'd be pot luck."

I stopped to think. Sylvie was three and a half thousand miles away on the other side of an ocean. She'd never know. And it wasn't as if we were engaged or anything.

Dave could see I was undecided.

"Come on, Steve. Give it a go. Nothing ventured and all that."

"I'll think about it."

As I sat there, feeling slightly guilty that I was even considering two-timing Sylvie, the younger of the two coffee drinkers at the corner table stood up.

"I don't think he's coming," he said to his companion. "I'm going to put something on the jukebox. You'll like this one if you've not heard it."

He turned towards us and realised that I must have heard what he'd said.

You'll like this record too," he added with a smile. "It came out last Friday. It's this guy's first national release and he's going to be huge. Absolutely huge. My friend here and I are poets from down in the West Village. I know some of the people who've been working with him. He's the real deal."

He walked over to the jukebox and put a dime into the slot. Then he pressed a couple of the cream-coloured buttons.

He caught my eye and lifted a forefinger as he headed back to his chair.

"You won't forget the first time you heard this," he said. "It might even be something you'll one day be telling your grandchildren about. Remember the name. Elvis Presley."

As we listened to the sad tale about a Heartbreak Hotel, and the sound of Elvis Presley's unforgettable voice filled the small, New York City coffee shop, I could feel the hairs starting to tingle on the back of my neck.

The record had everything.

An echo effect had been used to make the vocals even more astonishing. And the relatively raw and empty instrumental backing, provided by the illustrious Chet Atkins and Scotty Moore on guitars, Floyd Cramer on piano, Bill Black on bass and D.J. Fontana on drums, fitted the song perfectly.

The song was unlike anything I'd ever heard before. I could understand why Elvis, on first hearing the demo, had jumped up in excitement and exclaimed to Mae Boren Axton, who had co-written it with Jacksonville-based singer Tommy Durden, "Hot dog, Mae, play that song again."

Even before 'Heartbreak Hotel' came to an end I knew that, like Elvis, I had to hear it again. And I also knew that one day I would indeed be telling the grandchildren a story about a jukebox in a café, on a cold and foggy morning in New York City.

"That's a record we just have to take back to Liverpool," I said. "And I don't suppose it'll be turning up second-hand at Julie's for a while. We'll have to visit a record store before we sail."

Dave nodded his agreement.

I fished in my pocket for a ten cent coin and went over to the jukebox. As Elvis started to sing again I stopped at the table occupied by the two poets.

"It's brilliant," I said. "We'll definitely be taking a copy back to England with us. Our friends are going to love it."

The younger man shook my hand.

"Glad you like it. England, you say. Whereabouts?"

"Liverpool."

"Liverpool." He repeated the name and looked at the slightly older man who shrugged his shoulders. "I believe some of the ships from here in New York go there. But I can't say I know much else about the place."

"It's a big port on the west coast of England," I said. "On the River Mersey. I'm Steve. And my friend's Dave. We're stewards on one of the Cunard ships which sail between here and Liverpool every few weeks."

"Greg," said the young poet. "Gregory Corso. And my friend here is Allen. Allen Ginsberg."

I nodded a greeting to the two of them as Greg continued.

"We're supposed to be meeting our publisher. But it looks like the weather might've put him off. He doesn't much like the cold. Or the fog. Anyway. Good to talk to you. And now I know a little bit about Liverpool, maybe I'll see you over there one day."

By mid-February we were back home, listening to the latest records from the Thrift Store and the brilliant new release by Elvis Presley. He would quite soon be recognised as 'The King'.

'Heartbreak Hotel' was eventually released in England on 12th May 1956. It quickly reached Number Two in the New Musical Express chart but in Liverpool we'd already been listening to it for almost three months. As for 'Tutti Frutti', a huge hit in America which we'd very nearly left behind at the Thrift Store, it finally made it across the Atlantic two years later, hidden away on the flip side of Little Richard's biggest UK hit, 'Long Tall Sally'.

A month or two before our return, in November 1955, a banjo player from Chris Barber's jazz band called Lonnie Donegan had recorded an up-tempo version of Leadbelly's U.S. convict song, 'Rock Island Line'. It had stormed its way up the

British charts and triggered a craze for skiffle, a style of music which at its most simple required just three chords. Almost anyone could learn to play it.

Teenagers all over the country, including a lot of our friends in Liverpool, were soon buying cheap guitars and very basic sets of drums. With the addition of a washboard pinched from their mother's kitchen and played with borrowed clothes-pegs from the washing line, and an old tea-chest tied to a broomstick with a length of string to act as home-made bass, they were getting together to form groups and perform for their young friends.

As well as arriving on the ships from New York, American records were also reaching Liverpool from the U.S. Air Force Base at Burtonwood, about fifteen miles away, where Jean's husband, Carl, had been stationed. A man called Percy Phillips, who later set up Liverpool's first recording studio, had opened up a second-hand record store in the front room of his home, not far from the city centre, and boxes of used records from the Air Base could often be found there.

A lot of these American records were eventually released in England on labels such as London American, Top Rank and Oriole. But quite often Cunard Yanks and U.S. Airmen, and the records from Burtonwood in Percy Phillips' front room, had already introduced the emerging skiffle groups on Merseyside to some of the songs.

So our local groups, as they now called themselves rather than bands, had early access to a treasure trove of relatively unknown music which was not so easily available to teenagers in other parts of the country.

As they got hold of better instruments and more powerful amplifiers the Merseyside groups were able to add some Liverpool hardness and toughness to the songs. And loud, vibrating, bass notes which grabbed hold of the girls and shook up their insides.

Seasoned with a touch of Scouse humour it was a heady musical brew that needed a few years to mature fully. But with the Beatles leading the way it would eventually take the world by storm.

As would one of the other jukebox cast-offs which we brought home, Roy Hamilton's *'You'll Never Walk Alone'*.

Gerry Marsden loved the song, and the recording he made with the Pacemakers is still played at Liverpool's Anfield Stadium where fifty thousand fans lift their red and white scarves above their heads and sing the words which sum up their football club and the people who live in the city.

THIRTEEN

RMS QUEEN MARY

By the middle of 1956 Dave and I had been serving on RMS Media for almost two years, sailing backwards and forwards across the Atlantic. The relaxed and slow turnarounds in both Liverpool and New York gave us plenty of shore time and with Julie's help we'd managed to build up a very decent collection of American jukebox records which we'd continued to lend out to friends in Liverpool who were in groups and were itching to learn, and play, this exciting new music.

We had also started visiting record stores in Harlem where we'd find, and bring home, lesser-known African-American blues recordings along with rhythm 'n' blues singles which had never made it into the main Billboard charts. The result was that rock 'n' roll groups on Merseyside were playing Liverpool versions of songs which had originated in the United States.

These relatively obscure records were of little more than passing interest to the average U.S. teenager. That all changed on February 7th 1964 when four lads who had honed their skills playing these American songs in Hamburg and Liverpool turned up at Kennedy Airport in New York on Pan Am 'Yankee Clipper' Flight 101 from London Heathrow.

In the mid-sixties, thanks to the Beatles, Liverpool suddenly became the centre of the teenage universe.

In the mid-fifties, though, it was still the other way round. English youngsters were wide-eyed with wonder when they came across anything that was American. And it wasn't just the records. The American suits and the shirts, and the smart shoes which we brought home from New York, were all the envy of our Liverpool friends. And they went down well with the girls too.

I spent a lot of time with Sylvie when I was home in Liverpool. But in New York it was a different story. I felt very guilty about it, but I'd given in to temptation and started to see Julie's flatmate, Carol. She was attractive and good fun. I was young and spending long weeks away from home. Carol would never take the place of Sylvie. I was certain of that. So I sort of convinced myself that it was just a bit of innocent fun. And that Sylvie would understand.

Dave, though, was the cat that got the cream. He saw Julie every time he was in New York. And at home in Liverpool he got himself dressed up in his fancy New York outfits and hit the town, heading off to The Grafton or The Locarno and hoping to strike lucky. He wasn't usually disappointed.

Best of all, my mother was still doing well. The tablets were keeping her blood pressure normal and the doctors were very happy with her progress.

Life as a Cunard Yank was good.

The easy option would have been to carry on with what had become a very familiar, and enjoyable, routine. But as the late-night drinks in The Pig became more and more repetitive, and the same old jokes started to wear a bit thin, Dave and I both had the same feeling.

It was time for a change. Time for a new start.

Dave drained the last of the beer from his tankard and placed it very firmly on the table before wiping his lips with the back of his hand. We were sitting in The Pig and it was a sign I'd seen before. It meant he'd been thinking about something important. And he was about to come out with it.

"I've made up my mind, Steve. We should try for somethin' on the Mary."

It was the obvious fresh challenge. In fact, the idea of working on board the Queen Mary had been at the back of my mind ever since that early morning in New York when her twelve decks had towered over me as the tugs of the Port Authority had guided her gently to rest alongside Pier 90. I'd known even then that serving as a member of the crew on the flagship of the Cunard fleet, which for many years had been the fastest ocean liner the world had ever seen and which was still the most desirable and elegant way to cross the ocean for those who had the money and time, would provide me with plenty of tales for future grandchildren. Even if, by then, 'Heartbreak Hotel' and Elvis had faded into obscurity.

After almost two years on RMS Media we both had plenty of experience. I was quite certain that such a move should be possible. And that the time was right.

"I've been thinkin' the same," I said. "We'd have to get ourselves into First Class though. Or we'll lose out big time on tips."

"First Class is what we've both been doing here on the Media," said Dave. "So we've got loads of experience. I'm sure Graeme'll give you a good reference. And I'm well in with Jack Dixon now. He keeps saying I'm a natural as a waiter. I reckon a decent reference from him shouldn't be a problem at all."

"Okay," I said. "Let's go for it. It'll mean sailing out of Southampton instead of Liverpool which is a bit of a drag. And the turnarounds are a lot quicker. But I still think it's worth a go."

"To make up for the turnarounds being so quick," said Dave, "we'll get a fairly decent stretch of shore leave every few weeks. So it's swings and roundabouts."

"Okay," I said. "Decision made. We can put out a few feelers and see how the land lies when we get back to Liverpool."

●ー●ーーーーー●ー●ー●ー●ーーーー●ー●

We were in luck. With having many more crew members than the Media the crew turnover on the Queen Mary was significantly higher and several positions were available. Dave landed a job as one of the Stewards in the First Class Restaurant, while I was offered a post in the Verandah Grill which served simple '*a la carte*' meals to passengers who fancied an alternative to the Main Restaurant.

The two of us caught the train from Liverpool down to Southampton on the morning of Tuesday 31st July, 1956, and by the evening we were on board our new ship. We had one full day to learn the ropes and familiarise ourselves with the details of our new jobs.

The Queen Mary was quite unlike the Media. If the Media was like a small village where everybody knew everyone else, the Queen Mary was a floating city with over two thousand passengers and eleven hundred crew. Dave and I were confident that we would be comfortable in our new roles by the time we sailed because they were much the same as we'd been doing on the Media. But getting to know the layout of such a large and complex ship so that we could find our way around all twelve decks without having to stop and think for even a moment would take a few days.

Crossing the Atlantic on The Queen Mary was an iconic experience and Cunard presented every passenger making the journey with an illustrated, souvenir booklet. Within its pages they would learn that no British ship had ever before had so much care and expense lavished on the twenty-five public rooms, the staterooms and the cabins. Cunard's challenge to the architects and interior designers had been to create an air of contemporary elegance and lightness which spoke of luxury, while at the same time making passengers feel comfortable and at ease.

Within the souvenir booklet a typical stateroom was described.

'The walls are of ivory-white sycamore, with a faint ripple of grain as the light catches it. (A neighbour's stateroom may be birds-eye maple, African cherry, Pearwood, Pacific myrtle, or English yew.) All the furniture is made from the same, or blending, wood – chests of drawers, tall mirrors and deep, long-glass wardrobes. A little built-in clock ticks soundlessly and is timed from the ship's clock centrally. A colour-matching telephone sits by the bedside, while a lamp throws light upon the book being read, and nowhere else. The writing table is neatly furnished and the wide bed is sumptuous and comfortable. Carpet, curtains and chair coverings are of varied classic fabrics, and nothing obtrudes harshly upon a passenger's sense or movement. Nothing has been forgotten. A watered niche has been fitted above the mantlepiece to take flowers. At night there will be no intrusion of sound from outside, and by day the room will be bathed in light and colour. Each stateroom is, in fact, a passenger's delicate and lovely self-contained flat – at sea.'

Serving as a member of the crew on such a ship was a privilege and at eight o'clock on the Tuesday evening I reported for duty. Our passengers were yet to arrive on board and I was meeting Tommy Miller, the Head Steward in the Verandah Grill. He would take me through the various systems and procedures.

Situated at the aft end of the Sun Deck, high up in the ship with superb views over the stern, the Grill served lunch from 12 noon to 3.00 p.m. and dinner from 7.00 to 10.00 p.m. in the evening. Then, after 10 p.m., it turned into a night club in which a live band would provide music for dancing until the early hours of the morning.

"You've landed on your feet getting yourself a job in the Verandah Grill, Steve," said Tommy as he familiarised me with the layout of the tables and showed me where everything was kept. "If you're doing a good job and the passengers like you the tips you'll get up here are among the best on the ship. Our American guests in particular tend to be very generous. My predecessor used to pride himself on heading home with a couple of hundred dollars in his pocket at the end of each voyage. His plan was to save up enough to retire by the time he was fifty. Which is exactly what he was able to do."

My weekly pay on Queen Mary would be about fifty dollars. So two hundred dollars in cash after each two-way crossing of the Atlantic would be a very welcome bonus.

"Because the Queen Mary is such a special ship," continued Tommy, "a lot of our passengers are very wealthy. Or very well-known. And quite often both. Hollywood film stars, famous singers and musicians, Wall Street financiers and top politicians. They all love this ship and make every effort to travel with us whenever they can find the time. For many of them a meal in the Verandah Grill is a popular choice. The most well-known among them will expect to be seated at their special table in the Grill. And it's our job to make sure that it is always available."

He stopped and looked around to make sure nobody was listening.

"Don't say anything to anyone until it's confirmed because

she sometimes cancels at the last minute. But we're expecting Greta Garbo to be on board for the voyage to New York. She'll be with her regular companion, Mr George Schlee. They always travel together even though he's married. Mr Schlee is a financier who's based in New York and he lives in the same apartment building on 52nd Street as Miss Garbo. When they're in New York Mr Schlee lives in an apartment with his wife, Valentina, the fashion designer, while Miss Garbo has her own apartment a few floors below them. And when the two of them go travelling together Mrs Schlee stays behind in New York. It's not an arrangement my wife would approve of. But as the great American writer F. Scott Fitzgerald once said, 'The rich are different.'"

Tommy allowed himself a little laugh.

"During the day Miss Garbo generally keeps herself to herself. She takes twice daily walks around the Promenade Deck, but she always covers herself up in a big coat and hat so other passengers very rarely recognise her. Otherwise she tends to stay in their suite most of the time. Mr Schlee, though, is very different. He goes out and about and happily chats with our other passengers. But I suppose, as they say, opposites attract. The two of them take dinner here in the Verandah Grill most evenings. Always in the raised section of the Grill. Their table is the one by the wall with the red silk drapes behind it. It'll be one of yours."

It sounded like, once again, I was going to be jumping in at the deep end. I took a very deep breath and Tommy noticed.

"Don't worry, Steve. You'll be fine. If they're in tonight you should wish them a good evening, by name to indicate that you know who they are, but otherwise treat them just like any other passenger. One of the things our famous guests like about the Queen Mary is that we look after them well but we don't make too much fuss. For a few days they can feel almost like ordinary people and forget that they live so much of their lives in a goldfish bowl."

I liked Tommy. He was a decent chap. I'd already decided we were going to get on well.

⬦

At exactly two minutes past seven British Summer Time on the morning of Thursday 2ⁿᵈ August, 1956, Captain D.W. Sorrell up on the bridge gave the order for the final lines to be cast off. The men who'd been waiting on the dockside released the last pair of thick ropes and the Queen Mary's engineers, working away feverishly down below, gradually increased the power. The gently reassuring vibrations of the four, huge steam turbines, each producing 50,000 horse-power, could be felt throughout the ship but by the time she was fully under way they would hardly be noticeable. Slowly, almost imperceptibly at first, a line of oily water appeared between the hull and the black, rubber buffers which hung between the dockside and the ship. Shepherded by half a dozen tugs, the Queen Mary was leaving Southampton's Ocean Terminal. She was on her way, via a brief stop at Cherbourg in Normandy, to New York.

Using both of its magnificent ocean liners Cunard offered a regular weekly service across the ocean. Our sister ship, RMS Queen Elizabeth, had set sail from New York twenty-four hours earlier. In two and a half days, moving at a combined speed of fifty-seven knots, the two Queens would pass each other in the North Atlantic, almost certainly within viewing distance. For the passengers on both vessels it would be an unforgettable experience.

Two hours after leaving the Ocean Terminal we passed the Nab Tower lighthouse, manned by Trinity House, just off the coast of the Isle of Wight. This important lighthouse had been erected on the hazardous Nab rocks just after the end of World War One. It marked the eastern entry and exit point of the deep-water, Solent Channel.

The short passage across the English Channel to Cherbourg was completed in just over two and a half hours and by three minutes to four in the afternoon the Queen Mary was on her way again. She was heading west, passing to the south of the Republic of Ireland, and she would soon be in the open ocean.

The weather forecast was for light to moderate winds and a rough-to-rippled sea. Apart from occasional mist patches off the coast of Newfoundland the visibility was expected to be good and the skies would be clear. In just over four and a half days, at about half past three in the morning Eastern Daylight Savings Time, our ship would reach the Ambrose Lightship on her approach to New York Harbour.

I felt a little nervous as the guests started to arrive for dinner. The service at lunchtime had gone well, but only about half the tables were occupied so there was no need for me to rush. Everything felt relaxed.

The evening service was more formal. The gentlemen were all wearing tuxedos with white shirts and bow ties while the dresses the ladies had chosen were beautifully designed and made even more special by exquisite, and obviously very expensive, diamonds, emeralds and pearls.

At exactly quarter past seven there was an audible murmur in the room as Miss Greta Garbo and her companion, Mr George Schlee, entered. Miss Garbo, wearing a cream-coloured dress with lace details, was every bit the movie star that people knew from the silver screen while Mr Schlee, like all the other gentlemen, looked very smart in an impeccably cut dinner jacket.

Tommy greeted them and guided them to their table. Then, with the slightest of movement of his head, he indicated that it was time for me to move. I approached the table, two menus in hand, and addressed each of my guests in turn.

"Good evening, Miss Garbo."

I bowed my head slightly.

"And Mr Schlee."

Another slight bow of the head.

"My name is Stephen. And may I welcome you on board the Queen Mary. I wish both of you a very pleasant voyage to New York."

Each menu was presented inside an elegant, deep blue cover with Cunard livery on the front. I opened the top one and handed it to Miss Garbo, before doing the same for Mr Schlee.

The glasses on the table were empty.

"I'll bring you some iced water," I said. "Michael, our Head Wine Waiter, will be with you very shortly."

"Miss Garbo said nothing. It was Mr Schlee who spoke.

"Thank you, Stephen."

I bowed my head once again and moved away from the table, leaving them to read through the starters and main dishes on offer before making their selection.

I had four tables to look after but, while not making it too obvious, I kept a particularly close eye upon Miss Garbo and Mr Schlee. It was important that their first evening meal of the voyage passed off completely smoothly and without any problems.

Their conversation was easy and relaxed, while the two of them seemed to be equally comfortable sitting in silence at times during their meal. Miss Garbo looked straight ahead and didn't catch anybody's eye as she left the restaurant about an hour later. She didn't speak to me but Mr Schlee put a hand on my arm.

"A most enjoyable meal, Stephen. Thank you. Miss Garbo particularly enjoyed her poached sea-bass. At home in New

York she mostly follows a vegetarian diet but her nutritionist has assured her that fish is also very good for her. As long as it is absolutely fresh."

He let go of my arm and I felt a folded note being slipped into my hand.

"We shall see you again tomorrow evening, Stephen."

Miss Garbo was waiting for him by the door. Like a perfect gentleman Mr Schlee took her by the arm and guided her out of the restaurant.

As soon as they were out of sight I took a surreptitious look at the note in my hand. Ten dollars. Not bad. And the night was still young. The serious cocktail drinking and dancing had yet to get going. With a bit of luck a few more notes would be heading my way.

<hr />

"Anyone well-known in your restaurant last night?" I said to Dave as we were grabbing a quick bite in The Pig. I was ready to do a bit of gentle name-dropping while trying also to give the impression that I was completely unimpressed by my close proximity to fame.

"D'you mean apart from Bob Hope and Bing Crosby?" he said.

"You're joking?"

"No. They were in the First-Class Restaurant on a table for eight. But I didn't recognise any of the others."

"And you were their waiter?"

"Afraid not," he said, looking a little disappointed. "I was five or six tables away. Jack and Melvin were in charge of the service. But I got a good look. Bob Hope seemed to be cracking jokes the whole time. With Bing Crosby as his sidekick. The two of them had the whole table laughing throughout the meal."

"They've had plenty of practice over the years," I said. "How many of those *'Road'* films d'you reckon they've done now? It must be at least five. I saw *'Road to Bali'* three or four years ago. Just after it first came out. And I have to admit it was very funny."

"I never saw it," said Dave. "A mate of mine went to *'Road to Rio'* and didn't rate it much so I didn't bother. And what was your evening in the Grill like?"

"It didn't wind up 'til after three. I'm knackered. The tips were okay, though. I had Greta Garbo on one of my tables. Along with George Schlee, the man she travels around with. He's officially her manager but Tommy reckons it could be a bit more than that. Even though he's married to a New York fashion designer. Valentina I think Tommy said her name was."

"And they were okay?"

"Yeah. They were fine. She didn't say much. In fact she didn't say a single word to me the whole evening. He did all the talking. But he slipped me ten dollars when they were on the way out. And I made another fifteen or so later on in the evening. So I'm definitely not complaining."

"Looks like you're going to do better than me on the tips, then. I only got about five all evening."

"Yeah. But a lot of people in the restaurants leave it 'til the end of the voyage. You know. Rather than messing around with small tips every night they give you an envelope full of cash on the last night. At the end of the day you might do a lot better than you think. So keep being nice to them."

"We'll see," said Dave. "But the main thing is I really like the ship. There's a lot more happening than on the Media. There's apparently a couple of big name jazz musicians on board who'll be giving a concert tomorrow evening. There's a rumour it could be Duke Ellington and Ella Fitzgerald but it's a surprise for the passengers so nobody knows for sure yet. It's early days but it looks like switching from the Media will turn out to have been a good move."

"Apart from not having so much time ashore in New York," I said. "Does Julie know yet?"

"No. That's a rather tricky bridge I've still got to cross. She doesn't even know I've switched to the Mary."

"Nor does Carol," I said. "I thought maybe I'd use it as an excuse to stop seeing her."

"Why? Aren't you enjoying yourself? It sounded like things were going pretty well for the two of you last time we were over at their place."

"No. It's still great. It's just that . . ."

"I know. You're madly in love with Sylvie. Come on, Steve. There's no way she's ever going to know. I'm certainly not going to be telling her. And unless you're even dafter than I think you are I guess you won't be either. So what's the problem? Variety's the spice of life. The more the better, I say."

"I'm not sure. It just doesn't feel right. I'll give it a bit of time and see how things go when we get ashore. You know. Play it by ear."

"Well don't you go messing everything up for me, that's all. I don't want Julie turning all difficult on me because you've dumped her mate."

It was a real dilemma. We only get one shot at life. And as Dave said, Sylvie would never know. As long as what happened in New York stayed in New York it wasn't ever going to hurt her.

"I probably won't do anything about it anyway," I said. "I really like Carol. It's not the same as Sylvie, obviously, but it's good fun. I wouldn't want to upset her. So I'll make sure things stay nice and friendly."

Working in the Verandah Grill with Tommy was great. He was full of fascinating stories. He'd been on the Queen Mary, working his way up through various jobs, since before the war.

"I started off in the Merchant Navy as one of the 'Vindi Boys," he told me. "We got our training for going to sea on the Vindicatrix. It was an old hulk of a ship, moored up in a disused dock on the River Severn estuary. Near a place called Sharpness in Gloucestershire. It'd once had masts I think but they'd been removed and I'm not even sure it was still floating. It might just've been sitting in the mud. A tough experience it was though. We were only there for two or three months but none of us will ever forget it. The officers were like they'd been trained in some sort concentration camp. They were brutal. And there was no heating on the ship. I was there in the wintertime so a layer of ice formed on the inside of all the windows. And the food was disgusting. Worse than the stuff they serve up to prisoners in jails. But it was the making of us. We went in as innocent young lads and came out as proper men. Ready to take on the world we were. I decided to join Cunard and ended up as a very junior Cabin Steward. I was on this ship for her maiden voyage. Southampton to New York. May 1936." Tommy looked wistful. "Because it was the Queen Mary there were loads of really important dignitaries on board. And we were lucky with the weather. The Atlantic was flat as a pancake the whole way over. I don't think I've seen it that way since. Not in twenty years."

Tommy explained that on the maiden voyage Austin Reed, the men's outfitters, had fitted out a very smart store in the ship's Shopping Centre. To encourage passengers to call in and sample his wares the manager had sent a little publicity booklet to every stateroom with the title 'It May Surprise You To Know'. As well as providing details of his retail offerings it contained a few interesting and wryly amusing facts about the ship.

The Queen Mary is higher, from keel to funnel, than St Paul's Cathedral in London – but not quite the same shape.

For golfers on board, the length of the ship is equivalent to one glorious drive, one decent approach shot and a putt of sixteen feet.

The cheeses which are served in the ship's restaurants are all stored at exactly the right temperature – and every cheese does have its own, exactly right, temperature.

All the staterooms and cabins on board are equipped with a personal safe in which you can store precious items – which will obviously include gifts which you have purchased from Austin Reed in the Shopping Centre.

And lastly, the Verandah Grill is situated up on the Sun Deck – but I'm afraid someone has already beaten you to the rather obvious joke!

The maiden voyage had been a great success. But a return crossing to Southampton later in the year turned out to be an unexpected test of the Queen Mary's capabilities and seaworthiness. It was a test that the great ship very nearly failed.

Tommy told me it was his first experience of really bad weather. And members of the crew who had been with Cunard for many years said to him it was the worst storm they could ever remember.

"Two days out of New York we were," said Tommy, "when the Captain announced that a hurricane was heading our way and that it wasn't going to be possible to alter course to avoid it. We had twelve hours to prepare the ship for the coming onslaught. The order was given to rope down and secure all tables, chairs and other moveable pieces of furniture. And to store every smaller item away in locked cupboards and drawers."

I listened, awestruck, as he told me how as much as possible was done in the time available and everyone, passengers and crew, then prepared themselves to ride out the coming storm. The expectation was that the Queen Mary would both pitch and roll in the very heavy seas. A major worry for the Captain, however, was that while the ship had, on earlier crossings, shown her ability to cut through even the biggest waves when she was meeting them head on, she had also demonstrated an unexpected, and rather unnerving, tendency to roll from side to side in a big swell, particularly when the wind and waves were coming at her from the side. How badly she would roll in a hurricane was about to be discovered.

"You're not going to believe this, Steve, but there were times when we were keeling over at 44 degrees. The tops of the waves were breaking onto the Sun Deck which is normally a hundred feet above the water. Every time she rolled we thought she'd never come up again. She did, of course, or I wouldn't be here telling you about it. But it must sometimes have been a very close thing. It was terrifying. I remember thinking we weren't going to make it. That it was going to be my first and last experience of a proper Atlantic storm. We'd roped down as many items as we could but in places like the Cabin Class Lounge the furniture was very solid and heavy. Nobody had expected the ship to roll the way she did and at 44 degrees even the heaviest and most solid pieces of furniture were on the move. The thick carpets lost their grip on the highly-polished dance floor and the four-seater settees and big armchairs were sliding around the room on them. In the Tourist Lounge an upright piano which had been fixed to the wall pulled out all the plugs and screws which were meant to be holding it in place. Then it started careering around the room, smashing against expensively-carved wooden panelling and destroying every piece of furniture in its path. The piano itself was eventually reduced to just its iron frame. When we finally made it to Southampton there were twenty-seven ambulances lined up on the dockside to take injured passengers to hospital."

Tommy shook his head as though he could scarcely believe what he was telling me.

"I very nearly handed in my papers and looked for another job after that voyage," he said. "In the end I didn't. But it's not an experience I ever want to repeat."

According to Tommy the reason for the Queen Mary's excessive rolling was her exceptionally heavy engines and boilers. They had been fitted very low down in the ship which gave her an admirably low centre of gravity. But when combined with the height of the ship this arrangement created an unexpected problem. In big seas the ship behaved like one of those dolls with heavy, curved bases which always return to the upright position no matter how far you tip them over. Which works fine for a toy doll on dry land. But for the Queen Mary, tipping so far over created a very real risk of the ship being overwhelmed by lethal quantities of sea water.

The solution to the problem was to add some extra weight higher up in the ship. It was a fix which proved to be very costly for Cunard. But it worked.

Tommy told me he was also on board in 1937, by this time working as a Steward in the Verandah Grill, when the Queen Mary made an Atlantic crossing with a full complement of desperate Jewish refugees.

"Hitler had just invaded Austria," he told me as I stood there open-eyed, "and hundreds of Jewish people had been forced to leave their homes. Whole families, some with very small children and babes-in-arms, had to run for their lives, taking with them only what they could carry. Everything else, homes, furniture, pictures and photographs, had to be abandoned. There were doctors, teachers, lawyers, plumbers and every other kind of worker. All of them were making their way across the ocean, hoping to find safety and build new lives for themselves and their families in the United States. They'd been allowed to take a small amount of cash with them but most of their money they'd been forced to leave behind. And they would never see it again. Even those who had recently been leading a very comfortable existence were travelling Third Class. For the first time in their lives they found themselves having to accept charity and make use of the complimentary vouchers which Cunard issued so that they did not go short of food during the Atlantic crossing."

Tommy told me that a friend of his on the ship, one of the Engineering Officers, had described to him being on watch one night, far out in the Atlantic. At Verandah Grill level it was possible to walk round the Sun Deck of the Queen Mary and look down onto the Third-Class Deck far below. It was past midnight and this officer was strolling on the Sun Deck, taking some air. Peering down at the Third-Class Deck, crowded with refugees, all he could see was the occasional red glow of a cigarette.

Then, drifting up to him out of the darkness, there came the mournful sound of a violin.

It was a lament.

The saddest thing he had ever heard.

A haunting requiem for a way of life that had been lost for ever.

FOURTEEN

SECRETS

After three return voyages Dave and I were ready for our first shore leave. The Queen Mary would sail from Southampton without us and we'd be free until she returned to her home port eleven days later.

Jean had confirmed that our leave would coincide with her family's re-arranged visit to Liverpool. Carl had fortunately made a full recovery and his business was back on track. He had arranged their flights so that we'd all have at least a week to enjoy ourselves together. Ricky and Susan would be able to see something of their mother's home city. And most important of all the two children would at long last get to know their English grandmother.

A very special and memorable week lay ahead.

I'd been looking forward to seeing Sylvie, and I had the usual gifts for her. But when she came over to meet me at St Bride Street the evening after I'd got back to Liverpool she wasn't her normal self. I gave her a kiss and a hug as usual, but something wasn't right. She didn't seem to want me to touch her.

"What's the problem?"

"It's nothing."

"You're not happy, Sylvie. I can tell."

"I'm fine."

"But you're not."

"I told you, it's nothing."

"It can't be nothing. There's something wrong. What is it?"

"I said it's nothing. Forget it. I don't want to talk about it."

"Okay. What would you like to do then?"

"Go somewhere for a drink."

"Okay. Where?"

"The Phil."

"Great. Let's go. Anything, so long as it'll cheer you up."

The Philharmonic, on the corner of Hope Street and Hardman Street opposite The Philharmonic Hall, home of the Royal Liverpool Philharmonic Orchestra, was a Victorian public house. It was an elegant and interesting venue for a drink. Its full name was The Philharmonic Dining Rooms but it was known to everyone as 'The Phil'. And it was little more than five minutes' walk from St Bride Street. Built for the local brewer, Robert Cain it had been a Liverpool landmark, and very popular local watering-hole, for over fifty years.

As we reached the end of Catherine Street and turned left onto Myrtle Street, passing the Children's and the Ear, Nose and Throat Hospitals to our right and The Philharmonic Hall to our left, we could see The Phil straight ahead. Constructed in ashlar stone, similar to the ancient and accurately-worked masonry blocks that had been used by the Inca people at Machu Picchu in the Andes, the building was richly decorated with architraves and mullions. The icing on the architectural cake was an ornate and imposing, two-storey, oriel window which overlooked the junction where Hope Street met Myrtle Street and Hardman Street.

We made our way through a pair of Art Nouveau, metal gates which formed part of the main entrance and entered the main bar. It was even more sumptuous than the outside of the building. Half-moon, stained-glass windows with mahogany surrounds provided some natural light while the walls were decorated with detailed plasterwork and musically-themed, low-relief designs on hammered copper panels.

To our right a pair of comfortably-furnished rooms had name signs above the doors. One was called *'Brahms'*. And the other was *'Liszt'*.

When the pub welcomed its very first customers in the late 1890s, Philharmonic Hall regulars, calling in for a pre-concert drink, would have been very familiar with the phrase *'Brahms and Liszt'*. At that time it referred to two very different, and mutually exclusive, tastes in classical music.

To those of us who are more familiar with Cockney rhyming slang it now has a rather different meaning, but one which is very appropriate for a public house.

Sylvie glanced up at the signs.

"I think I'm going to get a bit Brahms and Liszt this evening."

I looked at her.

"You can get as pissed as you like. Just as long as it makes you happy."

The pub wasn't busy and we found ourselves a quiet corner.

"I'm having a pint," I said. "What can I get you?"

For the first time that evening Sylvie gave me a smile.

"A gin and tonic'd be nice. A double."

When I returned with the drinks I took hold of her hand.

"Right," I said. "Whatever it is that's bugging you we need to sort it out."

Sylvie didn't reply at first. Then she picked up the gin and tonic with her free hand and took a sip.

I gave the hand I was still holding a squeeze.

"Enjoy it. And no rush. But whenever you're ready you've got to tell me what's wrong."

She took another drink. This time rather more than a sip.

"I was getting some pains," she said, "and I went to see the doctor last week."

"Pains?" I said. "Where?"

"Down below. Like a burning. Every time I went for a pee."

"And?"

"She did some tests. And she said it was non-specific urethritis."

"Okay," I said slowly. "What's that?"

"It's an infection which makes your bladder and so on all inflamed. And you get this pain, sort of like cystitis. It's not very pleasant."

"And did the doctor give you something?"

Sylvie nodded her head.

"Yes. A course of an antibiotic called Tetracycline."

"And are you okay now? Have they worked?"

"Yes. I'm fine."

I put my arm around her and kissed her cheek.

"You had me worried for a minute. So that's what the problem's been. But I don't understand why you were bottling it up. Why you didn't want to say anything. I thought you'd gone off me."

"There's something else." Sylvie took another drink. "I'm not sure how to put it."

"Just tell me," I said. "Whatever it is."

"The doctor said it'd be best if you got some treatment too."

"Me? Why?"

"Because I could've given it to you." She paused for a minute. "Or you could've given it to me. She was asking me how many sexual partners I had at the moment and I said just one. You."

"Okay."

"She said the more people you have sex with, the more likely you are to pick that sort of infection up."

She took another drink of her gin and tonic. I had already downed more than half of my pint.

"I definitely haven't picked it up from anyone else," she said. "What about you?"

"Jesus, Sylvie. What are you saying. That I might've given it to you?"

"No, Steve." She shook her head. "Look. I don't know. It's just what the doctor said, that's all. That it'd be best if you got some treatment too."

I wasn't sure what to say. Inside my head I could hear Dave's voice as we were sitting together in The Pig just a week or two earlier. 'I'm certainly not going to be telling her. And unless you're even dafter than I think you are, I guess you won't be either.'

"I've been fine," I said. That at least was honest. "I haven't had any waterworks symptoms. No burning or anything. But if your doctor wants me to have some treatment just in case, I'll take it. I don't want to cause you any problems. I'll do whatever she recommends."

"She says you need to go and see your own doctor and get tested."

"Okay. That's what I'll do."

"You've not been with anybody else while you've been away, have you? On the ship? Or in New York or somewhere?"

"No."

"Promise me."

I heard Dave's voice again. 'I guess you won't be either.'

"No." I said. "I promise."

Sylvie gave me a kiss.

"I said to the doctor I didn't think I could've got it from you. And she did say it sometimes happens for no obvious reason. You can be carrying the bugs that cause it for years without them causing any problems. It's only if they get into your kidneys and your waterworks that you end up getting symptoms. But I could still have given it to you, she said. So you should definitely get tested. Just to be sure."

"Don't worry. I'll see the doctor as soon as I can."

Sylvie finished her gin and tonic in one while I did the same with my beer.

"Okay then," she said. "Now that's all sorted I think we need a few more drinks."

Later that evening, as we made our slightly unsteady way back to St Bride Street, hand in hand and more than a little 'Brahms and Liszt', I felt consumed by guilt. It was a mess. We were chatting away happily as we walked but all kind of thoughts were whirling round inside my brain.

Maybe I should have told Sylvie about Carol? But would that honestly have helped? I wouldn't have had to lie to her which would have been a big plus. But telling her the truth would have created an even bigger mess. Sylvie would have been upset and we'd have had an almighty row. And then most likely we'd have split up. Which would certainly have made me unhappy. And probably Sylvie too.

By the time we reached St Bride Street I'd convinced myself that I was a complete and utter bastard. But I'd learnt an important lesson. And done the most sensible, even if not the most honest, thing.

My mother and the two uncles were in the parlour.

"We've heard from Jean," said my mother with a broad smile on her face. "Their plane from New York landed in London a couple of hours ago. They're going to stay in a hotel near Euston Station overnight and catch a train up here tomorrow morning. It's due to get into Liverpool at lunchtime, just after one o'clock. I said you'd be there to meet them, Stephen."

I put both my arms round her and held her tight.

"That's wonderful news, Ma. I can't wait. What a great time we're all going to have."

Sylvie stayed the night in one of the spare bedrooms. Even though it was a night for celebrations the idea of the two of us sharing a bed was unthinkable. My mother's house rules were strict and admirably simple.

"If the two of you must sleep together, I can't stop you. You can do whatever you like elsewhere. But not under my roof."

Sylvie and I had anyway agreed that it would be best if we waited until after I'd been tested and, if necessary, treated.

———————

With an exciting day ahead I'd fallen asleep almost as soon as my head hit the pillow, hoping for a good night's rest. But at just after three o'clock in the morning I was woken by an urgent knocking on my bedroom door. I turned over and opened my eyes to see Uncle Georgie standing there.

"It's your mother, Stephen. She's not well. Your Uncle Jimmy was fast asleep and I heard a noise coming from the parlour so I went down to see what was going on. And I found her doubled up on the couch. She seems to be in a lot of pain and I think she needs to be seen at the hospital. I was going to call '999' for an ambulance but she just kept saying no, and that even if an ambulance turned up, she'd refuse to get in it. You need to come down. Maybe you can talk some sense into her?"

Wishing I'd not had quite so much to drink at The Phil, I grabbed my dressing gown from its hook on the back of the door and threw it on as I was rushing down the stairs.

It was as Georgie had said. My mother was half-sitting and half-lying on the settee, as white as a sheet and clutching her stomach.

"What is it, Ma?"

"I've got a bit of a pain." She was forcing the words out, almost grunting, and it was obvious that she was finding it difficult to talk. "It came on about fifteen minutes ago and it's not going away."

"Come on, Ma. It's more than a bit of a pain. You're not right.

There's something going on. Georgie thinks you need to be seen at the hospital. And I agree with him."

My mother sat forwards.

"No. We've got Jean and the children coming tomorrow. They're not taking me to any hospital. Your grandfather went off from here in an ambulance to the Royal Infirmary and he never came out again. I'll be fine. Just get me a drink of water and a couple of pain-killers."

She slumped back against the settee and continued to hold her stomach. Speaking just three or four sentences had been an enormous effort.

Georgie had followed me down the stairs. Sylvie and Jimmy had also been woken by the noise. The three of them were standing behind me, looking on.

"Come on, Barbara," said Georgie. "Please be sensible."

Even as he spoke my mother groaned loudly and gripped her stomach even tighter, bending forwards as she did so.

I turned to Georgie. The urgency of the situation had miraculously cleared my head.

"I know Jean's arriving tomorrow, but you're right. Ma needs to go to hospital and get checked out. I don't care what she says. I'm calling an ambulance. We can't just leave her like this and do nothing."

I lifted the receiver of the angular, Bakelite telephone in the corner of the room and put it to my ear to check for a dialling tone. Then I dialled the emergency number. '9-9-9'.

Within a couple of seconds a voice came onto the line.

"Which service do you require? Fire, police or ambulance?"

"Ambulance please."

"Hold the line."

There were a couple of clicks, followed by a different voice.

"Ambulance service. How can I help you?"

"My mother is in very severe pain. We know she's got an

abdominal aortic aneurysm. And I think she needs to be seen at the hospital urgently."

"What telephone number are you calling from?"

"Royal 2273."

"Is the patient conscious?"

"Yes."

"Can she speak to you?"

"Yes."

"Is she having any difficulty with her breathing?"

"A little bit. But I think it's just because of the pain."

"Is she bleeding?"

"No."

"What is your name?"

"Stephen Crane."

"And the address where the patient is now, please."

"19, St Bride Street, Liverpool 8."

"And the name of the patient?"

"Mrs Barbara Crane."

"You say she is your mother?"

"Yes."

"How old is she?"

"Forty-nine."

"And finally, her date of birth if you know it."

"30th June 1908."

"Thank you. Your request for an urgent ambulance has been logged. It should be with you within ten minutes. If the patient's condition gets significantly worse before the ambulance arrives please call me back."

"Thank you for your help."

"That's alright. You may put the phone down now."

I knelt down by the settee and took my mother's hand.

"There's an ambulance on its way, Ma. You've got to go to hospital."

"I'm not going, Stephen. Just get me some pain-killers. Please."

"There's some of my aspirin and codeine down in the kitchen," said Uncle Georgie. "I take them for headaches. I'll go and get them. I can't see that it'll do any harm if she takes a couple while we're waiting."

"I'm not going. You can't make me."

"Let's just see what the ambulance crew say when they arrive, Ma. They'll check you over and do what they can to help."

"I told you. I'm not going to any hospital."

My mother gave a little moan and closed her eyes.

I was still kneeling there, holding her hand, when Georgie returned with the tablets and a glass of water.

"Here, Barbara. I've got the tablets and some water. Let me give you a couple."

She opened her eyes and nodded her head. I let go of her hand while Georgie gave her the pain-killers, one at a time, and she awkwardly swallowed them down with some of the water.

"There you go," he said gently. "Give them a few minutes to work."

My mother closed her eyes again.

I looked up at Sylvie.

"You can go back to bed if you like. There's no need for us all to miss out on our sleep."

She shook her head.

"No, it's fine. I'll stay if that's okay. I wouldn't be able to sleep anyway."

My mother lay on the settee with her eyes closed, groaning from time to time. To try and give her some sort of comfort I held her hand while we waited for the ambulance in silence, each of us lost in our own thoughts.

I'd never found myself in such a situation before, watching the struggles of an obviously very sick patient who was also my mother. The feeling of helplessness was overwhelming. I could see that it was the same for Sylvie and my two uncles. And all the time, at the back of my mind, was the thought of Jean and her family down in London. After their three and a half thousand mile journey they would have gone to bed exhausted, but excited and happy at the thought of arriving in Liverpool and seeing the family. They would now be fast asleep, blissfully unaware of what was happening just two hundred miles away.

Our relief when two ambulance crew appeared in the parlour, carrying their emergency equipment and acting with totally professional confidence, was almost palpable.

One of them knelt down beside me.

"What's the patient's name?"

I told him, and he spoke to my mother quietly.

"Barbara. Can you hear me?" She opened her eyes. "My name's Frank. I'm an ambulance driver and I've come to have a look at you. My colleague's name is Vicky and she's a nurse. Is it okay if I ask you a couple of questions?"

"I've already told my son. I'm not going anywhere."

"That's fine, Barbara. We're not going to make you do anything you don't want to do. Just a couple of questions. Is that okay?"

My mother nodded her head and closed her eyes again. She seemed to be a little drowsy and not in quite so much pain. Perhaps the tablets were starting to work?

"Your son says you've been getting some pains in your stomach. Can you show me where?"

"In the middle." My mother let go of my hand and pointed to her stomach. "Just above my tummy button."

Frank placed the flat of his hand on the spot and let it rest there for a couple of moments before pressing, very gently. My mother winced.

"I'm sorry," he said. "I didn't mean to hurt you."

Frank removed his hand from my mother's abdomen and took hold of her wrist.

"I'm just going to count your pulse, Barabara. And then I'll check your blood pressure if that's okay."

The three of us watched as he carried out the necessary checks, calmly and efficiently. It was a huge relief to know that my mother was in such obviously capable hands.

After removing the blood pressure cuff from my mother's arm he turned to his colleague, Vicky.

"Pulse one hundred and twenty-two, sinus rhythm. Blood pressure one hundred and six over sixty-two with a definite pulsatile mass in the upper abdomen centrally, at the site of the pain."

Vicky jotted the information down in a notebook she was carrying while Frank stood up and spoke to us.

"I'd like the four of you come with me for a minute, please, so we can have a word? Vicky will stay in here and keep an eye on Barbara."

Frank led us out into the hall and Uncle Georgie pulled the parlour door to behind us.

"Someone told the ambulance controller that Barbara has an abdominal aortic aneurysm," said Frank.

"Yes," I said. "That was me."

Frank turned towards me.

"Well, I'm afraid it looks like she might now be developing what we call an aortic dissection. If I'm right it means a tear has developed in the lining of the weakened part of the aorta and it might be about to fail."

I felt my mouth go dry and my heart began to race.

"Is there anything that can be done?"

"That's a question for the specialists," said Frank. "The only thing I can tell you right now is that we need to get your mother to hospital as soon as possible."

"I don't think she'll agree to go," said Georgie. "I know my sister. She's frightened. And she's stubborn. Once she's made her mind up about something it's almost impossible to shift her. Added to which her daughter, Jean, is arriving here at lunchtime tomorrow with her family. Barbara has never met her two grandchildren. They've come all the way from America to see her."

I'm really sorry," said Frank, placing a hand on Georgie's upper arm to show that he understood. "But I still think we've got to have a go at persuading your sister to come with us to hospital. Even if it's only to be assessed. I'll be honest with you. If Vicky and I drive off and leave her here at home Barbara is very unlikely to survive. Even if we get her to the Royal Infirmary there may be very little that the specialists can do. But at least we'll have given her a chance."

He looked at each of us in turn.

"Let's go back in and see what we can do."

FIFTEEN

HOMECOMING

The distinctive shape and sound of the Royal Scot Class locomotive 'Royal Ulster Rifleman' emerged from a hissing cloud of smoke and steam at the head of a long line of carriages. I watched as the powerful steam engine puffed its way out of the deep Edge Hill cutting and made its way very slowly into Liverpool Lime Street Station, coming to a very gentle halt at the end of Platform Six, just short of the enormous buffers alongside which I was standing. Carriage doors were flung open and tired passengers, who had started their journey at London Euston almost four hours earlier, stepped carefully down onto the waiting platform with their bags and cases.

I scanned the faces of the bustling crowd as they hurried towards me, looking out for Jean and her family but they were nowhere to be seen. Then, just as I was beginning to think they must have missed the train, I caught sight of Carl. He was at the very far end of the platform with Jean and the two children. As always seems to happen when you're meeting someone they were right at the back of the queue to give in their tickets. They must, sensibly, have decided to let the initial rush subside before collecting their luggage together and shepherding the children off the train.

As they got closer Jean caught sight of me and waved excitedly. I waved back and managed to raise a smile, even though I knew I was about to break her heart.

Our mother's funeral took place at St Bride's Church on Percy Street, just a few hundred yards from her home. It was difficult to believe it was really happening. She was so young. Forty-nine was no age at all. While in one way we'd known her condition could worsen at any time, the medical reports had been so encouraging that we'd all convinced ourselves that everything would be alright.

It's what people tend to do when the alternative is too dreadful to contemplate.

Despite our best efforts that fateful night we had been unable to persuade our mother to go to hospital. Once it had become clear that she was determined to stay at home Frank had arranged for Dr Roxburgh, our family doctor, to attend. He and Vicky had very kindly waited until the doctor arrived, knowing that their calm presence would be a very welcome and much needed source of support and reassurance. They could not have done more.

Dr Roxburgh had himself spent a few minutes trying to get my mother to change her mind. But to no avail. She had, however, agreed to let him give her an injection of morphine after which, relieved of the worst of her pain, she had drifted off to sleep.

At just before nine o'clock the following morning Jean and her family had left Euston Station in London on the last leg of their long journey from Pennsylvania. As their train started to pick up speed, heading north towards Liverpool, occasional clouds of smoke and steam were blown past the carriage windows and the two children were almost beside themselves with excitement.

At almost exactly the same moment the grandmother they had travelled so far to see, but were destined never to meet, had very peacefully slipped away.

There would have been no time for the hospital doctors to attempt any treatment, which I think deep down our mother probably knew. If it is possible to find a silver lining in such a desperate situation it would be that her decision to refuse hospital treatment had turned out to be for the best. She died in her own home, surrounded by her immediate family. It was undoubtedly what she would have wanted.

As she drifted away under the influence of the morphine I like to think that she would almost certainly have believed that Jean and the children were there, in St Bride Street, with her.

Carl and I, along with Dave, my two uncles and Dave's father, carried her coffin.

Dave's father, Trevor, had been a pillar of strength to my mother in the long months since my father had disappeared. He and my mother had known each other since they were small children, long before my father appeared on the scene. They had always been very close. And with Trevor also being on his own we had sort of hoped that they might perhaps get together. Given more time I suppose it could still have happened. But it was not to be.

St Bride's Church was where our mother had been baptised in April 1909. And it was where her marriage to my father had taken place on 30th June, 1925. It was her seventeenth birthday and she was already four months pregnant with Jean. It was her pregnancy that had triggered the marriage but the news had not been shared with the vicar. Her condition was not obvious and he did not need to know. It might have complicated matters.

Dating back to the 1830s, like many of the fine Georgian

houses in the surrounding streets, the white-painted church of St Bride had the external appearance of a Greek temple. Six plain, Ionic columns formed an impressive portico across the front of the building and, as one of the undertakers pressed his right hand against the end of the coffin to stop it slipping backwards, the six of us very carefully ascended the stone steps and passed between the columns into the church.

Eight rows of polished, wooden pews sat on each side of the central aisle as we entered the body of the church, passing beneath an elegantly curved balcony which was supported by slim, cast-iron pillars. We then progressed slowly up the aisle and laid my mother's coffin on the twin supports in front of the altar before taking our places for the service.

The church was full and I could hear people sobbing. My mother had lived in St Bride Street all her life and many in the local community had come to mourn her untimely passing. Carl and I sat down alongside my poor sister, Jean, who was still distraught that she and the children had been so very close to seeing our mother before she died. Jean had told me it would come as some small consolation to her if she could deliver the eulogy. And as she was the oldest child I was happy to leave that difficult task to her. It would be her opportunity to tell my mother's many friends how much she had continued to love her despite being far away in America and how very much she would be missed.

And, most of all, how desperately sad she and her husband were that their two small children would now never be able to get to know their very special, English grandmother.

The whole service was a fitting tribute to a mother who turned out to have been more remarkable then we could possibly have imagined.

In her eulogy Jean referred very briefly to the disappearance of our father, saying how brave our mother had been, before recalling how, during the war when Jean was in her early teens, our mother used to go off to work five days a week. And quite often at weekends too. She had a job in a fairly ordinary office on Rumford Street in the business quarter of Liverpool not far from the river.

Jean told the congregation that on the few occasions when she was sufficiently interested to ask our mother what she did, she was told that it was just routine secretarial work in a boring office, far too boring even to be worth discussing.

Almost as soon as the war was over her job came to an end.

"It turned out," said Jean, speaking from the pulpit, "that our quiet and unassuming mother's boring office in Rumford Street contained the entrance to a top-secret, wartime bunker. This bunker, beneath Derby House, was reinforced in such a way that even the most powerful German bomb falling directly onto the building above would not damage or disable it. This was because it was the Operations Headquarters from which The Battle of The Atlantic was being run. Known in communications only as 'HMS Eaglet', it was the nerve centre from where the vital task of protecting the Atlantic convoys, and sinking Hitler's U-boats, was organised and coordinated. My mother told me that Winston Churchill himself used to make secret visits to satisfy himself that they had all the resources they needed. The great man even spoke to her several times, emphasising how very important her work was. The Battle of The Atlantic had to be won, Churchill would say. It was the key to success in the war."

Jean looked down at our mother's assembled family and friends who had all been stunned into silence by this remarkable revelation. Many of them were looking at the coffin and thinking about the extraordinary wartime exploits of the apparently ordinary and unassuming lady who lay within it.

"Like many of the men and women of the very special generation who helped to defeat Hitler," continued Jean, "our mother hardly ever talked about the war. We will never know exactly what her role was. But I am quite sure she would say that she was simply doing her bit to prevent the country she loved from being overrun by the forces of evil. I would ask you all to remember her. Not only with love. But also with pride. And with gratitude. She was one of the many unsung heroes who helped to ensure that our treasured freedoms were not taken away from us."

My mother's body was laid to rest in Toxteth Park Cemetery, just a mile or two from where she had spent most of her life. We all gathered afterwards for refreshments in the Thompson Community Hall in Toxteth, a beautiful Georgian assembly room with Adam-style decorations and panelling.

After everyone had gone I was standing there alone, lost in thought, when Dave came up to me, drink in hand.

"It's a sad day, Steve. But if it had to happen it's lucky that we were at home. Just imagine what it would have been like to get the news by telegram, somewhere out in the Atlantic. It would've been awful. The way it turned out, you were able to be there with your Ma at the end. It's a shame that Jean and her family didn't make it in time, but you all gave your Ma the send-off she deserved. You honestly couldn't have done more."

I wrapped an arm around his shoulders.

"Thanks for everything, Dave. What would I do without you?"

Dave and I had been granted compassionate leave on full pay by Cunard, and the Queen Mary had left Southampton without us three days before the funeral. With all the arrangements for the funeral needing to be sorted out there had been little time to entertain Ricky and Susan. Jean had quite rightly wanted to be fully involved with everything, so Carl had taken on the job of keeping the two children occupied.

We would be rejoining our ship in just over a week and I was certain that my mother would have wanted us to make sure that what remained of the children's stay in Liverpool was full of laughter and happy memories.

So, for Ricky and Susan, a busy and fun week lay ahead.

But there was another matter which first had to be addressed.

●·+————●·+·●·+·●————·+·●

At just after nine the following morning I found myself sitting in the consulting room of our family doctor, the same Dr Roxburgh who had come out to see my mother that night.

He offered me his condolences.

"I'm so sorry, Stephen, that there was nothing I could do for your poor mother that would have allowed her to see your sister Jean and the two small children before she died. Life can sometimes be very cruel."

"Thank you," I said. "Jean and her family understand that things are sometimes just not meant to be. They know there was nothing more you could have done."

Dr Roxburgh nodded his head slowly.

"So," he said, "what brings you along to see me today, Stephen. I'm assuming it's not just to say thank you."

"No," I said. "It's not. The thing is my girlfriend's been told she's got something called non-specific urethritis. And her doctor said I might need to be tested and get some treatment as well."

Dr Roxburgh took my fairly scanty NHS medical records out of the slim, brown folder within which they were kept and placed them on the desk between us. I was not one of his regular attenders.

"So, the two of you sleep together?"

"Yes. But I'm working for Cunard now so I'm away at sea quite a lot of the time. My girlfriend and I don't sleep together all that often."

Dr Roxburgh looked at me over the top of his half-moon, reading glasses and smiled.

"It only takes once to pick up or pass on an infection," he said, and looked at my record card. Then, after scribbling a few notes on it, he put down his pen.

"Do you use a condom?"

"No," I said. "We don't go all the way."

"Coitus interruptus. Not the most reliable of the various methods of contraception. I don't recommend it. A condom can prevent pregnancies. And infections. Remember that."

The doctor returned to his notes with a look of disapproval. I presumed to write down that I needed to be more sensible. Then he addressed me again.

"Right," he said briskly. "I'm afraid I'm going to have to ask you a few quite personal questions in order to get things straight and sort this problem out. You say you go to sea?"

"Yes. On the Queen Mary from Southampton to New York."

Dr Roxburgh removed his glasses and fixed his eyes on me.

"I think it'd be fair to say that men who go to sea, particularly young men like yourself, have . . ." He paused. "How shall I put it? A certain reputation. A girl in every port is the phrase people sometimes use. Would that apply to you?"

Did I really need to tell him about Carol?

After a moment's hesitation I decided that I did.

"Yes," I said. "I suppose it does. There is someone in New York I see from time to time."

"A girl?"

"Yes."

"And you engage in sex with her?"

"Yes."

"Again without protection?"

"Yes. She told me she's been fitted with something called an IUD. So she can't get pregnant."

"An intra-uterine device," said the doctor. "Not used all that commonly in the United States, I'm told. But yes, it is quite effective at preventing pregnancy. Unfortunately one reason why IUDs aren't more widely used over there is that they might increase the risk of infection. At least that's what the Americans think." He lifted his eyes again. "And what about on the ship? Have you had any relationships with other members of the crew?"

I shook my head.

"No."

"And to be clear, that means with both men and women."

"No," I said. A mental picture of Dr Hans stroking my buttocks after giving me his Krakatoa Cocktail on the Media suddenly flashed into my mind. "Definitely not. Not men." I paused for a moment. "And not women either. Not on the ship."

"Fine. And when was it you first had sex with this young lady in New York?"

I struggled to answer for a moment. Then another image popped into my head. The coffee shop and the jukebox. 'You'll remember this' the poet had said. What he hadn't foreseen was that it would be during an interrogation by my doctor.

"It was the week after 'Heartbreak Hotel' first came out in America," I said. "That's a record by Elvis Presley."

"Which was when exactly, Stephen? I'm afraid the dates of Mr Presley's transatlantic record releases are not something that I routinely take note of."

"I'm sorry. It was around the beginning of February."

"This year?"

"Yes. This year."

"And have you had any symptoms of an infection since then? Since February? Pain when you pass water? Going to the toilet more often than usual? Any sort of discharge?"

"No, nothing at all. I've been fine."

"And this girl in New York. She's never mentioned having any problems to you?"

"No. Never."

Dr Roxburgh picked up his pen and made a few more notes.

"So, to be clear. Your only other sexual relationship has been with this American girl?"

"That's right."

"And if it turns out you are responsible for your English girlfriend's unfortunate infection it will be from this American girl?"

"I suppose so, yes."

"And does your girlfriend here in Liverpool know about this other relationship? I'm assuming she does live somewhere round here."

"Yes. In West Derby. And no, I haven't told her about the girl in New York. Her doctor said this non-specific urethritis isn't always caught through sex."

"That's true. It isn't always. I have seen a few cases over the years where there's been no evidence of sexual transmission. Or at least nothing definite that could be identified. But I think it's fairly safe to say the vast majority of cases are down to sexual transmission in one form or another. So, what I need to do now is carry out a quick examination and take a couple of swabs which will be sent off for testing. Along with a urine sample. Is that alright?"

"Okay. That's fine."

"Let's get it sorted out, then. If you'd like to pop behind the screen and slip your trousers off, please. And your underpants. I'll be with you in just a moment."

Because I'd told Jean I was going to be tied up most of the day, she and Carl had decided to take Ricky and Susan for a ride on the Overhead Railway. They would never get another chance. The Dockers' Umbrella had been judged too expensive to maintain and the decision had been made to demolish the whole structure. The very last train was due to run from Seaforth Sands to Dingle on December 30th, 1956 and work to dismantle the railway would begin the following year.

Liverpool's citizens were up in arms. They could not believe that the city's decision-makers were so short-sighted and lacking in vision. By some miracle the world's first elevated railway with electrically-operated, automatic signals, had survived the Blitz. But the bean-counters were now in charge. And after sixty-three years of regular use by almost twenty million passengers each year they were planning to destroy it.

Protests took place and petitions were presented to the politicians, but the decision could not be changed. By the end of the decade a pioneering and important part of the world's railway heritage would have disappeared for ever.

⚫•⚫ ⚫•⚫•⚫ •⚫

That lunchtime, after my sadly necessary appointment with Dr Roxburgh, I was having a very welcome drink with Dave in The Phil.

"Honest," I said. "It was like The Spanish bloody Inquisition. One embarrassing question after another. About the only thing old Roxburgh didn't ask me was what positions Sylvie and Carol like best."

Dave lifted his eyebrows and gave me a grin. "And?"

"For God's sake, Dave. I can do without your little jokes just at the moment."

"Fair enough." He shrugged his shoulders. "It's of no great interest to me. Of very slight interest maybe. But I can survive without knowing."

"Stop your messing. Right now. Or I might have to hit you."

"No problem." He gave me another grin. "So, when do you get the test results?"

"They should be back tomorrow. I've got to call in at the surgery sometime after one o'clock."

Dave lifted up his pint and took a sip.

"So that's two things," he said. "I wonder what'll be next?"

"What are you on about?"

"You losing your poor Ma. And then Sylvie getting this infection. That's two things. My Ma used to say things always come in threes. So, as I said, I wonder what'll be next?"

"Did your poor old Ma really believe in that sort of stuff? You know. Old-fashioned superstitions?"

"Oh yeah," said Dave. "Very seriously. I know you and I were only about five or six when we lost her. And she was lovely. But you must remember what she was like. Her life revolved around them. One way of doing things was lucky and any other way was a recipe for disaster. Every single thing had to be done the lucky way. Even if it was seriously inconvenient. She once sat in our toilet all day because my Dad had gone out to work first thing in the morning when she was in there and left a ladder leaning against the wall in front of the toilet door. There was absolutely no way my Mum was going to walk out under it. So she just stayed there until my Dad got home. He thought it was hilarious, as you can imagine, but I don't think my Ma found it quite so amusing."

I'd heard the story before. But it was still very funny and we were both laughing as we recalled the delightful foibles of a lady we had both greatly loved.

Dave, who was a natural comedian, was now on a roll.

"And you must remember the way the floors in our house always seemed to be crunchy when you walked on them. If anyone in the house did something unlucky my Ma would throw a handful of salt over her left shoulder. The amount of salt that flew around our house was unbelievable. The world's salt mines are probably struggling to stay in business without her."

"I love it," I said, still laughing. "But I still think it's nonsense. Nothing else is going to happen."

"We'll see." Dave gave me a smile and shrugged his shoulders. "Anyway. How're you doin' with sorting out all your Ma's stuff."

"There's not that much to do to be honest. Jimmy and Georgie'll be still be living in St Bride Street. And the council transferred the rent book into Georgie's name when my grandad died because he was already living there. So he's been the official tenant ever since. The rest of us just chip in our bit towards the rent each week."

"Keeps it simple I suppose."

"Yeah. It doesn't half bug me though. Our family's been living in that house pretty much since it was first built. That's got to be close to a hundred years. It's daylight robbery. We must've paid for it in rent at least ten times over. If not more."

"It's the same for me and my Dad," said Dave. "And I reckon for most of the other families in the street as well. The thing is it's a nice place to live. Dead convenient for town. And the kids can play out in the street because it never gets busy. So people don't move away that often."

"I suppose we're lucky really," I said. "Living somewhere nice. I'm pretty sure Jean's really enjoyed being back here in Liverpool with the kids despite everything that's happened. And it's great that Ricky and Susan have been able to get to see some of the places where their Mum grew up. It's important, that is."

"Has she said how much longer they're stayin'?"

"About another week, I think. Carl says he needs to get back to his business. He doesn't want things going haywire again. Jean says a week'll give her the time she needs to get all Ma's bits and pieces sorted out before she heads home. She reckons Ma wouldn't have wanted us menfolk to be rooting around through all her clothes and so on. You know. The personal stuff. Which is fine with me."

"Everyone's been saying to me they thought your Jean did your Ma proud at the funeral. Not an easy thing to do and she got it just right. I liked the way she talked about your Dad. Not very much. Just a couple of little comments. But it was good that he wasn't completely forgotten."

"Yeah," I said. "You're probably right. But I'm not sure I can ever forgive him for disappearing the way he did and abandoning my Ma. And that letter just made it worse. It was cruel. She didn't deserve it. I don't know how she'd have coped if your Dad hadn't been there for her. He's been amazing."

"He's going to miss her," said Dave. "They were very close. I wonder how much he knew about your Ma. You know. Workin' in the secret bunker and havin' little secret chats with Churchill. He never said anything to me but I can't believe she wouldn't have mentioned it to him. It makes me proud to have known her."

"All I remember is her going off to work every day," I said. "And us being looked after by Jean and my two uncles. I suppose we were too little to notice very much about what the grown-ups were doing. I did once ask Uncle Jimmy why he and Georgie weren't in the army fighting the Germans. He said it was because they both had important jobs in a munitions factory somewhere near a little village called Kirkby where they made bombs and hand grenades. The work couldn't be done in the city, he said, in case of something going wrong and causing a massive explosion. It sounded pretty dangerous and I remember telling him to be careful."

"How did your Jean know about what your Ma was doing?" asked Dave.

"I'm not sure," I said. "I suppose Ma must've told her at some point. Jean was a lot older than us so perhaps Ma confided in her. I've been meaning to ask."

Dave looked at me.

"And what about your Dad in France? Do you know anything more about what he was up to?"

"Jean and I did talk about it when I was at their place in Manheim and she mentioned one or two things. But I sort of promised her I wouldn't say too much. She did tell me that he was in the Special Operations Executive though."

Dave looked blank.

"Yeah," I said. "I was the same when she said it. I'd never heard of them either. But apparently they were this specially-trained group of soldiers that Churchill set up to work behind enemy lines. You know. In Occupied France before D-Day. They were all parachuted in and Jean says they were fighting alongside the French Resistance doing their best to sabotage the German defences."

"I'd never have imagined your Dad bein' involved in that sort of stuff."

"Me neither," I said. "Though I can't remember if I actually said that to Jean."

"So what else did she say?"

"A few bits and pieces. Nothing much. Some of it might still be secret I suppose. I don't really know."

"Fair enough," said Dave. "But if you're ever able to tell me the full story I'd like to hear it."

I put my arms round him and give him a hug.

Dave and I didn't often admit how close we were to each other. But I couldn't stop myself. We were much more like brothers than friends really.

"You've been such a close mate for so long, Dave. You know most of it already. The letter and so on. There's probably stuff that I don't even know yet. But if I ever do, I promise you, you'll be the first to know."

"Thanks," he said. "And, by the way, those tests the doctor did. I don't know why, but I've got a feeling in my water that they're gonna be fine."

"That sounds like something your dear old Ma might've said."

Dave laughed.

"Yeah. She used to get feelings in her water all the time. It must've been pretty uncomfortable. But they were usually right."

Dave's water turned out to be right too. And after I'd called in at the surgery I gave Sylvie the good news.

"The tests the doctor did all came back negative. So I don't need any treatment."

"Thank goodness for that," said Sylvie with a smile. "I've been really worried I might have passed it on to you."

"Well you haven't Everything's fine. So now we can forget about it."

"It's a mystery how these things just happen, isn't it," she said brightly, giving me one of her lovely smiles.

I put my arms around her and immediately the guilt came flooding back. Sylvie was so lovely. So innocent. And I'd treated her very badly. I wouldn't ever forgive myself. But I could never tell her. Sometimes it's best to let a sleeping dog lie.

"I suppose so," I said, doing my utmost to sound normal and return her smile. "But let's just leave it now. You're all clear. And I'm fine. So, as I said, we can forget about it."

"It looks like your girlfriend has just been unlucky", Dr Roxburgh had said. "With all the tests being clear, and you having had no symptoms at any time, it's pretty unlikely that you picked up an infection in New York and passed it on to her. Not impossible. But very unlikely. And you seem to be fairly certain that she hasn't had any other partners while you've been away at sea. So it seems she must have picked up the infection some other way. Although if there's one thing that the practice of medicine has taught me, it is that life can be full of unexpected, and sometimes unwanted, surprises."

I hadn't been entirely sure what he was suggesting. But if he was saying that Sylvie might have been unfaithful I was as certain as I could possibly be that he was wrong. He didn't know her. And anyway, she'd surely have kept quiet about the infection if she thought she might have caught it from somebody else.

She didn't need to tell me. Unless, of course, her doctor had insisted she had to inform all her partners.

No, that was impossible. I was sure I could trust her.

Even though I knew for sure she shouldn't have trusted me.

SIXTEEN

PUZZLING TIMES

"So," I said to Jean. "What do we do about the letter? I haven't checked but as far as I know it's still tucked away in that book. Do we go to the police and tell them our father is still alive? Or at least he was six and a half years ago."

"We've got to, Steve. Although I can't help wondering if they might already know. I remember thinking at the time Dad disappeared that it was strange how quickly they seemed to lose interest in looking for him. They kept telling us the case wasn't closed. But it never seemed to be very active. At least not after the first week or two."

"So you think Ma might already have shown them the letter?"

"Don't you? I'm sure it's possible. Anyway, if we take it along we'll find out."

"And what about the uncles? And Sylvie? And your Carl? Do we tell them?"

"Let's wait and see," said Jean. "If it turns out the police know about the letter I suppose we might as well. It's not going to change anything. Dad's disappeared. And he seems to have made a pretty good job of it. If the new identities he seems to have created for the three of them haven't fallen apart by now I shouldn't think they're ever going to. We've got to take the letter to the police, I'm sure of that. But unless they tell us they're going to do something I think we're best just letting the others know. And then leaving well alone."

"And after we've shown it to the police, what then? Are we going to hang on to it?"

"I think I'd favour getting rid of it," said Jean. "It was written to Ma and there's no real need to keep it. I wouldn't want someone we don't know getting hold of it."

The letter was still there, in the book. So, as we'd agreed, Jean and I took it down to the police station on Hardman Street, opposite The Phil. It turned out that our mother had indeed informed them about the letter. Just two or three days after it had first arrived.

Because our father's trail was then still quite fresh the police had trawled through all the records of passengers leaving the UK for Europe around Christmas 1949. But they'd drawn a blank. As far as they could tell nobody using the name John Crane had left the United Kingdom between 21st December, 1949, which was the date of our father's disappearance, and 24th January, 1950, the date of the letter. So unless the records were wrong he must already have been using a different name and a false passport. His disappearance had obviously been carefully planned.

The case had never formally been closed but it had been marked as inactive. The Staff Sergeant on the desk at Hardman Street told us that in his view there was no good reason to change that designation and the three of us agreed that things were best left as they were.

Jean and I walked back along Hope Street and up Faulkner Street to St Bride Street where we tore the letter, and the envelope, into small pieces and threw them onto the coal fire.

We stood and watched as they were consumed by the flames.

Dave and I rejoined the Queen Mary as planned on Thursday 11th October, 1956 after our extended shore leave.

Rather than flying home Jean and her family decided to join us. They cancelled their flights and booked themselves a pair of cabins on the Queen Mary's voyage to New York from where they would return to Lancaster by train. Carl had already crossed the Atlantic in a troop ship during the war but it was a voyage Jean had always wanted to make. They both thought it would be a very worthwhile experience for the children. And it goes without saying that Ricky and Susan thought the idea of sailing home on a big ship was brilliant.

The crossing was uneventful and calm. On day three I managed to find time to sit with Jean for half an hour up on the open Sun Deck while Carl was playing deck quoits with the two children. It was eleven in the morning and the autumn weather was perfect. We found ourselves a secluded spot on the port side of the ship and lay back in a pair of steamer chairs, watching the ship's rail as it rose up and down. It was a regular, hypnotic motion which never changed, the varnished, wooden rail moving above and then below the distant horizon on the gentle, Atlantic swell.

At one point I took Jean to the stern of the ship where we stood for five or ten minutes, gazing at the straight, wide furrow which marked our passage across the ocean. Looking down over the stern rail the Queen Mary's quartet of manganese-bronze propellors turned the blue of the sea into a raging, white maelstrom as they drove us at a steady twenty-eight knots towards New York. It was an impressive demonstration of the power of the ship's engines, exerting the same, hypnotic fascination as white-water rapids or a mighty waterfall.

It was with some reluctance that we eventually dragged ourselves away from the mesmerising scene and returned to the comfort of our chairs.

"It's such a shame we weren't able to make it to Liverpool last year," said Jean as we sat there. "I know it couldn't be avoided. But poor Mum. Spending time with Ricky and Susan would have meant so much to her. Did she ever say anything to you about us putting off the visit?"

"No," I said. "Not a word. You know what she was like. She just accepted whatever life threw at her. When things happened they were meant to be and she just got on with it. She knew you and Carl couldn't help it. He had to get himself better and sort out the business. And as far as she was concerned that's all there was to it."

"It's still upsetting," said Jean. "And I suppose Ricky and Susan will never get to know our father either."

"Which may be no bad thing," I said. "They've still got Carl's parents. And having two grandparents has got to be better than none. In previous generations when people tended not to live quite so long they might not even have had that many. And they've met a lot of their Liverpool family. As well as getting to know the city a little bit. So there's lots of positives."

Jean smiled. "Yes. I suppose so."

"And don't forget crossing the Atlantic on a ship like this. That's a big plus. I'd have given my eye teeth to do that when I was their age. I don't think I even went on a Mersey Ferry 'til I was about nine or ten. You needn't worry about Ricky and Susan. They're great kids. And they'll be fine."

"I know," said Jean. "I know."

As we sat in silence for a few minutes gazing at the vast and restless ocean I thought about our mother, down in her secret lair, tracking and analysing the movements of Allied convoys and Nazi U-boats as they navigated these same, but then very hazardous, waters.

"When did Ma tell you about the bunker under Derby House?" I asked Jean. "She never mentioned anything about it to me."

"Just before I first left for America with Carl," said Jean. "She sat me down one day in the parlour and it all came out. She just said she wanted me to know. I got the impression she hadn't even said anything to Dad. She kept insisting that it wasn't anything special and that she didn't want to make a big song and dance about it. She said I could tell other people if I wanted. But not until after she'd gone. Which I suppose is why I decided to talk about it at her funeral. To be honest she didn't really say that much." Jean smiled. "I got the impression the thing she was most keen to tell me about was her little chats with Churchill. I think he knew how to make a lady feel a little bit special, so he might've had a twinkle in his eye. At times like that she probably felt as if she wasn't just a faceless nobody in a huge war machine. But she didn't go into any details."

"She'll have had to sign the Official Secrets Act," I said. "Which would have prevented her saying very much. But you were absolutely right to mention it. I'm really glad people know. It's the sort of thing that deserves to be recognised. Particularly when it's someone like Ma and it's the last thing you'd expect them to have been doing."

"Strange isn't it," said Jean. "Both our parents doing secret stuff in the war that they couldn't talk about."

"I'm sure quite a lot of people were," I said. "And most of them we'll never know about. They were a special generation. They kept us free. But in sixty or seventy years they'll all be gone. And their memories and wisdom will go with them. Future generations will probably end up having to fight the same old battles all over again."

I looked at the ocean on the other side of the ship's rail and gave a wry laugh.

"Makes you want to chuck yourself over the side, doesn't it."

"Don't you dare," said Jean.

The Meyers family took most of their meals in the Main Restaurant, Jean in particular hoping for close encounters with some of the famous names who might be on board. And she was in luck. On the day before we arrived in New York she tracked me down and whispered excitedly that Fred Astaire, one of her favourite Hollywood film stars, had been sitting at the very next table in the restaurant the previous evening. And he had been really nice, chatting away to both Ricky and Susan about Hollywood and film-making. For the two of them he was probably just another, rather talkative, grown-up. But for Jean it was one of the highlights of her voyage.

The big highlight for jazz-enthusiast Carl was meeting the British tenor saxophonist, Ronnie Scott, who was on one of his many transatlantic trips to check out the 52nd Street bebop scene in New York City. Carl's business sometimes took him to 'The Big Apple', the name given to the city by 1920s jazz musicians, so he was able to swap stories with Ronnie Scott about evenings at clubs like The Three Deuces and Birdland.

They were evenings which inspired the British musician to open his own modern jazz club in a small basement in London's Soho in October 1959. He called it Ronnie Scott's. It was the first club in England to feature American jazz musicians such as Dizzy Gillespie, Miles Davis and Buddy Rich.

Jean and Carl were delighted that they had decided to make the transatlantic crossing by ship. It was a great experience for the whole family, and the Queen Mary's arrival at New York was particularly special. The weather was perfect, making it something which none of them would ever forget.

As the mooring ropes were tightened and our ship was safely docked at Pier 90 we said our goodbyes. The family would be disembarking within the hour to catch their train to Lancaster.

As far as I was concerned it seemed that life would be returning to a more settled routine. Until Dave reminded me that there was still Carol to sort out. And that he expected me to conduct the sorting out as diplomatically as possible.

"So you really are going to finish with Carol, are you?" he said.

We were waiting in the now very familiar line to pass yet again through U.S Immigration.

"I think so. It's not fair on Sylvie. And I don't want to risk any further complications. I want to keep everything as simple and straightforward as possible."

"Fair enough," said Dave. "But simple and straightforward mightn't be half as much fun as continuing to see Carol. And anyway, what are you going to say to her?"

"I thought maybe we could just have a quick word with Julie. You know. Ask her to tell Carol."

"We can't do that," said Dave. "That's the coward's way out. You've got to come clean with Carol yourself. Face to face."

I knew he was right. But Carol could be feisty. I wasn't looking forward to the conversation at all.

"I just thought the other way might be easier," I said. "You know. In case Carol takes it badly. She can be quite fiery at times. You were the one who wanted to avoid any unpleasantness."

"Okay," said Dave. "We'll see what happens when we get there."

The line was shuffling forwards quite quickly and we were soon at the front of the queue.

"You go first," said Dave when the uniformed assistant pointed to a free booth. By this time we were both very familiar with the routine. The questions never seemed to change and we had the answers off pat. We were quickly through.

Because of the Queen Mary's rapid turnaround we couldn't hang about so we headed straight for the Salvation Army Thrift Store. Julie was in her usual place by the till.

"Great to see you both again," she said. "I thought you'd given up on me, Dave. I was expecting you a few weeks ago. I've put some more records aside."

Dave gave her a big hug.

"I'm really sorry. Steve and I changed ships. We're now on the Queen Mary not the Media. Which means we won't be in New York for quite so long on each turnaround. Then we had to take some extra shore leave over in England and there wasn't any way of letting you know."

"Complicated," said Julie, giving us her familiar, cheery smile. "But I forgive you. I'm still here."

I caught Dave's eye, wondering if he was planning to tell Julie about my mother. He must have read my mind because, quickly turning away from Julie, he put a finger to his lips and gently shook his head. I realised immediately he was right. Julie had never met my mother. It was best to say nothing. But he had decided to jump straight in and mention Carol.

"I'm afraid we've only got a couple of hours before we're due back on the ship," he said. "Hopefully we'll be able to get a bit longer next time. Steve won't have time to see Carol himself so he was wondering if you could give her a message."

I was just thinking how good Dave was at dealing with such tricky situations when Julie turned to me. She had a serious look on her face and I wondered for a moment exactly what she was about to say.

"I'm really sorry, Steve. But Carol's gone home to Miami. She woke up one morning a couple of weeks ago and said to me New York's too cold and she couldn't cope with another winter here. The next thing I know she's packing her stuff into a big rucksack and heading off to the Greyhound Station. And I haven't heard a thing from her since."

For a couple of seconds I felt a very genuine relief that Carol hadn't been injured in some way, or fallen ill. Then I remembered I should probably do my best to look upset. But it wasn't easy.

Dave could see I was struggling and put a comforting arm round my shoulders.

"Are you okay, Steve?"

"Don't worry," I said. "These things happen. I'll be fine."

"If it's any consolation," said Julie, giving me a grin, "quite a few decent records seem to have come in this time. I'll go get them. Oh, and we've got a couple of very interesting shirts which should cheer you up too. Pure lotus silk. I don't know if you've ever heard of it. I hadn't. But apparently it's one of the most expensive fabrics in the world. The guys who owned them must have had plenty of money. They're not in perfect condition, as you'll see, so you mightn't want them. But I thought I'd let you take a look at them anyway. As I said, they're very interesting. At the very least they'll cheer you up." She grinned at both of us and started laughing. "Wait here."

She went off through the staff door and I turned to Dave.

"What's up with Julie? Is it some kind of a joke?"

He shrugged his shoulders. "No idea. I suppose we'll find out in a minute. But Carol buggering off home to Florida like that is a bit of a bonus. Problem solved." He shook his head and gave me a smile. "You're a jammy sod, you are."

"It's better for you too," I said. "No risk of falling out with Julie."

Just as I was speaking Julie returned, carrying a sturdy paper bag in which were about ten jukebox records. And two shirts. She pulled one of them out of the bag and held it up. It was a very pale cream colour with what looked like expensive, tortoiseshell buttons down the front. Dave and I were about the same size and it looked as though it would fit either of us.

"Lotus silk," she said. "Feel it."

I rubbed the fabric very gently between my fingers and thumb. It was amazingly soft and smooth.

"That's fantastic," I said.

Dave followed suit and nodded his head approvingly at Julie who seemed to be finding our enthusiasm highly amusing.

"What's the other one like?" he asked her.

"Just as nice."

Julie laid the first shirt down on the counter, face up, and took the second one out of the bag. It was the same size and it felt equally luxurious. The colour was perhaps very slightly darker but the buttons were similar.

"How much are they?"

"The boss wants thirty cents for the two."

"Thirty cents?" said Dave. "Are you sure? It seems very cheap. Anyway, no problem. We'll have them."

"Hold on. Before you finally decide you'd better take a good look at them."

Julie was openly laughing now. She placed the second shirt on the counter, also face up.

"Go on then," she said. "Turn them over."

Dave looked at her and did as she suggested.

"Different, eh?" said Julie, continuing to laugh as Dave and I stared at the two shirts. There were three or four, perfectly round, evenly-spaced holes running across the back of each one.

Having finished staring at the shirts we looked at each other and joined Julie in her laughter.

"The blood washed out quite easily," she said. "But we couldn't do anything about the bullet holes. Mr Thompson reckons it was probably an automatic pistol."

Dave spoke first. "What d'you think?"

"We should definitely take them," I said as I continued to laugh. "I mean, unless you take your jacket off no-one's going to see the holes. And it's a great story."

"They came in with a whole load of other stuff from Brooklyn," said Julie. "Park Slope. I've never been there but

I believe it's a place where people tend to shoot first and ask questions later. We've no idea who once owned the shirts. But whoever they were I guess they're unlikely to be needing them again."

I could see that Dave was thinking the same as I was. Joe Zellin's friendly advice about Park Slope was spot on.

But that wasn't going to stop us having the shirts. I gave Julie one dollar and fifty cents which secured us the two unique shirts and all the records.

As we were leaving the store she took me by the arm.

"I'm sorry again about Carol," she said. "I've let a few people know there's a vacancy. So I should have a new flatmate by the time the ship's next over here. I'll introduce you to her."

"Thanks, Julie," I said, giving her a smile. "That'd be great."

She let go of my arm and hugged Dave.

"And as for you," she said. "Just make sure you're on the ship next time she's in. I want to see you as soon as you can get ashore. No more extended leave over in England. Okay?"

We walked slowly back towards the Pier, enjoying the pleasant warmth of the New York autumn.

"I think I'll give Park Slope a miss in future," said Dave.

I turned to him with a grin. "Wise move."

The leaves on the trees were just starting to change. Soon they would take on the spectacular colours of the fall. I looked up at the blue sky and thought of my mother. It was so sad. But life had to go on. She'd have been the first to say so.

We just had time, before reporting for duty, to look through the records. Julie had promised us a few good ones and we weren't disappointed.

In the bag we had 'Long Tall Sally' and 'Rip It Up', both by Little Richard. 'Be-Bop-a-Lula' by Gene Vincent. And 'Blue Suede Shoes' by Carl Perkins, with 'Honey Don't' on the flip-side.

Plus a pair of one hundred percent genuine, New York gangster shirts.

The records were brilliant. If they hadn't already got them we'd pass them on to our friends. And with the addition of a little bit of Scouse magic they would soon be a regular part of the repertoire of almost every Liverpool group.

Teenagers would be dancing to them in youth clubs and church halls across the whole of Merseyside.

What could easily have been a difficult day had turned out well.

SEVENTEEN

TROUBLE

I'd been landed with some extra duties to carry out and had to stay on board when the Queen Mary docked in New York on the first day in November, but Dave was granted a few hours' shore leave which he told me he'd naturally be spending at Julie's place in Greenwich Village.

When he got back to the ship he should have been relaxed and happy. But he wasn't. His face was pale. He was agitated and not at all like his normal self.

"I've got to speak to you, Steve. Not now. But soon. In The Pig. What time do you finish?"

"Most of the passengers won't be boarding until tomorrow," I said. "There's no band or late-night dancing in the Verandah so it shouldn't be late. If Tommy's in a good mood I should be able to get away by eleven."

"Okay. I'll see you just after. In The Pig."

Dave was obviously very worried. Something must have happened. The Grill was quiet so I spent most of the evening trying to work out what it might be. It was just after eleven when Tommy told me I could go. And when I got to The Pig Dave was sitting on his own, empty tankard in hand. His face was still just as pale.

"I'll get you another beer," I said. "You still look as though you've seen a ghost. We were very quiet up in the Grill but I had a couple of slightly tricky customers who we've not seen up there before. They didn't like anything that was on offer and after a lot of argy-bargy they settled for plain fillet steaks with chips which looked absolutely delicious. They were obviously the sort of people who are only happy when they're unhappy, you know the type, and they flounced off saying they were going straight to The Purser to get the Verandah charge removed from their account. They'll probably put in a complaint about me as well. But Tommy saw it all and he'll stick up for me. Anyway, that's enough about me. What are you having? Another pint?"

Passing me his tankard Dave nodded his head and I went over to the bar. Once it had been refilled I picked one up for myself and returned to the table.

"Okay," I said as I sat down. "First of all, how were things with Julie?"

"Fine, thanks. We had a great time. She understood that our swap to the Queen Mary would change things a bit, but she was okay about it. She's great. I like her a lot. It's just a shame we can't see more of each other."

"And what about her new flatmate? Not that I'm really interested."

"She moves in next week. But I told Julie you were getting very serious about a French girl in Liverpool so you probably wouldn't want to meet up with her. And that's not a problem."

"Great. So, what's bugging you?"

"Didn't I tell you things always come in threes?" he said, leaning towards me over the table to make his point. "And you refused to believe me. Well, here's number three. I think I'm being blackmailed."

"What?"

"No. Sorry Steve, that's wrong. I don't just think I'm

being blackmailed. I'm one hundred percent sure I'm being blackmailed."

"Come on, Dave. Don't be daft. What's the problem?"

"I'm not being daft," he said. "I'm dead serious. I was on my way back to the ship from Julie's in Greenwich Village. And I'd just got to the top of the steps. You know. The ones out of the subway at 50th. And all of a sudden I noticed these two men. And they seemed to be following me. I told myself not to be stupid. That I must be imagining it. So I started to walk a bit quicker. And they kept up with me. And then when I slowed down a bit they slowed down too. So I knew I was right."

Dave wiped his lips with his right hand. He looked really worried.

"Then, just as I got to the bottom of 50th. The place where you have to wait at the lights to cross over 12th to get to the Pier. Well, as I was waiting the two of them came up alongside me. One on each side. That was when I realised the one on my left was Spike from Park Slope. You know. The guy Eddie sent me to see and I got the stockings off. The other one I didn't recognise. He didn't say anything. He just kept his right hand in his coat pocket, holdin' onto something which looked like it was a gun. So it could've been the guy with the gun from Park Slope. But I'm not sure."

I think I knew what was coming. Joe Zellin had said it might happen.

"So, what did Eddie's friend, Spike, want?"

"He said he had a package for Eddie. Just a small one which'd fit in a jacket pocket so it'd be no problem gettin' it through Customs. Eddie was expecting it and he'd meet me off the ship. And that he'd be very grateful. Which I took to mean there might be some sort of payment when the package got delivered. But I didn't actually ask. It all happened so quickly and I wasn't thinkin' straight. This guy, Spike, was very friendly when we met in Park Slope. But he was different this time. There was something about the way he was lookin' at me that said he wouldn't take it all that kindly if I said no."

"So, what did you say?"

"By this time I was panicking. And even though I was terrified I sort of tried to say no. But Spike said I was the only person who could help him. That this package had to get to Eddie by the end of the week and the only way was on our ship. He told me he knew people and if I didn't help him Cunard might find out about the stockings. And the whole time I kept seeing those shirts with the bullet holes across the back. Honest, Steve, I was standin' there wettin' myself."

"He was bluffing," I said. "How's he going to make trouble for you with Cunard? And anyway, are they really going to be that bothered over a few pairs of stockings from ages ago?"

"Yeah, I know. But as I said, I kept seein' those shirts. And the bullet holes. And the other guy. The one I didn't know if I'd seen before or not. He kept twitching and looking down at his coat pocket. I'm sure it was a gun he had in there, Steve. I just didn't want to take any chances."

"So you agreed?"

Dave nodded his head miserably.

"When Spike showed me the package it wasn't much bigger than a man's wallet. And I thought the best thing would be to take it off him. You know. Bring it on board. And then worry about what to do with it later. The security guys at the gangway don't do much in the way of checks unless you're carrying bags. So I just slipped it in my jacket pocket and walked on. I've stashed it away in my locker for now."

"What's in it?"

"I don't know. It's all sealed up. Spike said I wasn't to open it. And that Eddie'd know if I tried."

"So, what're you going to do?"

"I'm not sure. I was hopin' you might have a few bright ideas."

I sat there in silence for a few moments, thinking.

"I honestly don't know, Dave," I said eventually. "A hundred pairs of stockings is one thing. But this package could be anything. It must be important if Spike and his friends are so keen to get it to Eddie. It could be a drug sample for Eddie to check out the quality. I think that's the sort of thing they sometimes do. Or maybe it's precious stones. Also to get checked out. You can get a lot of loose diamonds into a package the size of a wallet."

Dave's expression told me I wasn't making him feel any better. But if we were going to talk it through we had to be honest with each other.

"And if it is something like precious stones," I continued, "or especially if it's drugs, it's a massive risk. If you're caught taking that sort of stuff through Customs you can go down for years. And you can't say you didn't know what is was. The law says you're supposed to know what you're carrying ashore. And if you're not sure you've got to declare it. Otherwise everyone'd be smuggling serious stuff in and saying they didn't know what it was."

Dave looked at me.

"So, what d'you reckon?"

"It's a massive risk."

"I know. You just said that. But what else can I do?"

"What about leaving the package where it is until we're in the middle of the Atlantic and then chuck it over the side. At least you'd be rid of it."

"And say what to Eddie? That I lost it. And what then? I don't think Eddie'd be likely to do anything worse than have me beaten up. At least not in England. But he'd have to tell his friends in New York that I never gave him the package. And I got the impression they wouldn't think twice about doing me some very serious damage. The next time I set foot in New York I could end up full of holes."

"Okay," I said. "So what about if you go and see one of the officers on the ship and come clean? Tell them you're being blackmailed and give them the package. Let them sort it out."

"I've thought of that," said Dave. "But what if it is something like drugs and Cunard do me for bringing the package onto the ship. Or for smuggling the stockings. And even if they decided to let me off, Eddie's New York friends would still be very unhappy. And I don't think those guys mess about."

Poor Dave looked beaten.

"Honest, Steve, I've been through all the options and I think I'm snookered. I've got to take the risk and get the package to Eddie."

"And then what?" I said. "They'll just come back for more. They'll blackmail you again. As Joe said, that's how it works."

"Yeah. But if I take this one chance. You know. Take the package through and give it to Eddie. After that I can tell Cunard I'm jackin' my job in. I'll be no use to Eddie and his friends if I'm not working on the ships. They'll have to find some other poor sod to do their dirty work. Then all I need to do is steer clear of New York for a while. Give 'em time to forget about me."

I didn't know what to say. I knew he was probably right. The people who'd got their hooks into him were ruthless. And although we didn't know exactly what was in the package it could very easily be part of a big deal where serious money was at stake.

What Dave was planning should work. And I honestly couldn't think of anything better.

When we docked at Southampton Dave walked the package through Customs without any problem and Eddie was waiting as arranged. Whatever it was that he had reluctantly transported from New York, it was important enough for Eddie to have made the journey down from Liverpool to make sure it didn't go astray.

Dave handed the precious package over to him, along with a string of suitable obscenities, and pocketed a wad of notes in return. The money would help to tide him over until he could get himself another job.

Then the two of us jumped on a train back to Liverpool. And went straight to the Cunard Building so Dave could hand in his resignation.

It was very sad.

We'd expanded our youthful horizons together. And learnt a lot as we'd gone along.

I wondered what he'd do next. After more than two years at sea it wouldn't be easy to settle for a routine life back in Liverpool. Like me he'd been lucky enough to see the world beyond the River Mersey and the Irish Sea. He knew how much it had to offer.

•·•————•·•·•·•————·•·•

"Good morning," I whispered to her as Sylvie opened her eyes. "Are you okay?"

"Yes. I'm fine," she said sleepily. "This bed's really comfy."

My two uncles were men of the world. I can't say that they actually approved of Sylvie sharing my bed but the house rules were now more flexible and relaxed. Neither of them were ever going to say anything.

Sylvie stretched her arms out as I gave her a kiss.

"I had a really good sleep. I'm going to stay here more often."

She turned over and smiled at me with her blue eyes.

"If you don't mind, that is."

"I don't mind at all. You can stay here as often as you like. I'm just sorry that with me spending so much time away at sea it won't be as often as I'd really like."

"We'll manage somehow," she said.

She lifted up the sensuously smooth, silk nightdress which I'd brought home for her from New York and, reaching over her shoulders, she slipped it off.

"We'll just have to make the most of every opportunity we get."

I was already naked and I could feel my heart starting to beat faster as Sylvie knelt up and placed one leg each side of my hips. With her arms held tightly by her side she lifted her head slightly which allowed me to take in her beautifully soft and perfectly proportioned body. Then, taking hold of my wrists, she pushed them down onto the bed.

Afterwards Sylvie lay beside me with her eyes closed, breathing slowly as she ran her fingers over her lower abdomen.

"That was wonderful," I whispered, kissing her cheek. "You certainly know how to excite me."

She opened her eyes.

"I could say the same about you. It just gets better every time."

"One more night before I have to report back to the ship," I said. "Do you want to stay over?"

Taking hold of my hair Sylvie pulled me towards her and kissed me on the lips.

"Just you try and stop me."

EIGHTEEN

MANNY'S MUSIC

Dave walked down to Lime Street Station with me when I caught the train which would take me back to the Queen Mary in Southampton. He told me that Eddie hadn't been happy when he realised he was going to have to rethink his plans. But Liverpool wasn't like New York. Whoever Eddie was working with in England it was very unlikely that they routinely tooled themselves up with guns. Violence happened. But it usually tended to be of a slightly less lethal kind.

Although he no longer feared for his life Dave was well aware that settling for a humdrum existence in Liverpool wouldn't be easy.

"It's going to be tough, Steve. I'm sure I've made the right decision. I couldn't risk goin' back to New York. But I'll miss the life on board. And all the lads. And Julie too. Make sure you see her so she knows what's happened."

"Don't worry. It'll be the first thing I do when I get to New York. I'm hoping she'll still hang onto those records. Even though you sadly won't be there to supply the little extras."

"Don't worry. You can tell her I'll be back one day. And remember me to all the guys on board as well."

Dave stood at the end of the platform and I gave him one

last wave as the train pulled out of the station. Then, as it took the slow curve into the Edge Hill cutting, he disappeared from view.

We had lived in each other's pockets since we were small kids.

I was going to miss him.

The routines of life aboard the Queen Mary soon lifted my mood. We departed from Southampton on schedule and our passengers were in high spirits. Many were heading home to spend Christmas 1956 with their families in America, while others were excited at the prospect of enjoying the festive season in New York City and joining thousands of others in Times Square to celebrate the start of another year. As we left the English Channel behind and embarked on our four-day passage across the ocean, following the traditional Grand Circle route to the eastern seaboard of America, the ship was in party mode.

Over the next few days most of our passengers would be completely cut off from the outside world. A wealthy few might send and receive telegrams, but with no personal telephones or other mobile communication devices available to the majority their world would be defined by the steel hull of the ship which protected them from the hostile ocean. Sharing this space, and with nowhere else to go, the passengers would get to know one another. New friendships would quickly be forged and old acquaintances would be renewed.

For members of the crew like myself the experience of being at sea was different. The Queen Mary wasn't a relatively brief escape from everyday life. She was our home and our workplace. She restrained us and sometimes upset us. She protected and controlled us. We were as dependent upon her as she was upon us. For as long we were together, out on the ocean, she was our mother.

One of the attractions of life at sea tends to be its unhurried simplicity. Everyday life on land can be complicated but at sea things tend to be calmer and less hectic. There are regular, daily routines which do not change. Life is simple. And the further you sail from land, the less important the complexities of the outside world seem to become.

We always had a few passengers on board the Queen Mary who had booked a return Atlantic crossing simply for the pleasure of the voyage. Some had made the crossing and visited New York City many times. For such travellers the gentle rhythm of sea days was so seductive that they very often chose to remain on board for the whole time the ship was berthed at Pier 90. The quiet routines of shipboard life were more appealing than the hustle and bustle of a large metropolis. Even the many and varied attractions of a city like New York could not tempt them ashore.

In December the weather in the North Atlantic can often be wild and this voyage was no different. The first ten days of the month had been dull and mild, with thick cloud cover and very little sunshine. But then things changed. A low pressure system was developing in the mid-Atlantic and Tommy told me that one of the ship's officers had said a gust of wind, measured at an unusually strong 110 mph, had been recorded on December 12th at Stornoway in the Western Isles of Scotland.

By the time the Queen Mary was south of Greenland, an increasingly powerful storm was whipping up the sea and creating a noticeable, and very uncomfortable, swell. As we continued west the waves increased in size and we ran into squalls of torrential rain which gradually turned to sleet. The outside air temperature dropped to freezing, making the visibility very poor.

Having been designed and built by Cunard for the North Atlantic, the Queen Mary was exceptionally good in such heavy seas, slicing through and riding even the biggest of waves and seeming hardly to notice them. The early problems with excessive rolling had been completely cured but her bow would still, very occasionally, hit a particularly large or awkward wave at an angle that would send a shudder through the whole ship.

Because of the conditions the Captain gave the order to restrict access to the outside decks. Passengers who had donned cold weather gear in their cabins, expecting to take their usual, brisk morning walk on the open Sun Deck, found their way barred by yellow and black tapes marked with the words **'DANGER – DECK CLOSED – DO NOT PASS'.** Even though they were sailing on one of the world's great ocean liners, a glance outside quickly told them why the decision had been made. They would have to settle for circuits of the sheltered Promenade Deck, protected from the foul weather by its thick, plate-glass windows.

The high winds continued for almost twenty four hours and the ship's movements became very uncomfortable for those on board who were not good sailors. Empty chairs started to appear around the tables in the ship's various restaurants and the Verandah Grill, being high up on the ship and therefore subject to more movement, was often almost deserted. The Queen Mary's chefs were rightly proud of the quality and variety of dishes which they were able to offer at every meal, but even those passengers who were relatively unaffected by the weather found that their appetites were not quite as hearty as usual.

To everyone's relief, as we approached the rich fishing grounds to the east of Newfoundland known as the Grand Banks, the wind dropped and the sea became calmer. Appetites were quickly restored and the excitement on board the Queen Mary as we neared the end of our voyage was once again palpable.

At just before eight in the morning on Thursday 13th December, 1956 the last pair of mooring ropes were pulled tight by the powerful capstans on board and our great ship was once again safely berthed alongside Pier 90. There were only eleven shopping days to go until Christmas and New York City was buzzing.

As soon as I was able to get ashore I kept my promise to Dave and went along to see Julie at the Thrift Store. When I walked in through the door and Dave failed to follow me she immediately thought the worst.

"Where's Dave?" she said, looking worried as I approached the till on my own. "Wouldn't they let him ashore?"

There was no point in beating about the bush.

"I'm really sorry, Julie, but I'm afraid he's still in Liverpool. He asked me to tell you he won't be back in New York for a while."

Her reaction was unexpected. I'd assumed that for both of them their relationship was just a bit of fun. But I could see that Julie was blinking back tears and I suddenly realised that under the surface she wasn't the tough New York cookie I'd automatically imagined her to be.

"Come here," I said, putting my arms around her. "Look. There's nothing Dave would love more than to be here with you right now. But he's run into a problem. And he's had to give up his job with Cunard."

"Why?" Julie looked up at me. Her eyes were now full of tears. "He always said he couldn't imagine anything better than life at sea. And being able to spend time with me."

I didn't want to go into all the details about the package which the gangsters from Park Slope had blackmailed Dave into taking to England for Eddie. Mainly because I was pretty sure, for her own sake, that the less Julie knew the better.

"It's complicated," I said, "but Dave has good reason to think that some people here in New York might want to do him serious harm. Maybe even kill him. So he'll have to stay away from the city until he knows it's safe again."

"I don't understand," she said. "Why would anybody want to harm Dave? What's he done?"

"It's nothing terrible," I said. "And it's not his fault. But some pretty unpleasant people over here were trying to blackmail him into doing something illegal. Smuggling stuff over to England. Which he didn't want to do. And they didn't like it when he said no."

"So how soon will he be able to come back?"

"I'm not sure," I said. "I realise it's not what you want to hear, but I don't think Dave knows either. All I can say is he'll be back as soon as he possibly can. The last thing he said when he saw me off at Lime Street Station in Liverpool was that he was going to miss New York. And that he was going to miss you even more. He made me promise that I'd come and see you as soon as I got here and explain everything."

As I'd been speaking a few tears had started to run down Julie's cheeks but she quickly wiped them away with the back of her hand.

"Thanks Steve." She gave me a slightly sad smile. "Tell Dave it's okay. I'll be fine."

Her cheeks were damp but she was blinking to clear her eyes and most of the tears had already gone. The tough New York cookie was taking back control.

"No problem," I said. "I'll let him know. And can I tell him you'll still put a few records on one side for him as well? I think he'd like it, knowing they were coming from you."

"As long those records bring in a little bit of the money we need to help our clients we don't care who buys them. So if Dave still wants them they're his. In fact I'll go get you the latest batch right now."

I couldn't tell what she was feeling on the inside, but on the outside Julie was already back to her normal self. When I'd paid for the records and was about to leave I gave her a big hug.

"That's from Dave," I said.

She laughed and managed a smile.

My next stop was Manny's Music Store at 120 West 48th Street, between 6th and 7th Avenues, not far from the iconic Radio City Music Hall. Manny's was just one of a number of musical instrument retailers on that stretch of 48th Street. Rudy's, We Buy Guitars, Alex Music and Sam Ash, along with others that had come and gone. They had all clustered together there one time or another. For the many musicians, known and unknown, who had found their way to New York City over the years it wasn't West 48th Street. It was Music Row. And as I headed east along 48th I couldn't miss my destination. A huge neon sign with a large clockface beneath it said quite simply '*MANNY'S*'.

Manny Goldrich, who had started life as a saxophone salesman, first opened the doors of Manny's Musical Instruments and Accessories back in 1935. He was a cautious man so he started small. His original store was just twenty feet by twenty feet. But he kept his prices low. And as the years passed and his reputation grew the shop gradually expanded to occupy the whole building.

A violinist on the Queen Mary, who played in one of the six or seven highly professional bands that entertained the passengers, told me that Manny's had the best range of instruments in New York. And the best prices. It was the only place to go if I wanted to buy a guitar.

Music Row was within easy walking distance of the Piers so quite a lot of the Cunard Yanks from the various ships went there regularly. A few called in every time they were in New York. The instruments in all the music stores were significantly cheaper than back home. And most of the ones made by the top American companies like Gibson and Fender were quite simply unobtainable in England. Even in London.

Being too bulky to hide, the guitars and other musical items which were purchased were quite openly lugged through Customs on the ship's return to England. If the Customs Officers could be persuaded that the items were for personal use, a task which the average Scouser would not expect to find too difficult, they might not insist on any significant duty being paid. And even if duty turned out to be payable the instruments were still much cheaper than at home.

After getting home to Liverpool the Cunard Yank might convince himself that the guitar, or trumpet, or saxophone, was not quite what he wanted. So it would have to be sold, for cash, to a member of one of the groups that were sprouting up on Merseyside. The price was fair, but the profit would still be very healthy.

Before joining Cunard I'd quite often wandered into Hessy's or Rushworth's, the two most popular musical instrument retailers in Liverpool, to while away a bit of time looking at their wares. Frank Hessy tended to stock the widest choice of guitars, and he employed a man called Jim Gretty, a middle-aged and very experienced jazz, as well as country and western, guitarist. Jim Gretty's job was to demonstrate to potential buyers how very easy Mr Hessy's instruments were to play. Jim was a very fine guitarist and he certainly made it look easy. He had done his best on several occasions to persuade me to buy one of his employer's guitars. But I'd never taken the plunge.

At Manny's it would be different.

In comparison with Hessy's and Rushworth's the range and quantity of guitars and other musical instruments in his store was staggering. The post-war import restrictions imposed by the British Government to support UK-based manufacturers had simply served to starve music retailers of stock. The few companies in Britain who made guitars couldn't hope to compete with names like Rickenbacker and Fender, Gibson and Gretsch.

Manny's guitar-room was upstairs. Hanging on the wall were Rickenbacker Combos, Fender Broadcasters, Telecasters and Stratocasters, Gibson Les Pauls, and Gretsch Duo Jets, along with beautiful acoustic guitars by esteemed makers such as Martin and Epiphone.

Elsewhere in the store I could see bass guitars, banjos and mandolins.

I was no musician, but even so I was entranced. For a real musician, visiting Manny's would be like being a small kid again and walking into a sweet shop. The temptation to try out as many instruments as possible would be overwhelming.

Buddy Holly, it is said, called it his favourite place in the whole city.

To counter such urges Manny Goldrich had come up with a very simple rule. 'If you try it, you buy it.'

It wasn't realistic of course. No serious musician was going to spend good money on an instrument without trying several out first. As Jim Gretty had once said to me in Hessy's, "You've got to try them out, Steve. Guitars are like ladies. Two guitars may look the same. But when you sit them on your knee they feel completely different."

Manny was very well aware of that simple fact. But if you wanted to sit one of his guitars on your knee you had to convince him that you were a serious buyer and not some kid off the street looking to waste a bit of time by messing around with his precious merchandise.

A well-known fixture at Manny's was 'Old Yellow', an ancient and battered Danelectro guitar. It had left the factory black, but along with some other instruments, including a pink trombone and a jet black drum kit, it had been customised sometime in the distant past for a commercial photo-shoot at the store. The whole guitar, not just the body but also the neck, the fretboard and the headstock, had been painted in bright yellow. Once the shoot was over Manny had purchased all the now-unwanted instruments for a few dollars. Some went in the window to brighten up the display. But the mustard-yellow Danelectro he left out on the floor.

From that day on any musician, no matter how eminent or well-known, who wanted to try out an amplifier or other guitar accessory at Manny's had to use 'Old Yellow'.

In the years after my visit, numerous guitarists, many of them world-famous, would sit 'Old Yellow' on their knee in Manny's guitar-room and run their hands up and down her neck and over her body.

When the Beatles were at their peak George Harrison called in to see Manny, asking if he could buy her. As did Eric Clapton. According to Manny, George and Eric had similar tastes. Pattie Boyd was not the only lady who was able to trigger their passion.

What tales 'Old Yellow' could tell.

I showed Manny my cash and managed to persuade him that I was a serious buyer even though I didn't have the ability to play a single chord, or even the most rudimentary of tunes, on any of his beautiful instruments. I told myself it was the feel that mattered. And after handling a few of the guitars I found one that felt right. Just like Ivan, who sold his New York Gretsch to George Harrison in suburban Liverpool a few years later, I'd fallen for a beautiful, black Duo Jet.

I had yet to learn how to make music with such a wonderful instrument. But sitting down with the Duo Jet on my knee she appealed to me. Lacking the ability to play her I could do little more than feel the silky-smooth, mahogany neck and press each of the six strings firmly against the hard, rosewood fingerboard with my fingers while stroking the guitar's shiny and dark body gently with my right hand.

"She feels very light," I said to Manny. "I thought she'd be heavier."

He smiled at me.

"A Gibson Les Paul is heavy," he said. "But with the Duo Jet Gretsch have done something remarkable. They've created hollow chambers in the solid, mahogany body and fronted them with laminated maple. It enhances the tone as well as making the guitar lighter. And I noticed that just now you said 'she'. You are right. The Duo Jet has qualities which are not apparent at first sight. Just like a good woman. For less than three hundred dollars you will have a lifelong companion. And I promise that you will grow to love her even more as you get to know her better."

The violinist on the ship had warned me to be careful. Manny Goldrich was a master salesman and he had me well and truly hooked. But I didn't care. He had given me exactly what I was looking for.

Manny always offered a generous discount to Cunard Yanks so it was just two hundred and fifty-nine dollars that changed hands. I was the proud owner of a Gretsch Duo Jet.

There might be a little bit of duty to pay when I got back to Southampton.

But it was still a bargain.

NINETEEN

PLAYING ALONG

Once I'd got it back to Liverpool the Gretsch Duo Jet sat in its case in my room at St Bride Street for several weeks, waiting for my next long shore leave. To do full justice to such a beautiful instrument I needed some lessons. So it wasn't until late February that I had time to go along to see Jim Gretty at Hessy's, taking the Duo Jet with me.

Frank Hessy's guitar shop was right in the city centre, just off Whitechapel. It was still quite early so I took a detour past the Empire Theatre and the Walker Art Gallery before heading towards the Mersey along Dale Street. A left turn before reaching the Town Hall took me down North John Street from where I cut through Mathew Steet, a narrow, cobbled back-street with tall, dark warehouses on each side. It ran behind the Liverpool Fruit Exchange in Victoria Street and the whole area was bustling with activity. Groups of men were unloading crates of fruit from parked lorries onto small handcarts and then hurrying off to one or other of the warehouses.

About a third of the way down the street on the right, next to a warehouse belonging to a wholesale fruit merchant, Fell & Co, I noticed a roller-shutter door with a metal surround. Above the entrance were written the words *'THE CAVERN'*. Unlike other similar doorways in the street the shutter looked newly painted and I was pretty sure it hadn't been like that last time I'd walked past.

Two men in suits who appeared to be in their early twenties were standing alongside the doorway, smoking and chatting. They seemed to be a little out of place, surrounded as they were by all the bustling activity, and my curiosity got the better of me.

"Excuse me," I said as I approached them. "I hope you don't mind me asking, but do you know what this place '*THE CAVERN*' is? I've not noticed it before."

They looked at each other and one of them shrugged his shoulders.

"It's a jazz club," he said. "Down in the cellar under the fruit warehouse. We opened a couple of weeks ago." He reached into the inside pocket of his suit jacket and handed me a business card. "Come along one evening if you're interested. We're open most nights from about eight. And bring your friends."

His companion looked at the guitar case I was carrying.

"If that smart case is anything to go by you've got a nice guitar in there. We might be able to offer you some work if you're in a band. But it has to be jazz. We don't want to be attracting all sorts of riff-raff to the club by putting on rock 'n' roll and that sort of rubbish. We sometimes allow skiffle because it originated as a sort of poor man's jazz in the American South. But it's got to be good. And I'll confess that we've agreed to let Lonnie Donegan's fan club meet him here in the club when he's playing The Empire with his skiffle group towards the end of May. Mainly because they're paying us good money for the use of the space. And when you've just started a new business every little helps. We thought we might be able to get a bit of free publicity as well. We're doing our best to persuade one of the photographers from the Echo to come down here. Lonnie's got one of those big, long American cars. If we can get him to park it here in Mathew Street it'll stretch half-way to Bootle. It'd make a great picture."

"The Echo'd love that," I said, laughing. "And thanks for the offer of work. But I've only just got the guitar. I'm hoping Jim Gretty down at Hessy's might be able to give me a couple of lessons."

"Okay. Well, good luck. And if you want to hear some good jazz you know where to come."

I looked at the business card he'd given to me.

Alan Sytner
The Cavern Club, Mathew Street, Liverpool
The Home of Jazz in the North-West

"So you're Alan Sytner?"

The young man nodded. "That's me. And my friend here is Keith. Keith Hemmings. We started the club together. I came up with the idea after seeing a jazz club called *'LE CAVEAU DE LA HUCHETTE'* in a basement in Paris. I thought something similar might do well here in Liverpool. And up to now it seems to be working out okay. We're just waiting for some builders who are supposed to be doing a bit of work on the drains and typically they're twenty minutes late already."

His friend, Keith, looked at his watch.

"Let's give them five more minutes, Alan. And then call it a day."

It was my cue to move on.

"I'm Steve by the way. Nice to have met you both. I'll let people know about your new club. And I might see you down there myself."

Five or six minutes later I was standing outside Hessy's Music Centre gazing at the assembly of guitars and other musical instruments which were displayed behind the angled windows on each side of the door. It wasn't quite Manny's, but for a store in a provincial English city which must have been struggling with import restrictions the display was impressive.

Window-gazing done I went inside. To the left of the entrance just inside the door an attractive young assistant was standing behind a glazed, display counter.

"Hello," she said. "Can I help you?"

I lifted up the mottled-brown case which contained my precious Duo Jet so she could see it.

"I've just brought this guitar back from New York and I'm looking for someone who might be able to give me some lessons."

She smiled. I was obviously not the first customer to turn up on such a quest.

"I'm Thelma. But you'd best have a word with Jim Gretty. He knows all about guitars. That's him, down there at the back of the shop."

She pointed towards a man who I recognised. Wearing an off-white, short-sleeved shirt with loose grey trousers, and sitting on a stool, he was playing a semi-acoustic, electric guitar which he had resting on his knee.

"Thanks," I said. "I'm Steve. I've spoken to Jim about guitars a couple of times in the past."

"Let's go and have a word then," said Thelma.

As I followed Thelma through the shop Jim Gretty continued to pluck the strings with his fingers. He was leaning forwards over his guitar, swaying gently from side to side in a world of his own as a lazy, country and western melody emerged from the light-blue, Watkins Westminster amplifier into which his instrument was plugged.

"A little job for you, Jim," she said. He stopped playing and lifted up his head. "Steve here is in need of some lessons on a guitar he's brought back from New York."

"That's fine, love," said Jim, looking me up and down. "Leave it with me."

He stood up and placed his guitar on a stand. There was a loud click from the speaker as he bent down and switched off the amplifier.

"Okay young Steve. We've chatted before, I think. And now you've bought yourself a guitar in New York instead of coming to me. Let's take a look at it."

I clicked open the six fastenings on the hard case and opened it up before very carefully lifting the Duo Jet out of its protective cocoon.

Jim Gretty let out a gentle whistle of approval.

"A Gretsch Duo Jet, eh. We don't see many of those over here in Liverpool. In fact I've only ever seen one before. It belongs to a bloke called Ivan. He's one of the Cunard Yanks and just like you he brought it home from New York. He plays the occasional gig with a pal off the ship when they're on leave and he had it with him at The Locarno over Christmas. So I'm guessing you must be a sailor too."

"Yeah," I said, nodding my head. "I'm on the Queen Mary. Sailing to New York out of Southampton."

"It'd have to be New York," said Jim. "Or just possibly Hamburg. You can't get hold of guitars like that here in England. Do you mind if I see what it's like? I've never played one but they've got a really good reputation."

I handed my precious guitar to him and he sat down again on his stool. After plugging it into his Watkins, and adjusting the tuning on a couple of the strings, he began to play a solo instrumental version of 'Summertime' from Porgy and Bess. In his expert hands the Duo Jet sounded every bit as good as I'd hoped it might.

"Very nice," said Jim, as he finished the Gershwin tune with a little flourish. "Very nice indeed."

He switched off the amplifier and handed the guitar back to me.

"So you want some lessons," he said. "How long have you been playing?"

"I haven't," I replied. "This is my first guitar. That's why I need some help."

"That's one heck of an instrument to have as your first guitar," said Jim, shaking his head and smiling. "You're a lucky boy. Let's hope you've got a bit of natural talent otherwise it'll be wasted on you. A guitar like that does give you one big advantage though. The better a guitar is, the easier it usually is to play. Most beginners start off with a cheap Spanish guitar that's a bit of a nightmare even for someone who's been playing for a while. So they struggle and get discouraged. The good news for you is you've hit the jackpot with that Gretsch. The fretboard isn't too narrow and the action is exceptionally forgiving. That means it's nice and easy to press the strings against the metal frets on the fingerboard."

"So will you be able to give me some lessons? The problem is I'm away at sea a lot of the time. So I won't be able to get along all that often."

"I mostly play jazz," said Jim. "And country and western. But hopefully it's skiffle or rock 'n' roll that you've got in mind. They're a lot less complicated than jazz. If you're prepared to put in a bit of practice you should be able to teach yourself that sort of music. Some of the guitarists in the pop groups you see on TV are self-taught and they can only play about half a dozen chords. Sometimes not even that. And they manage to get away with it. The thing is Mr Hessy employs me in the shop here to help him sell guitars. So he likes me to restrict my lessons to people who've bought one of his."

He picked up his guitar and switched the Watkins amplifier on again before pulling a plectrum out of his pocket.

"Okay. Have a listen. This is just three simple chords. A, D and E."

I watched and listened as he played a few bars of *'Be-Bop-a-Lula'*. It didn't look all that hard.

The amplifier was switched off again and the guitar was put back on its stand.

"Okay," said Jim. "The first thing I need to point out is that your Duo Jet is a great guitar. But it's not much use to you without an amplifier. Unless you've already got one?"

I shook my head.

"No."

"It only needs to be a small one. Nothing too expensive or fancy. A practice amp might be your best bet. They're designed to be played at a low volume so you don't disturb other people when you're learning. I can fix you up with a decent one for less than fifteen quid. At that price it won't be new. But it'll be in good condition. And it'll do the job. If you want to pay a bit more we can do hire purchase. What do you think? Shall we take a look at what we've got in?"

In less than fifteen minutes we'd selected a nice, second-hand amplifier, a Selmer Truvoice:TV6. It wasn't really a practice amplifier but Jim said it'd be fine. Covered in a red and cream material with a white carrying-handle, the price was very reasonable. So there was no need for hire purchase. And Jim very kindly told me that since I'd bought the amplifier he'd stretch the rules and give me half-a-dozen lessons. Just to get me going. And throw in a used copy of a slim booklet by a guitarist called Bert Weedon.

It was called *'Play in a Day'*. In Jim's opinion the title was optimistic.

"*'Play In Three to Six Months'* might have been a more honest title," he said with a smile. "I get quite a lot of would-be, virtuoso guitarists turning up here asking me to take back a guitar they bought from me just a couple of weeks earlier. And they bring the book back too, telling me it's useless. But if you give it enough time you'll get there."

I was listening. And I hoped he was right.

"When you're lucky enough to have a beautiful guitar like that," he said, looking again at the Duo Jet, "it'd be a crime if you didn't teach yourself to play it."

A few minutes later Frank Hessy himself, short and serious in a well-worn, dark blue suit, watched carefully as I handed over the cash. He scribbled out a receipt and handed over what was now my amplifier.

Once I was back on the ship every spare moment was spent practising. It was hard work. Until they started to harden off the ends of my fingers were red raw from long hours of pressing them against the metal strings as I tried to work out how to move quickly from chord to chord and play some of the hit records of the day. As Jim Gretty had said, many of them needed only three chords. But getting even three chords to sound good was a struggle. Some days it felt like I'd never succeed but from time to time there were faint glimmers of hope as a particularly stubborn and difficult chord slowly started to sound the way it should.

'Play in a Day' was indeed optimistic. But Bert Weedon's slim booklet told me what I needed to know. I suppose if he'd given it a less optimistic title very few of the thousands of budding musicians who helped to make it one of the biggest-selling guitar tutors of all time would have purchased it. There must be some very wealthy guitar players who can thank Bert for their millions. But hopefully he did okay out of the book.

I owe him too. After a few months of looking at his chord diagrams and trying to hold my fingers in the right place I'd mastered the basics.

I was never going to be the next Les Paul or Chet Atkins. But

I was able to play straightforward skiffle. Along with a few of the easier rock 'n' roll numbers.

Be-Bop-a-Lula!

TWENTY

THE CAVERN

In the spring of 1957 I was on leave for twelve days, the Queen Mary having docked in Southampton early on the morning of the 23rd of May. I hadn't seen Dave for over a month. I also hadn't taken up Alan Sytner's suggestion that I should give his jazz club in Mathew Street a try.

To kill two birds with one stone I called in on Dave and suggested a night out together so we could catch up. A visit to The Cavern seemed as good a bet as any. He was free, and according to the Liverpool Echo there were three bands playing there on the 24th, which was Friday night. The Muskrat Jazz Band were the topping the bill. And they were being backed up by two local skiffle groups, the Gin Mill Skiffle Group and the Ravin' Texans.

The entrance to The Cavern hadn't changed, the only difference being that the roller-shutter door was now open. The metal casing which surrounded the doorway gave it a rather forbidding appearance, but at the same time it was enticing. There was the unspoken promise of something different, something exciting, in the darkness beyond.

Dave led the way down a steep and narrow set of eighteen stone steps from which we emerged into a cellar with an arched, brick-built roof, supported by a series of substantial brick pillars. They divided the space into three oblong aisles with a small stage at the far end of the central aisle.

The Gin Mill Skiffle Group were already on stage. But before we could get in to see them we had to join The Cavern Club by paying a membership and entrance fee to Alan Sytner who was seated at a small, square table at the bottom of the steps. In return for a shilling we were each given a pale green, pocket-sized Membership Booklet.

On the front cover was an animated sketch of a jazz trio with trumpet, trombone and clarinet, playing on the stage of the club.

Opening the booklet we could see our membership number, already stamped on the first page, and beneath it we each had to write our full name, address and signature, along with the date. On the opposite page there was a stern warning.

<u>IMPORTANT</u>
HANDBAGS, COATS
SHOES, UMBRELLAS, ETC.
Must NOT be Left Lying around the Club
UNDER SEATS
In the toilets . . . or anywhere
where you cannot look after them.

After two pages which were marked 'FOR OFFICIAL USE ONLY' and 'CLUB NOTES', there was a double-page '1957 CALENDAR' which was followed by two more pages, also marked 'CLUB NOTES' and 'FOR OFFICIAL USE ONLY'. The last two pages of the booklet had on them a sketch map along with a cartoon picture titled *'Show your friends how to get to the CAVERN!'*

On the back cover were a number of Club Rules, the most important of which stated that the Membership Card had to be shown, on request, to Door Staff, Desk Staff and any other Club Official who asked to see it. It also stated that possession of the card did not guarantee admission if the management deemed that the premises were full, or for any other reason.

As the membership numbers stamped into our little booklets were '3849' and '3850', this last rule was obviously essential for basic safety. Getting even five or six hundred people into the subterranean cellar would be a tight squeeze. In the event of an emergency such as a fire the escape route up the narrow stairway would hardly be adequate for even a third of that number. It was fortunate that there was very little in the way of combustible material in the slightly damp basement.

Alan Sytner was an astute, young businessman who understood that a crowded club was one of the essential ingredients for success. The word would quickly get out that if so many people were keen to become members The Cavern must be good.

Once we had completed the membership formalities we got ourselves a couple of Cokes from a small hatch marked 'REFRESHMENTS' and sat down on a couple of the very basic, bentwood chairs which were lined up in rows across the central area. We were about ten rows back from the stage and our chairs wobbled about a little on the slightly uneven, cobblestone floor.

The Gin Mill Skiffle Group, as well as playing popular skiffle numbers such as 'Freight Train', 'Cumberland Gap' and 'Rock Island Line', gave us some really great versions of traditional folk songs like 'D'Ye Ken John Peel' and 'The Lincolnshire Poacher'.

Listening to them, Dave thought they seemed much happier playing the folk music.

"These lot are good," he whispered to me. "But they should give up on skiffle and concentrate on the folk music. They've got a real feel for it."

He was right. By September of the following year the Gin

Mill Skiffle Group had become the Liverpool-based Spinners and very quickly gained a reputation as being among England's favourite and best-loved folk musicians, playing sold-out concerts at London's Royal Albert Hall and many other national venues.

The Ravin' Texans followed them onto the stage, fronted by a lead singer called Al Caldwell.

"Al Caldwell and the Ravin' Texans?" said Dave. "That doesn't sound very rock 'n' roll."

"That might be because they're a skiffle group," I said.

He gave me a gentle dig in the ribs.

"Still no flies on my friend Steve," he said with a laugh. "Me not being around doesn't seem to have blunted your razor-sharp sense of humour."

Al Caldwell and his Ravin' Texans couldn't be faulted for the energy they put into their performance. Al in particular made the most of the limited space on the small stage, moving constantly from side to side and swinging the microphone stand out over the audience as he was singing. Unfortunately his undoubted showmanship couldn't hide the fact that from a musical point of view the Ravin' Texans were still very much a work in progress. After just four numbers their set came to an abrupt end. This may have been because their limitations had been recognised by Alan Sytner and he had ordered them off. He was known not to hesitate to pull the plug if a band wasn't meeting his expectations, particularly if they weren't playing traditional jazz which was the only type of music he really wanted to put on at his club.

The stars of the evening, the Muskrat Jazz Band, must have made him happy. The seven-piece combo of trumpet, trombone, clarinet, piano, sousaphone, banjo and drums looked like amateurs. They were kitted out in rather nondescript white shirts and brown ties with loose-fitting brown trousers which were held up by well-worn belts. But appearances were deceptive. They blasted out straightforward jazz, New Orleans style. And they certainly knew how to play. They were already becoming firm favourites at The Cavern and their forty-minute set was enthusiastically received by the audience around us.

The Cavern didn't have a licence to sell alcohol so as soon as the Muskrats had played their well-deserved encore we said our goodbyes to Alan, who was still sitting at his desk, and walked the fifty yards or so along Mathew Street to The Grapes. We needed a couple of pints. And somewhere a bit quieter to catch up with each other's news.

"So," I said to Dave as we sat down at one of the tables with our beers. "What did you make of The Cavern?"

"Not bad. They need to do a bit of work on the toilets though. Did you notice the smell? They'd tried to hide it with loads of disinfectant. But you still got a whiff every now and then. There was a rather strange, sweet smell as well. Sort of organic and musty."

"Over-ripe fruit, probably," I said. "That's what's been stored down there for most of the past hundred years. Some of the juice could easily have seeped into the walls."

Dave nodded his head. "I liked the feel of the place though. It's a nice size. Not too big. And the acoustics were great."

"And what about you?" I said. "How are things?"

"Getting interesting." Dave took a generous mouthful from his pint. "I think I might join the British Army."

I gave him a questioning look. "Are you being serious?"

"Well, not definitely the Army," he said, taking another sip. "It could be the Royal Navy. Or even the Air Force. But I think most likely the Army."

"And what's made you decide on that?"

I didn't understand what he was up to.

"It's like this," said Dave. "After being with Cunard, which we know is the best there is, I don't really fancy any of the other shipping lines. And if I'm not in the Merchant Navy I won't be exempt from National Service. Which means I'll probably get called up pretty soon." He gave me a grin. "So I thought I might as well jump before I get pushed. And I quite fancy the idea anyway."

"But you've not actually signed up yet?"

"Not yet. I'm going along to see them at the Recruitment Office in town on Monday. To hear what they've got to say."

Dave certainly had a knack of springing surprises. It was the last thing I'd expected.

"And if you like what they say, how long might you give them?"

"I think it has to be at least three years. But to be honest I'm not exactly sure. Three years'd be fine though. It's not all that long. And I might get to see a bit more of the world. You know. Apart from just the Atlantic Ocean and New York."

"And you might get yourself killed as well," I said. "Has that occurred to you?"

"I don't think there's much chance of that. The Korean War seems to have settled down now and it doesn't look as though there's anything else on the way. And anyway, if your number's up, your number's up. That's how I look at it."

"Have you said anything to your Dad?"

"No. I thought I'd leave it until after Monday. I'll have a bit more to tell him when I've spoken to the recruitment people."

"And what about your Cavern Club membership? That's going to go to waste if you sign up. It says in the booklet it's not transferrable."

Dave looked at me and put on a serious expression.

"That's the price a man sometimes has to pay if he wants to serve his country, Steve,"

I wasn't sure if he was being serious or not. So to wind him up I started to sing the National Anthem.

"God Save Our Gracious Queen,

Long Live Our . . . ."

Dave leaned towards me over the table with a grin. "And you can sod off, mate. Right now."

"I'm only joking." I said.

And for once it was true. I admired his decision really.

"Our country needs a decent army," I said. "So good luck to you. 'If you want peace, prepare for war.' I'm sure I once came across that saying somewhere or other."

"Si vis pacem, para bellum." said Dave.

I looked at him in astonishment.

"It's Latin," he said. "It was in a book on military tactics written by an ancient Roman military expert called Vegetius. His proper name's a lot longer than that but I can't remember it. He wrote it around three or four hundred years after the birth of Christ. When the Roman Empire was still doin' well. I read about him in my Dad's old Encyclopaedia Brittanica. You know. That row of books he keeps in the front room. I was lookin' at it the other day to see what it said about the army."

He picked up his pint mug. It was empty.

"D'you fancy another?"

Dave would never cease to amaze me.

"According to the label this one's called *'That'll Be The Day',*" I said as I placed the 45 rpm vinyl on the turntable of the Dansette and moved the switch to *'PLAY'* before lowering the needle onto it. "It's by an American band called The Crickets. I've no idea what it's like."

I was with Dave, Sylvie and Greg and the record was another of the jukebox cast-offs which Julie had continued to put aside in the Thrift Store. I'd picked it up, along with a few others, the previous week.

Soon after our visit to The Cavern Dave had signed on for three years in the army and he was very shortly due to report for duty at Catterick Barracks, near Richmond in Yorkshire, where he would undergo his basic training. So this would be the last chance the four of us would get to listen to American records together for quite a while.

We wouldn't see each other again for at least six months. And it could be a lot longer if Dave ended up being posted at short notice to some far-flung part of the world.

'That'll Be The Day' was another of those unforgettable records. As soon as we heard the opening hook on the guitar we knew we were listening to something special. The song was more up-tempo than Elvis's 'Heartbreak Hotel', and the singer's voice was completely different, a lot lighter. But the spine-tingling effect was just the same.

We played it five times. And when I removed the record from the turntable and took a good look at it I saw that it had been released on America's Brunswick label.

According to the label the song had been written by Jerry Allison and Norman Petty. Along with someone called Buddy Holly.

The three names meant nothing to me.

TWENTY-ONE

A GARDEN FETE IN
WOOLTON

The first Saturday in July 1957 was hot. Well above average. And being near the centre of town St Bride Street felt even hotter. Even the stone cobbles outside the front door, baked by the sun, had been warm underfoot when I'd got back from Southampton the previous afternoon.

In what had become our usual routine when I was home Sylvie had caught a bus into town and stayed overnight at St Bride Street. It was good to see her again. My fling with Carol in New York had been fun but it had taught me a lesson. It had told me that Sylvie was special. And that variety, while it might be the spice of life, didn't always improve the flavour. I really regretted what had happened and I was very grateful indeed that I hadn't picked up an infection and passed it on to Sylvie.

Hopefully the whole sorry episode was now behind us.

Spending time with Carol had also told me the grass definitely wasn't greener on the other side of the hill. Sylvie was the one. Meeting each other when we did, although we were both so young, was very lucky. It had taken me a bit of time to fully realise it, but I was thankful to have her in my life. From now on I was determined to make the most of my good fortune.

And I think Sylvie felt the same.

"My friend Angie from college has invited us over to her place in Woolton today if you fancy it," she said as we were grabbing a quick breakfast of toast and coffee at the big table in the kitchen. "There's a garden fete on at her local church and anyone can go along. It might be okay. It looks like it's going to be really hot today so it'd be good to do something outside. She gave me this flyer. See what you think."

Sylvie handed me a sheet of paper.

She was right. It was definitely a day for getting out of the city centre and finding somewhere cooler.

A garden fete in Woolton might be the answer.

Woolton Parish Church
Garden Fete
and
Crowning of Rose Queen
Saturday July 6th 1957
To be opened at 3 p.m. by Dr Thelwall Jones

PROCESSION AT 2 P.M.
LIVERPOOL POLICE DOGS DISPLAY
FANCY DRESS PARADE
SIDESHOWS REFRESHMENTS
BAND OF THE CHESHIRE YEOMANRY
THE QUARRY MEN SKIFFLE GROUP
ADULTS 6d. CHILDREN 3d. OR BY PROGRAMME

GRAND DANCE
at 8 P.M. in the Church Hall
GEORGE EDWARDS' BAND
THE QUARRY MEN SKIFFLE GROUP
Tickets 2/-

"It looks as though it might be okay," I said. "If you want to give it a go it's fine with me. According to this sheet the procession's due to set off at two o'clock."

"I'll ring Angie and say we'll see her about one o'clock then. You remember her, don't you? She was on the Cake Stall at the Bring and Buy Sale the British Legion were running last Christmas. We bought a couple of her home-made cupcakes."

"She had short hair," I said. "Quite dark."

Sylvie nodded her head.

"That's her. And you told her that the cupcakes were disgustingly sweet."

"They were." I shrugged my shoulders. "I do remember that. If she'd told me up front that it was her mother that made 'em I'd have said they were lovely. Anyway, it was for charity. So I still paid up."

There was no point in getting to Angie's too early so to kill a bit of time we decided to walk into town while the weather was still relatively cool.

After meandering slowly along Blackburne Place we crossed Hope Street. Our plan was to cut through Mount Street and head for Church Street, the main shopping area in the city centre, where we'd be able to grab another coffee and then catch a bus to Woolton.

Half-way down Mount Street a couple of schoolboys with guitars were sitting on the sandstone steps of the Liverpool Institute. The Institute was one of Liverpool's top grammar schools so the pupils were sometimes expected to attend classes on a Saturday morning. Wearing their school uniforms, but with their hair swept back in Elvis Presley quiffs, the two young musicians gave us a smile as we passed. They were facing each other and I noticed that one of them, who looked slightly older, was playing his guitar left-handed.

Sylvie and I both recognised the song they were playing. It was Gene Vincent's *'Be-Bop-a-Lula'*.

"Easy," I thought to myself. "Just three chords."

Continuing down Mount Street brought us out onto Rodney Street. Many of Liverpool's fine Georgian houses had fallen into disrepair and been turned into student flats. But Rodney Street was the exception. Being convenient for the University Medical School and the Liverpool Royal Infirmary the houses were almost all occupied by private physicians and surgeons. It was often referred to as the Harley Street of the North.

We turned right and walked slowly along the street, passing the elegant doorways with their symmetrical stone columns and fanlights. Number 62 was the 1809 birthplace of a British Prime Minister, William Ewart Gladstone, while Number 29 boasted a very substantial sandstone portico. A swastika and large flag had flown from it when it was the German Consulate before World War Two. The Consul, Herr Walther Reinhardt, had been expelled in June 1939 for alleged involvement in a Nazi spying operation. His former Consulate, with its Adam-style marble fireplaces and elegant Georgian rooms, within which portraits of Adolf Hitler had once been proudly displayed, was now owned by the U.K. Government.

Further down the hill we reached Bold Street. Fifty years earlier it had vied with London's Bond Street as the epitome of retail elegance and fashion. But times had changed.

Having stopped off, as planned, for a coffee at the Kardomah it was just before quarter past twelve when we finally jumped onto a bus which would take us to Woolton Village via Sefton Park and the suburb of Allerton. Our journey would take just over half an hour.

Many years ago Woolton had been a small village surrounded by green fields. Now it was one of Liverpool's suburbs, but it had managed to retain its own, very distinct character. The small shops and cafes in the centre of the village were busy and thriving. With leaded windows and narrow doorways that were almost

Dickensian in appearance they were still the focus of local life. Most of the original village houses were still standing and Angie's family lived in one of them. Quite small, and built of sandstone from the local quarry, the house was set back from Allerton Road near to where the village had once given way to open fields.

We reached the house to find Angie sitting by a wishing well in the family's well-kept, cottage garden. The small lawn and colourful flower-beds formed a very necessary barrier between the house and what had once been a quiet, country lane but was now an increasingly busy, main road.

Angie made her way to the garden gate and greeted us. Sylvie gave her a kiss.

"Do you remember Steve?" she said. "He came with me to that Bring and Buy Sale at the British Legion."

Angie nodded a greeting.

"The chap who doesn't much like sweet cupcakes," she said as she opened the gate. "How could I forget?"

Was she joking? I wasn't sure.

"Tea?" she said, addressing us both. "I think we've got time. The procession isn't due to start for at least forty minutes. And they'll probably be running late."

"Tea would be great," said Sylvie.

"Me too," I said. "I'm thirsty."

"No cupcakes," said Angie, turning to me with a laugh. "I thought they were pretty dodgy too."

Angie didn't know what route the procession would be following. Or exactly what form it would take. So, having finished our tea we found ourselves a spot in the middle of the village close to the end of Church Road. Quite a few other people were standing around and Sylvie spotted someone she knew.

"That's my friend, Kathy," she said, pointing towards a girl wearing jeans and a loose, white pullover who was standing on the opposite pavement. "She might know something."

Sylvie gave her a wave and Kathy came over.

"The fete's supposed to be happening in the field round the back of the church," she said. "Someone I was speaking to has just walked past St Peter's and the procession seems to be starting from there. There's four or five lorries and a military band lined up along Church Road and they're all facing this way."

St Peter's Church was only a couple of minutes away. It looked like we'd chosen as good a place as any so we got ready to wait. Over the next ten or fifteen minutes more people turned up and quite soon the pavements on both sides of the road were comfortably full.

Then, at just after two o'clock, we heard the sound of military music. Fronted by a man wielding an ornamental mace the Band of the Cheshire Yeomanry came into view, all kitted out in smart, navy-blue uniforms. They were followed by Morris Dancers, Boy Scouts, Brownies, Girl Guides and Cubs, some doing better than others at keeping in step with the regular beat.

Young members of St Peter's Church Youth Club kept pace with the procession on both sides, shaking collection tins and encouraging the spectators to contribute to their funds.

It was much better than I'd expected. And there was more to come. A flatbed lorry came into view and as it drew level with us we could see The Rose Queen, seated on a throne with her back to the cab. She was dressed in a white lace gown and her pink velvet train had been draped around the throne which had been artfully created by decorating a high-backed chair with tinsel and other suitably sparkly items. There were hand-made roses and ribbons in her hair, and a wooden trellis, also decorated with roses and other flowers, formed a colourful backdrop and frame which arched over her head. Her young attendants from St Peter's Sunday School were dressed in matching pink and white satin. And they too had flowers in their hair.

A couple of very brightly-coloured floats followed, bearing children in fancy dress with young dancers surrounding them.

Finally, right at the back of the procession, another lorry appeared. The name G.A. Chadwick of Halewood, a local coal merchant, was displayed prominently on the driver's door. On the flat tail-board behind the cab a group of young musicians were trying hard to keep their balance and play their instruments as the lorry trundled slowly past us. I counted six of them, four seated and two standing. The two who were standing had abandoned any attempt to produce music. But a guitarist and a washboard player were still valiantly playing away, along with a lad who had his foot up on a black-painted tea-chest decorated with a silver treble clef and with silver edges. By altering the tension on a length of string which ran from the tea-chest to the top of a wooden broom handle he was producing rudimentary bass notes in time with the music. A drummer, with 'QUARRY-MEN' stencilled in a black V-shape on the front of his bass drum, completed the ensemble.

We carried on watching as the tail end of the procession continued down the road towards Kings Drive and then disappeared from view.

"That seems to be it," I said. "Are we going to fork out sixpence each and take a look at the fete?"

"Let's give it a go," said Sylvie. "Sixpence is hardly going to break the bank."

Decision made we followed the rest of the crowd up Church Road. Angie told us we were heading for a footpath which led past the grave of a lady called Eleanor Rigby and then round the back of the church. At the end of the path was an entrance to the field where the fete was being held.

There were quite a few people already wandering around in the field and after we had each parted with a sixpenny piece we were free to inspect the various exhibits and activities. None of the stalls were yet open and not much was going to happen until the procession had completed its circuit of the village. Happily it was a pleasantly warm afternoon, the previous two weeks having been unusually hot for an English summer. The grass would normally have been slightly damp but it was now sun-baked and dry. A perfect day, in fact, for lying around in a field and doing nothing.

A small stage, decorated with tree branches, foliage and Union Jacks, had been set up on one side of the field with a rudimentary microphone and Tannoy system. This was where the Quarrymen would later be playing.

We lay there, enjoying the sun, until the sound of military music told us that the Band of the Cheshire Yeomanry had arrived back at the church and at ten minutes to three they marched along the footpath and into the field. To the sound of applause from the onlookers they did a quick circuit before dispersing for well-earned refreshments.

The Rose Queen and her retinue then took their places on the stage, accompanied by various church wardens and other local officials. All was ready for the coronation.

The Reverend Morris Pryce-Jones stood up in front of the microphone and gave a short speech which was followed by a couple of prayers. Mrs Thelwall Jones then crowned The Rose Queen and, after a brief Children's Fancy Dress Parade, the fete was declared officially open.

Stalls selling the usual array of cakes, savouries, pies and home-made biscuits, along with a second-hand bookstall and a 'white elephant' stall, were now in business. And with several hundred people in attendance they were busy.

On the far side of the field a group of local boy scouts, who had also been marching in the procession, had erected a very impressive and popular zip wire called The Aerial Run. It ran from an elevated platform to a finishing point at ground level some fifty yards away.

Even more popular, though, was a stall where, having donated a further threepence to St Peter's Church funds, the participants wrote their name on a cardboard tag which was attached to a helium-filled balloon. The balloon was then released to be borne off on the wind, and the name tag which travelled the greatest distance before being returned to the church would win a prize.

The weather remained fine and at exactly quarter past four the Quarrymen made their way onto the stage. Although this must have been the biggest audience they had ever faced they looked confident. A teenager with tousled hair, wearing a checked shirt, was very clearly the leader of the group. He stood front-centre, legs slightly apart and lips close to the microphone, and sang several skiffle songs which had been hits in England.

'Rock Island Line', 'Cumberland Gap' and 'Come Go With Me' were certainly three of them, along with 'Maggie Mae' and Gene Vincent's 'Be-Bop-a-Lula'. He also attempted a couple of Elvis Presley numbers, 'That's All Right' and 'Mean Woman Blues'. It was fairly clear that he hadn't bothered to learn all the lyrics of the songs because in many cases he was making up the words as he went along.

Perhaps it was because the other members of the group were all dressed identically in white shirts and dark trousers that he stood out. But there was something about him that was different. Despite his youth he had a strange magnetism, and a stage presence that forced you to keep looking at him.

"That's John Lennon," said Angie. "I used to be in the church choir with him but he gave up on it when he discovered skiffle and started the group. He was always messing about anyway so the vicar wasn't sorry to see him go."

She pointed to two ladies standing by the stage watching him.

"The smartly dressed lady is his Aunt Mimi and the person next to her is his Mum, Julia. I don't know exactly why, but for some reason he lives with his Aunt Mimi on Menlove Avenue rather than his Mum."

The Quarrymen played for half an hour and as soon as they had finished their set the City of Liverpool Police Dogs took to the field for their display while the group disappeared into the nearby Scout Hut for refreshments. Before leaving the stage John Lennon had announced that his group would be playing again in an hour and fifteen minutes. At six o'clock.

"What do you want to do?" I said to Sylvie and Angie. "I wouldn't mind hanging round for their second set. There's a couple of stalls selling quite decent-looking food if you're hungry. But it's up to you. If you've had enough I'm happy to call it a day."

We weren't the only ones who decided to stay but the numbers in the field had definitely thinned out by the time the Quarrymen returned to the stage. Exhausted parents had taken happy, but now rather tired, young children home to bed and the much smaller audience for the Quarrymen's second set was mainly younger people like ourselves.

As the group's slightly low-key second set drew to a close Angie spotted a lad she knew.

"Hi, Ivan," she said.

He turned round and gave her a smile. "Hi there, Angie. How're you doing?"

He turned to another boy who was standing next to him wearing a fashionably long, white jacket. He was holding an acoustic guitar in his left hand.

"This is my friend, Paul," said Ivan. "He's pretty good on the guitar so I'm going to introduce him to John when the set finishes in case he needs someone else for his skiffle group."

"I'm Steve," I said. "And this is Sylvie"

We all nodded a polite hello to each other.

The Quarrymen had been asked to perform a short set that

evening for a dance in the Church Hall. So as soon as they had finished playing they gathered together their equipment and trooped off along the footpath, heading past the church and across the road to the hall. A few minutes later Ivan and Paul followed them, Paul with his guitar now slung over his back and pushing the bicycle on which he had arrived at the fete. His home was in Forthlin Road, about a mile away on the far side of Allerton Golf Course.

"Let's go and tell the Quarrymen we thought they were good," said Angie as she watched the two lads making their way along the path past the graveyard. "John might remember me from the choir."

As we entered the spacious Church Hall we could see John Lennon holding court in front of the stage on which the George Edwards Band, who were providing most of the music, had already set up their instruments ready for the dance. He was sitting in the middle of a half-circle of fold-up chairs surrounded by the other Quarrymen.

Several middle-aged ladies from the Garden Fete Committee were attaching colourful balloons and bunting to the otherwise bare walls of the hall in a valiant attempt to make it look more festive.

John saw Ivan come in and gave him a wave. Ivan walked over to him and introduced Paul who stood alongside them, hands in pockets, as the two friends chatted away. Then, instead of joining in with the conversation, Paul took his guitar off his back and began to strum away on it, holding it left-handed.

I turned to Sylvie. "I'm sure he's one of the two lads who were playing in Mount Street this morning. On the steps of the Institute."

As I was speaking Paul's strumming had changed to a very competent rendition of Eddie Cochran's hit single, *Twenty Flight Rock*. John Lennon stopped chatting and looked at the young guitarist as the Eddie Cochran song was followed by an equally impressive version of Gene Vincent's *'Be-Bop-a-Lula'*. Ivan's friend was definitely the same lad.

Despite being left-handed and holding his instrument upside down he certainly knew how to play a guitar.

Outside the hall there were crashes of thunder, and rain began to fall. The heat of the afternoon had triggered a brief, summer storm.

It was obvious by the look on his face as he watched Paul playing that John Lennon was quietly impressed. Should this younger lad, who clearly had talent, be in his group? Maybe he should? But to ask him right now would run the risk of a refusal and loss of face.

So it wasn't until a week or two later that he sent the group's washboard player, his close friend Pete Shotton, to ask Paul if he'd be interested in joining the Quarrymen.

His answer would eventually change the world.

TWENTY-TWO

RIVER BOAT SHUFFLE

In early August I took Sylvie along to The Cavern for the first time. We didn't know beforehand, but it happened to be the evening the Quarrymen were making their first-ever appearance at the club, albeit without Paul McCartney. Although Paul had accepted the invitation to join the group he was unable to make the gig at The Cavern because he was away from home, initially at Scout Camp and then on holiday with his parents and younger brother, Mike, at Butlin's in Filey.

Sylvie knew all about my visit to the club with Dave. I'd told her how incredibly atmospheric it was and as we made our way down the narrow stone stairs she was very excited. Alan Sytner was once again sitting at his desk and, the fee for membership and entrance having been paid, Sylvie joined me as a member of The Cavern Club.

Three other local groups, the Ron McKay Skiffle Group, the Deltones and the Darktown Skiffle Group, were also on that night. Having bought a couple of soft drinks from the small bar we found two spare seats in front of the stage.

In the confined space of the subterranean cellar the Quarrymen were a lot better than at Woolton. Despite their very basic equipment the hard bricks of the curved ceiling and walls amplified the sound and made it much fuller and more exciting, and the reaction of the audience around us seemed to indicate that they agreed.

Alan Sytner, however, who knew John Lennon because they lived a few hundred yards away from each other in Woolton, was less impressed. The Cavern was first and foremost a jazz club. Alan Sytner booked the occasional skiffle group only because it was a quite popular offshoot of traditional jazz, and young John Lennon knew the rules very well.

The Quarrymen had started their set with skiffle, as had been agreed, but he was keen to play the new music that he had discovered by listening to the American records that were increasingly starting to appear around the city and that were being played regularly at the nearby U.S. Air Force Base. Taking no notice of the club's strict 'jazz and skiffle only' rule, he led the Quarrymen into a couple of Elvis Presley numbers. Sylvie and I were sitting quite near the front and we watched as Alan Sytner, who'd moved from his desk into the small band room alongside the stage, handed the Quarrymen's tea-chest bass player, Len Garry, a note which was passed on to the singer. John Lennon slowly unfolded it and smiled. Then, still smiling, he looked at the audience and announced, "We've had a request".

Before he could say anything more Alan Sytner's head appeared out of the band room.

"Yes, Lennon. It's from me. And it's not a request. It's an order. Cut out the bloody rock 'n' roll."

A week and a half later Alan Sytner put on his first 'Cavern Club Riverboat Shuffle'. He was a man full of ideas who never missed a trick when it came to thinking up novel events. Having looked at the River Mersey, which ran just a couple of hundred yards away from his club in Mathew Street, he had decided that what Liverpool's jazz and skiffle enthusiasts needed on a summer evening was a New Orleans style trip. With music. On a riverboat.

For five shillings Cavern Club members would be able to cruise the River Mersey on a riverboat called the Royal Iris, while listening to the Merseysippi Jazz Band, the Gin Mill Skiffle Group and the Wall City Jazzmen. And for good measure the 'Miss Cavern 1957' Bathing Beauty Contest would also be judged during the evening.

I was still on leave from the Queen Mary. It was an event not to be missed.

The Royal Iris was fairly new to the Mersey having been launched only six years earlier in 1951. She quickly became a favourite, instantly recognisable from the shore with her distinctive green and cream livery as she cruised up and down the river. With a capacity of one thousand passengers for such events she had been designed with river cruises in mind. And having been fitted out with a dance floor and a fish and chip café she was perfect for the type of evening which Alan Sytner had so carefully planned.

The only element that was unpredictable was the weather. For the cruise to be a complete success the river would need to be as calm as possible. Teenage club-goers were not necessarily good sailors. To avoid an epidemic of sea sickness any 'rocking and rolling' would have to be limited to the music. Not that Alan had rock 'n' roll in mind. There was no John Lennon on board to push against the rules. The three bands he had booked for the trip would be sticking very strictly to jazz and skiffle.

Our boat was already moored alongside as Sylvie and I stood on the floating landing stage at the Pier Head waiting to go on board. We were excited. Everything looked promising and a fun evening beckoned. The sky was slightly overcast and it looked as though we might possibly see a little bit of light rain. But the evening air was warm. And the river was flat. Hardly a ripple disturbed the surface as the incoming tide carried the salt water in from the Irish Sea and swept it upstream.

We were due to cast off two hours before high tide so the Captain of the Royal Iris could set off up-river, towards Speke and the Runcorn Bridge, before turning back and allowing the ebb tide to return us gently to the Pier Head landing stage. Not having to fight against the powerful River Mersey currents would save fuel and make for a more comfortable ride for his festive passengers.

Fifteen minutes before sailing time a couple of deckhands appeared and lowered two permanent gangways noisily from the landing stage onto the ship. The chains and pulleys clanked against each other as the hefty walkways hit the deck with a crash. Once they had been roped securely in place we were waved on board. A few eager party-goers hurried ahead to grab what they hoped were the best places, but the evening was pleasantly warm so Sylvie and I decided to sit out on deck in the open air. We would move inside only if the weather turned cold and wet.

We were soon on our way, passing the tired-looking warehouses of Jesse Hartley's once magnificent Albert Dock on our left side, or to port as sailors would say. Over on the Birkenhead side of the river, to starboard, we could see the Cammel Laird shipyards where both the huge aircraft carriers which carried the famous name 'Ark Royal' had been built.

As we continued upstream the sound of the Gin Mill Skiffle Group drifted out to us from the dance floor area. They had started their set with the ever-popular sea shanty 'The Drunken Sailor', played skiffle style to be certain of not upsetting the boss, and we could see through one of the portholes that many of our fellow passenger were already enjoying a dance.

Further up the river, locals who were out for an evening stroll recognised the Royal Iris and waved to us from the recently-opened Otterspool Promenade which ran for several miles along the Liverpool side of the river, all the way from the Dingle to Aigburth. The river wall, along which it was now possible to walk, had been completed in just three years between 1929 and 1932 but a further twenty years had then been needed to fill in and raise the land behind the wall to form a large, recreational park. Clean domestic refuse had been used for the in-fill, topped by dirt and soil which had been laboriously excavated from beneath the river during the digging of the first Mersey Tunnel a few years earlier. This ingenious and economical method of construction, and the savings made by not having to dispose of the soil and waste elsewhere, meant that the ambitious project had been completed at no cost at all to the ratepayers of the city who were now able to enjoy the considerable benefits.

The weather remained warm and dry, and as we approached Runcorn Bridge the Royal Iris slowly turned for home. I'd have been perfectly happy just to sit and take in the ever-changing views but that was not an option. Sylvie had decided it was time for a dance.

"Come on," she said. "The Merseysippis have just started playing. Let's go and stretch our legs."

So we did. The Merseysippi Jazz Band were recognised as one of Liverpool's very best exponents of traditional New Orleans jazz and their lively set kept us on our feet for almost forty minutes. We returned to our seats exhausted, carrying fish and chips from the café and a couple of refreshing lemonade shandies.

Our boat got back to the Pier Head with an hour to spare. The water was still calm so the Captain decided to continue down river, towards Liverpool Bay, Seacombe and the resort town of New Brighton on the Wirral.

As we passed Salisbury Dock and the Clarence Graving Dock on the Liverpool side of the river I caught sight of the disused, six-sided Victoria Clock Tower. Designed by Jesse Hartley, like the Albert Dock, it had once told incoming and departing vessels the official time of day. Back in the nineteenth century clocks were unreliable, so the time on the Victoria Tower's clock-face very quickly became the standard for the entire Liverpool dock network.

"Over there," I said to Sylvie, pointing out the lights of ships in the Huskisson Dock. "That's where Dave and I first sailed out of Liverpool on the Media. It's difficult to believe it was only three years ago. It seems like a lifetime."

TWENTY-THREE

BUDDY HOLLY
AND THE CRICKETS

By Thursday 22nd August I was back in New York City and along with three others from the Queen Mary I caught the subway heading north from Pier 90. Two stops after Cathedral Parkway we got off the train and climbed the steps to the street. As we headed east along West 125th Street towards 8th Avenue I could see a vertical sign attached to the stone façade of a building and extending above it, supported by lightweight, boxed scaffolding. On the sign, in big, red letters, was the single word, '**APOLLO**'.

We were in Harlem. There, ahead of us, was the world-famous Apollo Theatre.

Clyde McPhatter, who had been the original lead singer of The Drifters, was topping the bill having scored a big, solo hit with his song *'Treasure of Love'*. It had sold over two million copies in the United States alone. But we weren't there to see Mr McPhatter, brilliant rhythm 'n' blues singer though he was. We were there to see the number two act on the bill.

His name was Charles Hardin Holley. But everybody called him Buddy.

Since hearing *'That'll Be The Day'* back home in Liverpool

I'd done a little bit of searching around and found out that the song had been recorded in July 1956 by the then unknown singer from Lubbock in Texas with a couple of friends. They had gone along to Bradley's Barn Studio in Nashville, Tennessee which had links with Decca. According to legend, the session producer, Owen Bradley, and Paul Cohen, an Executive with Decca, both believed that to be successful this young lad, Buddy Holly, should aim at the country and western market. So they persuaded him to record the song in a traditional country style at a slower tempo than the version of the song which was eventually released.

After a number of unsatisfactory takes Owen Bradley's verdict on 'That'll Be The Day' was said to have been that it was the worst song he had ever heard, and the session was abandoned. Even when a much improved up-tempo recording of the song was made at the Norman Petty Studios in Clovis, New Mexico, in late February 1957, the senior people at Decca weren't impressed. It was only when Bob Thiele, the A & R Director at the Decca subsidiary, Coral Records, pushed hard for it to be released that they agreed. The recording in Clovis had been intended as a demo rather than a finished record but Decca would spend no more money on it. It had to go out just as it was on their Brunswick label which was once very successful but had been allowed to fall out of fashion.

Although the more up-beat version of 'That'll Be The Day' had been recorded in February, and eventually released in America at the end of May, it hadn't sold well. The first pressing of the record on Brunswick was a mere one thousand copies. And as I had noticed at home in England Buddy Holly's name appeared on the record label only as one of the writers of the song. The lead singer of the Crickets, a uniquely gifted songwriter, was otherwise invisible. It was a strange decision, but Decca had good reasons for making it. Paul Cohen, who was the first person to work with the young singer from Lubbock, was said to have felt betrayed.

It wasn't until the end of July, eight weeks after its release, that Billboard Magazine, the most influential of the U.S. music papers, finally started telling people in America that the record was special. And that they should go out and buy it.

Buddy's seven night appearance at The Apollo was just one stop on a long, nationwide tour that had been organised by Brunswick to try and persuade people to do exactly that.

After hearing the jukebox recording back home in Liverpool I didn't need any persuading. Having discovered that The Crickets were doing a show in New York City while the Queen Mary was in port I'd managed to get hold of four tickets. And I'd told three of my fellow stewards, who were also off duty that evening, that they'd regret it for the rest of their lives if they didn't join me.

We entered the theatre through the main doors which were overshadowed by a very substantial, white canopy which was festooned with brightly-lit information about the evening's show. The doors took us straight into the main lobby. It was long and narrow, almost like a bowling alley, and there were numerous colourful murals on the walls.

Our seats were in the stalls, just to the left of the two aisles and about half-way back from the stage. The rows of seats were gently raked so we were confident of getting a great view even though people were still pouring in and it looked as though the show was going to be a sell-out. Looking round I could see that the main and upper balconies were also filling up fast.

It was the last of Buddy Holly's seven-night run at The Apollo.

The Crickets were the first white musicians for many years to appear at The Apollo, the week-long run having been arranged by mistake because Buddy Holly and his group from Texas had been confused with a non-white group of the same name who had previously played the theatre. The word on the street was that the reception Buddy Holly and The Crickets had received from the mainly African-American audience on the first couple of nights had been slightly lukewarm. That may or may not have been true. But if it was true the regular Apollo audience had been well and truly won over by the end of the run.

The Crickets opened the show with 'Bo Diddley', playing the song behind closed curtains so that the audience could not see what they looked like. The curtains were then pulled back to reveal the band. Buddy Holly was wearing his signature black, horn-rimmed glasses and a slim-cut suit which was a shade lighter than the similar outfits worn by Jerry Allison on drums and Joe B. Mauldin on double-bass. As the three of them appeared they launched into 'That'll Be The Day', following it immediately with 'Peggy Sue'. After a brief few words from the lead singer they played a couple of their more recent numbers, 'Words of Love', and 'Everyday', neither of which I had previously heard but the straightforward melodies felt almost instantly familiar. Then it was back to a series of more up-tempo songs, including 'Oh Boy' and 'Not Fade Away'.

At the end of the performance the audience all around us could not have been more enthusiastic. They were on their feet, whooping and hollering, and yelling out for more. As they took their final bows Buddy Holly and The Crickets looked very pleased.

Later in 1957 'That'll Be The Day' was released on the Coral label in the UK and reached Number One in November, staying at the top of the record charts for three weeks. Because it was such an easy song to play it quickly became a staple of skiffle groups throughout the country.

Ross Williams and Colin Miller, two of the stewards from the Queen Mary who had gone to The Apollo to see Buddy Holly with me, had been thinking of forming a group on the ship. There were six or seven professional jazz and dance bands on board the ship whose job was to keep the passengers entertained in the bars, restaurants and lounges. And several of my shipmates played instruments and sang in the amateur variety shows which the crew put on regularly. But strangely, given the huge popularity of Lonnie Donegan's music at home in England since the release of 'Rock Island Line' in November 1955, and the nationwide tours which followed, the Queen Mary did not have her own skiffle group. It was something that was crying out to be put right.

Ross was a drummer and Colin fancied himself as a bass player. And the long hours I'd spent with the Duo Jet and Bert Weedon's slim book paid off when they auditioned me and invited me to join them on rhythm guitar. All we needed was a washboard player. 'Slim' Whitty, one of the pastry chefs, volunteered his services.

'Slim' was very amusing and outgoing. A natural performer. He had acquired the monicker 'Slim' because of his very considerable weight and he was already the proud owner of a classic American washboard which he'd come across when working at a Creole restaurant in New Orleans before joining Cunard. Ever since finding it he had wanted to be in a group. And as soon as he demonstrated his natural skills and rhythm to us he had to be given the job.

We had a group. And 'Slim' came up with a name which the rest of us liked. We would be the Grand Banks Skiffle Group. We put in some practice and were soon good enough to play a couple of times on each crossing. One gig was for the crew, and one performance took place as part of an informal variety show for the entertainment of our passengers. We went down quite well and it was fun. We enjoyed ourselves. And their reaction suggested that our audiences enjoyed it too.

Because Ross and Colin originally came from London, and 'Slim' was from Jamaica, there was never any prospect of the Grand Banks Skiffle Group performing ashore. Which was a shame. Skiffle was really taking off in Britain and we'd managed to put together quite a decent set of songs.

Although we were unable to give people out in the wider world the pleasure of listening to us, other groups were still seeking out opportunities to perform. Playing for an audience was by far the best way to learn what worked and what didn't. And to improve. Towards the end of January 1958 the Quarrymen were on at The Cavern again, this time with Paul McCartney in the line-up. But Alan Sytner found it hard to be impressed.

"They came across as arrogant and couldn't play to save their lives," he would say in later years. "The main thing I remember is their cheek and their chat. They'd only been playing together for a short time so I suppose you wouldn't expect them to be much good. But to be fair they did eventually change their name and become one of the best. Some people say the best there is ever likely to be."

At the end of March 1958 Buddy Holly and The Crickets appeared at The Philharmonic Hall in Liverpool. There were two shows, 6.15 p.m. and 8.30 p.m., and tickets were like gold dust. Sylvie had a friend who worked in the box office so she was able to get hold of a couple of seats for the second show in one of the smart boxes which surrounded the stalls. She assured us that our box was just to the right of centre, one of the best in the house.

We didn't know it when we arrived at the hall, but the early show had been plagued by technical problems. The classical musicians who normally performed at The Philharmonic Hall did not use amplifiers and when Buddy Holly's amplifier was plugged in it wouldn't work. Nobody seemed to know whether this was because the American equipment used 110 volts rather than the standard UK 240 volts, or because the electricity supply to the stage area was dead. The only certain thing was that not a sound could be heard from Buddy Holly's microphone or from his electric guitar. It was looking like his performance might have to be abandoned.

The American group killed time in their dressing room as their British road manager fiddled around with the troublesome piece of equipment and tried plugging it in to every electric socket he could find. While all this was happening Ronnie Keene and his Orchestra, who were one of the supporting acts for the evening, were given the unenviable job of keeping a slightly restless audience entertained.

Miraculously, and to the road manager's slight surprise, the power to the amplifier was suddenly restored, possibly through an experimental feed to a ceiling light. But nobody was ever quite sure. All that mattered was that the amplifier was working and a slightly reluctant Buddy Holly, who had told himself that the evening was going to be a disaster, was persuaded to return to the stage and go ahead with his performance.

The audience for the first show had to leave before we were able to go in and take our seats. As they spilled out through the glass doors onto Hope Street they were all chattering away enthusiastically about Buddy Holly's brilliant performance. We couldn't wait to see him ourselves.

Our box had six chairs, arranged in two rows of three, and Sylvie and I grabbed two of the seats in the front row. We couldn't have had a better spot. It was just after eight-twenty and there were less than ten minutes to go so we sat back in our very comfortable chairs and waited for the show to start.

Buddy Holly had just scored a huge hit with 'Peggy Sue', the first single to have been released under his own name in England.

For obscure contractual reasons the recording of his earlier UK hit, 'That'll Be The Day', would continue to be attributed only to The Crickets.

The audience for the second house, most of whom like us were blissfully unaware of the earlier technical problems, sat there expectantly. Having seen Buddy perform at The Apollo in Harlem only nine months earlier I already knew just how good he was going to be. And if anything that made my expectations even greater.

But before The Crickets appeared we had to sit through the supporting acts.

The Philharmonic Hall had been designed for classical performances by an orchestra so there was no proscenium arch or curtain. Buddy Holly's drum kit, floor mike for the double bass, guitar amplifier and voice microphone were already sitting there on the stage which, if anything, increased the tension as we watched the first half of the show. They were concrete proof that before very long Buddy Holly and The Crickets would enter through the polished wooden door on the left-hand side of the stage and walk to their places, instruments and drum-sticks in hand. Their eagerly-awaited performance would then begin.

Many young teenagers on Merseyside were already playing in their own groups. And most of them were in the audience. But not the Quarrymen. John Lennon and Paul McCartney in later years invariably named Buddy Holly as one of the performers and songwriters who'd had the biggest influence upon them. But instead of turning up at The Philharmonic Hall to see him they had gone to the opening night of The Morgue Skiffle Club in the basement of a house in Oakhill Park, just a couple of miles away.

This new skiffle club would be a venue where the Quarrymen might be able to perform. A young lad called George Harrison, who was known to Paul McCartney, was close friends with a girl called Iris Caldwell, and her family were involved with running

The Morgue. If the Quarrymen wanted to get gigs there they had to support the brand-new club by showing up at the opening even if it meant missing out on seeing Buddy Holly.

It must have been a very tough decision to make. But because Buddy Holly was so young they probably told themselves there'd always be another opportunity.

One of the support acts was the Liverpool comedian, Des O'Connor, who was also the compere for the show. He came up with some good jokes but he didn't stay on stage for long. He knew we weren't there to listen to him, very amusing though he might have been on another night.

There was a brief interval before Buddy Holly's appearance, during which time the tension in the hall was palpable. And when Des O'Connor appeared again to introduce the singer he simply waved his hand towards the polished, wooden door.

"Ladies and gentlemen," he said. "Buddy Holly and The Crickets."

The three, young Americans appeared and made their way across the stage. Buddy Holly plugged his guitar into the now-working amplifier and walked up to the microphone. Looking out at the audience through his black-rimmed glasses he spoke in a soft, Texas drawl.

"It's great to be here in Liverpool. But you don't want to hear me talking. Let's play some music."

The whole place erupted. And the response of the performers was equally wild. They opened their set with 'Everyday' and continued with hits like 'Oh Boy!', 'Maybe Baby' and 'Peggy Sue'. They even did their own, very energetic version of the Jerry Lee Lewis classic 'Great Balls Of Fire'.

Buddy was playing a solid-body, Fender Stratocaster, a guitar that was almost unobtainable in England at that time, and at one point in the show he lifted it up and played it behind his head. It was a trick that Jimi Hendrix, another Stratocaster afficionado, would make a part of his act a few years later. The evening came to an end with *'Rip It Up'* and, of course *'That'll Be The Day'*.

Jerry Allison threw his drum sticks into the stalls and the three musicians left the stage.

It was a night to remember. A night which Sylvie and I, and everyone else who was lucky enough to have been there, will never forget.

* * *

By July of that year the Quarrymen had changed their line up and were gradually accommodating John Lennon's fervent wishes by moving from skiffle towards the increasingly popular sound of rock 'n' roll. By listening to *'That'll Be The Day'* time after time, and writing down the words, they had worked out how to play the song. They were now keen to make a record to show off their talents.

Having gathered together a few shillings they booked a brief recording session slot at a small studio which had been set up by Percy Phillips who had previously been selling second-hand records, including the ones from the U.S. Air Base at Burtonwood.

Their plan was to cut their own version of the Buddy Holly song on a 78 rpm acetate. It was the very first time that John Lennon and Paul McCartney, who had now been joined by Paul's young friend, George Harrison, had entered a recording studio. Colin Hanton was still their drummer. And another friend, John Duff Lowe, was now playing piano. At this session they also recorded an original song, attributed on the record label to Paul McCartney and George Harrison. It was called *'In Spite Of All The Danger'*. That acetate disc, almost certainly one of the most valuable records in existence, was lost for many years. But in 1981 John Duff Lowe came across it among some abandoned items at his home. It is now owned by Paul McCartney who keeps it securely locked away in his personal archive.

———•·•————•·•·•·•·•————•·•———

Tragically, just over six months later, Buddy Holly would be dead, along with his fellow musicians J. P. Richardson, known as 'The Big Bopper', and seventeen year old chart-topper Ritchie Valens.

They were on a long, twenty-four city tour of the Mid-West of the United States known as 'The Winter Dance Party'. It was February 1959, the coldest month of the North American winter, and at the beginning of the month the weather conditions were appalling. The heating on their tour bus was continually breaking down and one performer had already been hospitalised with frostbite.

It was a nightmare. The musicians were all calling it 'the tour from hell'. In order to avoid yet another exhausting three hundred mile journey in a freezing cold bus, Buddy Holly decided to charter a light plane to take him and two members of The Crickets from Clear Lake in Iowa, where they had just performed, to their next date in the town of Moorhead in Minnesota.

There were only three passenger seats on the plane. Buddy had expected group members Tommy Allsup and Waylon Jennings to join him on the flight. But Tommy Allsup lost his seat in a last minute coin-toss with seventeen year old teenage heart-throb, Ritchie Valens. Waylon Jennings then decided to give his place to The Big Bopper who was suffering from a bad chest and urgently needed to see a doctor before his next performance.

Having been told about the switch Buddy Holly is said to have joked to Waylon Jennings, who was watching nearby as he climbed in to take his seat in the tiny plane, "Well, Waylon, I hope your ol' bus freezes up." As the pilot fired up the engine, a laughing Waylon Jennings replied," Well, Buddy, I hope your ol' plane crashes."

They were possibly the last words that Buddy Holly ever heard.

The plane took off at just before 1.00 a.m. in freezing snow and mist. In such conditions even the slightest miscalculation can be fatal. Nobody can know for sure what went wrong, but not long into the flight the pilot, Roger Peterson, lost control. The tiny airplane ploughed at speed into a cornfield, the right wing hitting the ground first. The three passengers were thrown out of the shattered fuselage onto the frozen earth while the body of the pilot had to be cut out of the mangled wreckage

They were all killed instantly.

It was a tragic goodbye to youthful hope.

And to American Pie.

TWENTY-FOUR

THE ADELPHI HOTEL

Tuesday 2nd September, 1958 was the fourth anniversary of the day Sylvie and I had first met at The Grafton and we decided to celebrate by treating ourselves to dinner in the celebrated French restaurant in Liverpool's Adelphi Hotel, followed by an overnight stay and a late and lazy breakfast.

Determined to make the most of our time in the city's most celebrated, and expensive, hotel we checked in at exactly 3.00 p.m. and were shown to our room on the third floor by a liveried porter. The windows looked out over the front of the hotel, towards Lime Street, Ranelagh Place and Lewis's Department Store. Sir Jacob Epstein's immense bronze statue, 'Liverpool Resurgent', had been erected over the main entrance to the Department Store just two years earlier. It was fondly known by the locals as 'Dickie', for reasons that were very obvious when the pelvic regions of the statue were viewed from the vantage point of our room.

I was familiar with the elegant and sumptuous staterooms on the Queen Mary, the décor and fittings of which matched and sometimes exceeded the finest hotel rooms in the world, but our room didn't disappoint me. Sylvie, who was less used to such opulence, thought it was amazing.

As soon as the porter had left the room and closed the door behind him she flopped down onto the king-size bed, sighing as her body was cocooned in the softness and comfort of the satin eiderdown beneath which there would be fine, Egyptian cotton sheets.

She then went to check out all the toiletries in the bathroom, breathing in the gorgeous perfume from the soaps and the shampoo, and the complimentary eau de toilette.

"You're not going to find it easy to get me out of this place tomorrow," she said, emerging with a big smile and carrying a deep-red bathrobe over her arm. "I'm going to have a nice, hot bath right now to freshen up and then put this robe on." She handed it to me. "Doesn't it feel wonderfully soft and decadent."

"Do whatever takes your fancy," I said. "This room's all ours until noon tomorrow. And as we were saying earlier we'd be crazy not to make the most of it."

"I'll see you in a few minutes, then," she said as I returned the bathrobe to her.

"No rush. Our table for dinner's not 'til seven thirty. Relax and enjoy yourself. I'll unpack the overnight bags."

Knowing the anniversary was coming up, and that we were planning to celebrate, I'd packed one or two exotic items from New York City into my bag. I knew Sylvie's tastes and I was sure that she would like them.

After transferring all the contents of our two small bags, including the New York gifts, into one or two of the many drawers in the room I lay down on the bed and closed my eyes. It was every bit as comfortable and luxurious as Sylvie's reaction had indicated.

I had almost dozed off when the door to the bathroom opened and Sylvie emerged. Her hair was tousled and slightly damp, and although she had put the bathrobe on she had not secured the belt. It hung half-open, leaving little to the imagination and making it fairly clear that she was wearing nothing else.

"You look amazing," I said.

As she approached the bed Sylvie carefully adjusted her bathrobe to make it slightly less revealing while the look on her face told me that she was being deliberately provocative. Her eyes twinkled and she leant forwards to give me a kiss.

"Go and try out that bath," she whispered. "It's huge. I've left the water to save you time. And as soon as you're finished I'll be waiting."

On my way to the bathroom I took two beautifully elegant packages from one of the drawers and gave them to Sylvie. An assistant in one of the more risqué lingerie boutiques in New York had wrapped them for me.

"They're for you," I said.

I lay on my back, looking out at the patch of sky that was visible through the window on the far side of the room.

"It's six o'clock," I said. "They'll be expecting us down in the restaurant in an hour and a half."

Sylvie rolled onto her side and looked at me.

"How many more times do you think it's possible to make love in eighteen hours?" she said with a slightly naughty smile.

"Why eighteen hours?"

For some reason I didn't immediately get it.

"That's exactly how much longer we've got this room for," she said. Her eyes were sparkling mischievously.

I put my arms round her and ran my hands over the warm, softness of her gorgeous body.

"Two down, and two to go. How about that? But not now. We've got a four-course meal to tackle first. And I don't know about you, but I'm starving."

The Adelphi's signature French restaurant was elegantly decorated in French Renaissance style. The walls were panelled with sycamore, inlaid with rare woods, which had developed a beautiful silver-grey tone. The menu was also in that language so Sylvie was immediately at home. And even though I'd never studied French at school I'd picked up one or two useful words and phrases in the Verandah Grill. So, with a little bit of help from a very friendly, Scouse waiter, Pete, with whom we were quickly on first-name terms, we were able to come up with a very tempting order.

We passed on the 'Cuisses de Grenouille' and 'Escargots', plumping instead for 'Soupe a L'Oignon' served with 'Croutons Gruyere'. This was followed by the easiest choice of all, Chateaubriand for Two, cooked medium rare with a pan-sauce of butter, shallots and wine, accompanied by 'Haricots Verts' and 'Gratin Dauphinoise'.

Sheer perfection.

Following the French tradition of 'salty before sweet', our cheese course was served before the desert. The five different cheeses, each piece cut sufficiently generously to avoid it drying out, were served on an elegantly-crafted, cool platter.

"As I'm sure Sylvie will know," said our waiter, Pete, "most people like to start with the mildest cheese and finish with the strongest. So you might like to try the Port Salut first of all, then the Camembert, then the Gruyere de Comte. After that it's the Laguiole. And I recommend that you finish with the strong and salty Roquefort."

Once we had eaten the last of the delicious cheeses Sylvie was keen to round off a memorable meal with a classic French dessert. Pete went to speak to the maitre d' who came over to see us. He had a story to tell.

"My name is Alphonse," he said to Sylvie. Standing alongside her he looked suave and elegant in his white shirt and bow-tie, and pin-striped tailcoat. "About sixty years ago the future King of England, Edward, Prince of Wales, was dining at the Café de Paris in Monte Carlo with a beautiful French lady."

Sylvie was entranced and did not take her eyes off him.

"The Prince was in the same position as the lucky young man who is accompanying you tonight, Mademoiselle. Because your accent tells me that you too are French. His companion was an actress whose name was Suzette. In her honour the Prince asked for crepes, served with a sauce of caramelised sugar and butter, orange juice, and zest. 'The dish must be flambeed,' announced the Prince. 'Here at our table. With Triple Sec and Grand Marnier.' The Prince looked at his lady companion. 'And henceforth it will be called 'Crepes Suzette.'''

The maitre d' smiled at Sylvie.

"This evening, Mademoiselle, I shall myself prepare for you, at your table, a very similar dish. And in your honour I shall call it 'Crepes Sylvie.'"

Sylvie looked almost overcome. A dish served at the table in her honour. But how did the maitre d' know her name?

I looked over at Pete, who was already assembling the various components of the dish on a nearby trolley and getting ready to wheel it over. He caught my eye and gave me a wink.

Having completed his preparations Pete wheeled the trolley over and lit a small gas ring. Then he placed a shining copper pan on the heat. The stage was set for the maitre d' to commence his performance. And a performance it certainly was.

Sylvie and I both watched with admiration as our maitre d' went through what was obviously a well-practiced routine. Every ingredient was added to the copper pan with a flourish. A halved orange was skewered theatrically on the end of a fork and it sizzled as it was used to stir the caramelised sugar and the melted butter. He then held a second, fresh orange high above the hot pan and scraped the outer zest from it, the tiny flakes falling like the finest confetti into the pan. They would add a wonderfully delicate bitterness to the otherwise sweet sauce. Pete handed him the ready-prepared and folded crepes and they were placed carefully into the pan before being coated with the warm, bitter-sweet sauce.

Once the crepes had been given a little time to warm up and absorb the flavours of the sauce it was time for the climax of the show. Very generous quantities of Triple Sec and Grand Marnier were poured into the hot pan. Extra alcohol, in the form of Curacao, was then added.

"This Orange Curacao, Mademoiselle," said Alphonse, showing the distinctive, oval bottle to Sylvie before replacing it on the trolley, "is unique to your 'Crepes Sylvie.'"

While waiting for the alcohol to reach the required temperature he looked up to check that there was nothing easily flammable above the trolley. Happy that all was well he moved the pan a little to one side so that the flame from the ring was licking at its side. Then he tipped it slightly. The fumes from the alcohol ignited and a pillar of fire shot up towards the ceiling before quickly subsiding.

Holding a spoon and fork in his right hand, silver-service style, Alphonse lifted our 'Crepes Sylvie' from the pan and placed them on two very elegant, dessert plates, each with a scoop of vanilla ice-cream already in place, which Pete was holding out ready. He then returned to the pan and spooned the remaining sauce over our crepes.

They were delicious. The perfect ending to an anniversary meal after which we moved into the very relaxed and comfortable lounge alongside the restaurant for coffee and 'petits fours'.

When we got back to our room I flopped onto the bed, feeling very bloated, and loosened the belt on my trousers.

"Don't touch me," I said to Sylvie. "I'm too full."

Next morning we enjoyed a late breakfast. I took hold of Sylvie's hand and looked into her blue eyes.

"You're very beautiful," I said. "And very wild. Four times would probably have been too much. But three was just perfect."

TWENTY-FIVE

PETER KAVANAGH'S

Dave was home on leave and it was a couple of days before I was due to report back to the ship. So the evening after Sylvie and I had celebrated our fourth anniversary at The Adelphi we joined him at one of Liverpool's historic pubs, just a five minute walk from St Bride Street. It was Peter Kavanagh's. In Egerton Street.

A large sign which had been hanging outside the pub for years suggested that the name of the pub was 'The Grapes'. But nobody ever called it that. If the three of us had said we were nipping down to 'The Grapes', people would have been mystified.

Peter Kavanagh, you see, was a legend. Everybody knew him. He'd become the pub's landlord when he was in his twenties, back in 1897 when Queen Victoria was still on the throne. And he didn't finally call time on himself until 1950. Through two world wars, for a heroic fifty-three years, Peter Kavanagh had been in sole charge.

The layout of the pub followed the traditional northern pattern with front and back rooms opening off a central bar or lobby from which the drinks were served. The building had been constructed in 1844, at the same time as many of the surrounding Georgian houses, and during his long reign as licensee Peter Kavanagh had left his mark on the interior.

At the tail-end of the 1920s he had arranged for a Scottish artist, Eric Robinson, to decorate the walls with large murals which depicted traditional scenes from the tales of Dickens and Hogarth. People used to say that they had been painted to settle a debt. But that was never certain. At about the same time he had also installed some very fine stained-glass panels with seafaring scenes. And in what was a very personal touch, small carvings of Peter's own face had been added to the ends of the fixed, wooden benches in the bars.

So this unique and wonderful pub was known quite simply as Peter Kavanagh's. It couldn't possibly have been called anything else.

One day someone will get round to replacing the sign with an image of the pub's celebrated landlord. Beneath the image there will be just four words.

Welcome To
PETER KAVANAGH'S

"Oh, by the way," said Dave when I returned from the bar with our drinks. "We're being posted to Cyprus."

Sylvie and I both looked at him. "What for?" she said.

"To sort out a few little problems," said Dave. "There's been a bit of trouble over there for the past year or two. The Greek Cypriots on the island, who are by far the majority, are looking to become part of Greece. But the Turkish Cypriots are understandably less keen. And we of course want them all to remain British because their island happens to be in quite a handy place. At the eastern end of the Mediterranean, very close to the Middle East. We've had a big military base there for years which we'd quite like to hang on to. There's been quite a bit of fighting, on and off, so the big bosses have decided to beef up the armed forces we've already got on the island."

"And you're the beef," I said.

"Something like that. They're flying about a hundred of us out there on Friday. I've got to report back to the barracks by tomorrow lunchtime."

"It sounds like it might be a bit hairy," said Sylvie, looking a little worried.

"Nah," said Dave. "It'll be fine. One of our sergeants reckons it'll all be over by Christmas."

"That's what they said about World War One," I said, giving him a doubtful smile. "And look how that turned out."

"A barrel of laughs you are," said Dave. "Anyway, I knew when I joined up that I might have to do a bit of fighting. It's what we've all been training for. And if there's a problem which needs sorting out somebody's got to do it."

"Well," I said. "Full marks to you for giving it a go. But rather you than me. It wouldn't be my cup of tea."

Even as I spoke I knew that I admired his ability to overcome adversity and bounce back. Without people like Dave in it the world would be a much poorer place.

I lifted up my pint.

"Cheers, Dave. And good luck. I hope it goes well."

The three of us clinked our glasses together and I gave him a smile.

"See you at Christmas, then."

After three more New York crossings on the Queen Mary I got back to Liverpool to be greeted by some troubling news.

"Dave's gone missing," said Sylvie. They were her first words to me when we met.

Three weeks after arriving in Cyprus Dave and one of his fellow soldiers had mysteriously disappeared and their superiors in the army were very concerned.

I went straight round to see his father, Trevor.

The two of us sat together in his front room. It was a room I had known for many years, since I was a small child, and over all those years it had hardly changed. The three piece suite was the same and the floral carpet, now looking a little threadbare, had done very good service.

The increasingly bald carpet had been a joke for years. Trevor would never change it now.

"The Royal Family hardly ever replace the carpets and soft furnishings at Buckingham Palace." Trevor would say with a smile. "My cousin Douggie was a footman there for years. The only new carpets he ever saw were in the offices."

Everyone in the room would then join in with Trevor's closing refrain. It was always the same.

"And if it's good enough for Her Majesty The Queen, it's good enough for us."

I'd been there, and enjoyed the predictable routine, so many times. We'd all be crying with laughter.

But now there was no laughter. Instead there were tears in Trevor's eyes. Tears of almost unbearable sadness.

"I can't believe it, Steve," he said. "I keep thinking it's a nightmare and in a minute I'm going to wake up. But I don't."

I knew exactly how he was feeling. I felt the same. I wanted to comfort him but I didn't really know how to. Or what to say.

"I'm so sorry, Trevor." It was the best I could manage. "How long ago did you find out?"

"It seems like yesterday," he said, taking a deep breath. "But it's been nearly a month now. It was just after eight in the morning and there was this knock on the door. Quite loud it was. Almost like someone was trying to break in. The door bell doesn't always work and maybe I didn't hear a quieter knock. I don't know. I'd only just got up so I was still in my pyjamas and dressing gown. The kettle had not long boiled and I was about to sit down with the paper and a cup of tea. I goes to the door, expecting it to be the postman or something like that. And when I open it there's two people standing there. A man and a woman. Both of them in uniform. The man was holding a sort of plywood clipboard in his left hand, half under his arm. And there was a gold-coloured Parker pen under the clip, along with a set of black and white, pre-printed forms."

He paused for a moment.

"It's funny how you remember the little details isn't it. I tell you, Steve, my heart sank. I knew right away it wasn't going to be good news."

The tears which had filled his eyes were now running down Trevor's cheeks. I nodded my head and found myself making a sort of murmuring sound in sympathy. But I didn't say anything.

"The woman asked me if I was Mr Roberston," he said. "To make sure they were at the right house I suppose. So I told her I was. Then the man said his name was Major Scovel. Major Tom Scovel. And the woman with him was from the Army Nursing Corps, Senior Sister Alice Bowden."

"And what did they say about Dave?"

"First of all they wanted me to confirm that he was serving in Cyprus, seconded to the Queen's Royal Surrey Regiment. Well to be honest I wasn't sure which regiment David was with. So I told them all I knew was that he'd been flown out there a few weeks earlier. Then the Major came straight out with it. That David had gone missing in action."

He started to sob.

"Why couldn't he have stayed on the Queen Mary with you, Steve? I told him I didn't want him to join the army but he just said if he didn't volunteer he'd be called up to do National Service anyway."

The sobbing got louder and his shoulders were shaking.

"I don't understand what made him jack in a perfectly

good job. He always said he was loving it. And if he'd stayed with Cunard a couple more years he wouldn't have had to do National Service. He'd have been exempt."

I didn't know what Dave might have said to his Dad about Eddie and the New York gangsters. Probably very little, I thought. He wouldn't have wanted to worry him. So I didn't try to explain Dave's reasons for leaving the ship. I just put my arms around Trevor's shoulders to comfort him as he continued to sob and take very deep breaths.

"Did the army people tell you what happened?" I asked.

Trevor took a couple of even deeper breaths, then wiped his face with both hands.

"I'm sorry, Steve. It's just that I'm so worried. David's all I've got now."

I could see he was doing his best to keep himself composed.

"Don't worry," I said quietly. "I understand."

Trevor nodded his head to show he'd heard.

"When they were standing there outside the door telling me he'd gone missing I was in shock, Steve. I just felt completely numb. I didn't know what I was supposed to do so I asked them to come in and we sat down with cups of tea. I needed something. And I think they probably did too. Something stronger than tea would've been nice but it was only breakfast time. And I didn't want them to go away thinking I was a drinker."

Trevor looked at me and started to weep again.

"I wouldn't want their job," he said. "It can't be easy turning up at someone's house to tell him his only son has disappeared. I still don't believe it's real."

Some people say a problem shared is a problem halved. I don't know if they're right but I sort of felt that if I could just keep Dave's Dad talking it might help. And it surely couldn't do any harm.

"What happened to him, Trevor?"

"The Major said the British troops who'd flown out to Cyprus were based in a tented camp. At a place called Kermia. Not far from the capital, Nicosia. I know the name of the camp because it's been all over the news in connection with David and his friend going missing. I don't suppose I'll ever forget it now. You might've seen it."

I shook my head.

"All we get on the ship is a one page summary of what's happening in the world," I said.

I very nearly added that a couple of British soldiers going missing, and the name of their base, wouldn't have been important enough to make it into a brief news summary. But fortunately I thought better of it. I just told Trevor that I must have missed it.

"The name of the place isn't important, anyway," said Trevor. "David was sharing a tent with another lad who was also from Liverpool. They didn't tell me his name but I suppose that might be how the two of them got friendly. For some reason they'd both been transferred from Kermia to the main British base at Akrotiri, about an hour away. And from there they'd been sent out on patrol to a place on the south-west coast called Aphrodite's Rock. Just a mile or two from Akrotiri. It's apparently a well-known beauty spot where Aphrodite, the Goddess of Love, is supposed to have emerged from the sea. There's this ancient Greek temple nearby which David and his friend had been told to check out. Apparently the army had got wind of some rumours about it being used by local terrorists to store weapons and ammunition. They'd been given orders to take a look at it and report back."

Trevor had stopped crying. The focus required to tell me the story did seem to be helping him.

"And that was when they disappeared?" I said.

He nodded his head.

"They never reported back. According to the Major they were driving an Austin Champ. You know. A bit like an American Army Jeep. It was found abandoned on a dirt road between the temple and the beach. Close to Aphrodite's Rock. The strange thing was their army uniforms were there in the Champ. Lying in a pile as if they'd been thrown in very hurriedly. But their rifles and ammunition pouches, along with a few hand grenades, had gone."

"And there was no sign of them?"

"They found the other lad's body in some bushes by the beach. He'd been shot in the back. But there was no sign of David. The Major said soldiers from the Akrotiri base combed the whole area as well as doing a house-to-house search in the nearest town. A small place called Paphos. And they pulled some of the local supporters of EOKA, the Cypriot Fighters' Organisation, in for questioning. But David had vanished."

"And that's it?" I said.

"The nurse in particular was very kind," said Trevor. "I suppose that's what she was there for. And to be fair the Major was very sympathetic too. But his main job seemed to be telling me the facts. He said they wouldn't give up searching. And that British soldiers don't just disappear. Especially on such a small island. He seemed to be pretty confident they'd find David eventually, one way or another. The army have even been in touch with Colonel Georgios Grivas, the Leader of EOKA. And the Head of the Cypriot Church on the island, Archbishop Makarios, has offered to help. But there's been nothing." He shrugged his shoulders. "They've promised to let me know immediately if there are any developments."

Trevor looked beaten.

"I hate to say it, Steve. But I'm beginning to give up hope."

"See you at Christmas, then," I said to Sylvie. "Do you remember me saying that to Dave when we were with him at Peter Kavanagh's?"

It was the following morning. We'd just made love and Sylvie put her head on my chest.

"Poor Trevor," she said quietly. "It doesn't seem fair. First his wife, Jean, gets killed by a random bomb in the war. Then he loses your Ma. And now, Dave."

She continued to lie there, saying nothing. Then quite suddenly she lifted her head and turned to face me.

"Do you know," she said, "it's never occurred to me before. But do you think that could be why your mother chose the name Jean for your sister? You know, with Trevor's wife being called Jean."

"I suppose it could be," I said. "I can't say I ever really thought about it. It was just the way it had always been. My sister was called Jean. And Dave's Mum was called Jean. The idea that it might be more than a coincidence never crossed my mind. But I suppose it's possible. Ma knew Trevor and Jean long before my Dad arrived on the scene. The three of them were big mates. All in the same class in primary school. And Ma always said that Jean was her best friend."

"It can't just be a coincidence," said Sylvie as she gently stroked my chest. "I think your Jean must have been named after your Mum's best friend. Who was also Dave's Mum."

"My Ma never knew my Dad when she was young because he didn't live round here. He was born in Egerton Street, a few doors down from Peter Kavanagh's, but the whole family moved away when my Dad was very little. My Dad's father, my grandfather, was a landlord and he ran a pub out in Prescot for about fifteen years. Then he took over Ye Cracke. You know. The very small pub in Rice Street near the Philharmonic Hall. That's when my Dad moved back here."

"So how come your Ma got together with your Dad?" said Sylvie.

"Ma told me they met in Ye Cracke. My Dad was helping out. Serving drinks behind the bar and so on. And one day he saw my Ma in there and started chatting her up. She shouldn't really have been drinking in there at all because she was under age. And then she got pregnant so they had to get married."

"It's weird how that sort of thing happens and changes your life," said Sylvie. "You know, your Mum being in Ye Cracke when she shouldn't have been."

She paused for a moment.

"I'd never have met you if my boyfriend hadn't decided he'd rather go on a pub crawl in Manchester with some of his mates than see me that Saturday night. When Greg's sister said to me there was a blind date at The Grafton on offer it seemed like the perfect way of teaching him a lesson."

"Wonderful," I said, feigning annoyance that our first meeting had been to teach another lad a lesson. "You never told me."

"You never asked," said Sylvie with a laugh. "Anyway, I didn't expect to fall madly in love that night. And certainly not with a Cunard Yank who I hardly ever see."

"And what about this boyfriend?" I said. "The one who needed to be taught a lesson. What did he say about it?"

"I didn't give him a chance to say anything. He was a waste of space compared to you. So I just dumped him."

"And you've not seen him since?"

"No. Of course I haven't. I've got you now."

I put my arms around Sylvie and held her close, feeling her soft, warm skin against mine. It made me feel better. And with the news about Dave I badly needed something to make me feel better.

"I can't stop thinking," I said. "I keep wondering if Dave's still alive. And if he is, what he might be going through."

"Me too," said Sylvie. "It's awful."

I pulled her even closer to me. It was such an easy thing to do but it was more comforting than a thousand words. Skin against skin.

"That's so good," she whispered. "Don't let go."

We lay there in silence, letting the mysterious healing powers of warmth and the mutual touch of skin soothe us.

"My Ma once told me she went out with Trevor a few times before she met my Dad," I said. "And one time he got down on one knee and said he wanted to marry her. They were only fifteen so she told him to stop being so daft but that if he'd like to ask again in a year or two she might think about it. Then she went out with my Dad and got herself pregnant."

"And a few years later Trevor ends up marrying Jean," said Sylvie.

"Yeah. I'm not sure exactly when. But they'd been married a few years by the time Dave came along."

Sylvie ran her fingers through my hair.

"It'd be so sad if Trevor and your Ma had been in love with each other the whole time," she said quietly. "But they were too young to do anything about it. Then your Dad getting her pregnant meant she married the wrong man. And Trevor married her best friend, Jean, because he couldn't marry the person he really loved."

I stroked the top of her left shoulder.

"Dearest Sylvie," I said, giving her a kiss. "You're a real romantic aren't you. The next thing you'll be saying is that Trevor might be Jean's real father."

"That had occurred to me," she said. "But I don't think so. You and Jean are too alike."

"Maybe he's my Dad too?"

"Which would mean that Dave is your brother."

I caught Sylvie's eye. By holding on to each other and sharing crazy ideas we'd managed to block out the real world for a few minutes. But as soon as she mentioned Dave it all came flooding back in.

"Or was my brother," I said.

For a few minutes we lay there in silence again. Turning things over inside our heads.

"What do you really think?" said Sylvie. "Could Dave still be alive?"

"I hope so." I gave her a reassuring squeeze. "My heart tells me he could be. But Major Scovel who came to see Trevor told him that if Dave had been taken prisoner by EOKA someone would have said something by now. Or his body would have been found. Like the other poor lad's. He didn't say so but the British Army must have people working secretly inside the terrorist groups. So they may well know a whole load of stuff they can't tell us because it'd put their informers at risk."

My mind was working overtime. Trying to figure it out.

"What I don't understand," I said "is the uniforms. Why would they have thrown them into the Champ? And the missing rifles. Why would they take off their uniforms but keep their rifles and so on with them?"

"Unless someone didn't want them to be identified as British soldiers and made them remove their uniforms. And took their rifles and ammunition as well. They'd be useful to terrorists."

"To me it all suggests they were captured rather than killed," I said. "At least at first. So maybe Dave is in the hands of some breakaway group. EOKA may not have had anything to do with it. But we're just guessing. If you really want to start thinking outside the box, maybe they decided to go for a swim?"

Sylvie frowned at me.

"No, seriously," I said. "Trevor told me he looked Aphrodite's Rock up in an old set of encyclopaedias he's got because he wanted to be able to sort of visualise the place where Dave disappeared."

"I can understand that," said Sylvie. "I'd probably want to do the same."

"It said Aphrodite's Rock is beautiful. But the sea around it is very dangerous with a lot of powerful currents and undertows. The locals say it's Aphrodite guarding the place where she was born. But they also say if you manage to swim round her rock three times without being dragged under and drowned she will grant you eternal love."

"Can you imagine Dave and his friend stripping off and trying that?" said Sylvie. "And then getting captured without their uniforms? When they'd have known there could be armed terrorists in the area."

"No," I said, shaking my head. "I don't think so. Definitely not."

"Then they must have been captured. And the other poor lad got himself shot in the back for some reason. Maybe he was trying to escape? Which could mean that whoever took them prisoner has still got Dave."

We both lay there quietly. There were so many possibilities. Would we ever know what really happened?

Sylvie broke the silence.

"What are you going to do about Julie? I've obviously never met her so I've no idea what's best. But I suppose she'll have to be told."

It was something I'd been thinking about ever since I heard the news.

"I went to pick some records up off her last week," I said. "Before we got the news. She was asking about Dave and how he was getting on in the army so I told her he'd been posted to Cyprus. It's been a while now since they last saw each other and she knows he's signed up for three years. So she might well have moved on. I hope she has in a way."

I stopped to think.

"I'm sure they were very fond of each other. But with him being at sea and her living in New York Dave never acted like it might get serious. At least not as far as he was concerned. Julie was the only girl he saw regularly, but he had plenty of others dotted around Liverpool as you know."

"She still needs to be told." said Sylvie. "I'd want to be if I were her."

"What do I tell her?"

"The truth, of course" said Sylvie. "What else? That Dave's gone missing. At the moment that's all we know."

I nodded my head. As always she made it sound really straightforward. And she was absolutely right.

"I'd like you to come to New York with me one day," I said. "I could book you onto the ship without any problem. There's always a few spare cabins. And it wouldn't cost a lot. You'd love New York. And you could meet Julie. The two of you would get on really well. The difficulty is the turnarounds on the Queen Mary are so quick it wouldn't be worth it. Unless maybe I could arrange to take my shore leave over there instead of here? That might be possible."

"I'd love that." Sylvie snuggled up to me. "Promise me you'll look into it. And let's not leave it too long."

TWENTY-SIX

NEW YORK AND NIAGARA FALLS

May 18th, 1959

"I can't believe this is really happening," said Sylvie as the Queen Mary sailed slowly past the Statue of Liberty and approached the southern tip of Manhattan. "You've tried to describe it to me but words can't do it justice. I've imagined it so many times but the reality is even better. It's absolutely brilliant."

It had taken six months to organise everything. But Sylvie and I were at last going to be together in New York.

The skyscrapers were getting closer as our ship entered the Hudson River with the Battery to starboard and the New Jersey shore, a little further away, on our port side. It was early summer and the days were getting longer. It was already light enough to see that it was going to be a clear day with not a cloud in the sky. A perfect day for Sylvie to be seeing the city for the very first time. The geometrical shapes of the tall buildings, outlined against the blue of the sky, were sharp and clear as they caught and reflected the rays of the early morning sun. I'd seen it all before. But this time it was extra special because I was with Sylvie.

"The low-lying area we've just passed with a few trees on it," I said. "That's Battery Park. It's where the original cannons to defend the city were placed by the Dutch when it was still called New Amsterdam. The whole area was closed off for about fifteen years so they could build a tunnel to Brooklyn under the East River. It was re-opened three or four years ago and it's still being landscaped."

I pointed ahead and slightly to the right.

"See over there. The tallest skyscraper. That's the Empire State Building. And the one beyond it with the art-deco design at the top is the Chrysler Building."

"How long is it before we dock?" said Sylvie. "I can't wait to walk down the gangway and actually set foot on American soil." She gave me a big smile. "It's so exciting."

"Some tugs will be with us in a minute," I said. "They're to make sure there aren't any problems as we move alongside Cunard Pier 90. That's always our berth because it's the only one long enough to take this ship. In theory we should be able to manage the docking without assistance but the Captain and the Port Authorities like to have the tugs in place. Just in case something unexpected happens and last minute adjustments which the ship can't manage on her own are needed."

The Queen Mary reduced speed and the tugs moved alongside, keeping pace and guiding our much larger vessel as she began slowly to turn and manoeuvre herself towards the waiting Pier. I stayed up on deck with Sylvie, watching as the Captain placed his ship parallel to the Pier and then, ever so slowly, allowed her to drift gently sideways. There was a squeaking and squealing as the steel sides of the Queen Mary compressed the rubber buffers which stopped her from hitting the hard wood and concrete of the Pier itself. Small, round weights, about the size of tennis balls and attached to thin ropes, were thrown ashore into the hands of waiting stevedores who used them to pull thick mooring ropes onto the pier which were then looped over and secured around massive, steel bollards. The first couple of mooring ropes were tightened up after which several more were added until we were safely and securely berthed.

"That's it," I said to Sylvie. "We just need to wait for the Captain to announce that the arrival formalities have all been completed. It usually takes half an hour or so. Maybe an hour. And then we'll be able to head ashore."

• •• ———— • ••• • ◆ ••————— •• •

"What would you like to kick off with?" I asked Sylvie as we made our way down the gangway and headed towards U.S. Immigration and Customs. "There's no great rush to decide because we'll be in the queue for a little while. U.S. Immigration is thorough. And very slow. Getting into the Land of the Free has never been easy. And you won't officially have arrived in America until they've stamped your passport and given you the all-clear. As Les, our Head Steward on the Media, said to me and dear old Dave the first time we arrived here. No messing. Answer their questions as simply as possible. And no jokes. The Immigration Officers aren't selected for their sense of humour."

"What did the immigrant say to the Officer at the desk when he was asked if he had a criminal record?" said Sylvie, grinning at me. She paused before delivering the punchline. "I didn't know you still needed one!"

Sylvie burst out laughing at her own joke. As always it was infectious and I couldn't help joining in.

"You're an idiot," I said. "The British convicts were all transported to Australia, not America."

"A minor detail. And you've got to admit it's a good one."

We were both still laughing as we joined the queue which

snaked ahead of us between the guiding ropes. A uniformed attendant looked at us and frowned.

"Okay," I whispered to Sylvie. "Serious face from now on. Or we might get transported. Back to the ship."

Half an hour later we were standing at the junction of 12th Avenue and 50th. It was almost exactly the spot where Dave's fateful conversation with Spike and his gun-carrying accomplice had taken place but I didn't say anything to Sylvie. It would have spoilt the moment for her.

Knowing that we were going to be moving around from hotel to hotel we'd made a conscious decision to travel light. The two cases at our feet were small and very easily carried.

For our stay in New York I'd booked a room at The Alonquin Hotel, close to Times Square.

"I think what we need to do first of all," I said to Sylvie, "is go and leave our bags at the hotel rather than carrying them around New York with us. The Alonquin's only five or ten minutes' walk away and I can easily manage both bags. Then we could maybe pop along and see if Julie's on duty at the Thrift Store. It's only a couple of blocks from the hotel and I'm sure she'd like to meet you. She'll obviously want to know if there's been any news about Dave with things having been sorted out in Cyprus."

The fighting in Cyprus had come to an end three months earlier. The British Government had agreed that the island would become an independent republic and Britain would retain sovereignty over the military bases at Akrotiri and Dhekeila. With the cessation of hostilities it had been hoped that missing British soldiers who might still be in the hands of Greek Cypriot terrorists would be released. But there had been no sign of Dave.

Almost as soon as we walked in through the main door we both knew that The Alonquin Hotel would suit us well. It had been open for over fifty years and was very traditional in style, with wood-panelling and a large grandfather clock in the lobby. And unlike almost every other New York hotel the lifts were still operated by uniformed attendants. But, as a sort of quirky nod to modernity, it had been the very first hotel in the city to replace room keys with electronic key cards. It was a rather appealing mix of the old and the new.

As it turned out our room was ready and they were happy to let us leave our cases in there. Up on the eighth floor, with a bay window looking down onto West 44th Street, the room was small but comfortable. It would be more than adequate for our three-night stay before catching the train north to Buffalo and Niagara Falls.

On our way out to see Julie we popped our heads into the hotel's famous Blue Bar with its blue lighting and blue-toned, backlit bookshelves. It had first opened its doors in 1933 with the end of Prohibition and it looked like the perfect place for a nightcap.

When we got to the Salvation Army Thrift Store Julie greeted us with her usual smile, but before any introductions could be done she had an anxious question which needed to be answered.

"Any news about Dave?"

I shook my head.

"Nothing, I'm afraid. At least not when the ship left Southampton. And I think his Dad would have tried to let us know if there'd been anything since."

"Oh well," said Julie with a shrug of her shoulders. "If there's one thing the last six or seven months have taught me it's not to build my hopes up. But you never know."

I turned to Sylvie.

"I've brought my girlfriend, Sylvie, to meet you, Julie."

Julie gave Sylvie a very genuine smile. Julie was very worldly-wise and although I hadn't said anything to her she would know not to mention her old flatmate, Carol.

"Hi, Sylvie. It's good to meet you."

"I've heard so much about you from Steve I feel like I know you already," said Sylvie, returning her smile. "And I've listened to all your amazing American records. So it's really good to meet you too. I just wish we'd been able to bring some better news for you about poor Dave."

"It's really hard not knowing," said Julie. The smile had gone and she looked sad. "I think about him a lot. And I still miss him. He was fun. We got on really well even though we weren't able to spend all that much time together. Dave was a sailor. And I was his girl in New York City. I knew that. But what we had was still a bit special. And until I know for sure he'll never be coming back I'll keep on hoping that maybe we'll see each other again one day."

"Come here," said Sylvie, holding her arms out. I watched as the two of them hugged each other. They were already like old friends. The store was quiet so we were able to spend a bit of time together. Julie made us a coffee and the two of them never stopped talking. I hardly got a word in.

As we were finally leaving Julie called us back.

"I nearly forgot," she said. "There are some records for you in the back if you're interested."

"Definitely," I said. "But is there any chance of you hanging on to them for a few days? We're taking a train to Buffalo in a day or two. To see Niagara Falls. And then we'll be in Washington DC for a couple of days. We'll be back here next week. We can call in and pick them up then if that's okay?"

"No problem. I'll see you both next week then."

As we walked back to The Algonquin I had a question for Sylvie.

"You and Julie already seem to understand each other," I said. "She's not seen Dave for ages. And I suppose she may never see him again. But am I right in thinking she still cares quite a lot about him?"

"I'm sure she does," said Sylvie. "You can tell by the way she talks about him. They were obviously very fond of each other. And maybe they still would be if things had worked out differently."

"And you think Dave might have felt the same?"

"Julie's smart," she said. "I hardly know her but I don't think she'd have let herself get fond of Dave unless she was getting similar vibes back. I don't know what he might've said to you. And I could be completely wrong. But if he'd been based in New York instead of coming and going from England on a ship I think they could easily have ended up as a couple."

I nodded my head slowly.

"That's what I think too. So let's hope Dave's still alive. And that by some miracle he turns up in one piece."

Our three-day stay in New York was a whirlwind. We did the Empire State Building, Central Park, Fifth Avenue, The Staten Island Ferry, Bloomingdale's and Macy's. We ate Nathan's Famous Hot Dogs on Coney Island. And we tried out various New York Delis.

And, most unexpectedly, we got to see the original production of West Side Story. We were wandering along Broadway when Sylvie spotted a lady taping a hand-written notice to the doors of The Winter Garden Theatre where the show had premiered. The lady disappeared into the lobby and we crossed the street to take a look. The notice said that a few tickets had unexpectedly become available.

The box office was just inside the main Broadway entrance. And there was no queue.

"I'm sure they won't have anything," said Sylvie, "but I'd love to see a Broadway musical. So let's just ask. They can only say no."

The two of us went in. The lady who'd been putting up the notice was now sitting behind a glass screen.

"Have you got anything available in the next three days?" I said.

The lady yawned. "Sorry. Late night. I didn't get much sleep." She looked at Sylvie who was standing behind me. "Two tickets is it?"

"Yes, please," said Sylvie. "If that's possible."

An oblong box was pulled out from under the counter. The lady placed it in front of her and began to flick through the dozen or so brown envelopes it contained. Each envelope had a date and a number on the outside. I could see that on most of them the number was '1'.

"These are returns," she explained. "Nearly all singles. I only opened the door a couple of minutes ago and they'll go very quickly because the show's closing next month. A lot of people still want to see it. Tickets are like gold-dust."

She looked down at the box as her fingers continued to work their way through the contents.

"Aha." She stopped at the last envelope. There was a '2' written on it. "It looks like you're in luck. A pair of seats in the stalls. Friday May 22nd. That's tomorrow. In the evening. Row G. Seats 17 and 18. Twelve dollars fifty. They're good seats. And they're yours if you want them. Yes or no? You'll need to be quick."

I turned to see Sylvie nodding her head. I also saw that an eager queue of seven or eight people had already built up behind us.

"I guess that'll be a 'yes'," said the lady, passing me the envelope as I took the required dollars out of my pocket.

"Trust me," she said. "West Side Story is the best show to have hit this town in years. Your accents tell me you're from England. So now you'll be able to tell people back home you saw the very first production of West Side Story. In New York City. On Broadway."

On the way out of the lobby Sylvie spotted a framed poster.

> *"This show is my baby ... If it goes as well in New York*
> *as it has on the road we will have proved*
> *something very big indeed*
> *and maybe changed the face of American Musical Theater."*
> *– Leonard Bernstein 1957*

We had struck lucky. And the show was stunning.

To have seen the original production, in New York City, of one of the twentieth century's most iconic and important musicals was a huge privilege. And an unforgettable experience.

●‧‧————————●‧‧●‧‧●‧●————————‧‧●

The functional waterproof capes with hoods which had been supplied to all the passengers by the crew on the 'Maid of the Mist' kept us drier than we would otherwise have been as our vessel's powerful diesel engines fought against the swift current, taking us ever closer to the curved curtain of water which was known as the Horseshoe Falls. But we were still very wet.

We had already passed the American section of the Niagara Falls, at the base of which a slope of broken boulders slightly lessened the force of the plunging water, and our relatively small craft had now crossed over to the Canadian side of the Falls. We were very soon being soaked by the droplets of mist which were being thrown high into the air as the Niagara River reached the lip of the Falls and dived one hundred and seventy five feet into the Great Gorge, creating as it did so the treacherous Whirlpool Rapids which we were now approaching. A mere 66 feet long and carrying 101 passengers, our vessel had been brought into service just four years earlier, in 1955. It was difficult to imagine how the previous, wooden-hulled boat with its old-fashioned, steam-driven engine had coped with the treacherous conditions.

The close-up view of the Horseshoe Falls was breathtaking, made even more so by the thunderous, crashing roar as almost six million cubic feet of water cascaded over the crest every minute and hurtled down into the gorge. We were looking at the greatest volume of falling water on the planet.

Sylvie, who had been staring ahead transfixed by what she was seeing, turned to me. Her eyes were bright, and even though her hair was plastered to her forehead and water was running down both her cheeks the look on her face told me she was ecstatically happy.

"I've wanted to come here ever since I saw a picture of this little boat when I was about nine," she said. "I never dreamed it'd actually happen."

She threw her wet arms around me and we exchanged a very damp kiss.

"Thank you. Thank you. Thank you. It's unbelievable. Amazing."

"Next stop, Washington D.C." I said. "That should be pretty amazing too. And hopefully not quite so wet."

Washington was indeed amazing. The White House, the Capitol Building, the Washington Monument, the Lincoln Memorial and the Arlington National Cemetery. We saw them all. And we walked the whole length of the National Mall, looking to our left and right at the magnificent Smithsonian Museums which flanked the long expanse of grass.

We had a great time. But two days wasn't enough to even scratch the surface of the capital city of the United States. We promised ourselves that one day we would be back.

It was time to return to New York City, pick up some records, and catch a big ship back to England.

As Sylvie gave her new friend, Julie, one final hug she promised to let her know immediately if there was any news about Dave.

•–•–––––••–•–•–•–––––––••

That day came almost as soon as we returned home.

A letter had arrived at the British Sovereign Base at Akrotiri in Cyprus which contained information that could only have been supplied by Dave. Enclosed with the letter were several photographs of him in captivity.

The source of the letter was unknown. But having checked the information it contained, and examined the photographs very carefully, the military authorities in Cyprus had concluded that it was genuine.

Trevor was never shown the letter or the photographs. Perhaps the information was too sensitive. Or maybe the pictures were thought to be too upsetting. But the army confirmed to him that Dave and his friend had been captured by a group of terrorists who had broken away from EOKA because they did not agree with the political tactics of its leader, General Georgios Grivas. Dave's friend had indeed been shot when trying to escape. And Dave had then been held prisoner by the group as a potential bargaining counter.

The writer of the letter explained that when Britain granted independence to Cyprus, bringing the fighting to an end, the possibility of changing the political outcome of the war no longer existed. Dave was no longer of any value to them and he should have been released. But there had been a most unfortunate misunderstanding and he had instead been shot. To minimise the risk of their group being traced his body was now in a place where it would never be found.

His death was very regrettable, the letter had said. It should not have happened. The message was being sent to give Dave's family some sort of closure. The writer himself was seriously ill. He did not have long to live and he did not want to take the information to his own grave.

Dave's father told me that once the ceasefire had been agreed and weeks had passed without any news he had known in his heart that Dave could no longer be alive. Although it was something that no father ever wanted to hear, the news from Cyprus had come almost as a relief.

He would probably never know his son's final resting place. But it had indeed provided him with a degree of closure.

It was better, said Trevor, than never knowing anything at all.

"I can now," he said, with tears in his eyes, "abandon all hope. And properly grieve."

For me, if it was true that Dave need not have died. That it had been a mistake. An unfortunate misunderstanding. That was very hard to take.

A Memorial Service to honour Dave's all too brief time in the British Army and the ultimate sacrifice he had made on behalf of his country was held at St Bride's Church. Representatives from Cunard were there, along with senior officers from Dave's regiment who arranged for a commemorative plaque to be installed inside the church. He would not be forgotten.

I gave Julie the sad news on my next visit to New York City. She too said that it came as a strange sort of relief.

"I loved him, you know," she whispered as we held each other. "He was special. It was more than just a bit of fun."

I couldn't say anything. I just held her even tighter.

Life had to go on.

TWENTY–SEVEN

THE CASBAH COFFEE CLUB

"While you were in New York I signed us both up as members of a new place called The Casbah which is going to be opening soon in West Derby Village," said Sylvie as she handed me a couple of membership cards, one pink and one blue.

"Your card's the blue one," she said. "The pink one's mine. It's only five or ten minutes down the road from us in a big Victorian house and it sounds like it might be good. So I thought it'd be an idea to add our names to the membership list. It's half-a-crown each for twelve months. Mrs Best, the lady who owns the house, is setting the club up in her basement. She says they've got over a hundred members already."

I looked at the two cards.

"The Casbah Coffee Club," I said. "Great name."

"Somebody said it was Mrs Best who came up with it," said Sylvie. "She remembered seeing a film called 'Algiers', and one of the leading men saying, 'Come with me to The Casbah'. She thought it sounded cool."

"It does," I said. "And if she really has got that many people signed up before it's even opened she could be on to something."

"Remember my friend, Kathy?" said Sylvie. "The girl we met at the garden fete in Woolton? Well, her little sister's been helping them do up the basement. And she stayed the night there a couple of weeks ago. With some other girls and a few of the boys. She's only fifteen so her mother went spare. She had words with Mo. That's Mrs Best. And Mo just said she keeps a close eye on things to make sure the kids are all behaving themselves, but because they've all been working so hard she's not going to chuck them out if they're having fun. Having said that, the house has got a massive garden with lots of bushes and hiding places. So all sorts could be going on."

"She sounds like a fun lady," I said, raising my eyebrows. "What gave her the idea of starting up a coffee club?"

"According to Kathy's sister she heard about The Two I's in London which is doing really well, putting on live music and serving proper Italian coffee instead of the usual instant stuff. So she thought about the big basement in her house which wasn't being used for anything other than storage and decided to do something similar in Liverpool. Her husband's been in charge of the stadium in the city centre for years. So the idea of running a coffee club in their basement wouldn't really have phased her. And she's got hold of a proper Italian espresso machine too. It'll be the only one in Liverpool."

"And is she going to have live music?"

"I think so, yes," said Sylvie. "A lad she knows called Ken Brown is getting a group together. John Lennon, the singer with that skiffle group we saw in Woolton, is in it. Along with the other lad who was there in Woolton, Paul McCartney. And a boy called George Harrison. Kathy's sister said he's played with John and Paul in the Quarrymen a couple of times and he's also been in another group with Ken Brown. So he's joining them on lead guitar. They still think the Quarrymen is a good name so that's what they're going to carry on calling themselves."

I nodded my head. "Yeah. It is a good name. They'd struggle to find anything better."

"Mo has agreed they can definitely do the opening night," explained Sylvie. "And if it goes well she's promised to keep them on as the resident group every Saturday. They're all dead keen to stay in her good books so they've been helping out in the basement with all the other kids. Kathy's sister says they've painted stuff like rainbows and stars on the ceilings. And some Aztec-type hieroglyphics on one of the walls which Mo was apparently keen on having. John Lennon's a student at The Art College in Liverpool so he and his girlfriend, Cynthia, have done an amazing, life-like silhouette of him in white on another of the walls. When it's all finished it's going to look great."

I gave Sylvie a kiss.

"I owe you half-a-crown for getting us onto the membership list, then," I said. "Smart move."

Sylvie laughed.

"Forget it. I'll treat you."

"In which case I'll pay for both of us on opening night," I said. "When's the big day?"

"In just over three weeks," said Sylvie. "August the 29th. It's a Saturday. I've checked. And you'll be back here in Liverpool unless the date of your shore leave gets changed."

On Wednesday 26th August, 1959 I was on board the Queen Mary as she made her way slowly and steadily across the Atlantic on her return journey from New York to Southampton.

As we were crossing the mid-Atlantic ridge a jet aircraft passed high over our heads, also heading towards England. Nobody on board our ship saw or heard the brand-new Boeing 707-320. But it was a flight that was going to change everything.

The plane had been developed at the request of Pan American airlines. They had asked Boeing to make them a passenger jet that could fly from New York to London without needing to stop for refuelling at Gandar in Newfoundland. The 707-320 was the result. And it would land at London Airport just over eight hours after leaving New York.

The non-stop flight was all over the news. The headline writers were saying that transatlantic travel was about to enter a new era. That the world had suddenly become a much smaller place and that even the fastest and most luxurious of the great passenger liners would struggle to compete.

The press were predicting that travelling by ship as a way of crossing the Atlantic would very soon become the exception rather than the rule. The new passenger jets would allow people to make the journey much more quickly and easily.

The more I thought about it, the more I realised they were right. Being a Cunard Yank would no longer carry quite the same cachet. With New York City being just eight hours away and easily accessible it would no longer be so exotic or special.

Looking ahead I could see that Cunard Yanks could very easily go the way of the dodo. And become extinct.

I needed to start thinking about my future.

Sylvie and I walked from her place in West Derby, along Eaton Road, to the Best family's big Victorian house. It was about fifty yards up a tree-lined, side road called Hayman's Green. Not far from the centre of West Derby Village.

"It's on the right. Number Eight," said Sylvie as we made our way along the pavement, stepping into the road in two or three places to avoid overgrown and overhanging hedges. "The entrance to the basement is round the back."

The official opening time was seven-thirty but Kathy had warned Sylvie that lots of her friends were planning to be there. She didn't think the small basement could possibly hold all the people who were now signed up as members. So we turned up early to be on the safe side. We didn't want to risk being locked out.

As we reached the entrance to the driveway we discovered that we were not the only ones who had decided to play it safe. Although it was only just after six o'clock a queue already stretched half the length of the drive and disappeared round the corner of the house.

It looked like Mrs Best's Casbah Coffee Club was going to be a success.

We joined the queue and waited. Then, all of a sudden, it started to move forwards. Because so many people were waiting outside they had decided to open the doors even though the Quarrymen weren't due to start playing until eight. Coffees and Cokes would be on sale. And getting people in early would allow time for plenty of excitement to build up.

I paid our entrance fees and we made our way down a couple of newly-constructed, stone steps which took us into a corridor. To our left some stairs were signposted as leading to a cloakroom and toilet. On the right was an open doorway beyond which there was an oblong area. Three well-worn amplifiers lined up at the far end behind a microphone told us it was where the Quarrymen would be performing.

Their set had already been put back by forty-five minutes because of the unexpected crowds and a young man called Bob Stuart, who told us he was the club's disc-jockey, was playing records at full volume on a small, dark-blue and cream Dansette record player. The Best family had their own collection. And club members had been encouraged to bring their own favourites along. So Bob had a decent selection to choose from.

At the end of the main corridor was a bar where one of Mo's sons was dealing with the non-stop orders for coffees and Cokes as more and more people crowded in. The queue outside was still growing so Mo Best decided to open up the kitchen door on the ground floor. A second entrance would speed things up a bit.

The atmosphere in the increasingly crowded basement was expectant, but friendly. Mona Best had insisted that The Casbah should be *'Members Only'* so that she could easily identify, and exclude, troublemakers. Liverpool's city-centre clubs, most of which still concentrated on jazz, were plagued by undesirables who had little interest in the music. They just wanted to create mayhem and get involved in fights.

Mrs Best was on a mission. The Casbah Coffee Club was going to be different. It was going to present beat music, not jazz. And because it was part of her house it was going to be a place where everyone could feel safe and secure.

Rule Number Four on the membership cards spelled it out.

'Any member found creating a disturbance will be BARRED.'

●·+·————————●·+·●·+·●————————·+·●

As we waited for the Quarrymen to start their set we drank Cokes and listened to the records which Bob had carefully selected. The portable Dansette had never been designed for public performances. Even at full volume it struggled to compete with the chattering club members. But it didn't matter. The atmosphere was so relaxed and friendly that it felt more like a family party than a club.

It was exactly what Mona Best had been hoping to achieve.

Finally, at a quarter to nine, the Quarrymen appeared. We watched as they made their way to the area where they were due to perform and plugged in their guitars. John Lennon, as the leader and the original founder of the group, approached the microphone.

"Hello everyone. Welcome to The Casbah. We're the Quarrymen. And we're going to play some rock 'n' roll."

Everybody started clapping and cheering. We were more than ready to be entertained.

John's place at the microphone was quickly taken by Paul McCartney who went straight into their opening number, Little Richard's 'Long Tall Sally'. They ran through a selection of rock 'n' roll standards which they had learnt by listening to the records which were now available in Liverpool. Having jotted down the lyrics they would work out the chords. Which wasn't too difficult. As Jim Gretty had demonstrated to me, most of the songs used the same three or four chords and followed the same twelve-bar pattern.

The four Quarrymen played two forty-five minute sets, taking a fifteen minute break between them. They wound up the evening with their own extended version of the Ray Charles song, 'What'd I Say'. George Harrison introduced the song by saying it was currently his favourite and that he'd very recently attended an all-night party at which the Ray Charles record was played almost non-stop.

The reception the group got as they unplugged their instruments and shouted 'Thank you' to their new fans was loud and enthusiastic. We had all arrived determined to enjoy ourselves, whatever happened, but even so we were completely knocked out by what we had heard.

This particular line-up of the Quarrymen had only been playing together for a couple of weeks and it had been their first public performance. So it wasn't all that professional or polished. And their equipment, apart from George Harrison's recently-acquired electric Futurama, was fairly basic.

But the music was live. And it was loud. And that made it thrilling.

It had been a memorable evening.

As Sylvie and I walked back along Eaton Road, hand in hand, we were both thinking. We'd been talking earlier in the afternoon about the effect the new jet planes might have on transatlantic travel. And on my job.

And it wasn't just transatlantic travel that was changing. Music was changing too.

We had just spent an evening in Liverpool's first proper beat music club.

No jazz. No skiffle. And no blues.

As John Lennon had told us right at the beginning of the evening. It was pure rock 'n' roll. Played Liverpool-style.

Quarry Men? Or Quarrymen? It is a question that has been asked for more than sixty years.

The original members of the group state on their website <originalquarrymen.co.uk> (Feb 2024) that they prefer their name to be spelt 'Quarrymen', all one word, as in the Quarry Bank School Song from where their name originated. In this book I have therefore used their preferred spelling.

The original Quarrymen at the Garden Fete in Woolton were John Lennon (guitar), Eric Griffiths (guitar), Colin Hanton (drums), Rod Davis (banjo), Pete Shotton (washboard) and Len Garry (tea-chest bass).

TWENTY-EIGHT

THE KAISERKELLER - HAMBURG

It was October 1960.

The nineteen-fifties had come to an end and we had entered the sixties. Greg and I were listening to the latest batch of records from Julie in New York.

"D'you remember a kid called Geoff from school?" said Greg.

"Which one?" I said. "As far as I can remember there were three kids called Geoff in our year. There was the Geoff who had bad acne. And there was the Geoff who did magic tricks. The only thing I remember about him is he was very good at making money disappear. He conned me out of a whole week's pocket money playing 'Find The Lady'. Even now I don't know how he did it. He offered me double or quits on the last game and that was it. Every penny I had in the world. Gone."

"Unless you did much better than me for pocket money you can't have had that much," said Greg. "Enough for a couple of packets of chewie. Or maybe a few cheap fags. Anyway, it wasn't either of those Geoffs."

"In which case," I said, starting to laugh as I remembered

the story, "it's got to be the Geoff who claimed he'd been seduced by Miss Frazer in the Art Room. He said she had a tattoo of a butterfly on her bum but we never believed him. Then she seduced big Robbo as well. And he said it was true."

We were both now laughing at the memory but with an image of the lovely Miss Frazer, our very accommodating young art-teacher, now fully occupying my mind I'd completely forgotten Greg's original question.

"Sorry, Greg," I said, "but what you were asking?"

"I asked if you remembered that Geoff," he said. "Because he's now the drummer with a Liverpool group who've just come back from Germany. I bumped into him the other day and he told me they'd been playing at a club in Hamburg. Allan Williams, the Welsh guy who owns The Jacaranda in town, arranged for them to go on a tour of Scotland which fell through. So he asked them if they'd like to go over to Hamburg instead and do a few weeks at this place called the Kaiserkeller. Allan Williams told him he'd got chatting to the owner, Bruno Koschmider, when he was down in London. And this Bruno was keen to get hold of some English rock 'n' roll groups for his club. The money was good so they said yes. And when they were up on stage in Hamburg Geoff saw a bloke standing by the bar who was the absolute spit of your Dad."

"Was he sure?"

I could feel my heart beginning to race.

"Not at first, he said. He couldn't be certain. So when he saw this bloke again he went over to say hello. Just to be sociable. He hadn't heard about your Dad going missing so he'd sort of assumed he must be in Germany on holiday. Or working."

"And what happened?"

"'Geoff asked him if his name was John Crane. And the bloke just said his name was Ian and told Geoff he must be mistaken. But Geoff says he's sure it was your Dad. He can remember what your Dad's voice sounded like. And this bloke's was exactly the same."

"And how long ago was this?"

"A month or so, maybe. Not much more."

"Thanks, Greg. I'll have a word with Sylvie. It looks like we might have to go over to Germany and see if we can find this chap 'Ian.'"

I told Sylvie what Greg had said. She didn't even need to think about it. It was a no brainer. We both wangled a bit of time off work and a couple of weeks later we were there. In Hamburg.

I'd done a bit of asking around and discovered that the Kaiserkeller was in a street called the Grosse Freiheit in St Pauli, a fairly rough part of Hamburg, which was regarded as the city's red-light district. The Grosse Freiheit was on the northern side of a major road called the Reeperbahn. It was home to numerous burlesque and strip-clubs where Animierdamen, or 'beauty dancers', entertained their mostly male clientele.

I'd also found out that, in one of those curious paradoxes that crop up in life, the German words Grosse Freiheit mean 'Great Freedom'. The street acquired its name in the seventeenth century when the German Count Ernest of Schaumberg and Holstein-Pinneberg granted religious freedom to non-Lutherans such as Mennonites and Roman Catholics, whose faiths were not widely practiced in Germany. As long as they remained within the proscribed area they were permitted to worship with complete freedom.

The Count's edict also allowed individuals making handcrafts to practice their trade without being obliged to join one of the powerful guilds which controlled such activities elsewhere in the city.

As a result of what were initially intended to be religious freedoms, however, St Pauli started to change. It quite soon became a place where people who existed on society's margins and didn't easily fit into the establishment way of doing things liked to work and live.

We wandered along the street looking for the Kaiserkeller, ignoring the shouted invitations to stop and sample the delights of the street's various striptease and other illicit joints. The fact that I had Sylvie with me didn't make any difference. The hustlers seemed to think I might still be interested. Or maybe that their more exotic offerings might be of interest to both of us?

As well as the rather seedy clubs, the area was full of interesting restaurants serving Italian, Indonesian, Chinese and Swedish food, along with more traditional German fare. Sylvie and I decided that St Pauli was undoubtedly rough, and we certainly needed to be careful, but it also had a cosmopolitan feel that Liverpool at that time was definitely lacking.

Both the Mennonites and the Roman Catholics had taken full advantage of the freedoms which had been granted to them and they had constructed churches on the street. The Mennonite church had moved away from St Pauli during World War One, but halfway along the Grosse Freiheit we came across the Roman Catholic St Joseph-Kirche. The fine, baroque building looked slightly out of place among its rather less salubrious neighbours but the church provided much needed help and support to the homeless and the destitute who were inevitably drawn to such an area.

Almost opposite St Joseph-Kirche was the entrance to the Kaiserkeller. A poster on the door told us that two groups from Liverpool, 'Rory Storm and his Hurrican' and 'The Beatles', were providing non-stop, live music.

The young rock 'n' roll musicians from England who came over to play in the St Pauli clubs used the close proximity of

St Joseph's to reassure anxious parents that they needn't worry about the notorious flesh-pots of Hamburg. The Roman Catholic Church of St Joseph, they would say, was a stone's throw from the clubs. They would, of course, be attending Mass there every week. And the priest would be keeping a very close eye on them, making sure they were okay and giving them appropriate moral guidance.

In truth the youthful Scousers were much more likely to be receiving a very different sort of guidance from the strippers and prostitutes of St Pauli who shared their nocturnal lifestyle. Or getting together with the German girls who congregated at tables close to the stage in the Kaiserkeller, arranging between themselves which of the exotic, foreign musicians they would try to seduce at the end of the night.

The girls didn't need to try very hard. Having escaped the restrictions of home the still relatively inexperienced young men were extremely keen to receive as much guidance as possible from these very knowledgeable and worldly-wise ladies.

After going through the entrance marked *Kaiserkeller* Sylvie and I discovered that the club itself was actually in the basement down a flight of steps.

It was just after nine in the evening and the receptionist at our hotel had told us that the live music in the various clubs usually started at about eight and continued until the early hours of the morning. The two groups would be taking turns on stage, playing four ninety-minute sets each, the aim of the management being to keep the club rocking, and their clients drinking, for as many hours as possible.

As we made our way down the steps we could hear the familiar sound of rock 'n' roll and on reaching a small, dimly-lit lobby we found ourselves outside an unexpectedly large space, illuminated by ultraviolet lights. A burly, tattooed bouncer was stationed in the lobby. Without saying anything he took hold of my wrist and stamped the back of my hand with some sort of pass. He then did the same to Sylvie and, after parting with a small entrance fee, we were permitted to enter.

Once our eyes had got used to the ultraviolet light we could see that drinks were available from long bars on both sides of the room. A number of shelves, each supported by floor-to-ceiling poles which looked like repurposed scaffolding, were dotted around the space. They served as make-shift counters for drinks and several were already occupied by customers who were sitting on high stools each side of them. Other people were standing, moving from side to side with the beat of the music which was coming from a decent-sized stage at the far end of the room.

To make the flat ceiling a little more interesting a number of coarse fishing nets had been hung from it, decorated with the sort of large, coloured-glass balls that were used to keep the nets afloat. In the middle of the room there was a rowing boat, or maybe an old lifeboat. It had been sawn in half and some of the drinkers were sitting in it.

Although the stage was spacious, giving plenty of room for the musicians to move around and entertain their audience, it was a very basic and cheap affair. It consisted simply of long planks of wood supported by empty beer crates and orange boxes. As far as the management were concerned the focus was on keeping the costs down. And maximising the profits.

The on-stage musicians were elevated no more than about eighteen inches above the level of the spectators and drinkers. The poor sight-lines encouraged the clientele to dance and drink, and make frequent visits to the bar to relieve their thirst, rather than sitting down all evening and keeping their deutsche marks in their pockets while watching the musicians play.

On the stage a lean, blond singer was accompanied by three guitarists and a drummer who were pounding out a steady beat. The group on stage were 'Rory Storm and his Hurrican'. 'The Beatles' would be taking to the stage at about nine-thirty.

"Let's find somewhere to sit," I said, "and then I'll get you a drink."

Sylvie nodded her agreement and we made our way over to an empty table not far from the stage.

"What're you going to have?" I asked her as she sat down.

"Just a beer, thanks."

I went up to the bar and ordered two beers. A small one for Sylvie and a larger one for myself. Like most young Germans of his generation the barman spoke fairly decent English and as he handed me the drinks I decided to see if he could help us.

"I'm Steve," I said.

He nodded a greeting.

"Manfred," he said. "You are English, yes?"

"That's right. From Liverpool. I'm here in Hamburg for a few days with my girlfriend, Sylvie."

"Ah," said Manfred with a smile, looking over at the stage on which Rory Storm was belting out his own version of Buddy Holly's 'Rip It Up'. "Liverpool, eh. So you are here to see your friends. They are good. But I don't know how they keep going for so many hours. Maybe Bruno he gives them pills for the energy? Or maybe our German girls keep them happy?"

"Probably a bit of both," I said, smiling back at him. "But this group. They're not our friends. We've never seen them before."

"So maybe you know the Beatles then?"

I shook my head.

"No."

"But they are very famous in Liverpool. Yes?"

"I suppose they might be," I said. "I don't really know. I work on one of the Cunard ships, the Queen Mary. We sail regularly from Southampton to New York. So I don't spend all that much time at home."

"I understand," said Manfred. "So, this is your chance. You must see these Beatles. They are very good. The German art students here in the Kaiserkeller are all saying they will be famous one day. More are coming to see them all the time. The sailors from the docks and their ladies are always here of course. And the working men who come here only to drink. But now it is the students from the Art College as well. These students, they never came to the Kaiserkeller before. For them it was always the jazz clubs. Now your Liverpool Beatles have made a spell on them. They sit by the stage in their smart leather clothes every night and watch them playing the rock and roll. They will be here later, the students. Stay and you will see them. Existentionalists. Like the French philosophy students. That is what they call themselves. 'Exis.'"

"Thank you, Manfred. Sylvie and I, we'll definitely stay. But would you mind if I ask you about someone we're trying to find? A man called John. He will be about fifty years old now. But I have a picture of him from a few years ago."

I took a small, black and white photograph from my jacket pocket and handed it to Manfred. He looked at it intently but didn't say anything.

"He's English," I said. "It's possible he could be with a younger French women called Anna. The reason I ask is because someone I know saw him here a couple of months ago."

Manfred gave the photograph back to me.

"I will tell you," said Manfred quietly. "Bruno – that's the big boss – he'd kill me if he heard me talking to you like this. So you must not say anything. But, yes. This man. He looks different now. And I don't think his name is John. But I do know him. Maybe he will be here later."

He gave the photograph back to me.

"That is all I can say. Please. No more questions."

With that Manfred moved away to serve another customer and I picked up the two beers.

"Sorry I was so long," I said as I took a seat at the table alongside Sylvie. "I was showing the picture of my Dad to Manfred. That's the young chap behind the bar. I thought it might be worth asking him if he'd seen my Dad and Anna in here."

"And has he?"

"He was a bit cagey," I said quietly. "He told me his boss, Bruno, doesn't like him chatting to customers about people who come in here. But he did seem to be saying he's seen my Dad. Here in the Kaiserkeller."

"Recently?"

"I think so. He's frightened of his boss so he was very reluctant to tell me anything. But he seemed to be saying that Ian, or John, or whatever it is he now calls himself, might turn up later. I think Manfred's got to be careful. So I didn't push it. But it looks like my Dad might come in here quite regularly."

"And Anna?"

I shook my head.

"Manfred didn't say anything about a woman. But I obviously didn't have a picture of her to show him. Or maybe he just thought he'd said enough."

"So what now?"

I shrugged my shoulders and gave Sylvie a smile.

"We could just have a few drinks and see what happens if that's okay with you. Manfred said the other group, the Beatles, are really good. They're attracting a different sort of audience. Art students and so on. The type who usually stick to the trendy jazz clubs. Apparently they're starting to come down here. Just to watch them." I glanced at my watch. "They should be on in about fifteen or twenty minutes so we might as well stay and have a listen."

"That's fine," said Sylvie, looking at the stage. "Rory's good too and he seems like a nice guy. I went up and had a very quick word with him between numbers while you were at the bar. I told him we were from Liverpool so he's going to have a chat with us when he's finished this set."

"I'll show him the photograph if I get a chance," I said. "The more people who see it the better. It seems unlikely. But he might know something."

Rory Storm appeared at our table about ten minutes later. He was accompanied by one of the three guitarists.

"I'm Al," he said. "Al Caldwell. That's my real name. Is it okay if Johnny joins us?"

"Sure," I said. There were two spare seats so the musicians sat down. "What can I get you to drink?"

"A Coke'd be good if that's okay," said Al.

Johnny thought for a moment. "I'll have a beer, please."

"That's fine," I said. "I'm Steve, by the way. And this is my girlfriend, Sylvie."

To my surprise Al spoke with a slight stammer, even though in the guise of Rory Storm he'd been singing without any obvious hesitation at all.

"Another beer?" I said to Sylvie, before going to the bar. She nodded her head.

When I returned she was deep in conversation with the two musicians.

"Johnny here is Johnny Bryne," she said, turning to me. "But he calls himself Johnny Guitar."

"We all changed our names last year," said Al. "And the name of the group as well. We used to be called the Texans, or sometimes the Ravin' Texans, but we didn't seem to be getting anywhere. So I decided I was going to be Al Storm. And then someone said if I was going to be Al Storm the group had better be the Hurricanes."

"We used to play quite often at a place called the Jive Hive in Crosby," said Johnny Byrne. "And there was this Crosby girl I used to see after the gigs. She said Al Storm didn't sound right and she thought Rory Storm would be better."

He turned to Al.

"And you liked it, didn't you?"

"Yeah. So that's been my stage name ever since."

"It was the same girl came up with my new name," said Johnny. "'You've got to be Johnny Guitar,' she said. So that's what I went for. And Ritchie Starkey, our drummer. He's been calling himself Ringo Starr for ages."

"That's when things started to take off for us," said Al. "When we changed our names. We're probably one of the most popular groups on Merseyside now. It doesn't make any sense really because not much else has changed. We've learnt a few more numbers and so on, but not that many. I suppose we probably have got better, though. With playing so many gigs."

I'd thought Rory Storm had looked vaguely familiar when I first saw him on stage as we'd walked into the club. His voice, and the way he held the microphone, somehow rang a distant bell. And now I remembered.

"I think I might have seen you before," I said. "In Liverpool. When you were still the Ravin' Texans and playing skiffle. You did a session at The Cavern in Mathew Street. Not long after it first opened. With the Gin Mill Skiffle Group and the Muskrat Jazz Band?"

"That was our first time at The Cavern. Alan Sytner pulled us off after three or four numbers. He told me he couldn't stand skiffle even when it was played well. And the way we were playing it was a crime against humanity." Al laughed. "He didn't book us again for quite a while."

"I was there that night," I said, "with a mate of mine called Dave."

"Were we as crap as Sytner said?" asked Johnny, who was also laughing.

"Let's just say you're a lot better this evening."

"Coward!" said Johnny, continuing to laugh. "But don't worry. You can be honest. I thought we were pretty average that night at The Cavern too."

"Anyway," I said. "What are you doing over here in Germany if things have been going so well back home?"

Johnny Guitar looked over at Al.

"Money basically," said Al, shrugging his shoulders. "The clubs here pay a lot more than they do in Liverpool. There's loads of groups on Merseyside now. So if a promoter thinks you're asking for too much they just tell you to get lost and book someone else who'll play for a few quid less. And there's plenty in Liverpool who'll turn up for almost nothing."

He picked up his Coke and downed half of it in one go.

"The money's not bad," he said. "But it's thirsty work. Six hours we'll be playing tonight. The Beatles will be doing the same. Bruno pays well. But this is Germany. Everything's down in writing. We all had to sign a contract which says we've got to play six hours a night. Bruno Koschmider, the guy who owns this place, makes sure he gets his money's worth. And Bruno's not someone you want to mess around with. Some of the customers here can be rough. When sailors, hookers and gangsters are all in the same room with a skinful of alcohol inside them it's an effin' toxic brew if you'll excuse my German. So Bruno carries an extendable truncheon inside his jacket. And so do all the waiters. If they see any trouble starting the truncheons come out and the offenders get beaten to a pulp before being chucked out into the street. We've been up on stage and watched it happen."

He turned to Johnny Guitar who nodded his head.

"Al's not exaggerating," said Johnny. "Before we came here we did a season at Butlin's in Pwllheli. In North Wales. That could get a bit wild at times. But it was like playing for a convention of committed pacifists compared to some of the psychopaths and nutters that hang out in this place."

Just as he finished speaking a murmur spread through the audience which had increased in size over the past ten or fifteen minutes. A figure dressed in a black shirt and trousers and a light-coloured jacket had appeared on the stage. He was carrying a guitar and there was a toilet seat draped round his neck. I watched, fascinated, as he stood bolt upright facing the audience and thrust his arm out at forty-five degrees.

"Sieg Heil!" he shouted. "Sieg Heil you load of bloody Nazis. Are you ready for some rock 'n' roll?"

I couldn't believe it. We were in Germany. Not much more than ten years after the war. And he was standing there doing a Nazi salute. To my astonishment his antics were greeted by laughter and applause. And even a few cheers.

"I said are you ready?"

The audience responded with more cheers and laughter.

"Okay then," the figure shouted. "The Beatles are on their way. Sieg Heil to the lot of you!"

Then he left the stage, toilet seat still in place.

"What was that about?" I said to Johnny.

"That was John Lennon," he said. "One of the Beatles. The audience love him. He can make jokes and insult Hitler and the Nazis as much as he likes and they just laugh and cheer. Most of them probably agree with him. His group weren't even supposed to be here. Bruno wanted us. But he needed a group who could start in mid-August and we were still tied up at Butlin's. So we had to say no. Allan Williams from The Jacaranda was organising things for Bruno at the Liverpool end. And when we said no he asked Gerry and The Pacemakers if they'd be interested. But they were booked up too. Or Gerry didn't fancy it. I don't know. So Allan ended up asking the Beatles. They weren't getting many gigs in Liverpool and John Lennon was the only one who wanted to carry on. The others were pretty close to giving up on music and getting ordinary jobs. They didn't even have a drummer. This job in Germany might well have been their last chance. Allan Williams said Bruno wouldn't take them without a drummer but if they could find one he'd fix it all up for them. They sort of knew a guy called Pete Best whose mother runs a place called The Casbah in West Derby. So they persuaded him to join them on drums. And Allan Williams got them the job. They didn't have any transport so Allan actually drove them here himself in his own beat-up van with all their stuff roped onto the roof. How they managed to talk him into doing that I've no idea."

"Steve and I were at The Casbah the night it opened," said Sylvie. "It's near where I live."

"It seems to be doing well," said Al. "We've played there quite a few times. Johnny and I used to have a place ourselves a little while ago called The Morgue Skiffle Club. In the basement of a big house in Broadgreen. But it didn't last for long." He shook his head ruefully. "Too many complaints from neighbours about noise late at night. And empty Coke bottles getting chucked into their gardens. So we had to shut it down."

"Manfred behind the bar says the people over here really like the Beatles," I said. "Some of the students from the local Art College are in almost every night."

"Yeah," said Al. "They seem to be going down really well now. I'm not sure what's happened because some of the people who saw them in Liverpool didn't rate them much. My kid sister, Iris, went out with George Harrison, their lead guitarist, a few times before he joined up with them. When they were both about thirteen or fourteen. She used to stuff cotton wool inside her bra to make it worth her while wearing one."

Johnny Guitar shook his head. "You can't go around saying things like that about your sister, Al. Are you sure?"

"Okay," said Al, laughing. "Forget that bit. But what I do know for sure is that Pete Best, their drummer, only got together with them a couple of days before they left England. So they hadn't really rehearsed at all. When they first got to Germany Bruno had them playing at a strip club called The Indra which he also owns. But he was getting complaints about the noise they were making. So he moved them here. And it's done wonders for them." He paused and looked at the stage. "And here they come."

There were further murmurings from the crowd as John Lennon, this time without the toilet seat, made his way onto the stage followed by four other young men, all with Elvis-style quiffs and wearing identical black shirts and trousers. Three of them had the same pale-coloured jackets as John Lennon, but the one who took his place behind the set of drums had a darker jacket on. He was moody-looking and, unlike the others, he was wearing a tie.

Sylvie leaned over and whispered in my ear. "That guy, John Lennon, who was doing all the Nazi stuff. I thought I recognised him. And Al talking about The Casbah reminded me. Wasn't he in that group we saw at the opening there last year?"

"The Quarrymen?" I said.

"Yes. The Quarrymen. I'm sure it was him."

As they plugged their guitars into the battered amplifiers and prepared to play, John Lennon said nothing. But another guitarist who had his instrument slung upside down, which had to mean he was going to be playing left-handed, approached one of the three microphone stands.

"Good evening folks. I'm Paul McCartney and I hope you're all okay. If you are, let's go. We're The Beatles and we're going to kick off with a song released last year by a singer called Chan Romero. It's called '*Hippy Hippy Shake*.' One... Two .. Three .. Four!"

Sylvie leaned over again. "It's definitely them. This singer, Paul McCartney. Playing left-handed. He was one of the Quarrymen too."

Al would probably have confirmed that the Quarrymen were now the Beatles. But I didn't need to ask him. Sylvie was right. Even though they seemed completely different. It might have been the new name. Or just the long hours playing for an audience. Whatever it was there was no doubt that they now had something special. Their sound was still raw. But there was a primitive energy about them which was compelling. And just as we'd noticed at the garden fete with John Lennon they had a strange magnetism which drew you in. Sylvie and I couldn't stop looking at them.

Their bass guitarist, though, seemed to be doing very little. In fact I could hardly hear him at all. And he didn't look familiar. I was sure he hadn't been with them at The Casbah.

I leaned over to Al. "Who's the guy on bass?"

"That's Stu Sutcliffe. He's an old Art School friend of John Lennon's. John wanted him to be a member of the group. And it's John's group. So he's in. But Stu's not that bothered about playing music. He's okay with simple rock 'n' roll but he can't be doing with the slower stuff. So he doesn't turn his amp up as loud as the others."

"He's a brilliant artist though," added Johnny. "The Walker Art Gallery in Liverpool have got one of his paintings which won a prize in their John Moores Art Competition. If he's got any sense he'll stick to painting and forget about music. He's only in the Beatles because they were short of a bass guitarist and John Lennon was his best mate at Art College. It was John that persuaded him to spend the John Moores prize money on that very nice Hofner bass guitar."

"Even though he's not that keen on playing it?"

"Yeah," said Johnny, laughing. "Lennon can be very

persuasive if he wants something. Stu'll be okay though. He's got himself a lovely German girlfriend. She's one of the Art Students who come in every night. And he's got a place at the Art School here in Hamburg next year. So he probably thinks buying the guitar and coming over here with the Beatles was a good move. He told me the other day that he's planning to stay here in Hamburg permanently and not bother going back to Liverpool."

He pointed to some younger people who were sitting round a table on the other side of the stage.

"That's his girlfriend over there. The blonde with the short hair and the smart leather jacket. You can tell from here it's expensive. Her name's Astrid. She's lovely. And she's a great photographer too. Stu's done very well for himself with that one. She's crazy about him. She styles his hair. And buys him nice leather clothes. About the only time they don't have their arms round each other is when he's on stage. He's a really nice guy so I'm pleased for him."

I leaned over to speak to Sylvie. "I didn't notice them come in but those people over there are the Art College students Manfred was telling me about. The ones who come in every night to see the Beatles."

As I was talking to Sylvie, Al suddenly stood up and waved to someone before sitting down again.

"I've just seen a guy you and Sylvie should meet, Steve. He's originally from Liverpool but he's lived over here for a few years now. Although he speaks German like a native he's still got a slight Liverpool accent. He's a bit older than us so I shouldn't think you'd ever have come across him when he lived in Liverpool. But he's a nice guy. He looks after the club when Bruno wants to take a night off."

I looked towards the door. In response to Al's wave a man was making his way through the crowd towards us. As he reached our table Al stood up.

"Hello again, Ian. Good to see you. Is Anna with you?"

"She decided to stay at home with Karin. You know. Enjoy a bit of quality mother and daughter time without me interfering."

Hearing his voice left me in no doubt. It was my father. I didn't move. I sat perfectly still and watched him closely. He would have seen me very clearly as he approached the table, even in the ultraviolet light. But now he was ignoring me. He obviously didn't want to look at me. Even from the side I could see that his face had changed. He was three years past his fiftieth birthday, a time of life when men often start to look older. And he had lost weight. But there was no doubt at all who he was.

Being much younger I'd hardly changed at all. So I was sure he must have recognised me.

Al looked towards the stage. "It's the support group on at the moment, Ian. But we'll be back on stage in about an hour." He turned to me and Sylvie. "Meantime I've found two fellow Scousers for you to meet. Sylvie and Steve."

My father could ignore me no longer. As he caught my eye I stood up and held out my hand. My mouth had gone dry and I wasn't at all sure if the words would come out.

But they did.

"Hello, Ian," I said quietly. "It's good to see you."

⸻

"I can't believe you never said anything," said Sylvie. "You're quite certain it was your father?"

It was the following morning. Sylvie and I were sitting in the coffee bar of our small hotel having a late breakfast. After the introductions the previous evening Ian had quickly excused himself, saying he had work to do. We'd hung on at the Kaiserkeller until about midnight, listening to the Beatles and the Hurricanes, and even having a quick dance. But he hadn't reappeared.

"You've heard the word *'doppelganger?'*" I said. "The Germans use it to describe an apparition or a double of a living person." Sylvie nodded her head. "Well if Ian wasn't my father, that's what he was. And I don't believe in *'doppelgangers'*."

"If you were so sure, why didn't you say something?" she said. "I don't understand."

"Because I had nothing to say to him. He knew who I was. I could see it in his eyes. You must've noticed the way he wouldn't look at me until Al introduced us. If he was going to come clean he'd have done so as soon as he recognised me."

"I just wanted to give him a mouthful," said Sylvie. "Tell him what an evil bastard he was."

"I did too. But what would that have achieved? He'd probably have said he didn't know what we were talking about. I'm pretty sure he wouldn't have told us the truth."

"So what are you going to do now?"

"Nothing. I'm happy just to leave him to rot here in Germany. It was his choice to walk out on Ma. And now that I know that's definitely what he did, and that he's not prepared to face up to it, I don't ever want to see him again."

TWENTY-NINE

THE END OF THE GAME

As the year 1960 drew to a close it felt like things were on the mend. After the horrors of war and the shortages of rationing there was a sense of renewal and optimism in the air.

Cities like Liverpool were still scarred by the effects of bombing. Living among shattered buildings and bomb sites, which nature was slowly recolonising and turning green, had become almost normal. It would take many years for all the damage to be repaired, but there was a definite feeling that in the months and years ahead our lives would get better.

I'd written a letter to my sister, Jean, in Manheim, telling her about the meeting with our father in the Kaiserkeller and his reaction to coming face to face with me. I hadn't yet received a reply. But I had little doubt that her opinion would be the same as mine.

I arrived home from Southampton two days before Christmas. I didn't have to report back to the Queen Mary until after New Year. Eleven days of very welcome festivities lay ahead.

Sylvie would stay at St Bride Street for the whole of the holiday season and her Dad would join us on Christmas Day. Dave's Dad, Trevor, would be with us too.

My uncles, Jimmy and Georgie, had made a real effort with

the house. It looked properly festive with a Christmas wreath on the front door, paper decorations and strings of coloured lights in all the rooms, and Christmas cards from family and friends on display everywhere. In the parlour a Christmas tree, festooned with baubles, tinsel and twinkling lights, reached almost to the ceiling. And carefully wrapped Christmas presents had been gathered around its base.

Late on Christmas Eve we would all walk down Blackburne Place and along Hope Street to Liverpool's Anglican Cathedral where we would join the congregation in the traditional Midnight Service.

Our Christmas turkey was in the cool larder along with an alcohol-laced Christmas pudding and a rich, sherry trifle. All that remained was to visit St John's Market where we would be able to pick up a few last-minute, fresh items.

Everything was ready.

Then, on Christmas Eve, an envelope with a Hamburg postmark was delivered. Inside was a German Christmas card. And a letter.

16th December 1960   *Grosse Freiheit 779e*
Hamburg
Deutschland

Dear Stephen,

I am sending this letter and card to St Bride Street in the hope that you still live there and that it might reach you in time for Christmas.

I'm afraid I didn't know what to do when I saw you sitting there in the Kaiserkeller. Was it only six weeks ago? It feels like a lifetime. I have not stopped thinking for one moment since that evening.

I understand now that I should have been braver and

*shown more courage. You knew that I was not 'Ian'. I
could see that. And I chose to turn tail and run.*

*I sent a letter to your mother soon after I left England,
telling her that I was alive and that I intended to start a
new life. She may have shown it to you. I do not know.*

*In the letter I told her that I had fallen in love with
a girl when I was fighting in France during the war. Her
name is Anna and we have a daughter, Karin, who is now
fifteen years of age and your half-sister.*

*There is far too much to put in a letter. But there are
things I would like you to understand while I am still
around to explain them.*

*If you can find it in your heart to forgive me I would
like to meet. It would have to be here in Hamburg. For a
number of reasons I am unable to travel to England.*

*I hope to hear from you. And that perhaps we might
one day see each other again.*

With love from your father,
John

"What are you going to do?" said Sylvie when we'd both
finished reading the letter.

"I don't know," I said. "But until Christmas is over I'm going
to put it away. Then maybe I'll give it some thought."

—

Two days after Christmas we were at Litherland Town Hall. A
few miles north of Liverpool city centre.

A hand-made poster which had been pinned up outside the
door said, '*Direct from Hamburg – The Beatles*'.

The Beatles were back home. Long nights playing for the
hookers, sailors and students in Hamburg had transformed

them. They had left Liverpool as relatively inexperienced teenagers and fairly average musicians, and they had returned as a group who would very soon become the tightest and most influential rock 'n' roll outfit of all time.

They didn't yet have their own van. Or a manager. Allan Williams, who'd arranged the booking in Hamburg and ferried them there in his van, had tried to manage them. But the word was they'd fallen out with him over money.

George Harrison loved cars but there was no way he could afford one. He had travelled to Litherland from his home in Upton Green, Speke on the bus. A friend, who he would later employ, had travelled with him carrying his Futurama guitar so he could get into the Town Hall free. In six months' time George would walk from the same family house to buy an American guitar from a Cunard Yank to replace the Futurama which no longer matched his ambitions.

The Beatles were still living from hand to mouth. Relatively few people, even in Liverpool, had heard of them. But they were on the cusp of greatness.

The last few pieces of a complex jigsaw just needed to fall into place.

Nine days earlier Sylvie had gone with several of her friends to see them play a 'Welcome Home' gig at The Casbah. I was still in New York that night. But now we were both inside Litherland Town Hall with the same group of West Derby friends.

We were surrounded by a young audience who had turned up, curious to see this unknown German group from Hamburg. They had no idea at all of what was about to hit them.

Paul McCartney screamed the opening words of Little Richard's *Long Tall Sally* into his microphone and hurled them out across the dance floor. It was electric. Almost everyone in the audience stood there, heads turned towards the stage, mesmerised by the sound, and by the look, of the leather-clad figures.

There was a loud roar as the song came to an end. The singer waved to the cheering crowd.

"Thanks for that. It's great to be playin' fer yer all tonight."

A girl near me turned to a young lad who was standing alongside her.

"Jesus Christ, Tony. You'd almost think 'e was from round 'ere the way 'e speaks."

Before he could reply she was gone, heading towards the stage. The Beatles had arrived.

In a few short years they would change almost everything.

Next morning in St Bride Street I sat with Sylvie in front of the fire in the parlour. The envelope which contained my father's letter was in my hand.

Sylvie looked at me as I slid the letter out of its envelope and unfolded the paper. I glanced at it briefly but didn't bother to read it. There was no point.

"I realised what I had to do last night," I said to her quietly. "While John Lennon was singing 'Please Mr. Postman'. I remembered the letter and I didn't even have to think about it. The answer was obvious. There was only one thing that was important. Only one thing that really mattered. And that was not to let Ma down."

I folded the letter up and put it back inside the envelope. With the German Christmas card.

"Ian," I said. "Or John. Or whatever he wants to call himself. He had his chance when we saw him in Hamburg. It's too late now."

I took hold of Sylvie's hand.

"He's the past. And for Ma's sake that's where he's got to stay. Anything else wouldn't be right."

Sylvie put her arms around me and kissed my cheek.

As she did so I placed the envelope containing my father's letter and the card on top of the red-hot coals.

We both watched as the edges of the envelope curled up very slowly and turned a golden brown. Then, in a sudden burst of flames, the past was gone.

"So that's it," I said. "It's done."

I stared at the fire, watching the last embers of the letter burn away. Then I turned towards Sylvie.

"There's something else," I said. "I've been thinking for a few weeks now. And I suppose in a way we've already talked about it."

Sylvie smiled at me. She knew what I was going to say.

"How would you feel if I wasn't a Cunard Yank anymore?"

There were tears in her eyes.

"I've done over six years with Cunard. And it's been great. But it's not the same without Dave. I miss him. And I miss you too."

Still holding Sylvie's hand I spoke very softly.

"Perhaps it's time for a change?"

She didn't need to answer.

We just looked at each other. And saw the future.

ABOUT THE AUTHOR

JOHN WINTER was a teenager on Merseyside in the nineteen sixties.

He worked as a songwriter and got to know some of the musicians and poets who were making Liverpool famous.
He was there as Merseybeat developed and a tidal wave of popular culture, led by the Beatles, emerged from his home city and changed the world.

He later qualified as a physician and spent time researching altitude sickness on Everest and working in the Australian outback, as well as running a general practice on Merseyside.

Liverpool had close links with America thanks to the transatlantic shipping trade. One of his relatives was a Cunard Yank, serving as an electrical engineer on the original Queen Mary.

*If you enjoyed this book and want to know what happens next
you can find out by reading Tony's story in the companion book*

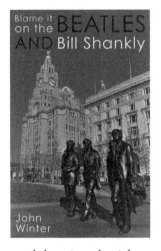

Blame It On
The Beatles…
And Bill Shankly

The Beatles are back home from Germany. Long nights playing at clubs in the red-light district of Hamburg have turned them into the tightest rock 'n' roll outfit of all time. The great Bill Shankly is in charge of Liverpool Football Club. Tony and his friends on Merseyside start to realise that everything is changing. By 1964 their city is being hailed as the centre of the teenage universe.

'Absolutely brilliant story. Sad, uplifting, sorrowful and joyous – all within its pages. At times almost like a biography. I haven't enjoyed a book so much in ages.' A.B.H. – Glasgow UK

'I thought this book was great. If you lived through those times it will take you back to the streets and the clubs – and the dripping ceiling of The Cavern. And if you weren't there, it'll make you feel as if you were. Can't wait for the film!' A.G. – Birmingham UK

'I was a mini-skirted teenager in the sixties. This book made me laugh, and it made me cry. Brilliant! I loved it.' J.H. – Liverpool UK

For more information go to <blameitonthebeatles.com>

Also by John Winter

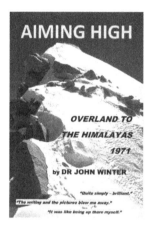

Aiming High – Overland to the Himalayas 1971

A drive from Liverpool, in England, following The Hippie Trail to India and the high Himalayan peaks. It is a journey which it would now be almost impossible to make. Read about the medical and physical challenges of high-altitude Himalayan mountaineering as seen through the eyes of a doctor who had previously not even walked up to the summit of Snowdon, the highest mountain in England and Wales.

'The writing and the pictures blew me away. It was like being up there myself' B.K. – Cape Cod USA

'Quite simply – brilliant! J.D. – Kirkby Lonsdale UK

For more information go to <blameitonthebeatles.com>

Also by John Winter

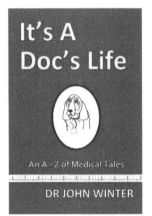

It's A Doc's Life

General practice in England. Researching altitude sickness on Everest in Nepal. Outback medicine in Australia. These various experiences as a doctor provided Dr John Winter with the stories which appear in this book. Some will make you laugh. And some might make you feel a little sad.

'*A triumph of a book. I laughed out loud at several of the stories.*'
C.R. – Worcester UK

For more information go to <blameitonthebeatles.com>